REVA KORDA

HAVING IT ALL

A SIGNET BOOK

SIGNET
Published by the Penguin Group
Penguin Books USA Inc., 375 Hudson Street,
New York, New York 10014, U.S.A.
Penguin Books Ltd, 27 Wrights Lane,
London W8 5TZ, England
Penguin Books Australia Ltd, Ringwood,
Victoria, Australia
Penguin Books Canada Ltd, 10 Alcorn Avenue,
Toronto, Ontario, Canada M4V 3B2
Penguin Books (N.Z.) Ltd, 182–190 Wairau Road,
Auckland 10, New Zealand

Penguin Books Ltd, Registered Offices:
Harmondsworth, Middlesex, England

Published by Signet
an imprint of New American Library,
a division of Penguin Books USA Inc.
Previously published in a Dutton edition.

First Signet Printing, February, 1992
10 9 8 7 6 5 4 3 2 1

 REGISTERED TRADEMARK—MARCA REGISTRADA

Printed in the United States of America

PUBLISHER'S NOTE
This is a work of fiction. Names, characters, places, and incidents either are the product of the author's imagination or are used fictitiously, and any resemblance to actual persons, living or dead, events, or locales is entirely coincidental.

This book is not biography or reportage—it is fiction. I dedicate it with love, and gratitude, to William Korda—a man who never ceases to surprise me, and who always knows how to make me laugh.

Two bawdy pigeons were crazy about the air conditioner that jutted from the Gagarins' bedroom window. They found it a delightful trysting place; they would check in every morning around the crack of dawn and start beating their wings and carrying on.

They were very lewd pigeons, and very loud.

And then it wasn't just the pigeons bothering Becky. Alex stood like an indictment at the foot of their bed, holding out the blue sweat suit he'd given her on her last birthday.

"It's not as if I'm asking you to run a marathon. Just once around the reservoir. At your own speed."

"What speed? Everyone passes me. People with walkers. People on crutches. Yesterday a woman pushing a baby carriage passed me. A baby carriage with *twins* in it." She sat up and began to pull on the pants of the sweat suit. Because Alex was watching, she tried to hold her stomach in and discovered it was difficult to hold your stomach in and pull on pants at the same time.

"If you stopped worrying so much about who passed you, you might even learn to enjoy it." He spoke in the offhand tone of someone convinced he was saying something of profound importance.

"Come on, Becky. Nobody's going to *grade* you. We're just running."

"And you wanted to stay in bed! Look at it, it's gorgeous out. You know those stupid overcoats they put on the little dogs as soon as it gets the least bit cold out? They don't have them on yet."

Becky hugged herself and watched Alex step back four feet, brace his hands against the trunk of a tree, and begin pushing, careful to keep both heels on the ground for maximum agony to the muscles of his calves. She looked around for little dogs but didn't see any. They were all probably still at home, asleep in nice warm apartments. No, over there, a lady in a beaver coat was walking a small dog. The woman was smiling. The dog didn't have a beaver coat. The dog was shivering.

As usual, the Gagarins began together, Alex holding back, staying close beside Becky, encouraging her with useful advice.

"Lift your feet. Get them off the ground. The reason people keep passing you is you don't get your feet *off* the ground. You *shuffle*. Be a gazelle. Be Bambi. Tell yourself, the hell with gravity!"

It was his mentioning gravity that did it. As soon as he said the word the earth began tugging at her, dragging her down. Just seconds ago she had been soaring Bambi-style, but now she was sprawled on the ground, gravel embedded in the skin of both palms.

Alex sighed. This happened fairly often. "Did you hurt yourself?"

She tried to keep her scraped and smarting palms hidden as she struggled to her feet. "Alex, it must be agony for you hanging back this way. Why don't you go on ahead and I'll meet you back home?"

"You promise to do the whole thing? All the way around?" He waited long enough to dust her off and point her in the right direction and made sure she was in motion before he did what she knew he had been longing to do ever since they set out. He took a deep breath and really started *running*. Soon he was almost out of sight on the path, a tall spare man in a well-worn track suit. Even in the mangy suit, with his hair gray now and more forehead showing every year, he still looked good.

She began to run again too, but carefully now. Her mother ran beside her whispering caution. Becky's mother was always on hand whenever Becky did anything that could be remotely classified as dangerous. She had been there in the backseat of the automobile when Becky took driving lessons, her invisible presence prophesying loss of control, collision, disfigurement, death . . .

A seventyish man in shorts, his body covered with white fuzz—surely the end of October was too cold for shorts?—passed Becky and waved a jaunty good morning.

Two sixtyish women, obviously girdled under their pants and speed-walking instead of running, passed her and burbled, "Nice day!"

Anyone she could classify as over forty either waved or said good morning or, at the very least, smiled. To be sure the smiles were sometimes grim, considering the pain of hauling one's body the mile and a half around the running path, but they were friendly gestures nonetheless. Whereas the young ones, those of the gleaming skin and thick manes of hair and no evident cellulite, those who took such long easy loping strides—male or female, they all just *loped* along— never greeted each other, much less her. They moved in their own private worlds of youth and grace. They weren't running to live longer. They weren't running to lose weight. They ran because they simply, incredibly, actually *liked* it. She only got the "we are all in this together" salutes from runners with thinning hair and flabby bottoms. They recognized Becky; they claimed her.

Forgetting her vow to Alex she turned and began to walk the rest of the way home.

But she did try to walk briskly.

Joseph thought that right now Mrs. Gagarin didn't look like the kind of killer career lady you saw in the movies. Faye Dunaway, Jane Fonda, in the old days Joan Crawford, that type. She was kind of a shy woman, but funny—lots of times she said things that made him laugh, and she always looked pleased when he laughed, as if entertaining an elevator man mattered. Now her short blonde hair was sweaty and her running pants were ripped at the knee. Of course later, when she came out of her apartment the second time, she would have makeup on and be wearing a nice dress and high heels and carrying a briefcase. And then the chauffeured car from her firm would pick her up, like it did every day. Joseph thought Mr. Gagarin couldn't be as successful as his wife was, *he* always turned toward the subway when he left the building.

Joseph gave Mrs. Gagarin the day's most important news. "The Salmons in 10W just sold. Almost a mil."

She looked properly impressed. "A million *dollars*? Wow. That's high."

He nodded. "*I* thought it was pretty steep too, considering that 10W is a back apartment without a park view. When are you going to sell yours, Mrs. Gagarin?"

"I'm *not*."

"Hate to leave us, huh? Well, come to think of it, you are one of the old-timers here."

"Watch it, Joe."

"Oh, I didn't mean *you're* old, Mrs. Gagarin," he said smoothly. "I just meant you've been in the building a long time. Why, you were here before we went co-op."

Joseph knew everything about the lives of everyone in the building. He knew how much maintenance the Gagarins paid on their apartment, he knew when they were getting along with each other and when they were not, sometimes Becky suspected he knew how old she was. Something she no longer let drop in casual conversation. He even knew that once Alex had had a serious drinking problem but was now a sailing, skiing, white-water-rafting, reservoir running, sober member of The Program. Becky thought that Joseph must have once seen a French movie with an all-seeing, all-knowing concierge in the plot, and had taken him as his role model ever since.

The elevator had reached her floor but Joseph made no move to open the door and liberate her. Joseph's elevator was not just transportation. It was his private salon, and he never opened the door to let you out until the conversation ceased to interest him. "How is Charlotte?" he asked gravely, and Becky repeated what she had told the dry-cleaner and the butcher and the various maids in the building who had rung her bell to ask.

"The doctors say it's only a matter of time now. But they won't say what *time* means. Whether months or weeks or only days."

Charlotte had been the Gagarin housekeeper for more than twenty years. She had done more than the usual cooking, cleaning, marketing, child-minding housekeeper chores—sometimes Becky thought that she had anchored the whole family. Now she was dying of cancer. When the Gagarin children were very little, sometimes they used to call *both* Becky and Charlotte mama.

"Mrs. Gagarin? It's Daphne Schwartz again. I know it's sinfully early to call, but we *must* talk. Have you had a chance to think some more about my client's offer? It's top dollar, you're not likely to do better . . ."

It was her own fault. Any sensible woman knows you do not answer a phone when it is late and you are halfway out the door. It will always be someone who wants to sell you dance lessons or mutual funds or buy your apartment. And Daphne Schwartz had been pursuing Becky for months.

"I'm afraid we haven't changed our minds, Mrs. Schwartz."

"Oh, Mrs. Gagarin! Are you being practical?" The voice was sweetly reproving now. "You've got one child out of college and the other halfway through. An empty nest of nine rooms could feel awfully barren. And you're sitting on a valuable property you know, those grand old West Side apartments are hot now. Thick walls. High ceilings. Working fireplaces. Parquet floors. Huge closets, no, *humongous* closets. I don't care what anyone says about the West Side, some of those apartments make what's available on the East Side look sick."

The voice became less sugary. "And if you move fast, before they start fiddling with the tax laws again, you can take advantage of the 'over fifty-five' deduction . . ."

"I happen to be nowhere near fifty-five. I happen to be forty-nine," Becky said stiffly. Although the little girl inside her, who still counted ages in installments (five-and-a-half, six, six-and-a-half, seven) immediately corrected: forty-nine-and-a-quarter.

"All right, let's forget about *selling*. That doesn't mean you can't let somebody peek at the place? Surely you want to get some feel for its current value? Things *happen* you know. Just the other day I had a man in your business, you're in advertising aren't you, and this very nice man was suddenly terminated and believe me he was glad to know what his apartment was worth when he had to make new plans."

In the mirror over the telephone table Becky looked at her hair. Somehow, overnight, a seam of gray had sprouted in the middle of all the expensive blonde. Also, there was a new line leading from her left nostril to the corner of her mouth—it was more than a line, it was a fissure, a crevice, it was a *wrinkle* that had definitely not been there when she had gone to bed the night before.

"If by *terminated* you mean *fired*, that isn't going to happen to me. I've been with my firm for twenty-seven years."

"My, isn't that nice! I heard there was a lot of turnover in advertising. They must think highly of you."

Something about her tone made Becky feel like an old governess nobody had the guts to pension off. "I'm afraid I don't have time to discuss this now Mrs. Schwartz, would you mind calling me back? Call me back—next week. In my office." What were secretaries for if not to save you from the Daphne Schwartzes of this world?

And besides, next week she would be in London.

"We can't discuss it sooner? All right, all right! I'll be back in touch Monday!"

Becky was still repeating, "But I don't intend to sell," when a firm click at the other end told her Daphne Schwartz had hung up.

She knew she should be rushing to make up for the time that Daphne Schwartz had stolen. Instead she walked to the window and looked out at the park. Becky's park. Becky's joggers circling Becky's reservoir. In the bedroom behind her there was a bed with a mattress three times as thick as the one she had slept on in childhood. On the bedroom floor, instead of the linoleum of childhood, there was a Bokhara rug. In the

bathroom there was a tub so long that Becky had to
steady herself with one foot set against the soap dish
in the wall to keep from floating as she bathed. And in
her *humongous* closets there were clothes she had sometimes bought just because she liked a neckline or a
pleat, without giving a thought to how long the thing
might wear. And yes, Daphne, the living room had a
working fireplace and a ceiling so high that when the
children were little they used to have Christmas trees
twice as tall as Alex, who was more than six feet tall.
There was even a light-drenched room large enough for
an artist's studio: Alex's studio.

Dressed now, high heels, attaché case, armored
for the day, she walked past the bedroom where Miranda was sleeping the comatose sleep of a healthy
twenty-one-year-old. Past the room where Peter's records and books and pennants still resided, even though
Peter himself was in college in California, theoretically
studying hard. She leaned against the wall of Alex's
studio for a moment to watch him work.

Gone was the morning's stern drill-sergeant face.
Now he looked abstracted, mildly pleased. He was hum-
ming "Mairzy Doats," the way he always hummed when
he was painting and things were going well. A few hours
after she'd been driven downtown in one of Seton &
Cecil's cars, he would take the subway to the Artists'
Alliance, where this year they'd given him *two* classes
to teach: Adventures in Art for Teenagers, and the
Make-a-Mess Workshop for Under-Sevens, offering in-
struction in clay, collage, crayon, paste, and paper, with
special emphasis on finger painting.

The Alliance brochure insisted that *all* children
were born creative. Alex said that the more he had to
do with them, the less he believed that. But the classes
paid a regular stipend and left his mornings free for his
own work.

Alex was beginning to sell now. His old paintings

used to move slowly, if at all. The forms had been formidable, almost threatening. He used to work in raw muddy colors: ochres, browns, somber reds and greens heavily laced with black. But this year he had switched to a gentler palette. Light vernal greens, pinks, violets, blues, a lot of white. Becky adored these new paintings. She would have loved to tell Alex how charming she thought they were. Except that you had to be very careful about what adjectives you used to an artist about his work. For all she knew, "charming" might be a terrible insult now.

But the portrait he was working on this morning *was* charming. It was the startled face of a raven-haired young girl, chewing on her nails with adolescent uncertainty. It was an unusual painting for Alex, who almost never did portraits. The last one he had done was of Becky, way back when Becky's hair color was a gift of God and not Clairol . . .

"Who was that on the phone?"

"That same real-estate lady. Still in hot pursuit. As if we would think of selling."

"Hmm," he said, peering down at the canvas on the floor, and suddenly stooping to deposit a brushload of white just *there*! "Hmm," he continued, smiling, the color must have landed exactly where he wanted it, "I think of it sometimes. I'd like to find a place where I could do some welding. You can't weld in an apartment. Now if we had a loft . . ."

Alex always turned first to the Real Estate section in the *Times* on Sundays. He clipped advertisements for firehouses being auctioned in Vermont, old churches newly come on the market in exotic venues like Hoboken or Flatbush. He dreamed tempting dreams of his work suddenly taking wing and soaring in larger spaces than the ex-dining room of a New York City apartment. But Becky loved their apartment. She had found it, she had paid for it, she was never going to leave it. Until she died, or until her wheelchair couldn't make it through the doors . . .

She remembered her mother always asking, whenever Becky wanted something they couldn't possibly afford, "Where do you think we live, Rebecca? Central Park West?"

Now she smiled and thought: Yes, mama. I live on Central Park West now. I'm married to Alex, who is Christian, and who paints. No, not *walls* Mama, *pictures*. I have two gorgeous children, they're both six feet tall, a boy in college and a girl who just finished. I wish you could have lived to see them, Mama. And I have a job, an important job, exactly the kind of job I always wanted. I'm very happy with my life, Mama.

Blood.

Becky looked away as a cheerful young nurse pushed a needle into her arm. One of the executive perks at Seton & Cecil was an annual checkup at Corporate Body. Once Becky had been the only woman among dozens of men being shifted from doctor to doctor, as they were all vetted, explored, investigated in areas she didn't even know she had.

Her first years of coming here she'd sat among the men, all of them looking like overage interns in identical white pajamas. But now there were so many women reporting to Corporate Body that they had their own special day: Fridays. Now women were issued pink Liz Claiborne smocks and sat in their own pink waiting room, with copies of *Vogue* and *Harper's Bazaar* and *Mirabella* distributed around the coffee tables and (lest Corporate Body be accused of sexism) also copies of *Fortune* and *Forbes*. Idly she wondered, did the men get to wear *blue* pajamas now? Did the men wait now in a room painted blue?

The nurse weighed Becky and furrowed her brow. "Gained a few pounds since last year, haven't we, Mrs. Gagarin?"

"Oh, you too?" But the nurse didn't laugh. She checked Becky's height, announced "Five feet five," and began to enter that on Becky's chart.

"No, I'm five *six*."

"But Mrs. Gagarin, we just measured you."

"I'm *positive* I'm five six. I've been five six since I was twelve years old. It says five six on my *passport*."

"I'm sure it does, Mrs. Gagarin. But we all tend to shrink a little as we grow older. Especially women. Now why don't we just pop in and see the gynecologist? Then we can visit the internist, and then we'll be all done!"

The gynecologist was a woman. Indian. Dark gray hair pulled back into a chignon, doctor's coat over a patterned woolen dress. She poked about inside Becky, making soothing little affirmative noises. "Do you still have menstrual periods?" she asked, casually.

"Of course!"

"And they are still regular? I ask because you are fifty now . . ."

"Forty-nine!"

". . . and soon you will enter the menopause. Your periods will start tapering off. Or they may end abruptly—one month will be your last, and then there will be no more. But there is no reason for you to experience discomfort. Women like you, women who have interesting, fulfilling jobs, generally breeze right through it."

It was like a painting of the Annunciation. There was Becky, looking astonished, legs hoisted in the air in the embarrassing posture of the examining table. There was the lady doctor, unwinged and unhaloed, bearing her terrifying news as gently as she could. Except that this announcement was about an end, rather than a beginning . . .

The internist was fifty years old. He said that in his opinion Becky could stand to lose a few pounds. "Once we start putting it on at our age, it becomes very hard to take it off."

But he finally allowed her to return to the pink dressing room and remove the insipid pink smock and put on her real clothes and return to her interesting, fulfilling job. Where she was not just a body—a trifle too heavy, a year older now, an inch shorter—where she was *somebody*.

Rebecca Gagarin. Creative head of Seton & Cecil.

~~~~~~

When Becky Gelb—before she'd become Mrs. Gagarin—had first joined Seton & Cecil, the agency had been so tiny that nowadays it would be dismissed as just another boutique.

All they'd had then were a few piddling soft-goods accounts.

But the little agency also had Angus Seton. The marketing messiah who wrote their first advertisements, hypnotized the first clients, and presided over the kind of growth that has become a textbook example in business schools everywhere.

And with Angus Seton at the helm, Seton & Cecil had prospered. After New York, other offices had opened in Atlanta and Chicago, Minneapolis and San Francisco, Detroit and Dallas. Then in London and Paris, Milan and Bombay, Nairobi and São Paulo, Hong Kong and Jakarta. Today, Seton & Cecil had offices on six continents. Today, Seton & Cecil was larger than Ogilvy & Mather, larger than Interpublic, running neck and neck with Young & Rubicam, within sight of Communicorp.

But New York still headquartered the firm. And in New York, the grandest office—the one with the terrace high above Park Avenue—still belonged to Angus Seton. Although most of the time that office was empty and silent now. Because Angus Seton, the man who had founded the firm and nursed it from a tiny boutique to a huge international advertising and public relations and direct mail empire, now spent most of the year in England.

And Becky Gagarin hadn't done badly either. She now headed a department of several hundred people, the initials R. G. had to appear on every piece of creative work before it could be shown to any client, she occupied a corner office on the fifteenth floor—you had to go through her secretary's room to get to it.

Not bad, she thought, for a kid from the Bronx.

Because Mrs. Gagarin was late, a traffic jam had built up in the corridor outside her secretary's door.

"I'll have to start giving out tickets soon. Like a bakery," Eileen told her. "Loren Odell's on the phone. And Victor Cameron is in your office. Remember, he asked if he could be a fly on the wall this morning? Sit in on your meetings?"

Eileen repeated "Odell" and put the phone into Becky's hand. Eileen had been Becky's secretary for eight years; they no longer had to talk much to understand each other. Eileen knew Becky would always accept a call from Loren Odell.

"Help," Loren said. "I have three people from your client here, two of your account guys, one of your art directors, they are all screaming at me at the same time and countermanding each other's orders, and where the hell are *you*?"

His voice sounded exactly the way it used to when they had first worked together all those years ago: smiling, funny, clever, altogether engaging—and altogether aware of it.

"I'm sure you're coping brilliantly. I'll get there on my lunch hour."

"Lunch *hour*? Madame Gagarin, it has been years since you gulped lunch in an *hour*. Come on, it's a beautiful location. And it's a very good commercial, one that you'd like to watch being produced."

"I know—remember, I wrote it? I'll be there. I promise. Later."

She was smiling when she gave the phone back to Eileen. Loren Odell had come to work for Becky right out of school, when he was still in his early twenties. And Becky had been what? Thirty-five, maybe thirty-five-and-a-half then, but already venerable in the agency. The Odell boy had been a promising junior copywriter, and Becky had thought that one day he might be more than promising . . . except that one day Loren had decided that the new medium, television, would be more fun and a lot more lucrative and had headed to California to open his own production company: Odell & Comrades.

For a long time there had been no comrades, only Odell. But now his production house had built a reputation, and Becky had heard that larger outfits were circling and sniffing, interested in gobbling him up and making him more successful than he already was. By now Loren Odell could pick and choose which commercials he wanted to produce, and even then he usually didn't handle them himself—just assigned one of his minions. He was doing Becky a great favor to cross the country personally to direct a spot for her. Of *course* she would join him later.

"Does that price include batteries?"

She was behind her desk now, a small mob of account men clustered around her.

A junior account man placed his hand on an invisible Bible and swore, "*Everything* is included. Batteries, lotion to prevent stretch marks, little suitcase for going to the hospital, everything." He opened the wee suitcase and took out a tiny booklet. "There's even a Helpful Handbook covering the Lamaze Method, postpartum depression, nesting instinct, all in simple sentences for ages four to eight."

A senior account man twinkled. "Everything except the baby, ha ha."

Feet comfortably outstretched, Victor Cameron watched the scene from a couch against the wall. Cameron was creative head of Seton & Cecil's office in Australia.

Only Radiant Ruthie said nothing. The World's First Pregnant Doll sat erect and silent, her china-blue eyes (eyes that could both open and close) fastened on Becky.

The junior account man grabbed the meeting back. It was supposed to be *his* chance to shine. "How do you like her name? *I* came up with it. The client was considering Expectant Elsie or maybe Pregnant Pat, but as soon as they heard Radiant Ruthie they flipped! See, you can inflate her from first to ninth month with the merest twist of this teensy dial under her dress. An authentic two-piece maternity dress, with bow at the collar and elastic waist and look, sensible flat shoes."

The Group Executive puffed on his pipe and looked wise. "*Flat* shoes, because the strategy is for Ruthie to be sold as an educational toy. And you know how healthy walks are for pregnant gals. So, the client is asking, what does Rebecca Gagarin think? And will you assign a creative team to knock out some ads I can show them?"

Becky gazed out the window, avoiding Radiant Ruthie's stare.

"I think, before we start knocking out ads, we

should ask the client to widen the sidewalks around the factory. So there will be room for both picket lines. The one the Sanctity of Birth ladies will send, and the one from NOW."

The account group argued for a while. They did not like returning to the client with anything but hosannas from Gagarin. When they had finally left her office, she turned to Victor Cameron.

"Educational, my foot. We'd be teaching a whole generation of little girls that babies get made by someone fiddling with a teensy dial under a dress."

"Is that so terribly far from the truth? By the way, luv, what on earth is a 'nesting instinct'?"

Crossing his legs, Victor Cameron swung one foot in casual circles. Was that so Becky could admire his boots? Soft glove leather, they looked as if they had been *chewed* to order for him by a bunch of aboriginal women. She wondered, did all the men in Australia wear boots to the office? So they could be ready to fling themselves into the saddle at a moment's notice?

"Nesting instinct—it's when a woman starts stocking the pantry, putting extra dinners in the freezer, cleaning house, bustling around in general. It's supposed to be a surefire signal that labor is imminent."

"Did that happen to you, Becky? When you had your little ones? Did you suddenly find yourself on your hands and knees scrubbing the kitchen floor?"

"Sorry. I don't do floors. Or windows."

But the night before Peter was born she remembered heading to the desk in her bedroom, typing a status report on all her assignments, meticulously explaining what stage each project had reached. She had finished the report at midnight, to be jolted awake an hour later by the first contraction. And when she'd roused Alex, the first thing she'd told him was how important it was for that report to get to the agency first thing in the morning, even before she mentioned that it might be a good idea to head for the hospital right away . . .

"Today is an eye-opener for me, luv. All of us natives out there in the bush know about Rebecca Gagarin, but I never really understood how much clout you have. No creative work seems to get near a client without your approval, and now I see you also have veto power over new products."

"Far from veto power. It's just that since we're happy to take the commissions for the advertising, the clients like us to help with new products, too . . ."

She paused. Cameron was not listening. He was looking around her office as if he planned to redecorate it.

"Your office reminds me of a revolving door. I can't believe how quickly you get them in and out. Do you make all your decisions that fast?"

Becky grinned. "I thought I was slow this morning. Listen, new products are the part of my job I like best— I get such a nice warm feeling when I can defend the American consumer against Radiant Ruthies."

"That, plus the nice warm feeling you get on the way to the bank? What kind of salary does the creative head of the New York office pull down, Becky? If you don't mind my asking?"

Becky didn't mind. In fact, she rather enjoyed telling him.

Cameron raised his brows. "I must say I'm surprised."

"At how much it is?"

"No. To be honest—how little."

She didn't know if it was meant to be taken seriously, because he laughed and went on smoothly, "I'm sure you know what you're doing, but a doll that gives birth sounds pretty exciting to me."

"Ah, but she never actually gives birth. There's nothing in that tummy except batteries. We'd be lying to our customers, disappointing little girls everywhere."

She tried not to think of what Victor's idea of the proper salary for a New York creative head might be. And how far short of that her own might fall. Of course she probably wasn't paid as much as she might have been if she'd hopped from job to job—that was one of the penalties of staying in the same place for a long time. She was smiling brightly at her visitor, and answering his questions politely, but Becky thought—not for the first time—that she didn't like this Victor Cameron very much.

"Well. It's good to have you with us again, Victor."

"Oh, I wouldn't dream of missing a Creative Caucus. It's always enlightening to see the kind of work my colleagues in the big-time offices are doing. The lucky devils in London and Paris . . . and New York."

She remembered that visiting firemen expect to be entertained and steeled herself to form an invitation.

"If you don't have any special plans for Sunday, perhaps you'd like to come to the Metropolitan Museum with Alex—my husband—and me? Alex says there are four good shows there now. And afterwards, maybe Chinatown for dinner?"

He looked sincerely sorry when he said, "Oh, luv, I'm afraid old Ham's preempted me. Asked me to his place in Virginia. He's going to fly us down there in his plane. It's for the whole weekend too, which does make Sunday impossible."

He sounded so sorry to miss the cultural treat the Gagarins were offering that Becky hastened to comfort him. "Oh, the museum will always be there. And I hear Hamlin's little plantation is great. A thousand acres. Horses. Black Angus cattle. I bet he even has slaves in the old slave quarters. I'm jealous, I've never been invited."

Eileen reappeared in the doorway. "You have to review the stuff on your desk before the Friday meeting.

Uh, Mr. Cameron, I thought you might like some coffee?"

The cup she handed him was china and came with a cunning china creamer and cute little sugar bowl on a silver tray that Eileen must have kept hidden in her desk for visiting Australians. The beleaguered expression Becky's secretary had worn all morning had disappeared from her face. She was smiling a gentle smile now and kept her eyes down while she talked to Cameron. It was as good an imitation of a woman in purdah as Becky had ever seen done without a veil.

"Well, you heard my orders, Victor. I have to get back to work now, I have a meeting with Hamlin."

"So do I. He's invited me to eavesdrop a little."

That was surprising. Friday meetings were when the most important decisions of the New York office were deliberated: hirings, firings, promotions, which loose business would be pursued and which accounts were in danger and would need tender loving care. Strangers, even visitors from other Seton & Cecil offices, were never invited to "eavesdrop a little."

She was finally alone in her office.

She leaned back in her chair and, for a moment, gave herself to the pleasure of just being there.

She loved this room. She had told the agency decorator, "When people come in here, it's going to be with problems. I want this to be an oasis, a place where they can relax and draw breath."

The decorator had taken "oasis" literally. The room was done entirely in liquid shades. A green glass coffee table swam in the center of four squashy sea-green chairs. The couch that Victor had finally vacated was covered in cerulean blue linen. All the frantic paraphernalia of advertising—projector, screen, VCR—had been hidden behind sliding doors. A recent painting of Alex's hung on the wall. Nobody was ever sure what it represented, but it was all greens and grays and blues and serene brushstrokes. Everything was calm in this room, and sexually neutral. Only the thick white rug hinted, "A woman works here."

"Works." She said it out loud, prodding herself into action.

Eileen had already typed the memos Becky had left in her OUT box the night before. She had stacked proofs of the agency's latest print advertisements in a neat pile for Becky's inspection and put the memos and letters that needed immediate attention on top of the pile in her IN box.

Some were signed in orange ink. Those would be from Horatio Hamlin. Some were signed in brown ink. Those would be from Wilbur Rank. She didn't see *any* with the familiar A.S. scrawled across the bottom in green crayon. Green: the color of the "Go" signal in traffic lights, the color of cash, the color of profits. The color Angus Seton reserved for himself.

She went through the IN box once more. She hadn't heard a word from Angus for months now, and she was used to being bombarded with notes from him daily. (Sometimes cranky: *I cannot believe that you approved the attached abortion!* Sometimes exhilarating: *Rebecca Gagarin, you are worth your weight in gold.*) But for months now there had been *nothing* in the mail from Angus. Not to worry. Whatever the reason, she would discover it next week. In England!

Eileen hurtled in with a new warning: "Ten minutes till the Friday meeting. After that there's the Creative Caucus. You'll have some visitors from Japan today, they've been all over the place all morning bowing and taking photographs. As soon as that's over, you have the Eve meeting. Do *not* get waylaid in the corridor and start holding conferences there because the Eve people say they need all the time they can get. Oh, and Mr. Hamlin wants to see you privately, this afternoon. At five. If you're free. And after that there's that reporter from *Ad Hoc*. You've postponed her three times already, you *cannot* do it again."

"If you're free" meant Becky *would* be free. Horatio Hamlin was president and chief executive officer of Seton & Cecil, U.S.A. He stood second only to Angus Seton in the Seton & Cecil hierarchy. But she was careful to play her role in the business fictions they all lived by and peered thoughtfully at her calendar before announcing that yes, Eileen could cancel the five o'clock screening so that she could meet with Horatio Hamlin then.

"I've already canceled it. Look, I'm putting this galley for the next *Who's Who* on your desk in front of you. Read it right away, I have to send it back."

Obediently, Becky read about Rebecca Gagarin, who was also Mrs. Alexander Gagarin. Born in New York City, the daughter of Louis and Frieda (née Sussmanovich) Gelb. Began her career in the advertising department of Omni's Discount Department Store. Joined Seton & Cecil as junior writer. Promoted to senior writer. Promoted to vice-president. Promoted to senior vice-president and creative director. Promoted to executive vice-president and creative head. Elected to board of directors, Seton & Cecil International.

You don't *have* to give your age in *Who's Who*, and a surprising number of men do not. But Becky's age was there for all the world to see. Would she still have courage enough to let them print it again next year? When that critical first digit changed from a *four* to a *five*?

~~~~~

Since power fills a vacuum, and since Angus Seton now spent most of his time in England, the U. S. office of Seton & Cecil had been run for the past five years by Horatio Hamlin.

Becky knew she should like Hamlin. He was, after all, the man who had appointed her creative head the first year he'd been in command. While Angus Seton had never been able to get past the fact that Becky was female, and therefore ineligible for high office.

But try as she might, like everybody else she was too afraid of Hamlin to like him.

Hamlin's office reeked of work. The furniture had no personality and the lighting was harsh; he had obviously instructed the decorator not to pamper visitors with pretty pictures or soft draperies.

There were only a few things that offered clues, purposely of course, to Horatio Hamlin, the man.

First clue: A wall of framed black-and-white photographs showed Hamlin at play. Rough, grainy photos, obviously unretouched. Here was Hamlin, sweaty from tennis. Hamlin, frogman-suited, hauling himself aboard deck after a morning spent diving. Hamlin, someplace in South America, caught in a snapshot after having skied a trail so high you had to be *flown* to the top of it. Hamlin, arm in arm with a Sherpa pal, waving triumphantly from atop a mountain no amateur had ever climbed. But these pictures proclaimed that Horatio Hamlin was no amateur climber. In fact, the whole wall of pictures was there to remind you that although short in stature, Horatio Hamlin was a powerful man, unafraid of enormous physical risk.

Second clue: another wall of pictures, this one devoted to Hamlin's love of opera. (*Opera?* one was meant to react. Yes, the wall insisted, you are dealing with a complex man of many facets, not just another Neanderthal executive.) One picture showed Hamlin with an arm around Placido Domingo's shoulders. Another showed him buddy-buddy with Pavarotti, and there was one with Kiri Te Kanawa, and one with Maria Callas. Hamlin had been a very young man in the Callas picture—but he had already discovered that you do not need to contribute all that much to an opera house to get a diva to stand next to you in a photograph.

Third clue: pictures of Hamlin's children, in their twenties now, smart-looking overachievers gazing confidently at the camera. There were no pictures of Hamlin's wife. They had recently divorced. She had permitted her arms to flab and her rear to expand; the children were photogenic young men and women. Rumor had it that the next Mrs. Hamlin would be an ambitious thirty-two-year-old already high in the echelons of a well-known global bank . . .

Fourth clue, and the one that said the most to Becky: Behind Hamlin's desk, on a table against the wall so that all he needed to do was swivel his chair to reach it, was a *typewriter*. Almost all the male executives Becky had ever worked with would rather have died than type a memo. Even while using computers—permissible, because unisex—they would make a show of hunting for the right keys. Typing was the obedient task of females. Horatio Hamlin had no need to be ashamed of typing his own notes and memos. And he often did, because many of these little notes were too cutting even for the eyes of his secretary.

Today, when Becky Gagarin opened the door to Hamlin's office, the scene was not the usual Friday meeting. Horatio Hamlin was *smiling*. On the desk in front of him was a birthday cake, with WELCOME TO THE BIG FIVE-O! lettered on it in orange icing. Next to the cake, champagne flutes stood at attention. Wilbur Rank—like Becky Gagarin, an executive vice-president—was posted behind Hamlin with a bottle of Tattinger in hand, ready to pour.

Victor Cameron was already there, in the chair closest to Hamlin's desk. Becky dropped into the seat she always took. In the back. Against the wall. Far away from the two guys who liked to smoke cigars right after breakfast.

As usual, she was the only woman in the room.

"So, how does fifty feel, chief?" Wilbur Rank was asking Hamlin. "Or maybe you don't want to talk about it?"

"Why shouldn't I want to talk about it?" Hamlin replied, digging into the extra large hunk of cake he had carved for himself. "I'll tell you how it feels. It feels wonderful. If you guys think I've done a few positive things for Seton & Cecil so far, just keep on watching me now that I'm *fifty*."

Everybody laughed politely. "Listen, I mean it. Fifty is a glorious age. An age when—if a man has any power at all—it's a hell of a lot easier to get more. Power is like compound interest. The more you have the more you get. People pay closer attention, suddenly you're walking taller . . ."

He wiped an orange crumb from his face. "Yes, even a little runt like me." There was another ripple of polite laughter, the way Napoleon's aides might have chuckled at the Emperor confessing that he was somewhat lacking in stature. Hamlin didn't pause for the laughter. He was in an expansive mood, he wanted to reveal his plans for the agency's future.

Eyes dreamily half-shut, he leaned back in his chair and waved a casual hand to dismiss the good old days, when all anyone at Seton & Cecil talked about was how to make better advertisements. Soon, very soon, the agency would expand beyond the mere making of ads! Soon, Seton & Cecil would be a different place. A sleek space-age ship, computer-nourished, multinational, mind-boggling, ready for brilliant hands to pilot into a profitable new future. He did not need to explain whose hands they would be.

"That Japanese agency I brought into the fold last year? It's doing better than any of our other subsidiaries! Of course it's a joint venture, they don't like to give foreigners complete control in Japan. But when *all* our offices can display that kind of bottom line, our stock won't be dead in the water the way it is now.

"And I've got other ideas I want to fool with. We're heading into a new age, the Age of Information, and advertising is only a minuscule part of getting information to people! Any child with a box of Crayolas and a toy typewriter can make an ad—Seton & Cecil should be in things like data distribution and satellite broadcasting! Seton & Cecil is a business, we're in the business of *information*, let's find out how to mine it for gold!"

The man who was in charge of the media department offered, "I've always thought S&C should get into cable . . ."

From the head of research: "Religion! Every lifestyle study I've ever seen shows America has more churchgoers than any other industrialized nation. We can buy a few lists of preachers, get the copywriters to start writing sermons in their downtime, put out a catalog . . ."

"Or start a new TV network. Who says there have to be only three biggies!" From one of the cigar smokers.

"Politics, Ham, we haven't touched on politics!" Wilbur Rank was so excited he jumped to his feet. A short man too, he was waving his hand back and forth to catch Hamlin's eye. As if they were all back in school and Hamlin was teacher. "We can do more than just prepare ads for the guys who are running. We can formulate the whole damn strategy for them. We couldn't run the country any worse than it's been run lately!"

"How are we planning to pay for all of this?" Becky wondered. And was surprised to find that she had wondered it out loud.

"What?" asked Hamlin.

"Can we afford to start spending money with such abandon? All those new services, we'd have to staff up for them. Our writers don't *have* any downtime now."

"Believe it or not I have some ideas on how we can fund everything that's come up this morning," Horatio Hamlin said slowly. Then he laughed. "I didn't know you wanted to take over our comptroller's responsibilities too, Rebecca. I would have thought you'd have your hands full trying to keep our creative house in order."

He turned to the others in the room. "But we're lucky to have Becky with us, lucky Rebecca has *always* been with us, to remind us when we're wasting our time on dreams."

He picked up his phone to tell his secretary that the birthday party was over. She could collect champagne glasses and distribute spreadsheets.

The next time Becky glanced up at Horatio Hamlin, he was staring at her, his face shuttered.

When the meeting broke, he put out a hand to stop her before she could leave the room. "Becky, I hope you won't mind that I've invited a small delegation of Japanese businessmen to sit in on your Creative Caucus today . . ."

"My secretary mentioned it, of course I don't mind . . ."

". . . and I also told Vic Cameron that he ought to follow you around a lot while he's here in the States. Watch how you do your job, handle your people, that kind of thing."

"He's already following."

And *that*, she minded. Although she wasn't sure why.

She went into Conference Room 1 the back way, through the projection booth. Max, her favorite projectionist, was already there, chewing on a bagel. Why did Becky like Max? Because she knew Max liked *her*. Max said he liked her because she would usually approve, or disapprove, a spot after only one viewing. Max said he never had to stay late and screen anything sixteen times for Becky while she tried to make up her mind whether she *should* like it or not. Becky thought she'd probably made some ghastly mistakes with her famous quick decisions. But not as many as she would have made agonizing over them.

"I want to show the latest new business reel today, Max."

"I bet you thought I didn't see you steal the other half of my bagel? And the new business reel is already up."

Max had already been through five Creative Caucuses with Becky; he knew the routine as well as she did. Every delegate got to show one reel of his office's best work, the reel that he would present to prospective clients. New York, as host city, always showed its work last. Today was the last day of the Caucus, so it was New York's turn.

Promising herself she would start losing weight tomorrow, she nibbled on Max's bagel and peered through the window set into the wall that separated the projection room from the conference room.

Up and down the long table little flags represented the countries the delegates had come from: Max had stolen the idea from TV coverage of the United Nations. The delegates were the brightest creative lights of Seton & Cecil's offices, and Becky had arranged eighty hours of lectures for them—on media, research, direct mail, corporate advertising, package-goods advertising, drug advertising, food advertising, you name it.

Besides the lectures, they had been lunched and dined and stared at by all the New York brass. Notes had been entered into their dossiers on which ones asked the most piercing questions, which ones presented the best reels, which ones were likely to make it to the top, and which would get shoved off the ladder long before then. They were all ambitious, all talented—otherwise why would they have been chosen to come to New York at such great expense? But at this point it had become clear to all of them that Victor Cameron had already emerged as winner of the tournament. That he had probably won even before it started.

Through the projection-booth window, she saw the gentle writer from the office in Bombay, who had taken her to a tiny Indian restaurant in the theater district and quoted poetry to her in Punjabi.

And over there was the tall Dutch art director, a fierce and unpleasant young man who had arrived at the Caucus with greasy black hair touching his shoulders and a headband around his forehead. Sometime in the past two weeks he had looked around him in New York, gotten rid of the headband, started shaving, and acquired a haircut.

And there was Victor Cameron, in the middle of a circle of Japanese visitors. There were seven or eight of them, all with the same horn-rimmed glasses, the same pinstriped suits, the same Nikon cameras slung about their necks. Had they all been cloned from one oriental cell? They stood there deferentially as Victor chatted up the leader of their group. He *had* to be the leader, otherwise why would Victor Cameron have picked him to talk to?

Swallowing the last crumb of bagel, Becky went into the conference room.

Cameron looked startled to see her—who did he think was going to chair this meeting?—but quickly introduced the man he had been talking to. "Ichiro Yamaoto of Hiro Motors," he said, as cozily as if Ichiro and he had been pals for years. ("My old friend Itchy.") With a popping of flashbulbs the rest of the Japanese swiveled to photograph her.

"Good afternoon, gentlemen. I'm planning to

screen the New York reel for all of you this morning—
I'm afraid I haven't prepared any special introduction
for it. It will just have to speak for itself."

She waved at Max in the projection booth. "Here
goes, for better or worse." Which was false modesty.
This was the reel that had brought in five major new
clients in just one year.

When the lights came up again, there was applause.
From the Seton & Cecil delegates, and, vigorously,
from the visiting Japanese.

Only Victor Cameron sat quietly, hands folded.

"Victor? You don't seem thrilled by our reel."

"Oh, Becky, that's not fair. I thought it was first-
rate. Well, a lot of it was. Only . . ."

He furrowed his brow, as if he wanted to say something else but could not quite find the words. Which
was strange. Becky had never seen Victor Cameron
unable to locate precisely the words he wanted and
without visible strain.

"Please, Victor. Say whatever you're thinking. Be
frank. That's what the Caucus is all about—we have to
be frank with each other, so we can help each other."

"Well, okay, here goes. I couldn't help wondering
why New York's creative product is so, ah, so incon-
sistent. Of course most of the time it's first-rate, luv,
which is what one expects from New York, after all this
is Seton & Cecil's capital city. But I'm afraid that fairly
often it can be a little ah, old hat? A little passé?"

He shook his head. Neither was quite the word he
was looking for. Then his mouth curled into the smile
of a small boy who had been warned to stay away from
the pitcher of milk, and really he didn't intend to, but
somehow, he doesn't know how, his hand got too near
the pitcher and all the milk just . . . spilled.

He came out with exactly the word he'd been
hunting.

"I hate to say this luv, but I'm afraid that now and then I found your reel somewhat . . . *boring*."

Only the Japanese, who hadn't understood what had just been said, were still smiling. At the far end of the room, Max's face peered with interest through the projection-booth window. Becky knew there was a button in the booth that permitted one to overhear every word spoken in the conference room. She had often switched that button to the "off" position herself, before sensitive meetings. It was obviously not on "off" now. Which was too bad. Max liked to gossip.

"I'm sorry you find New York's work boring . . ." she began.

"Oh, not fair, luv. I did say that a *lot* of it was first-rate." Victor leaned back in his chair now, smiling encouragingly at her, as if it were she who had spilled the milk and needed reassurance in her amateurish mopping-up.

She began speaking faster: ". . . but I think you should know that one of the commercials on that reel took a brand that was really a terminal case, they couldn't *give* the stuff away any more, and created a whole new market for the product. And another campaign on that reel is considered so warm and human that it gets Christmas cards from its fans every year . . ."

Her voice was beginning to sound high and squeaky. Like a blond Minnie Mouse. "Don't misunderstand, *I'm* not taking the credit, it belongs to a lot of exceptionally talented people in our creative department. By the way, did you know that Seton & Cecil has the lowest turnover rate of any creative department in any major U.S. agency?"

Victor ran a relaxed hand through his hair, smiled again, and cheerily said, "Well, I suppose it's not hard to keep people if nobody else wants them."

This was not what the Creative Caucus was supposed to be about. Seton & Cecil did not transport people across oceans for them to have ugly public confrontations with each other. Becky forced herself to laugh, as if Victor had just said something witty rather than nasty.

"Okay, Victor, you've earned the right to be critical. Compared to what *your* office turns out, the work of any other place could easily seem second-rate."

Later, while they were walking together toward the Eve meeting, she managed a gracious, "I'll have another look at our reel, with your comments in mind."

"I suppose I could have been more tactful. Don't *worry* about it."

She hadn't thought of *worrying* about it.

Should she?

The scene bore no relation to the glass-and-chrome conference rooms you see in movies about advertising.

The length of the table was punctuated with half-empty Coke bottles, overflowing ashtrays, scribbled-on yellow pads, wadded-up pages on which ideas had been quickly written down and just as quickly discarded.

Twenty-five years ago Eve had been the first important new product Becky had ever worked on. Eve looked like a soap, but it had none of the ingredients that make soap impolite to skin. Eve contained creams, and sunscreens, and all sorts of other therapeutic goodies. It had been Becky's idea to shape Eve to fit a woman's hand and color it *black*. She had thought the black of the product would be a surprising counterpoint to the image of gentleness and purity she was going to build.

Eve had been her first triumph. And 20 percent of the women in America still said "Eve" when asked what product was best for washing the face. But 20 percent was a figure that no longer satisfied Eve's management. There had been ominous rumors about other companies using obscure midwestern cities as test markets for new products that would try to invade Eve's market share.

The language of war is always used in advertising. Companies "invade" each other's territories. They "battle" for market share. Commercials and print advertisements are not just placed: "Campaigns" are waged. When an important new piece of business is being pursued, the conference room that is headquarters for the effort is called—and nobody laughs!—the War Room.

Becky looked around at the copywriters and art directors who had worked so hard on the layouts festooning the walls. They had barely glanced at Victor Cameron when she introduced him, they were all so busy staring at her. Rebecca Gagarin was the first hurdle they would have to clear before they could show their work to the account people, and then to The Client. And today she was more than a hurdle. Today she was also Competition. The commercial that Loren Odell had crossed the country to produce was an Eve spot that Becky had written herself.

Ordinarily Rebecca Gagarin did not write commercials. Not since becoming creative head. She would be competing with her own people if she did—how could she be *in* the race, and judge it fairly?

But the natives were restless in Winosha, where Eve's corporate headquarters were freezingly located, and Horatio Hamlin had suggested that she return to her typewriter and write yet another commercial for the product she had launched all those years ago. Hamlin suggested, Gagarin obeyed. The purpose of this meeting was to find other commercials to test against hers.

Because of the importance of the Eve problem, the people in the room today were a task force Becky had drawn from different groups. She'd chosen a copywriter from one group, an art director from another, a producer from a third.

For two decades now Becky Gagarin had directed

every nuance of Eve's presentation to the public: how Eve should look, what it should say, what it should *be*. But this year the account people kept talking nervously about the new management at Eve. They said the new management would want different advertising, advertising that blazed new trails, *clever* advertising. So, for the first time since Eve had been launched, Becky had set no guidelines for her creative people but left what they would do wide open.

She asked Lilah James if she would present her work first.

If Lilah James had cared enough to try, she might have been a beautiful woman. Tall and thin, so thin that her full breasts were startling, hers was a good body for clothes. *If* Lilah had given any thought to clothes. Her hair, although shot with gray now, was thick enough to have looked good in almost any style. *If* Lilah had ever bothered styling it. She usually just yanked it up and fastened it into a haphazard bun at the nape of her neck.

At forty-five or thereabouts, Lilah James's lifestyle had become very simple. When she was in the office, Lilah wrote ads. Brilliant ads, often. When she was not in the office, she drank. There were even rumors about drugs. And her boyfriends seemed to tend toward violence. On days when Lilah arrived in the agency with a black eye (and once, a missing tooth, unfortunately a conspicuous incisor), she would explain that she had, the night before, been mugged. Lilah could easily have run for the most-mugged woman in New York.

Yet Lilah James, as unlike the ordinary suburban housewife as was possible to imagine, always seemed to understand how the suburban housewife thought. What pictures, what words, what promises would open her purse.

Today, Lilah's glasses were held together with

Scotch tape and her hands shook as she tried to light a cigarette. "Just a sec," she mumbled, and clicked her stopwatch rapidly at the tip of her Marlboro. Until it occurred to her that her stopwatch was *not* her cigarette lighter.

The campaign Lilah presented was a slice of life. Two women sat at a kitchen table discussing the challenges of hanging on to beauty, husbands, self-esteem when too many pages have fallen from the calendar. The prettier of the women recommended Eve to the other. The payoff came when the husband of the plainer lady (after a slow dissolve signifying weeks of Eve) looked at his wife with new interest. He didn't sing to her, he didn't shower her with diamonds, he simply looked at her with *interest*. Which, after a couple of decades on the same pillow, stretch marks on the belly, and gray roots in the hair, is all most women will ask of their husbands.

Becky thought you'd have had to be a woman in her forties or fifties or sixties to realize the power of the work that Lilah was showing. Would it qualify as the "clever" advertising the Eve client was now demanding? Probably not. No client would get congratulated on advertising like this at the next trade conference he attended.

Keith Andrews, the television producer, was up next.

Today Keith wore a gray suit from the shop in London that had his measurements. The ascot around his neck was heavy Italian silk, fastidiously knotted.

Before Becky had become creative head, when she was still working closely with Keith as his group head, for a while he had decided to take an interest in her appearance. Every morning Keith would look her over and mercilessly criticize her hair (the cut was always wrong) or her dress (too long, or else too short) or her makeup (horribly unprofessional, better to wear none at all than *slap* it on like that).

And then, one day, the criticism had stopped. After a week, oddly enough, Becky had started missing it, and asked Keith why he no longer took any interest in the way she looked. Keith had folded his hands on his desk top, lowered his lashes sadly, and said, "Because, my dear, I have decided you are hopeless."

Keith would have liked them all to believe he came from the Old South of fine manners, tall tinkling glasses, polished door knockers. But Becky (who had read his personnel file) knew that his father managed—didn't own, just managed—a drugstore in an Atlanta shopping mall, and his mother augmented the family income with Tupperware parties.

Keith was a Harvard graduate, magna cum laude, a member of Mensa, even though he never went to their meetings (*"Bor-ing!"*). English was the language he had been accidentally born to; when he whispered to his friends on the phone in his office, he was as likely to be speaking French or Italian. Keith was a citizen of the *world* and wanted everyone to appreciate that.

The storyboard Keith presented today had nothing as pedestrian as words. Keith said the entire tale would be told in visuals. The new Eurostyle in advertising.

"We open on this ravishing girl lying on a deserted beach. We come in for an extreme closeup and see that her eyes are closed, lashes fluttering just a little. Cut to a dark handsome man swimming towards her. He strides out of the ocean, leans over and strokes her face broodingly, turns, reenters the water, and swims away. The woman opens her eyes. She touches her face, where *he* had touched her, and smiles mysteriously. We cross-dissolve to a beauty shot of the product as the lapping of waves segues into music—I think we should shoot this in Agadir. I hear there are great beaches in Agadir and it would be cheaper than California." Besides, Keith had always wanted to see Agadir.

Becky put her head in her hands. This was what came from not setting guidelines. "That's it? I mean, there isn't more to it than that? Something about the product, maybe?"

"I thought you gave us carte blanche to be *original* on this assignment? I can't believe you want a voice-over to come in and start yakking about the product after something so subtle, so sophisticated, so *new*."

It was Rae Ashley's turn. Today, Rae was all in white. A knife-sharp crease in white pants. A white linen jacket over a white shirt. White ankle-high boots, with the surprise of scarlet soles when she crossed her legs. The white was a calculated contrast to the short-cropped black hair and the black-framed glasses that kept sliding down her nose, giving her a chance for charming pauses in her presentation as she pushed them back up with the tip of a scarlet fingernail.

Rae was an art director; she resented it when copy-writers presumed art directors could not *think*. Her presentations were famous—meticulously detailed, complete with charts explaining her thought processes. Today she took twenty minutes to explain that the only advertising tool that had not been thoroughly explored for Eve was *music*. She fed a tape into a Wollensack.

"I want them to shoot their whole budget on a *jingle*. But what a jingle!"

The message was delivered by drums, bass, piano, and a strident female voice. "Buhbuhbuhbaby your skin's gonna start luh-luh-livin' with Eve . . . Oh sweet buhbuhbuhbaby your skin never had it so go-oo-ood . . ."

Becky listened to the pounding rock and thought of the millions of women who had rushed to buy Eve when it had first been introduced twenty-five years ago. And who still bought enough to guarantee it shelf space today. Eve was a wrinkle fighter. Every woman's friend in the cruelest war she would ever have to wage, the war against age. She listened to the thumping, blasting music and saw a woman peering into her mirror, desperate over the first warning signals of time. A woman who had just been told she was shrinking, and overweight, and would soon disappear as a woman, the way the Cheshire cat had disappeared in *Alice* . . .

There was one more writer to hear from, a junior. Becky had hired her herself just a few months ago, in spite of the employment agent who had phoned and said, "She's terrific. A *young* Rebecca Gagarin."

Her name was Gandhi.

Really. Gandhi Hendricks.

Becky usually didn't interview inexperienced juniors, but she could not help being curious about a *young* Becky Gagarin. Especially one named Gandhi.

Well, the employment agent had been wrong. There were certain differences no one could miss. To begin with, Gandhi was black. Almost six feet tall, lean, and stunningly black.

Because she was in the creative department Gandhi was allowed eccentricity in dress, and she liked to wear Mexican outfits to work—a straight pleated white *guayabera* hanging loose over tight black pants. She plaited her hair into braids, dozens of skinny braids spinning off in all directions, with tiny silver and gold and bronze beads twined into them, creating a gleaming nimbus around her head.

Gandhi's temper was already famous throughout the agency. The new writer was known to be ferociously intelligent, and sometimes just plain ferocious.

The day Becky had interviewed her, she'd said, "My mother named me Gandhi because she liked his ideas about nonviolence. She linked it up with what Martin Luther King was preaching around the time I was born. She didn't know she'd be getting the meanest-tempered little girl on the block."

The day after it happened, the story of Gandhi's explosion during a research session had flown through the agency.

It had been one of those sessions with a two-way mirror. A group of consumers sat around a table discussing beauty products like Eve, while on the other side of what looked like an ordinary mirror, unheard by them and hidden from their view, Seton & Cecil copywriters and art directors and account people took notes on what they said.

Except that one young account executive was not taking notes. He was too busy mimicking the plump, middle-aged matron on the other side of the mirror. He was hilarious about the woman's flowered polyester pants suit, her teased hairdo, the romance novel she'd been clutching when she came in.

And Gandhi had blown up. She'd told the young account man that the woman he was ridiculing was paying his salary. That without all the tiresome women who bought the products Seton & Cecil advertised, he would be unemployed. And she'd finished by ordering him from the room. "You get the hell out of here now, buster, because everyone else is here to *learn*, and you already know it all."

Horatio Hamlin often rebuked Becky for being too fond of the people who worked for her. Hamlin insisted that all a good leader needed to care about was how his people performed. Not where they come from, what they dreamed about, who they *were*.

But Gandhi Hendricks reminded Becky Gagarin of herself, when Becky had been Gandhi's age. Becky too had blown up easily; she too had never cared what she said, or to whom she said it. And although junior writers and creative heads did not often attend the same meetings, Becky was always pleased to see Gandhi.

Now Gandhi had a stack of storyboards facedown on the table in front of her. "The research sessions we had on Eve convinced me that women don't want *promises* any more. They want *reasons* to believe that Eve might be different from all the other stuff they've bought, and swore they wasted their money on."

The campaign the tall black junior copywriter went on to show was packed with information. The sentences were short, each one dealing with a specific ingredient. Explaining exactly what that ingredient did. And (although this was heresy in the beauty business) admitting what the product could *not* do.

Instead of the standard twenty-year-old model used in all cosmetic advertising, the girl with perfect skin and gleaming teeth and windswept hair, Gandhi said she wanted to use real women. She presented candid photographs she had taken herself on Manhattan streets. Pictures of intelligent, energetic, attractive women in their thirties and forties and fifties . . . one was in her sixties.

"Go find me one of our customers who *believes* those incredible dames in the Hiro and Avedon and Scavullo photos. But you show her the product, you tell her what's in it and what it can do for her, you show real women who use it, terrific-looking dames who look as if they might inhabit the same planet she does, then you get out of the way and let her buy."

When Gandhi had finished, Becky looked around the room. Victor Cameron was no longer there; she remembered seeing him stroll out as soon as Rae Ashley finished playing her jingle. But everyone who was left understood what had just happened. This apprentice, with only a few months' experience, had trounced her elders. She had shaken the puzzle box and come up with an original and honest solution.

No one was surprised when Becky said that the idea they were all going to work on now, the idea they would polish and make ready for submission to the client, was the idea that young Gandhi Hendricks had just submitted.

Rae Ashley and Becky wound up being the last in the room. Rae put a hand on Becky's shoulder. "Don't you think you should at least test the jingle?"

"I'm sorry, Rae, I can't see rock and roll in an Eve campaign."

"Okay. You're the creative head." Then, in a lower tone, "While it lasts."

"What?" Becky turned toward the woman in the white suit. "What did you say?"

Rae knew what she had just said. She had probably lingered after the others left just to have a chance to say it.

"Look, Becky, you helped me transfer to New York from the Detroit office, where God knows I was miserable enough. And I feel I owe you something. I think you should know the kind of gossip I've been hearing."

"I hate gossip. It's rarely accurate."

"I can't swear this is accurate. But it sure as hell is ubiquitous. And it's about *you*."

Mrs. Gagarin looked unimpressed. "So what else is new? There's always gossip about creative heads. Their work is always right there in the morning paper for the whole world to see. And tear apart."

Rae shook her head. "This isn't the usual carping, memo-war stuff. Everybody knows *something* is going to happen to you, Becky. I mean, to your job."

"We're the same thing." Wasn't it Descartes who said, *Je pense, donc je suis*? With Rebecca Gagarin it had always been, I *work*, therefore I am.

Rae picked up the memo pad that Becky had brought with her to the conference room. One of the oversize white pads with REBECCA GAGARIN

printed across the top in Franklin Gothic. Rae selected
a pencil from the debris on the conference table and
closed the opening of the first *C* in REBECCA, so that
it became a zero instead of a *C*. She drew an arrow
from the top of the little zero, pointing up.

"Most of them are saying that you're going to be
kicked upstairs. They say you'll get a fancy new title . . ."

"Maximum Creative Head? Lord of All Crea-
tion?" Becky laughed. Rae was not going to *frighten*
her.

"Whatever the title is, it won't matter. Because the
job won't matter. It will be so 'above' what is happening
that you'll never know what's going on until after it's
over. You'll still sound important, but you won't *matter*
at all."

A tickle of unease formed in Becky's gut. She
forced herself to laugh again. "You said most. The rest
of your prophets, what are they predicting?"

The point of Rae's pencil hovered around the second *C* in REBECCA. And turned that into another
zero. Only this time the arrow attached to it pointed
down.

"They don't think you'll be kicked upstairs. They
think you'll be forced to leave."

"Rae, don't be ridiculous. I've been with Seton &
Cecil since the flood."

"Can't you see, that's part of it? I know you came
when you were a baby, but how old are you now?
Almost fifty? That means you were already important,
already part of the big decisions, already close to Angus
when a lot of the account guys who are in charge now
were just coming in. Except the kids you used to send
out for coffee are now calling the shots. Okay, so they
know that the agency never lost an account while Becky
Gagarin was writing the ads. They know you work fast,
you think fast, you make decisions fast . . ."

"At least I'll never be a bottleneck . . ."

". . . but they don't like working with you. You're not in the club. You're not a team player. You don't give a damn what they think about copy, casting, music, strategy—whatever. You have a disgusting habit of zeroing in on a problem, all by yourself, and then just solving it, *by yourself.* Your motto seems to be Becky Knows Best. The fact that you usually do doesn't make it less irritating. Of course, they're not admitting that. What they're saying—more important, what they're saying to *Hamlin*—is that Becky Gagarin is passé. That a woman who's too *mature* shouldn't be in your job. They're saying you might have been an *enfant terrible* once, but you're over the hill now."

Becky's eyes stayed riveted to the two zeros (one with an arrow pointing up, the other with an arrow pointing down). "I thought maturity was good. I thought it implied all sorts of dandy things. Wisdom. Judgment. Stuff like that."

"When I said mature, I was being polite. It was a euphemism, like saying ladies room when you mean toilet. What they really mean is that you're *old.*"

"Forty-nine isn't old!"

"When it's one of the guys on the international board with you it isn't. When it's a *woman* it is. Confucius say: Men get distinguished, women get *old.*"

"That's nonsense! More than half of our account executives are women now . . ."

"Sure, there are lots of bright little gals hanging around the bottom of the ladder. How many do you think will make it to the top? Listen to me, Becky. Everybody's saying that Gagarin is on the way out, that her taste is boring, that what the place needs now is a *young* creative head."

Becky thought of how much harder it had suddenly become for her to get raises for her people. Just last week Hamlin had said she had to get approval from him—or from Wilbur Rank!—for anyone she wanted to hire who made more than $50,000 a year. The most important part of any creative head's job is hiring, and she had always had total control there before.

She remembered the pressure the account group had put on her not to set her own guidelines for the new work on Eve. That also had never happened before.

And she thought of the strange confrontation less than an hour ago, when Victor Cameron had used the same word Rae had just used to describe her taste. *Boring.*

It hurt the muscles around her mouth, but Becky smiled. "Rae, this nonsense you've been spouting, don't you believe a word of it."

She plucked the pencil from Rae's hand and erased the pencil marks that had changed the *C*s in REBECCA to zeros. So that the name on the top of the page read REBECCA GAGARIN once more. In the middle of the page she printed LOOSE LIPS SINK SHIPS and held up the pad to show Rae what she had written.

"It was before your time. It was a slogan that was all over the place during the war. World War II, not the Civil War, I'm not *that* old. It means too much gossip can be a dangerous thing."

"That's what I've been trying to tell you." Rae gripped Becky's wrist more tightly than she had probably intended. "I was trying to tell you the ship that's sinking might be *yours*."

The army of girls marched over the crest of the hill, the castle in the distance behind them. Their heads were held high and their hair bounced in the breeze. They were heading directly at Becky.

Irrationally, she felt that they would not pause when they reached her but would keep on coming and coming and coming until they trampled right over her.

Then one girl in front, in the middle of the first row, stumbled, nearly fell, did not fall, regained her balance, and did an embarrassed little jig before managing to get herself back in step with the others.

"Cut. Print that," Loren said.

"*Cut!*" an assistant screamed and jumped up and down semaphoring his arms wildly. The nubile little army scattered into chattering groups of teenagers. They were fourteen and fifteen and sixteen years old—it had been a formidable strain for them not to talk to each other this whole long morning.

"Don't worry, we have it," Loren said comfortably. "We'll just fade before her stumble and cross-dissolve to the older women."

In the finished spot, the marching girls would become twenty years older before your eyes. That was why the casting had taken so long. Becky had wanted

each girl to resemble the woman she was going to fade
into. No, *blossom* into. She'd told Loren, "I want
women to be able to look at this spot and believe that
you never have to lose the confidence of youth. That
you can march happily forward through your thirties
and forties and fifties and beyond . . . with a little help
from a product called Eve."

Loren relaxed his body from the cowboy squat he
had dropped into when they had started shooting, and
stood up and up and *up*. That was a new trick he must
have learned since she had seen him last, that easy
Western squat, that slow unfurling. She remembered
Gary Cooper used to be especially fond of that piece
of business. Now Loren seemed at least seven feet tall
as he sl-o-owly stood.

Becky thought how much Loren relished casting
himself in different roles. How full of invention he had
been in bed, charming little surprises calculated to leave
a girl amazed and delighted . . .

Now, how did Rebecca Gagarin happen to know
how Loren Odell behaved in bed?

She knew because once upon a time, a long *long*
time ago, when Loren Odell had been a cub writer
working in the group that Becky headed—the two of
them had, quite briefly, been lovers.

That was the time when Alexander Gagarin had
been drinking heavily. Yes, the same sweet Alex who
now skied and ran around reservoirs and taught art to
little children had been making ugly scenes and passing
out and sometimes blacking out: disappearing into
black holes of open-eyed unconsciousness.

And Loren had been there, young and sexy and
reaching out for Becky. And, although he had been
fifteen years her junior, after a while Becky had reached
out for him.

Their affair had been exciting, lecherous, and carefully hidden. Even if the boss is female it does not do

to sleep with the staff. *Especially* if the boss is female.

She did not feel she was betraying her husband.
While Alex was drinking so heavily, the man she had
married had disappeared, and Becky had been terri-
fyingly alone.

Then Alex had joined The Program and the man
she had married came home. Like a car sputtering into
life after being left out in the cold all night, the Gagarin
marriage had started up again.

A few months after that Loren Odell had left for
California. Not because his affair with Rebecca Gagarin
was over. Because Odell was an ambitious youngster
and had learned all that was of interest to him at Seton
& Cecil.

Still, it was always lovely when Loren came in from
California. Old friends who were no longer lovers, they
had no need to conceal anything from each other. It
was comforting to unburden yourself to somebody who
understood your problems, knew the cast of characters
where you worked—and was located a safe continent
away. It was like having an analyst you didn't have to
see three times a week.

"Loren, do you know why I picked this location?
Because I used to come here all the time when I was a
little girl. That's *my* castle on the top of that hill. Do
we have time to climb up to it and say hello?"

"*Your* castle?"

"Bits and pieces of old monasteries the Rockefel-
lers picked up in France and Germany and Spain, and
put together on the edge of the Bronx, of all places.
It's called the Cloisters. When I was growing up it used
to be my special place."

*She would go down into the subway at 167th and
come up at Fort Tryon Park, and there it always was.
Always sunlight around her castle, the banners slapping
in welcome . . .*

"Sure, we have time. I'm using a cherry picker for

the next scene and it'll take them a while to set up."

He climbed effortlessly beside her. "You're looking good, Marchbanks," she told him.

"You're in good shape too, Candida."

Candida and Marchbanks. Those had been the code names they had used to keep their trysts secret. (A pink WHILE YOU WERE GONE message on her desk: Mr. Marchbanks called, wants you to call him back . . . and Becky would hurry the few feet from her office to Loren's cubicle.)

Companionably, Loren asked, "So, how are things in Rebecca Gagarin's world these days?"

"Oh, just fine. Only, everybody is so much *older* suddenly. Yesterday Peter was a sweet little scabby-kneed boy, now he's a sophomore at U.C.L.A. And Miranda's *out* of college. The funny thing is I can't remember it happening. I must have slept right through it."

"You didn't sleep through it. You *worked* through it. Tell me, what's all this I hear about a class-action suit?"

"Class-action suit? What are you talking about?"

Loren stopped climbing to stare down at her. "I don't believe it. Only you could be so involved with your job that you don't even know what's going on around you. Haven't you heard about all those dames at Seton & Cecil, the place where you hang your hat every day, who are getting together to sue the joint?"

"*Sue* Seton & Cecil? What on earth for?"

"Sexism. Age-ism. Actually, a combination of both. They claim the agency discriminates against older women—women over forty—in hiring, salaries, promotions, little things like that. You *really* haven't heard about it?"

"They'll have a tough time proving it. Loren, you used to work at Seton & Cecil. You know how honest and decent and fair the place is. How could I have gotten as far as I did if they were biased against women?"

"Maybe by working twice as hard as any of the guys? By being twice as good?" Loren answered blandly. "I'll tell you one thing, Becky Gagarin, if the case comes to trial you'll make an unbeatable witness for the defense. Since deep in your heart you've always believed that Seton & Cecil wasn't incorporated in Delaware, it was incorporated in Heaven."

"Don't be silly. I've never said Seton & Cecil is *perfect*. Why, only this morning some nasty things happened . . ."

And Becky told Loren about Victor Cameron panning her work *publicly*. In front of the creative heads of all the other offices, not to mention a visiting Japanese tour group.

Loren frowned. "Who is this guy Cameron? Sounds like a real operator. Tell me about him."

She spoke carefully, trying hard to be impartial. "He runs the Australian office, and for its size it's one of the most successful in the entire agency. Real macho guy. Does the whole macho bit, the pub crawls, the women, the soccer, the women, the sailing, the snorkeling, the women . . . And you should see his shirts! You know the kind of denim shirts laborers wear, with big snaps instead of buttons? Only his are made of *silk*, not denim. He wears them open at the throat so a bit of chest and manly hair can peek out. No neckties, perish forbid. I mean, he's in charge of the whole office in Sydney, not just their creative department, but he always tries to look as if he'd just come from herding sheep in the outback."

Loren shrugged. Becky's attempt at sounding objective hadn't fooled him. "Isn't the outback arid? What would the poor sheep eat?"

"Oh, he'd scrounge something for them. This is

one clever man I'm telling you about. Tall guy, nice body, quite attractive I suppose."

Attractive enough, and clever enough, to have charmed everyone he met in the upper echelons of Seton & Cecil. At least everyone who'd gotten to Australia. Which was rapidly becoming a popular Seton & Cecil place for top management to visit—wonderful seafood, surprisingly good wines, smashing girls, and Victor Cameron to show you where to find them all.

Loren put his hands on Becky's shoulders and peered down into her eyes.

"Listen, Becky, take my advice. Watch that Cameron. You can't make what he pulled today disappear by pretending it didn't happen. Why did he pan your work in public? From what you tell me—the clothes, the way he turns himself inside out for visitors from New York—this is a man who knows how to use publicity. I'll bet he staged his little flareup at the Creative Caucus as a good attention-getting device. Here I am, the brilliant young genius from Down Under, ready and willing to take over old Gagarin's job. And do it better."

They were standing now before the Cloisters' most famous possession: the unicorn tapestries. Hunters surrounded the unicorn, their faces intent. They were going to capture the unicorn. They were going to destroy it. Becky did not want to hear what Loren was saying. Seton & Cecil was not a television miniseries or a paperback novel about the Byzantine world of advertising. Seton & Cecil was *home*.

She remembered how once, years ago, at the end of a long and tedious meeting in a client's office, Angus Seton had turned to her with a question about the research on that client's advertising.

"I don't have the numbers with me. I'll look them up as soon as I get home."

"Home?" Seton had asked, eyebrows rising. "You keep your research files at *home*?"

It had been a slip of the tongue. A silly certified Freudian slip. She had meant to say I'll look them up as soon as I get back to *the agency*. But even then, after only a dozen years or so of working with Angus Seton, she already thought of Seton & Cecil as the place she'd most belonged in all her life. Home.

"Loren, don't worry about me. I'm built into Seton & Cecil. Like the filing cabinets. The place would fall apart without me! Now pay attention, I've got a brand-new 'how many' joke for you. This is a good one: How many copywriters does it take to change a light bulb?"

He gave up disappointingly fast.

"No copywriters. But ten account men. Before you can change a light bulb, you have to *position* it correctly."

Loren still wasn't smiling. "I miss you, Becky. They don't make them like you in California."

She put a finger on an imaginary dimple and simpered up at him. "So what am I like?"

"A loner. Too much of a loner. Often difficult, sometimes abrasive, but always intelligent." He paused, then continued, "So intelligent that occasionally you can't see what's going on right under your nose. Listen, come to California? I want to show you how Odell & Comrades has grown."

She leered at him and twirled imaginary mustachios. "Come up to my office, little girl, and I'll show you my balance sheets? No, thanks. Candida doesn't want to be someone who pops into Marchbanks's mind when he's between young ladies."

He laughed, and together they walked back down the hill toward the huddle of reflectors and cameras and crew.

When she left, Loren was high up on a cherry picker with a cameraman, directing a repeat of the marching shot. It was late in the afternoon and he was working fast because he was losing the light. She would have loved to hang around and watch Loren play director some more. But she had an appointment with Horatio Hamlin. And no one kept Hamlin waiting.

From his perch on the cherry picker, Loren watched the car with the S&C license plates drive off. He waved and shouted, "California! See you in California!"

As the car drove south on the parkway, back home to Seton & Cecil, she was sorry that Loren hadn't had a chance to get a better look at the unicorn tapestries. Especially the happy ending. Because yes, there was a happy ending. The mythical creature had been hunted down, destroyed—and then, miraculously, was reborn.

Horatio Hamlin was typing.

He was completely focused on the task at hand, his fingers battering the keys, rat-a-tat-tat.

It was the same when he just *talked* to the people on his staff. His chin would jut as he machine-gunned words at them, clipped, curt. Rat-a-tat-tat.

Ah, but when Hamlin talked to *clients*, it was a different matter. Then he would stand close, there would be a friendly tap on the shoulder, a pat on the back, a cordial handshake, his voice would become obliging, reasonable. Sometimes, when the client was an important one, controlling a budget of many millions, Hamlin would greet the man with a fervent Mexican-style abrazo.

Becky sat down silently. He knew she was there. For reasons of his own he wanted to keep her waiting. On the wall facing her, blown-up snapshots of the athletic, adventurous, risk-taking Hamlin stared down at her, such sharp and candid snapshots she could almost smell the sweat.

Horatio Hamlin was the only top-level executive

Becky could remember who had been brought into Seton & Cecil from the outside; Angus Seton liked to promote from within. But when Seton started spending more and more time in England, he had said it would be an opportunity to bring fresh leadership to the New York office. Someone who would look at his agency with eyes that were not misted with the fondness of having grown up there. Someone new. Hard-working. Tough.

In his first year at the agency Hamlin had presided over what was nearly a bloodbath, cutting the staff by a sixth, wiping out whole departments.

And then, announcing that he wanted a Chief to run the creative department, not a committee, Hamlin had humiliated three male creative directors by inventing a new, higher echelon. Creative *head*. And promoting Rebecca Gagarin to it.

The day he had announced her promotion, Hamlin had called Becky into his office and read her a letter from Angus Seton, doubting the wisdom of the move.

Angus had asked in his letter, how could Hamlin expect men to work for a woman? It was well known that women could not be leaders. What would happen to the morale of the creative department with a female at the helm? Besides, Angus had cautioned, the account men always complained how difficult it was to work with Gagarin. She was so unyielding in her opinions, so uninterested in theirs.

Seton's letter had concluded, "Besides, if you let Becky Gagarin run the whole department, she will stop *writing*, which would be a tragedy for the agency. There isn't anyone in the place, male or female, who can hold a candle to her."

Becky had known why Hamlin had read her that letter from Angus. He had wanted to make sure she understood that she was beholden only to *Hamlin* for her advancement. But even as Hamlin had read her the reasons Angus listed against her moving ahead, she had swept them from her thoughts and clung to that last glorious sentence. The words she would treasure and turn over and over in her mind for months to come: "There isn't anyone in the place who can hold a candle to her."

"Rebecca. I didn't hear you come in. Have you been sitting there long?"

"A few minutes."

"Here's what I wanted to talk to you about. Have you heard about this class-action thing?"

She nodded and silently thanked Loren for having told her about it.

"Well, do you know that one of your writers is mixed up in it?"

His eyes dropped to a paper on his desk. "Gal named Lilah James. Seems she's decided she's one of the elderly female geniuses that this agency discriminates against . . ." He furrowed his brow. "James. Didn't I hear she hits the bottle? If so, I'm surprised you've kept her this long."

"She has personal problems, yes. But she's a wonderful writer. I wish she'd told me what was troubling her instead of doing this."

But Hamlin wasn't interested in what might have been troubling Lilah James.

"I thought these female class-action suits had gone out of style—they were popular in the sixties and seventies. But suddenly they're back, hitting banks, insurance companies, all kinds of places where lots of females work . . . And now us. They began with the girls in billing and the girls in media and now it's the girls in creative. Well, I guess we'll have to leave it up to the lawyers for the time being, they're certainly charging us enough . . . How's the Creative Cotillion coming? All your little lambs having fun, spending our money in the Big Apple?"

The Creative Caucus had been one of Angus Seton's ideas, and Horatio Hamlin never hesitated to point out what a waste of the agency's funds he thought it was. But today he did not really want to talk about the Caucus. Only about one participant in it.

"*Victor Cameron*," he announced. "Have you thought about finding a place for Vic in New York? Heading one of the creative groups, maybe? Of course, it could be considered a step down to transfer from being the head of an office to just running a group, but the move would bring him to New York. Where a man of his ability belongs. The clients in Australia tell me he is first-class. A natural leader. Runs a tight ship. Even has a good second in place, ready to step into his shoes as soon as he comes here." Then he laughed and added, "He also plays a wicked game of tennis."

Becky could not believe what Hamlin was saying. He had gone around talking to people in Australia about Cameron joining her department, he had half-arranged it without a single word to her.

"Another thing, Becky. Have you ever considered that the low turnover in your department might not be as much a sign of stability . . . as of stagnation? Are your people not being raided because they're so incredibly happy with us, or because nobody else wants them? In fact, would you do me a favor and send me a list of the people *you* consider your real stars? Our standards ought to be the same. You may run the creative department, but *I* run the agency."

Loren was right, she thought. Victor Cameron's strategy of a public confrontation had worked. Hamlin had not been in the room, yet here he was repeating everything Victor had said, practically word for word. Either it had gotten back to him already—or Victor had dropped by personally to tell him.

"I can name my real stars, as you call them, right now. There's . . ."

"No. I'd rather you gave this some *thought*. It can wait until we get back from London."

Hamlin's meaning was clear: If he didn't caution her to think, she would rattle off the first names that popped into her head. "I'm coming in tomorrow anyway. I'll put the list together for you tomorrow."

She would agonize over it. She would review the files of everyone in the department. And she would probably wind up with exactly the same names she could have ticked off today. "Real stars" weren't easy to forget.

"One more thing. Howard Pullett asked me to speak to you about your attitude on United. Howard says the account group thinks consumers are bored with the campaign. It's been running for eleven years."

"Because it's been selling for eleven years. The customer isn't bored."

Hamlin sat back and studied her. "Could you be acting so stubborn about the United campaign because it was your idea?"

"Actually, that idea came from Angus."

"Really? Then that makes *three*. I always thought there were just the immortal two. The one for the vodka, and the one for the car."

His voice became light now, teasing. Anyone eavesdropping would have had to know Horatio Hamlin was just joking about Angus Seton's celebrated oeuvre having been limited to two campaigns.

But Becky had heard these jokes before. She knew that underneath them, Hamlin was furious about not having been appointed chief executive officer of the entire international agency by now. Everyone on the board knew the extent of the tension that had grown up between Seton and Hamlin. The famous Founding Father, now within sight of seventy, and the aggressive younger man who felt he had really been running the agency for the past five years, or at least the most important part of it, and wanted the whole world to applaud that fact.

Hamlin waited for Becky to laugh with him. But she couldn't. Yes, it was Hamlin who had promoted her to creative head. Who had made like a homing pigeon to her, on his arrival in the agency. Who said that she should be running the department, because she thought like a man and could belt out tough and hardhitting presentations . . . and look sweet and demure even as she was going for the jugular. And it was Hamlin who had nominated her to the international board and pushed the nomination through—despite Angus's incredulous reaction to the idea of little Becky, a copywriter, and a female at that, having a vote on the most serious issues facing the agency.

Any of the men who sat with Becky at board meetings now could have told Becky what she ought to do. She ought to laugh when Hamlin laughed. And vote the way Hamlin voted. But when Hamlin mocked Angus, as he had been doing more and more publicly of late, her palms would begin to sweat, her heart would thump angrily, and she could not join in. Because Angus—well, Rebecca Gagarin never felt that Angus Seton had just hired her.

It was more as if Angus had *invented* her.

Hamlin waited a beat for the woman sitting across the desk to join him in his joke. Then he bit his lip and changed the subject. "How's the Eve presentation coming? We having trouble there?"

"We filmed a new spot I wrote today. And I threw it open to a number of people from different groups, to find something to test against it. You'll be surprised who won."

"Victor said he sat in on that meeting, and Rae Ashley was out in front by a mile."

"*Rae?* No, it was Gandhi Hendricks."

For a moment, Hamlin sat staring at her silently.

"The black girl? With the peculiar hairdo? I hope you know what you're doing. Eve is an important account, not the sort of thing one throws open to juniors, whatever shade they are. I think we're finished, don't you?"

When her hand was on the doorknob, he added, "If you've reached the point of desperation with Eve, the point where you're assigning it to just *anybody*, you might want to see what Vic Cameron could do with it. Of course, providing you agree with me that Vic belongs in New York."

Now nobody would be able to say that he had shoved Victor Cameron into her department without consulting her about it first.

She had the strange sensation that somewhere an ominous clock had begun ticking for her—and that she was the only one who hadn't heard it.

Back in the sanctuary of her office, she would have liked to shut her eyes and put her head down on the desk like a kid in grade school. The way the teachers at P.S. 42 in the Bronx used to let kids rest for a while, when they were overextended.

But Eileen had followed her in.

"The girl from *Ad Hoc* is here. She's been waiting an hour."

Becky heard Hamlin's voice again. Hamlin was saying, "It spread from the *girls* in the billing department to the *girls* in media."

"Don't call her that."

"Don't call her what?"

"*Girl.*"

Eileen looked tired too. It was obvious that she too longed to get this day over with. Finished. In the OUT box.

"What should I call her? The lady from *Ad Hoc*? The woman? The person?"

"She has a name, doesn't she? Why not say Jane Doe—or whatever her name is—is here?"

Wordlessly, Eileen handed Becky a card. Becky
read the name on it: *Placidia Brubaker Pennysworth-
Klein*.

Becky looked up and said, "Send them *all* in."

"Rebecca Gagarin! I can't believe I'm meeting you at
last. Oh no, I didn't mean that, it sounds as if I'm
complaining about being kept waiting! Believe me, I
know how busy you are. What I meant was, I've been
hearing about you all my life. It's like meeting a
legend."

Becky's visitor shook her hand with reverence, gazing at her as if she were an icon, smiling at her with
perfect teeth. Becky could price that orthodontist's
smile. She had paid for two of them already: Miranda's
and Peter's. She was about to offer her visitor a smile
too, but closed her mouth instead. Dentists had been
for toothaches in the Bronx.

"Well, Ms. Klein, ah, Ms. Pennysworth-Klein?
What can I do for you?"

"You've already done it! You've been an inspi-
ration to women everywhere! You've had it all. Marriage, children, running the creative department of one
of the world's biggest agencies, how on earth did you
manage?"

It was the question interviewers always asked. And
Becky would usually babble about the importance of
organization, setting priorities, thinking ahead for
emergencies. Today she heard herself saying, "It was
easy. I just neglected the children."

There was a horrified silence.

Then Placidia chortled. Ms. Gagarin was *joking*.

"Well, actually, I did want to ask you to do something for me. You know every year *Ad Hoc* chooses a
different agency to honor? This year we've chosen Seton
& Cecil! We've already phoned Angus Seton, he's going
to send us a half-hour film explaining how he made the

agency great. But what creative name do you think of right after Seton's, when you think of Seton & Cecil? Rebecca Gagarin, of course. We'd be so pleased if you would introduce Mr. Seton's film. Everybody knows Angus Seton was your mentor."

Ad Hoc was the most prestigious of the advertising trade journals. And the *Ad Hoc* Festival was one of the most significant events of the advertising year. Every June *Ad Hoc* would bring together the most important advertising agencies in America to honor one of their own. That meant three days off at an expensive resort hotel. Speeches in the morning. Golf, swimming, tennis, riding, squash, racquetball, whatever made you look good in the afternoon. Rumors were exchanged. Grown-up men swapped business leads the way they had swapped baseball cards as small boys. Very quietly (because this was high-level stuff), people looked for better jobs.

"We always have a woman make one of the speeches. And if you introduce Angus Seton's film this year, we'll have our woman, and we'll also have a great creative leader from Seton & Cecil. The agency we're honoring. We'll be killing two birds with one stone!"

It couldn't have come at a better time. Becky had felt surrounded by assassins all day. She didn't go through any of that nonsense about consulting her calendar to see if she had conflicting engagements, but accepted immediately.

Placidia was taking off her jacket. She also took off her vest and rolled up her sleeves, the way she'd seen the guys do it at meetings, to signal that they were ready to get down to business.

"Of course, we wouldn't dream of telling Rebecca Gagarin what to talk about in her speech. But there is one topic we thought might be of special interest coming from you."

She blushed the modest blush of any client saying,

well, I'm not a copywriter, but I do have some terrific ideas now and then.

"We thought you might like to talk about the role of *mentors* in career development. Especially for a woman. Most people say a woman can't make it in the corporate world today without a strong mentor." Placidia turned on her tape recorder, looked at the woman across the desk earnestly, and demanded: "Rebecca Gagarin, who were your mentors?"

"First, let's make sure we know what we're talking about." Becky walked to the big dictionary enshrined on its mahogany stand in a corner of the room. The dictionary that had traveled with her from office to office, until they both made it to the office in the corner.

"*Mentor*," she read aloud. "Faithful teacher, guide, counselor, loyal advisor. In Homer's *Odyssey*, a sage, appointed by Odysseus to be the guardian of his son before Odysseus departed for the Trojan War."

"Mentors," she repeated, closing the dictionary. "Well, my father was a big influence on me."

Placidia looked disappointed. "Ah, yes, of course. To be successful, a woman—and also a man I suppose—must have a supportive father . . ."

"Supportive. yes, he sure as hell supported us. And it wasn't always easy, there were times when the world didn't need another sign painter."

Becky was in the sign shop again.

Her father's blue-veined hand held a stick of charcoal as he sketched out the big black desperate words: SALE. CLEARANCE. LAST TWO DAYS. EVERYTHING MUST GO. She learned to read watching the pleading words appear on glaring sheets of white cardboard. Also watching were Myrna Loy, Paul Muni, Don Ameche, Sylvia Sydney, Robert Taylor, Clark Gable, and all the other glamorous movie stars on the posters thumbtacked to the walls. The posters came to the shop with the pictures of the stars already on them, and with rectangles of empty space where her father would letter in the name of a local movie house—the Fenway, the Blenheim, the Loew's Fordham—and the dates the movie would show.

Every ten minutes or so, the Third Avenue elevated train would roar overhead and rattle the little shop. The stool the little girl sat on shook. The ancient desk with its spindle of past-due bills shook. The long wooden worktable covered with open cans of brightly colored paints shook, and the paints inside sloshed back and forth. Whenever Becky went near the paint cans or brushes the colors would jump off onto her skirt or middy blouse. But her father worked with them all day long, and his white shirt remained white while the words spilled magically from his fingers, each letter deftly and elegantly outlined.

Sometimes the telephone on the wall would ring. If there was a train passing overhead her father would clap the receiver tightly to his ear and yell into the mouthpiece. "What? You haven't got them yet? But the boy left here with them an hour ago. They're on the way. On the way!" And then he would set aside the sign he had been working on and start on whatever it was that the telephone had demanded. He would outline the letters with charcoal and fill them in with bold yellow or red or black paint. Sometimes the letters slanted like a line of skaters heading across the page against the wind. That was called Italics. Sometimes they stood upright and staunch, like brave Roman soldiers defending a castle. That was Roman. The little girl sounded out the letters, surprised and pleased whenever she could turn them into words . . .

"Ah. So it was your father's influence that led you to become a writer?" Placidia's flat midwestern voice jolted Becky back into the Now.

"A writer? Well, no, I think he hoped I'd be able

to get a job in somebody's office. A secretary. Maybe a bookkeeper, if I was lucky."

Placidia's eyes glittered. She sensed a dramatic touch of conflict for her interview. "Was his ambition for you so, ah, limited because you were a *woman*?"

"No. I was born into the tail end of a Depression. The big one, the one with the capital *D*. It was so big that even after it was declared officially over, there was still an awful lot of poverty around. Enough for us, anyway."

The pencil halted and the *Ad Hoc* reporter flushed. Becky suspected that her talking about being *poor* had struck the younger woman as, well, tacky. Unnecessary. Would she understand if Becky told her that even now, years after the sign painter's death, whenever anything of importance happened to her, whenever she got a raise or a promotion, she would find herself reaching for the phone to tell him? To earn his nod. To bask in his approval.

"Er, could we talk about some of your *other* mentors? I mean, like, well, like Angus Seton. Everybody knows what an enormous influence Seton has had on your career. It's true, isn't it, that he discovered you working in a *retail store*, back when no agency would consider hiring a retail writer, much less a *woman*, and *lured* you to Seton & Cecil?"

"He didn't have to do much luring. He paid me fifteen dollars more a week. Fifteen dollars was a hell of a raise in those days. Suddenly I was making more money than my father made in his whole life."

But Placidia was rushing ahead on her own track. Her eyes gleamed as she asked, "Tell me, is Angus Seton really as egotistic as everyone says he is?"

"You have to have a strong personality to build an agency from nothing to the size of Seton & Cecil. In fact, in many ways I think he's rather a *shy* man."

"*Shy?*" Placidia was incredulous.

"Yes. I think the outrageous memos, the famous stunts, the way he shows off when there are a lot of strangers in the room, I think it's all a cover for shyness."

Talking about him now, suddenly, surprisingly, Becky found herself missing Angus. He had been spending more time in England than in New York for years now, but it had been a horrible day. Like a little kid, she wanted Angus to come home and make it all well again.

Placidia was asking if there were any warm and human Seton anecdotes Becky could give her.

Becky told her about the traffic lights that had hung over Seton's office door when the agency was new. Seton had controlled them from his desk. When the green light was on, anyone could come in with a question, a problem, a piece of copy. But when the red light was on, you were not supposed to enter. Angus Seton was writing. Or, even more impressive, *thinking*. People tiptoed past the closed door then. It was like being in the Vatican and knowing that the Pope was on the other side of a partition, praying.

"My. You really do worship him, don't you?"

"Isn't that what you're supposed to do with a mentor? Worship him?"

It was late enough in the day for Placidia to get frank. "*Men* don't worship their mentors. They *use* them. Pick their brains. Borrow their clout. But you, when you talk about Seton, do you know your eyes light up?"

"You've never seen a man's eyes light up when he talks about someone who helped him?"

Placidia settled back in her chair. She'd never dreamed she would wind up teaching Rebecca Gagarin anything. "Oh sure, they'll *talk* about the warmth and friendship they share. But it's still the old buddy system. You do something for me, I'll do something for you.

Quid pro quo. They're both using the corporation for their own benefit. Whereas women—because of their nurturing natures, I suppose—don't take from the corporation, they're always delivering back into it."

Nurturing. If there was one word Becky disliked it was that wet and vapid *nurturing*. "Quid pro quo? What on earth can a mentee"—she smiled at the word she had invented—"do for somebody grand enough to be a mentor?"

"Succeed," Placidia said briskly. "Climb the ladder. Show what great wisdom the mentor demonstrated in choosing this particular lad to sponsor. Or, less frequently, lass. Which is why women today are *obsessed* with finding mentors. It's the kind of public endorsement not many men are willing to give a woman. Placing a public bet on anyone is dangerous. You should see how fast the most important man will dump a kid he's sponsored who isn't making it. And betting on a woman is even riskier, because any kind of failure will be that much more noticeable . . . Listen, this is going to be one damn good interview. Rebecca Gagarin, the first female creative head of a top-ten agency, tells you *How to Get a Mentor*."

She stood and threw her arms around the older woman. "My secretary will call yours to set up a good time for photos. See you in California. In June!"

Placidia rolled down her sleeves, put her jacket on again, picked up her briefcase, and was gone.

It wasn't until she was ready to leave herself that Becky discovered the vest Placidia had left behind on the chair. A natural oversight for someone who hadn't been wearing three-piece suits very long.

"Mom, this lady's been phoning and phoning. She said for you to call her back the minute you got home."

Becky recognized the number printed on the back

of the envelope that Miranda handed her, and sighed. She wanted to take her clothes off and put on a bathrobe, the oldest and shabbiest robe she had. She wanted someone to appear magically and produce dinner. She wanted the shoes and scarves and records and assorted debris to disappear from the floor in Miranda's room. She most definitely did *not* want to talk to Daphne Schwartz.

She dialed the number on the envelope.

"Mrs. Gagarin, I know you asked me to wait until *next* week before calling you again, but I've got such wonderful unexpected news! My client has raised her offer!"

"Mrs. Schwartz, now is not a good time . . ."

"Mrs. Gagarin, you didn't hear me. My client has *raised* her bid before she's even looked at your apartment. Presuming that it is in reasonable shape, she's actually offering . . ."

She paused dramatically, and whispered a figure.

"Mrs. Schwartz, that's very impressive. Only, you're forgetting one thing. I live here. My husband lives here. My children grew up here. This is my *home*. I think I already told you, I am not going to sell it."

And for the first time in her life Rebecca Gagarin hung up on someone, without saying goodbye.

"It's truly mysterious. Half my stuff has disappeared."

Miranda was packing, her thick blonde brows furrowed over the enormity of the task. Becky had given Miranda the color of her brows, but Alex had donated their thickness. Becky thought that soon she would be persuaded to pluck them by someone in the new world she was about to enter. Just as some high school friend had once gotten her to dye a platinum streak down the natural ash blonde of her hair.

The apartment Miranda was moving to was on 110th and Broadway. She had proudly told her mother that it was an elevator building. And then added honestly that of course the elevator usually didn't *work*. But the apartment was only on the fifth floor.

"Did you try calling Annabelle? She might have some of your things. Because . . . ," and Becky retrieved from the floor a skirt she recognized as Annabelle's, ". . . you seem to have some of hers."

On the floor next to the skirt, Becky noticed a Bennington catalog of courses.

"Taking this with you?"

"Nope—that part of my life is *over*. Kaput. Finito."

Becky thumbed the catalog's pages. What marvelous courses! Dance, theater, philosophy, Latin, Greek, Sanskrit. Independent tutorials with professors if you could not find exactly what you wanted to study listed in the catalog. Private studios for art majors, rehearsal rooms for music majors. Nothing labeled *pre-teaching, pre-nursing, pre–social work*—the dull, hard, poorly paid jobs that had been the female choices of Becky's time.

Becky ordered herself not to be jealous of Miranda. Why had she fought so hard to go to Hunter, she asked herself sternly, if it wasn't to be successful enough to send her daughter to Bennington?

"Where's your father? I thought we'd throw together something to eat, then I'll give you a hand with your packing, crawl into bed early . . ." She sighed and remembered the days when Charlotte would have dinner on the table when she got home. She hadn't made any attempt to find somebody to replace Charlotte yet. Miranda's eyes always filled with tears if Becky even mentioned it.

"Dad said not to wait up for him, he'll be late. He's helping them hang the show for tomorrow."

Becky had forgotten. Tomorrow was the yearly show at the Artists' Alliance. It was always handled as seriously as a Biennale. All the students exhibited their work from the summer, even the little children in Alex's classes. And since Alex came with Becky to advertising parties, she would have to go with him to tomorrow's vernissage.

Searching for her telephone in the midden heap on the floor, Miranda said, "I'll call Annabelle and see if she has my bomber jacket." But the phone rang before she could dial.

Osceola, Charlotte's sister, was calling Becky person-to-person, long distance.

Becky whispered, "Osceola, is she . . . dead?"

But no, Osceola only wanted to say that Charlotte was hanging in there. She was really amazing.

"Like yesterday. Yesterday, she even wanted to start crocheting Christmas presents, she said she'd start with Peter's. Well, of course when she found she didn't have strength in her fingers to hold a crocheting hook, she did cry a little. Do you know what she was going to crochet for Peter? A bunny rabbit. Charlotte knows how old Peter is, she raised him from the day you carried him home from the hospital and put him right into her arms, she *knows* Peter's a grown man now, her mind is sharp as yours and mine, but she wanted to turn the clock back and make him into a little baby again so she could be young and strong again herself."

Miranda was plucking at her mother's sleeve. "Tell Osceola I have to talk to Charlotte!"

Becky whispered, "I don't think Charlotte can make it to the phone . . ."

"*Ask!*"

Becky remembered when Charlotte had had the flu. It was one of the few times Charlotte had admitted that she was too sick to come to work and had stayed home. Miranda—a year old then—had kept crawling through the kitchen to the maid's room, and scratching at Charlotte's closed door. And scratching and scratching, even though Charlotte would not come out of the empty room . . .

Osceola said, "I hate to rouse her when she isn't in pain. But soon as she wakes up I'll tell her Miranda wanted to talk to her. I won't forget. I know Miranda and Peter were her babies."

When Becky had said good-bye and hung up the phone, she turned to Miranda. And found her tall grown-up daughter sobbing.

Becky got down on the floor and wrapped her arms around Miranda.

The two of them sat there, rocking back and forth, the way Becky used to sit in a rocking chair with Miranda every night. Sometimes reading to the little girl, sometimes singing, sometimes just rocking. Miranda had demanded it until she was so big that her heels had scraped the floor when Becky sat in the rocker with her child in her lap. Becky used to think she was doing it for Miranda's sake. An hour of "quality time" for her child. But she had been doing it for herself, too. An hour every night to hold someone in her arms, to feel the pressures and struggles of the day drop from her, as she rocked . . .

"I can't believe you saved these."

They had nearly finished packing when Becky found the shoe box full of nameplates. Round nameplates, oblong nameplates, cardboard and plastic nameplates, some with pins, some with Velcro, all saying the same thing: REBECCA GAGARIN, SETON & CECIL. They represented overnight trips to Chicago and St. Louis and Dallas and Boston, location trips to L.A. and Santa Fe, conferences in Paris and Mexico City and Toronto and once even Helsinki.

"Don't you remember? You used to bring me the name tags from wherever you went. Sometimes when

you were away, I'd pin them on all over me and make
believe *I* was Rebecca Gagarin."

Becky flushed. "Was it horribly lonely, having an
absentee mother?"

"Of course not. I had Charlotte."

Then Miranda looked at her mother, realized the
way that must have sounded, and added in a rush, "Of
course I missed you . . . but Charlotte was *here*."

And that sounded worse. Except it was true. It
was Charlotte who had taken her shopping for clothes,
Charlotte who had come to the ballet and piano recitals,
Charlotte who had been there in the kitchen that day
she'd run home from school with the news that today
she was a woman, today she'd found blood on her pan-
ties . . .

Alex was not home yet—how long could it take to hang
a bunch of children's drawings?—so Becky went to bed
alone. She lay there thinking that she had to send something to Charlotte. A little present to say they were
thinking of her. But what would be right to send? Osceola had said she was eating almost nothing and reading only her Bible.

She knew! She would send Charlotte's *babies* to
Charlotte. She would find a picture of the children when
they were little, when Charlotte had filled their world
while Mommy kept vanishing.

She got out of bed to ransack the desk in the bedroom, until finally, triumphantly, she found the snapshot she wanted.

And here is the Gagarin family clustered around
a kitchen table, celebrating a birthday. No, not the
whole family—Alex is missing from the picture, Alex
is taking it. Front and center, wearing a silver crown
that Charlotte has snipped out of tinfoil, sits the birthday girl, Miranda. Her eyes are shut tight and her
cheeks puffed out—she is all set to blow out five little

pink candles and make a big wish. In back of her, cheeks puffed out too, ready to help, stands a strong and smiling Charlotte. Next to Charlotte is three-year-old Peter, looking cranky even though Charlotte has just finished explaining that he will have a crown when it is his birthday. In back of Peter, a little apart from the others, still in suit and heels because she's gotten home only minutes ago and hasn't had time to change, is Becky.

Becky stared at the Becky in the photograph, the Becky in the feather-cut hairdo and harlequin eyeglasses of the time, and felt a rush of pity for the younger woman, who looked so tired and anxious and every bit as cranky as Peter. Could it be that she too was longing for a silver crown?

3

Joseph stood in front of the building and listened to Apartment 4A having a good old-fashioned fight.

Their Audi was parked in front of the building canopy, blocking the entrance. This was strictly against regulations, and Joe should have asked them (nicely, of course) to move it. But Saturdays were slow, and this might be the most interesting thing that would happen all morning.

The trunk of the car was jammed with rolls of blankets, cartons of books and compact disks, a birdcage, a guitar, a computer, a typewriter, skis, ski boots, and two large black boxes that Joseph thought must be amplifiers. The trunk was so loaded that the top wouldn't stay closed until finally Mr. Gagarin tied it to the rear bumper.

Mr. Gagarin said, not even looking at Mrs. Gagarin now, "It's just a few hours out of your life but it's a milestone event for Miranda."

Mrs. Gagarin answered, "I would if I could, but this particular morning I can't. I have this morass of reports to read."

"Can't you read them Monday? Why can't you work weekdays, like normal people do?"

Mrs. Gagarin said, "Remember, we're flying to *England* on Monday? Both of us."

Miranda, the daughter, was looking nervous the way kids do when they think their parents are behaving like nerds in public.

"That's all right, Mom, don't worry, you helped me with all that packing last night, please go along to the office, I know you have a lot to do."

"Well . . . if you really need me to help you move in of course I'll come."

"Don't be silly. When the place is all fixed up I'll invite you guys to dinner."

Mrs. Gagarin waved at the car as it turned into the park and drove away, and kept on waving as long as she could see it. She wiped her eyes with a Kleenex, turned, and said, "There's an awful lot of pollen in the air this time of year, Joe."

From Monday to Friday, the revolving doors on the Park Avenue side of the building would be in constant motion at this hour, as people spun into the lobby and the offices above. But it was Saturday so only one side door was unlocked.

The security man in the lobby had the *Daily News* on the reception desk, open to the daily murder. A portable heater sat on the floor near him. On Saturdays the heat went off at one o'clock, and the building would become cold within the hour—Becky had her own portable heater in her office upstairs. The security man's name was Nick, and he looked so comfortable that she felt guilty about disturbing him.

Nick had been making her feel guilty every Saturday morning for years.

From Monday to Friday the elevators ran automatically. But this was Saturday so the elevator was on "manual" and Nick had to take her up. On the fifteenth floor it was dark. "I'll walk ahead of you, Mrs. Gagarin, and turn on the lights," he offered, as he offered every Saturday morning.

"That's okay, Nick, I know where they are," she answered, as expected.

The first bank of light switches was to the left of the elevator, and the reception room leaped into brightness when she clicked them on.

She switched on light after light as she walked to her office in the corner. From Monday to Friday there would be a hum of typewriters as she passed each secretary's desk, but on Saturday the typewriters were covered and still, and the thick carpets swallowed her solitary footsteps.

Mrs. Gagarin: I wonder if you know how unpleasant that Dragon Lady you've got outside your office can be? She won't let me get past her, but I happen to know there is an opening for a junior writer in your department. So I'm going to wait until Dragon Lady goes back to her cave tonight and I'm going to leave these storyboards on your desk! We've never met but I'm sure you can recognize BIG IDEAS when you see them. I've been working in the media department at Seton & Cecil for eleven boring years, and I can hardly wait to start working for you. Wanda Schiavone, Ext. 919.

The note sat on a tower of amateurishly drawn storyboards. Becky picked up the top board. A stick-figure Cleopatra confided how much she regretted not having been born in the twentieth century, when she could have removed eye makeup more easily with Eve.

Becky sighed. A thousand commercials opening on Cleopatra had been submitted to her by young writers over the years. But when she saw the next board, she knew this Wanda could not be a *young* writer. She would have had to have lived many miserable years, a whole long unhappy lifetime, to come up with anything so awful, so mind-bendingly tasteless.

One of Seton & Cecil's accounts was Arrete deodorant: Wanda Schiavone proposed using a blind man as presenter in the Arrete commercials. A real authentic blind man, complete with seeing-eye dog. The blind man would appear in public places—ball games, theaters, maybe even on the floor of Congress—sniffing out and exposing people who had neglected to use Arrete.

Becky made a mental note to thank Eileen for having kept Wanda Schiavone away and turned to the stack of reports she was here to read.

Becky always used Saturdays for tying up loose ends. She would do things that could not be done during the week, when the phone rang insistently and meetings were penciled on her calendar back to back. And this morning she had awakened with Rae's warnings echoing in her ears from yesterday. Of course she would have liked to go with Miranda to inspect Miranda's new apartment, she would have loved doing that—except that suddenly it seemed more important than ever that there be no loose ends.

She had only finished the first page of the first report when the phone shrilled at her elbow.

"Becky. I have to see you. I'll take a cab. I can be in your office in ten minutes."

It was Lilah James, and her voice was slurred.

One of the many lessons Becky had learned from Angus Seton was that if you're not absolutely sure what is going to happen at a meeting, *do not have it in your own office*. That way you can always leave if things get sticky.

She said, "No, I'll come to you."

Lilah James had no lock on her office door. The sumptuary laws of Seton & Cecil decreed you had to be at least a vice-president to rate the privacy of a lock. Lilah's office was empty and Becky dropped into Lilah's barber chair to wait for her. Because that was what

Lilah had in front of her desk: a barber chair. An American flag hung over her window, doing duty as a curtain. A Bob Dylan poster looked down from one wall. Facing Dylan was another poster: Madonna in bustier and tap pants.

Becky was appalled at all the effort that had gone into making the room look as if it were inhabited by a cub writer or junior art director. And Lilah was one of Becky's contemporaries!

Lilah had not said that Gandhi Hendricks would be with her, but the two women walked in together. Was it a morning after for Lilah, or still the night before? She was wearing the same dress she had had on yesterday.

Becky had been sure that Lilah would want to talk about the class-action suit. She would want to explain to Becky how she had managed to get herself mixed up with the whole foolish enterprise. But that wasn't what Lilah was here to discuss at all.

"Want to fill you in on what happened yesterday, Becky. After we showed you the Eve stuff, we set up a meeting with the account guys to show it to them."

Lilah said that Wilbur Rank had arrived at the meeting arm in arm with Victor Cameron. It seemed the two men had lunched together. It must have been a pleasant meal, because they'd dropped cozily into seats next to each other at the conference table.

"Cameron kept calling us 'luv.' He kept nodding at the campaigns when we showed them, like he was saying hello to old friends. Or maybe he just wanted to let Rank know that he'd seen them all before, that he was now an expert on Eve.

"But when we said that the campaign we were recommending was the one that Gandhi had done, Cameron put up his hand like a traffic cop. He said that it wasn't his decision to make, but never in a million years would he have chosen that one."

Lilah stretched out her legs and leaned back indolently, hands folded behind her head, in a surprisingly accurate imitation of Cameron. " 'The only campaign that has a prayer of doing anything for the brand is the one with the music. The one that girl Rae did. It isn't geriatric like the other campaign. And remember, the client did say they wanted something *new*.' "

Gandhi spoke for the first time. She looked like a little girl in her Saturday jeans, sneakers, and sweatshirt. "That was when Gandhi Hendricks started yelling."

Lilah protested faintly, "Oh, you didn't really *yell*."

"So why did three security men show up?" Gandhi laughed at Becky's shocked face. "Only kidding. No security men. But I did tell Cameron that he was right, it *wasn't* his decision to make. I said that Becky Gagarin had practically invented Eve, we should all shut up and trust Becky's instincts when it came to that product . . . But Cameron wasn't about to argue with a junior writer. A nothing. He said he thought he'd just give Hamlin his opinion on the direction Eve should be taking, since he happened to be spending the weekend with Hamlin. Then he ambled out with Wilbur Rank, his arm slung over Rank's shoulder."

Lilah James began to cry. "What is this guy Cameron doing here, Becky? I'm scared of him. Tell me what he's *really* here for."

Becky poked about in her handbag for a Kleenex, found a clean one, and tucked it into Lilah's hand. "Well, actually, he might be coming to work in New York. I suppose it wasn't tactful of him to start handing out advice so soon, but Victor is a talented man, and like all talented people he has a lot of confidence."

Even while she said it she thought, confidence, hell. "Gall" was the word. Or arrogance. (Becky's mother, who sat invisibly beside her, suggested, "Maybe *chutzpah*?")

Gandhi said, "Come on, Lilah, let's get some coffee into you, you'll feel better."

Lilah stopped in mid-sob. Becky was her boss, she said, but Becky never rubbed it in. And Gandhi was now her best friend in the whole world. She wanted to treat both these wonderful women to brunch. She knew the sweetest little place for brunch not far from the office, they would adore it.

"Come off it, Lilah. We don't serve *brunch* here and what's more, we never will. Orange mimosa? Eggs Benedict? Not here! We can fix you a burger if you like. Plus the usual?"

The waiter folded massive arms over his chest. Lilah's sweet little place was a bar on Second Avenue.

Becky remembered her mother's warnings about ground meat and dirty kitchens. "Uh, can you make mine sort of well done? Sort of *burn* it, you know?"

With the courage of youth, Gandhi devoured one hamburger and ordered a second. Lilah concentrated on the usual: a glass of beer accompanied by a shot of bourbon.

Gandhi applied half a bottle of ketchup to her second hamburger and abruptly confessed, "You know, I feel I owe you a lot, Mrs. Gagarin—"

"Becky."

"—I've learned so much from you."

Becky moved her own hamburger around on the paper plate so it would look lived with, if not actually eaten. "So why do I have the funny feeling that it was you who lured Lilah into this class-action thing? If you owe me so much, why'd you do that?"

In answer, a smile lit the corners of Gandhi's mouth.

Becky repeated, "If you owe me so much, why the

hell did you get Lilah mixed up in this whole ridiculous charade?"

"Okay, I'll ask you one. Why, when Lilah wrote two of the best-selling campaigns we had last year, why hasn't she ever been made a group head? It *has* to be because she's a woman that she never got anywhere in the agency."

Becky glanced at Lilah and saw that Lilah heard nothing. Except for her boilermaker, nothing else in this room existed for Lilah right now. "Have you ever thought it might be because she is not the world's most abstemious woman?"

Gandhi grinned. "Have you ever seen some of the guys coming back from lunch? Listen, Mrs. Ga . . . Becky, why don't *you* join us in the suit? Now *that* would get publicity, Rebecca Gagarin coming out and saying that Seton & Cecil is unfair to women! And we've found a terrific lawyer to handle the case, she specializes in class-action suits."

Becky stared at the tall black girl. How long did it take to plait those intricate braids? Two hours? Three?

"You've got to be kidding. How could I, of all people, say that *I've* been discriminated against in the agency?"

Gandhi raised her brows. "From what I hear, you've always had to run twice as fast as any man, to get to the same spot."

Becky wasn't angry. At least, she didn't think she was. But she *was* irritated. "You want me to join a bunch of women sitting around and whining about their lot? Everything I've ever gotten at Seton & Cecil I've *earned*."

Deliberately, Gandhi said, "Gee. Then it must hurt like hell when they still won't let you into the club."

"Club? What club?"

But Becky knew exactly what Gandhi meant. Wasn't it pretty much what Rae had said yesterday?

There was a club in every business. Run by the people—run by the men—who talked each other's language, who backed each other up in meetings, who knew where the bodies were buried. Of course Becky was not a member of the Seton & Cecil club. She never had been. It didn't matter. She had gotten where she was by working harder. By being better.

"Gandhi is dandy," Lilah anounced. "But liquor is quicker." She waved at her pal the bartender: She was ready for a second boilermaker.

"No," Gandhi swiveled to her. "It's time for *coffee* now, pal. I know you want to keep that nice buzz going, and I promise the coffee won't sober you up. It will just make you a wide-awake drunk. So we can get you home in one piece."

Becky settled the bill with cash (the waiter finding the idea of American Express even more hilarious than the idea of serving brunch), and together the head of the creative department and the agency's newest junior writer put Lilah James into a cab.

Gandhi watched the taxi disappear. "I'd hate to have her head tomorrow. I wonder what got her started on that crying jag."

"I don't think you know Lilah very well, Gandhi. She's *always* teetering on the edge of hysteria. But I guess Victor Cameron trying to overturn one of my decisions really upset her. I mean, she could accept my choosing your campaign over hers, but a stranger walking in and trying to turn that around—Lilah looks on me as her protector, and I guess now she isn't sure where her protector stands in the scheme of things."

"Are *you* sure?"

"Of course I am. How old are you, Gandhi?"

"Twenty-four."

"I was working at Seton & Cecil before you were

born. Now let's find you a taxi too, so I can get back to my desk. Where do you live?"

"Don't make me laugh—we won't find a cab that will take me there. I live in the Bronx. I'll take the subway."

"The Bronx?" Becky didn't know why she felt so surprised. After all, this girl had been presented to her as a young Rebecca Gagarin. "I was born on 173d Street!"

"But I'll bet it wasn't a ghetto when you lived there."

Becky laughed. "Wasn't it? It was 100 percent Jewish. You couldn't find an open store on a Jewish holiday to save your life." *People walk gravely along the streets in tight family clusters, the children always at the center of the groups, small emblems of obstinate faith. But Becky's father says that religion is the opiate of the masses. And not believing in G-d in that particular neighborhood, going about ordinary pursuits on the Day of Atonement, makes Becky feel like an outsider, an infidel, a pariah . . .*

"I only knew one Christian girl while I was growing up. I used to think she was terribly exotic. She was born in Chicago and she went to church! To me, it was like being friends with a Fiji Islander. The Bronx may have been a different kind of ghetto in those days, but believe me, it was a ghetto."

Becky spotted a cab and hailed it. The driver looked betrayed when it was Gandhi, not Becky, who climbed in. And he *wouldn't* take Gandhi to the Bronx. He insisted he'd never get a fare back.

The next driver swore he was just getting ready to put his OFF DUTY sign on, he had to get to a toilet . . .

Gandhi didn't tell the third cabby where she was going until she was inside the cab, arms grimly folded.

"Lady, I can only go downtown. My engine's acting funny and I have to get to the garage."

Gandhi leaned forward until her lips were against the BurglarGard separating them. "You are going exactly where I tell you to, or else we are going to the Hack Bureau. So I can have them lift your effing license."

The cab swung around and headed Bronxward.

Although Gandhi had looked angry enough to kill, Becky had a strange feeling that she had enjoyed the little scene.

It was an Open Meeting (friends and family permitted) in the badly ventilated, crowded basement of a Catholic church.

It was nothing new to Becky. She had gone with Alex to many Open Meetings in the subterranean rooms, the back rooms, the cramped auxiliary rooms of synagogues, Baptist churches, Methodist Presbyterian Christian Science Seventh Day Adventist you-name-it churches. She spotted Alex sitting in the back and slid into the seat next to him. They had arranged to meet here, then they would go on to the show at the Artists' Alliance together.

The girl who was talking in front of the room was surprisingly young. She wore sweater and pants, the uniform of her generation, but they were definitely not cheap. With her eyes Becky stroked the silkiness of cashmere, the nubbiness of a very good tweed.

There was a hint of a stammer in the girl's voice, but it had been worked on, coached, there must have been good teachers in charge of the near-conquest of that stammer. She was a slight girl, ivory skin, delicate bones, dark eyes almost too large for her face. It was a pity she had cut her hair so short—it was thick, richly textured hair, as black as Alex's used to be when Becky had first met him. The girl lifted a hand to brush the marvelous hair out of her eyes, revealing nails that had been cruelly bitten, raw flesh where she had kept on chewing after she had gotten down to the quick. She clenched and unclenched the poor punished fingers as she described a childhood of affluent poverty.

Becky used to think that alcoholism was a disease of the poor. That alcoholics were shambling men who drank out of paper bags in doorways, who surrounded your car to swipe at your windshield with filthy rags at intersections and then whined for handouts. That was what she had thought—until she met the serious men and women who had joined together to do something about their common problem in the group to which Alex now so fervently belonged. Until Becky had started hearing stories like the one she was listening to now.

She was introduced to the pretty twelve-year-old with a room of her own in an expensive East Side brownstone. A bright little girl who passed the canapés at her parents' cocktail parties and then proceeded to finish whatever anyone had left in any glass.

Becky listened to the memories of the little girl— now grown up—who had polished off dregs of martinis, scotch, brandy, whatever was there, and then tripped upstairs to a room full of stuffed toys and games, where she would sometimes pass sweetly out.

The people in the room with Becky, the people listening to this story with her, *laughed*. Alex, sitting beside her, made a funny half-snickering half-chortling sound.

The speaker described having been thrown out of Brearley, Nightingale-Bamford, and Miss Hewitt's classes, because of drinking. And fired from a teenage bicycle tour of France. The wine was so delicious, and so available.

Everyone laughed.

She said that no college would keep her for very long, so her parents had zoned in on a minor, very minor, talent for drawing and sent her to the Artists' Alliance. And then, because it would get her out from under their roof (a problem that no longer lived with you was a problem half-solved), they had bought her an apartment of her own.

She talked about creeping on hands and knees toward her apartment door late one night (there was no way she could have made it upright) and bidding a polite "good evening" to the neighbor who had heard her creeping past his door and opened it.

They all laughed.

Becky had once asked Alex why everyone laughed so hard at the lacerating memories recounted in these meetings.

"Because we've all been there, and we know what it's like. We're really laughing at *ourselves*."

The speaker's voice was rushed now. She talked of expensive therapists purchased by parents who were still trying to solve everything with their checkbooks. Speaking more to a spot on the table than to the people in the room with her, she talked about the gratitude she felt to the man she had met at the Artists' Alliance, the man who had recognized her despair and persuaded her to join The Program.

"It's only ninety days since I stopped drinking, but with this wonderful guy's help, I'm beginning to think that I'll never have to start again."

Everyone joined hands for the Lord's Prayer. As soon as it was over the girl who had spoken rushed toward Alex. Standing on the tips of her toes, she threw her arms around his neck and kissed him.

Alex smiled down at the glowing young face. "See? You did it. You spoke at a meeting. Now, it wasn't so hard, was it?"

"Alex," Becky said, lightly, sociably, "won't you introduce me to your friend?"

Alex peeled the girl away. Not too far away; she still had one arm pasted to him.

"Oh, sorry. Becky, this is Zoe. Zoe, I'd like you to meet my wife, Becky."

The girl's hair had been cropped severely since Alex had begun the painting. Nevertheless, Becky recognized the dark-eyed girl in the picture that had preoccupied her husband for months now.

"You're her sponsor, aren't you? The man she was talking about."

He beamed proudly. "Yes. It's one of the best things that's ever happened to me, being able to help her."

They were in the faux-marble building that the Artists' Alliance occupied on upper Fifth Avenue. The top-floor gallery was a high-ceilinged room with an Italianate skylight, always used for exhibitions. Alex's two classes had been allotted favored space toward the front. (Parents who could pay hefty tuition for toddlers might also be generous at fund-raising time.)

None of the little artists was here. They were safely tucked into bed at home, guarded by nannies, sitters, au pair girls. The parents drifted around the paintings, wineglasses in hand, exchanging compliments.

"Carter invented the technique himself. What he does is drip Jell-O from a squeeze bottle directly onto the canvas . . ."

"After that kind of effort, I wasn't going to lecture Hilary about *spelling* . . ."

The effort was an expensive Laura Ashley bedsheet, streaked with green, purple, and orange crayon. On the hem of the bedsheet, someone had printed in shaky red crayon, *In Sumr we go to Sowth Hamton*.

Next to the Sowth Hamton landscape, Becky examined a collage constructed of Magic Marker, bits of felt, clay glued to cardboard, and what looked like the remains of treasured old family photographs. "Meredith got into the desk where I keep all the photographs, but when she said it was for *Mr. Gagarin's* class, how could I scold her? She's absolutely wild about him . . . ooh, he's going to talk now."

And the parents assembled into an obedient little circle around Alex, who said, "Small muscle manipulation . . . sensory awareness . . . group interaction . . . positive approach to materials . . . kinetic synthesis . . ."

Becky asked, "Why were you spouting that jargon? It isn't your usual style. Hey, don't grab all the blanket, it's *November* tomorrow."

"They tell me it's the kind of thing parents like to hear. And after all, they are giving me a week off next week, right at the beginning of term, so I can come with you to England."

"But you have an assistant. He can handle the classes while you're gone, can't he?"

"She." And after a pause: "Jimmy started Oberlin this year. Zoe's my assistant now."

Becky stared at the ceiling and remarked warily, "Zoe? That child who kissed you at the meeting?"

He was silent for so long that she thought he had fallen asleep. "So she might have a little schoolgirl crush on me. It's nothing to *worry* about, Becky."

Then he turned on his side, away from her.

4

"The little girls in the village sing about it when they jump rope. *Cecil Hall, it's the color of honey, it's made of glass and stone and bags of money* . . . It nearly ruined the Cecils, you know. They built it at hideous expense to entertain Elizabeth and her crew on one of the old girl's progresses . . ."

Angus Seton puffed on his pipe and leaned on the railing, gazing out over his countryside. Becky and Seton were up on the roof of Cecil Hall, a huge flat leaded expanse bordered all around with a carved oak balustrade so that sightseers wouldn't fall off.

The house was a dazzlement of glass. Enormous windows punctuated a stone facade—a warm honey-colored stone that seemed to absorb sunlight instead of merely reflecting it.

"But wouldn't you know, Bess stayed only a few days and tottered back to London to die, and then they had to begin all over and start bootlicking James."

He sounded as if he were chatting about people both he and Becky knew well, and things that had happened only yesterday. While he stood there, smiling down at her, Becky felt stout, unsuitably dressed, poorly made up—her usual reaction to any encounter with Angus Seton.

"Actually, the place is a hopeless muddle of Italian,

Dutch, French, and English architectural ideas. Plus a lot of expensive plumbing installed recently by an American advertising chap." Seton looked pensive for a moment, as if brooding on the outrageous price of plumbing, then cheered up.

"The locals say, 'Cecil Hall, more glass than wall.' So much glass was an exciting idea for its time; up to then windows had been smallish and cozy. As I said, the place is something of a muddle, but don't you think it joins together to form rather a pleasing whole?"

Becky granted that yes, she thought it did.

It was a beautiful clear afternoon. Crowded London was two hours away, frantic New York was eight hours away. Here all was order, space, and calm.

"I'm glad you agree. I think it's nothing short of a miracle that so many generations have added to the place, edited it, put in their own two cents about it, and yet it still looks halfway decent."

Cecil Hall, when Seton had found it, had been a sad heap with eighty decaying rooms, acres of overgrown gardens, and stables that any civilized horse would have champed at entering. But now the house had been redecorated, the gardens replanted, the Augean stables swept. Now there was an orangery and tennis courts and a swimming pool. Angus waved his pipe and talked about a pagoda, a pavilion, pediments, pilasters and porticos, fountains, a folly, a buttery, stables and a dovecote, a topiary and a temple, and down there, very far down (where Becky was trying not to look), there was a maze.

Angus had pounced on Becky as soon as she arrived. "Let's you and I have a look round before people start piling in. They'll be here all too soon." He had given Alex into the charge of a charming young wife (Seton's third) and taken Becky up to the roof to show her the scenery—he said. She knew it was really so that they could gossip. Angus adored gossip. He liked to maintain a certain lordly reserve and still be kept up to date on everything going on in the scullery.

"Cecil Hall? Were they related to *the* Cecil, your original partner?" Seton & Cecil had been in business for a few years before Becky had been hired, and she had always taken it for granted that once upon a time there had been a Mr. Cecil.

"My dear Rebecca, I had no original partners. In the beginning there was just Angus Seton, alone against the world. But I was worried that might sound a bit threadbare to client ears, so I *invented* a Cecil to share the letterhead with me. And lo and behold, one day when I had made my pile and was looking about for a place to hang my hat in England, they showed me *Cecil Hall*. I had no choice. I had to buy it. It was obviously destined."

While they talked, a quarter of a century faded away, and Angus Seton was once again the handsome young head of a tiny advertising agency, in the first stages of building his empire. And Becky was once again the worshipful young retail writer he had hired on the telephone, sight unseen, because he admired an advertisement of hers in his morning paper.

At Omni's Discount Department Store she had shared an office with three other copywriters. And somehow they had all been able to write, despite the ringing of each other's phones and—in those days before computers—the banging of each other's typewriters.

But on her very first day at Seton & Cecil she'd been given an office of her own. Tiny, but her own. With a desk of her own. And a window of her own. And a *door* of her own.

The door was the most thrilling of all. It meant other people had to stay out unless she wanted them in, and that morning she had stood, opening and closing her very own door, for the sheer glory of it.

Until once, when she swung the door open, there was a man on the other side, hand raised, ready to knock. Tall. Chestnut hair, with glints of gold, and a natural wave that—she later discovered—always appeared in humid weather. Gray, witty, appraising eyes. No jacket, just a white shirt with sleeves folded back at the wrists. No tie. Green suspenders.

"Rebecca Gelb," the man accused. It wasn't a question. If she weren't Rebecca Gelb, that was who she would have to become.

"Yes, that's me." Or should it have been, I am she?

She didn't know yet that this would be the pattern of all conversations with Angus Seton. That whatever she said, she would worry about it later. Had it been intelligent enough? Interesting enough? Good God, had it even been grammatical?

"Welcome aboard. My name is Seton. Angus Seton. We've spoken on the phone. I brought you something I'd like you to look at, if you can find the time." The man was carrying a heavy proof book and looked about for a place to set it down.

"I call this my Bible. I have put into this one book everything I know about advertising. Everything anyone *needs* to know about advertising. Don't bother with that first page, it's a barefaced lie."

Becky immediately looked at the first page. It read: *Private. For the eyes of Seton & Cecil copywriters, only.*

"We use the book to impress clients at new business meetings. It appeals to the voyeur in them. Says on the first page they aren't *meant* to read it, so of course they become desperate to. But listen, Rebecca Gelb, you *are* meant to read it. Study it. Think about it. Dream about it. Commit it to memory. I'll be back to hear you recite."

And without saying goodbye, he had turned and walked out.

It took Becky years to get used to that. Years of Angus Seton walking out of meetings without telling anyone if he were going to the men's room or, perhaps, to Europe.

Mortals said goodbye. Angus Seton simply left.

That first day, looking at the door through which all that radiance had disappeared, she had been swept with the strangest feeling. Not sexual attraction, although God knew the man was gorgeous enough. But it was a kind of roped-off gorgeousness. You expected to hear a guard hiss, "Don't touch" if you came too near. In a life that had been empty of charm, Becky had just been completely, quickly, expertly charmed. If it had been the Middle Ages she would have suspected witchcraft. Angus Seton had just done to her what witches or warlocks do to their familiars: enchanted her enough to make her willing to follow him anywhere. Enough to stay with him for twenty-seven years, a loyal, and most people said brilliant, retainer, but unfortunately not one he could place in the highest reaches of his agency. Because she was, after all, a woman . . .

But that was the past, and now Becky Gagarin was a guest of Seton's in his home, a member of his company's board of directors. Even if she had been placed there by a man Angus Seton had now decided he detested.

Leaning on the balustrade, Seton quizzed her about the Creative Caucus. How had it gone this year? Which of the visitors had impressed her most?

Planting her elbows on the balustrade next to his— and trying hard to keep her eyes from drifting down to the stone courtyard below—she spoke in glowing terms of reels shown by the creative heads of the Bangkok office, the offices in Oslo and São Paulo . . . and oh yes, the office in Sydney.

She was honest enough to include Sydney, although she could not help including it last.

But Angus picked up on Sydney immediately and said yes, he understood that Victor Cameron would be transferring to New York in a few weeks. That must be welcome news for Becky!

She assured Seton that she was ecstatic about it.

It was the first she had heard that a date had been set for Cameron's arrival.

Angus sucked on his pipe and said, "They tell me Horatio Hamlin intends to marry that girl he's been squiring about. Works in some bank, I believe . . ."

He made it sound as if Hamlin's bride-to-be stood behind a counter cashing checks. Becky said it was an international bank, with branches all over the world, and that Hamlin's betrothed was involved in their most important foreign operations.

"So she's got a man's job? I might have guessed. Hamlin always relishes ambition in women."

Put that way, *ambition* sounded like pretty breasts or good legs—something a man might savor in a woman, something that was there for *his* amusement.

There was a pause. As always, whenever Becky was with Angus, she was positive during the silence that he was thinking of twenty other people he would rather have been with.

She hurried to fill the gap and babbled about flying to London on the Concorde.

"I hated that thingumabob that kept clicking away in front of us. I was conscious every second I was up there of smashing sound barriers, and it made me feel so vulnerable and so mortal. Pilots should have to worry about sound barriers, not passengers. And the price! In retrospect, it seems ridiculous to have shelled out for it."

Angus looked wicked. "*You* didn't. Seton & Cecil did. Listen Becky, I'm glad we have these moments to talk privately. I want to ask you to do something for me at the meeting tomorrow."

"Of course!" She would swim the channel for him. She would journey forth and bring back the Holy Grail. She would ride naked through town à la Lady Godiva.

"I've put an important subject on the agenda for tomorrow: the future of the agency. Sitting in this tranquil place, away from all the action, does give one perspective. Here, divorced from the hustle and bustle, I have had a clear realization that the agency has come to a dangerous turning point. The creative work of Seton & Cecil is going down. Don't turn pale. I don't mean New York. It's the international shops that worry me. The Creative Caucuses are helping, but not fast enough. The agency's work isn't nearly as impressive now as it was in that Golden Age we both remember."

They both knew he meant the days when Angus Seton had been in charge of the creative work, and doing most of it himself.

"It strikes me that our creative people are no longer *reaching*. 'Ah, but a man's reach should exceed his grasp, or what's a heaven for?' All present management seems to care about is gobbling up smaller agencies, megamergers, intricate financial schemes, the harder to understand the better. My God, last year Hamlin insisted on a joint venture in Tokyo! I don't think he gives a hoot for anything as pedestrian—and difficult!—as the mere making of advertisements."

He breathed the word "advertisements" the way a charismatic Christian might say "prayers."

"We are changing from an agency that used to explode with creative energy to one that thinks of itself as a branch of Wall Street!"

Becky nodded happily. From the first year that Seton & Cecil had been in business, Angus Seton had worried that the agency was losing its creativity. She felt at home now, listening to the familiar lament.

"This thing I would like you to do for me. I can't do it myself. Whenever I start complaining that Seton & Cecil is no longer interested in creating the world's best advertising, every man jack at the table starts defending his own turf. Everyone says that it might be true of the other offices, but it isn't true of *his*. I want it understood once more that the future of Seton & Cecil depends on how creative we are! I want the question of raising creative standards all over the world brought up at tomorrow's meeting! And Rebecca, *you* are the logical person to do it. Since you are the only person on the board from the creative side."

"Not the only one," she said shyly. "There's you."

"Ah, I *used* to burn with creative fire. Centuries ago. No more. Do you know how I think of Seton & Cecil now? As if it were a garden that I planted and pruned and watered a long long time ago. A garden that others have taken over, and now they fancy it belongs to them. Nevertheless, I cannot help feeling grieved when I see weeds grow in my flower beds . . .

"So . . ." and his voice became brisk, ". . . Will you do it? Raise the question of our declining creative standards at the meeting tomorrow? Scold a little, so they at least *think* about it? Remind them that *au fond* we are still an advertising agency, and that it is time for the shoemakers to return to their lasts?"

Becky nodded gravely.

And now, since they were here in this secret place, she ventured, "You've stopped sending me notes. I was beginning to think you were angry at me about something."

"Angry at you? Don't be silly. I stopped writing because Hamlin asked me to stop interfering in New York creative matters. After all, New York is now his office to run."

She suddenly wondered, could Angus Seton be jealous of Horatio Hamlin? Which was nonsense, of course. Seton was godlike. Mentor, hero, deity. And Horatio Hamlin, while scary, was merely human.

"And now, let's go down and visit my maze! It's my favorite place of all . . . did you know that these mazes were probably inspired by the early Christian church . . . they used to lay out penitential mazes in stone or tile inside churches, for sinners to journey through on their knees . . ."

They went down into the labyrinth together.

As she walked through it with Angus Seton, the shrubbery walls kept her from seeing where they were really going, which she supposed was the whole point of a maze. But of course Seton knew the way.

She remembered the time she had visited the Garden for the Blind with her father.

She'd been ten years old. Her father had read about the extraordinary garden designed for blind people, and that very weekend they had taken two subways to Brooklyn to see it.

No, not *see* it. Her father had said, "It will be more exciting for you to discover the garden the way blind people do. Through the feel of the flowers as you touch them . . . through the fragrance of each flower." And even with her eyes tightly shut she had not been afraid of stumbling because it had been her father guiding her. With the merest hints of pressure from his hand he had steered her, showing her when to turn left, when to turn right, when to go straight ahead, when to stop.

When Angus Seton and Becky Gagarin came out of the maze, Bentleys and Daimlers and a Jaguar were drawn up in the courtyard and servants lugged suitcases inside. The rest of the board had arrived, along with their chic and laughing second wives. The board members were successful men: They had almost all rewarded themselves by now with second wives—prettier, skin-

nier, better-dressed, and better-natured than the haphazard choices of their youth.

"Are you sure this is only for the two of us? Shouldn't
we agree on somewhere to meet in case we lose each
other?"

Alex scrunched deeper under the coverlet. The bed
might have been designed for royal accouchements: It
was eight feet long and just as wide. Over their heads
a canopy swung on golden chains, and from the canopy
fell curtains of Genoa velvet.

"And would you believe it, somebody *unpacked*
for me? I thought there was a sneak thief around, until
I looked in that fancy chest over there and found my
stuff all laid out in it. And I never thought I'd see the
kind of little drama we had at dinner outside of a movie.
Seton sending the ladies out of the room, so the gentlemen could linger over their port and make decisions
about the empire. There was a scene like that in *Four
Feathers*."

Becky remembered the hum of conversation and
the tinkle of glasses in the Great Eating Room. The
minstrel's gallery at one end. A Jacobean fireplace at
the other. The long table stretching on either side of
her into eternity, Angus dimly perceived at one end,
his wife at the other. All the other marvelous rooms
she had glimpsed on the way in to dinner—the music
room, the billiards room, the conservatory, with a tiled
pool surrounded by palms and giant ferns and huge pots
of lobelias . . .

Alex continued, "Those fancy cars your pals rented
to arrive in. It will all wind up on the expense accounts,
so who are they trying to impress? Each other? You
know Becky, I don't think I want to come with you to
any more of these shindigs."

"I'm sorry if you feel out of place."

"I don't. I happen to be completely at my ease in stately homes. I watched 'Upstairs Downstairs' faithfully for years, just so I would know how to behave if I ever got invited to Angus Seton's place. *You're* the one who's uncomfortable, and that makes me uncomfortable."

"Don't be silly. I'm having the time of my life." And to prove it, she told him about the mission Angus had entrusted to her, for tomorrow's board meeting.

Alex whistled. "That's typical of generals. They love to send the junior officers out to storm the barricades first. If you do what Angus is suggesting, won't it irritate every guy in the room? Especially Hamlin? Won't Hamlin feel it's a criticism of the way he's running the store?"

"It's only a subject Angus wants discussed. How could just talking about it irritate anyone?"

"Becky, you know you could get hurt if you wind up in a shootout between those two guys? Angus Seton and Horatio Hamlin. In this corner, the aging titan, and in that corner, the wave of the future."

"Angus wouldn't let me get hurt."

He raised himself on an elbow to stare down at her. "Dear God, I think you really believe that."

"Angus *hired* me for the agency in the first place. If he hadn't found me, I'd still be writing copy on 34th Street."

"You had nothing to do with it? Your brains, your talent, your bloody—as the Brits would say—hard work? You're nothing but another good idea that Angus Seton had?"

Becky said that was not such a bad thing to be. And that it was midnight. And that she had to get some sleep to be fresh for tomorrow's meeting.

When she woke the next morning she was menstruating. This was not supposed to happen. She was not due for another two weeks. The Indian doctor had said that she would start *missing* periods. Not that she would get bonuses.

Breakfast was not in the Great Eating Room, nor in the morning room. Although it was already the first week in November, it was such a glorious day that breakfast had been laid outside, on the terrace near the pool.

Wilbur Rank's wife poured herself a second cup of coffee. "I feel sorry for you fellows," she cooed. "As for me, *I* plan to go riding. I'd absolutely loathe being stuck in a little room poring over numbers on a day like today."

"Well, *somebody's* got to do it," Alex Gagarin pointed out blandly, and reached for another scone to slather with butter and fresh strawberry jam. There was a moment of silence as the prettily dressed women digested what Becky Gagarin's husband had just said, and then there was a ripple of embarrassed feminine laughter.

In the annual report they were called *directors*. In Seton & Cecil slang they were *rajahs*. Each man had his own emirate. Pieces of Europe, South America, Asia—each rajah was responsible for his portion of the world, its profits, its growth, its reputation.

Angus Seton, the chairman of the international board, sat at one end of the table. Horatio Hamlin, vice-chairman and head of the New York office, sat at the other. Although every person at the table was equal when it came to voting, it was clear that Seton and Hamlin were the most equal of all.

The meeting began, as usual, with each rajah reporting news from his own realm.

Germany had had to sue a client for nonpayment. In England, the printers' union was launching yet another strike. The two English directors summarized frantic efforts to shift billings into television.

The best figures of the year came from Japan, the office that Horatio Hamlin ran as a joint venture with a Japanese agency. One of the European directors said jokingly, "Maybe the Japanese will wind up owning *us* soon. Eh, Ham?" But when Horatio Hamlin swiveled and stared at him, he placated feebly, "Just teasing, my friend," and the meeting continued.

In New York, there were rumors of a class-action suit. Some women were trying to form themselves into a group and threatening to sue the agency.

Wilbur Rank fielded this one. "It's a bunch of older gals. They claim they're not as well paid as men, and promoted slower. Of course no one takes them seriously. I doubt that it will ever reach a courtroom, but any time you get near a lawyer his meter starts running, and it will probably cost us a bundle in legal fees."

The Compensation Committee reported. As in most corporations, only outside directors—men who did not work for the firm—served on the Compensation Committee. The outside directors were recommending salary increases for ten executives, among them a dramatic one for Rebecca Gagarin. They said they had been checking into executive compensation at other agencies and had discovered that hers was at the low end of the scale for a creative head.

Becky took a deep breath. The figure they were recommending would make her salary higher than Wilbur Rank's. Or Howard Pullett's. Her fellow executive vice-presidents. Both account men, both protégés of Horatio Hamlin. Both were sitting with her at the board table right this minute, Wilbur seeming to scribble notes to himself in his pocket memo book, and Howard seemingly absorbed in figures they had already finished reviewing.

Becky told herself that she had been at the agency

longer than either one of them. Besides—could they
build campaigns? Could they come up with ideas that
seduced customers into stores? But she knew that they
both believed they did something far more important
than writing. They kept clients happy. They steered the
ship.

Anyway, they were not neglected for long.

That day lunch was wheeled in. But Horatio Hamlin invited the Compensation Committee for a little
stroll first. And when the afternoon proceedings began,
the outside directors took the floor again to announce
that there had been an inadvertent omission. They now
believed that Wilbur Rank and Howard Pullett should
receive raises too, equal to the one recommended for
Mrs. Gagarin. Looking at Hamlin to make sure they'd
got it right, they said that would help keep the account
forces and the creative forces in the proper balance.

The matter of executive compensation being disposed of, the meeting moved on to the day's critical
question: What could be done about the lagging price
of the agency's stock?

Horatio Hamlin sketched a dollar sign on his pad
and framed it with black mourning bands. "Everyone
knows Seton & Cecil is worth more than what we're
selling at now! Our stock has been dead in the water
for a year now, and if we can't get the price up, it could
leave us exposed to a takeover."

The room was silent. The class-action suit had been
dismissed quickly, a bunch of disgruntled women making frivolous demands. But a takeover would affect the
pocket of every person in the room.

Hamlin looked at the sorrowful frame he had
drawn around the dollar sign and began surrounding it
with happy little exclamation points.

"But there *are* things we can do to defend ourselves! We can split the board into groups, so the directors will be elected in different years, not all together

in a bunch. That would make it harder for a raider to take over the whole board.

"We can buy back as many of our own shares as possible, which will drive the price up and make us less tempting. We can put in a shareholder rights plan—you know, those "poison pills"—that would also make us more expensive.

"We can keep in better touch with our most important stockholders, the pension funds, so they'll be less likely to dump us at the first hostile offer . . . But the first thing we *have* to do, immediately, is appoint a committee to put all these plans into motion. I'll be happy to chair it."

Around the table smiles bloomed at this list of specific steps that could be taken to secure their jobs and titles and pleasant lives. And, while no one was delighted with the thought of Horatio Hamlin heading the rescue squad, no one minded his taking on the necessary work.

But Hamlin was still speaking. "However, we mustn't be naive. The history of the past few years shows that most of the companies that have tried to defend themselves against takeovers have lost out in the end. Despite all the safeguards we put in place, we could still be vulnerable.

"And so, if in spite of all our best efforts there is a change of management, I believe that it is only fair that people who have worked hard to build Seton & Cecil should be protected."

And Hamlin passed out a list of agency executives he was recommending for golden parachutes. In the event of a takeover, each person would bail out with a little gift of three years' salary, stock options redeemable immediately, and all benefits—insurance, pensions, any bonuses that had not yet been paid—intact.

"Special arrangements for special people," Hamlin

smiled, as other smiles bloomed contagiously around the table.

Becky studied the names on the list. She thought, Seton & Cecil is an advertising agency. The most important thing we do is make advertising. Yet—except for herself—on this list of twenty people there was not a single creative person.

She took a breath and raised her hand.

Even to her own ears, her voice sounded soprano and flutey, in contrast to all the baritone that had gone before.

"Doesn't the Bible say something about not muzzling the ox that treadeth out the grain? Don't you think that if we're going to start handing out golden parachutes, our best creative people have a right to some of them too? Seton & Cecil is supposed to be one of the world's great creative agencies. But once these 'special arrangements for special people' becomes public knowledge, it will be quite clear whom the agency values. *Not* our creative people."

And she went on to cover the points she and Angus had discussed the day before—the importance of the shoemaker sticking to his last, of Seton & Cecil returning to its original mission: creating great advertisements.

Throughout her plea, Horatio Hamlin did not look at her once. He stared down the length of the table at Angus Seton, as if it were Seton who was speaking.

"We can't afford to start handing out these goodies to *everybody*," Hamlin growled.

For someone who had spoken so passionately just the day before, Angus sounded mild when he answered. "I have to say I agree with Rebecca, it's always a good idea for an advertising agency to consider the effect of its actions on creative morale . . ."

There was some debate. And when the debate was over, three additional names had been added to the

golden-parachute list. The creative head of the London
office. The creative head of São Paulo. And Victor
Cameron, formerly of Sydney, Australia, soon to be of
New York.

Horatio Hamlin did not appear shaken by the set-
back, although he had the closed, bland look on his
face that he always wore when things did not go his
way.

"I see the next item on the agenda is a discussion
of the future of the agency," Hamlin said. "Mr. Chairman, if I may, I would like to lead off that discussion."

Then, without slides or notes of any kind, Hamlin
took the floor again, for an hour.

"London should have foreseen the printers were
going to strike and laid plans to switch print advertising
to broadcast before it happened! Germany should have
checked more carefully on the credit rating of that de-
linquent client. I am sure we are not the first supplier
they have tried to cheat! And I hate to remind you that
it was I, Horatio Hamlin, who just had to initiate steps
against a takeover, steps which should have been taken
long ago."

Hamlin stood rigidly in one spot as he talked, his
hands clasped behind him. When he finally moved, circling the table, all the rajahs followed him with their
eyes, mesmerized. Now his voice was less sharp; there
was actually warmth in his tone as he spoke of Angus
Seton's long years of valiantly preventing the kind of
problems Hamlin had just lamented.

"And now, with his usual foresight, Angus has put
the future of the agency on our agenda. It is clear that
our founding father feels that the time has come to
change the way we operate, before this creeping ca-
sualness ends up torpedoing us all. And, while he has
never complained about it, I am sure that Angus would
also like us to clarify the line of succession at Seton &

Cecil, so that he can enjoy his semiretirement and know the agency will still have firm direction . . ."

"Are you running for chairman now, Ham?" It was Seton's voice. Mildly interested, somewhat amused.

"Don't be silly, Angus. We have an excellent chairman, long may he live. What we need is a CEO. A chief executive officer who is young enough, and firm enough, to prevent *messes* . . ." his voice took on a revolted note, as if he had just noticed a puddle of vomit on the floor, ". . . while he leads the agency bravely forward into the twenty-first century!"

"I wonder, who can that be?" mused Angus.

Hamlin smiled. "I suppose we ought to vote first on whether or not the directors believe a CEO is *needed*, before we talk about who it should be?"

Becky had never sat on any other board. Even so she knew that Angus could have stopped such a vote from happening. Because it was quite clear that Angus did not want Hamlin seizing the reins that he had not yet dropped, did not want Hamlin trying out the feel of a throne he had not yet vacated. But perhaps Angus was confident about how such a vote would turn out?

All of the directors from New York (with the exception of Rebecca Gagarin) thought that having a CEO was a wonderful idea.

But all the other directors—the Europeans, and the men from Canada and Southeast Asia and South America and the smaller offices of the United States— saw no need for a new hand at the helm. (And besides, none of them liked Horatio Hamlin all that much.)

It was a majority for no CEO. Becky's vote would not have changed things no matter which side she had come out on.

But Horatio Hamlin did not see it that way. In fact, he did not seem to see Becky at all, anymore. She was the only director from the New York office who had not followed his lead.

After she had voted, as far as Horatio Hamlin was concerned, the only woman in the room had disappeared forever.

Now Becky had to cope once again with this thing that was happening in her body. She had feared, *Après moi, le déluge*, but the back of her dress and the seat she'd been sitting on looked fine. She breathed in relief.

Rebecca Gagarin may have been a new breed of woman, but she had inherited anxieties dating back to Eve.

When Alex and Becky took the train back to London, five solemn little girls jumped rope in front of the train station. As they jumped they chanted: *Cecil Hall, it's the color of honey, it's made of glass and stone and bags of money* . . .

Their voices shrilled when they got to "bags of money." They sounded like tiny banshees as they shrieked the words.

Alex and Becky sat side by side flying home, but they didn't talk much. Becky felt troubled, and Alex seemed preoccupied, too.

Again, a device in front of them ticked off the miles until they would break the sound barrier.

She watched the numbers click by and thought about Angus Seton.

Working for Angus had been unlike anything Becky Gagarin had ever experienced. She remembered those first years, when she used to bring her copy in to show him—how his pencil would hover over one of her sentences, and stop at exactly the word she'd suspected might be a little weak. Then he would gaze into space for a few seconds and pull out of the air the sharper word that would make the sentence vibrant and firm—make the whole paragraph spring into life.

She remembered how he would sometimes throw temper tantrums at agency meetings, but of course she always forgave them immediately. He had the right to be impatient with minds that *plodded*.

She remembered how he could direct his charm at an unsuspecting group of businessmen who thought they were choosing an agency. And how, within an hour, they would submit to the charm, enjoy the submission, wag their tails, and beg to be chosen by him.

She'd always believed, until she met Angus Seton, that Southerners *thought* in the same sleepy way they spoke. And then she discovered the crisp edge of Seton's mind, ideas so sharp that they sliced through the prattle of any meeting.

For her, Angus Seton had always been incandescence, luminescence, the marvelous flash of lightning that had selected Becky from all the other girls working in all the advertising departments of all the retail stores in New York City, and plunked her down into a shining new life.

Angus was the sun; she was only a minor planet. To Rebecca Gagarin, Angus Seton was mentor, hero, father, all bound into one. Her life had been spent in the warmth of his glory. She never stopped to think that she might have done better to kindle a candle of her own.

5

Victor Cameron did not pretend to be surprised when, a few days after Rebecca Gagarin got back from the board meeting in England, she invited him to stay on in New York and run one of her creative groups.

He looked without enthusiasm at the list of the accounts she wanted him to handle and the list of people who would be transferred to his group.

"Don't mean to start carping right away, luv, but can't you give me anyone less geriatric than these? *Young* writers, *young* art directors? People who can give me stuff that sparkles?"

People who would follow his banner without a lot of questions. Who would not waste his time by arguing with him.

The Cameron group kept different hours from the rest of the agency. Victor let it be known that he loathed mornings, didn't really wake up until midafternoon, and only hit his stride around midnight. All his young people thought that was romantic. The Cameron group worked into the early hours of each morning and drifted in one by one late the next day, bleary-eyed and self-important.

Victor gave TGIM parties. Thank God it's *Mon-*

day. Every Monday evening, one of the paste-up tables was cleared. Wine and beer and cheese appeared. Victor's very young staff relished these parties; they enjoyed knowing the whole agency was talking about the stylish goings-on in the Cameron group.

It became *the* group to work in.

Victor explained to them, "Our group says Thank God it's Monday because we *like* working. We like it better than anything else! Most people spend all week waiting for the weekend. *We* spend all weekend waiting for the week! We know making ads is the most fun you can have with your clothes on."

They ate his words.

Victor fired two art directors and one copywriter.

Becky Gagarin went to his office to tell him, "I like to be consulted before anyone in my department is let go."

"Sorry, luv. But you'll be amazed at how morale shot up as soon as I got rid of the stragglers. Those who are left feel they're working in a place that has *standards* now."

Victor rented an apartment on Sutton Place. He announced that he also planned to take a house on the ocean for the summer and told his young troops that the ones who did the best work would get weekends in Easthampton as an extra, nontaxable reward.

Becky Gagarin had thought she knew what Victor's salary was. It began to occur to her that Horatio Hamlin might have made some special arrangement with Cameron. Extra hardship pay, for the discomforts of Sutton Place in winter, Easthampton in summer?

Long after all the men on Rebecca Gagarin's level would be calling a new client Al, John, or Joe, they remained Mr. Smith, Mr. Doe, or Mr. Jones to Becky. In fact, she rather liked hearing her own voice still calling the clients "Mister," while the account men were already on a first-name basis. To her own ears she sounded modest, polite, charming in a Jane Austin sort of way.

She didn't realize the honorifics had been invented to create barriers, to set people apart, and that by continuing to call the clients "Mister" she was keeping them at a distance.

She never took part in the small talk that starts business meetings in America and encourages the birth of business friendships. The chat about baseball, football, tennis, golf, sailing, whatever the seasonal sport happens to be. Because she didn't *care* about sports. Because they didn't interest her. She refused to realize that this small talk was only the same ritual savages go through when they raise their hands, palms exposed, to show strangers they have no weapons. That when you begin a meeting by reviewing last night's football game, you are not just sizing up the man across the table, you are also showing him how unthreatening you are, that you have no weapons. Rebecca Gagarin sat silent through these important preliminaries . . . rarely bothering to hide how bored she felt.

But there was one client who never wanted to talk about basketball. One client with whom Rebecca had always felt as easy as if she were sitting with her mother, across a kitchen table in the Bronx.

Princess Lyubov's secretary telephoned. "What strings do I have to pull to get you over here again? The old girl's been screaming for you." It was time for Becky to pay a call on the Princess.

And so at seven o'clock one morning in late November, Becky Gagarin followed a Japanese manservant through the marble entrance hall of a triplex on Fifth Avenue. Up a curving marble staircase. Down a corridor with recessed cases of African and oriental art. Past many closed doors and one opened door.

That particular door was always open. It wasn't just a bedroom, it was a shrine devoted to the memory of the Prince, the Princess's last and favorite husband. He had been the favorite because he had come equipped with a title she could use for the rest of her life. And because he hadn't had the effrontery to give her anything besides that. He hadn't helped plan her cosmetics empire, as her first husband had. He hadn't given her children, like her second. He hadn't introduced her to people she wanted to know—dancers, singers, artists, poets—like her fashionable third. He was simply something she had *bought.* And because she had owned him totally, she was devoted to his memory.

So his bedroom remained the same—hairbrushes in place on the inlaid ivory-and-teak chest, embroidered silk slippers beside the bed, silken bathrobe fastidiously arranged atop a coverlet that was turned down, ready and waiting. Waiting for a long time now. The Prince had been dead for thirty years.

The Japanese manservant knocked delicately and opened ebony double doors to Princess Lyubov's bedroom. The curtains that banked the wall of windows were not open. Not because it was early, but because Princess Lyubov liked rooms to be dim. Long before doctors had started to fret about the dangers of sunlight, when wealthy women were still advertising their money with year-round tans, the Princess was already preaching that sunlight aged the skin. Now she had her worries about electric light.

At the end of the room, in an immense glass bed made up with pink satin sheets and covered with pink cashmere blankets, a tiny Chinese empress waited for Becky.

At least, Natalia Lyubov always looked like a Chinese empress to Becky, with her long black hair parted in the middle and hanging loose around her shoulders (later in the day it would be coiled into a bun at the nape of her neck), her slightly slanted black eyes, and her incredibly smooth amber skin. Becky knew that when the Princess took her frequent vacations in Switzerland, it would be to have that smoothness restored in some arcane manner, in a clinic that only the world's richest women knew existed.

This morning, the Princess wore a bed jacket embroidered with dragons. She didn't loll against the pink satin pillows plumped up behind her; she sat upright, erect as a girl. Small rectangles of paper covered with numbers were strewn around her on the coverlet, some slipping to the floor. They were brokers' confirmations, recording stock transactions the Princess had made the day before on exchanges all over the world.

Lyubov Cosmetics was Seton & Cecil's oldest account. And at ninety-three, Natalia Lyubov was the agency's oldest client. But the cosmetics were only part of the Princess's empire. She had made other fortunes playing the stock markets of the world. Becky had often heard her put through calls to one or another of her five brokers: the fat one, the skinny one, the tall one, the short one, and the dead one. ("The dead one" was a man who had replaced another man who had died while serving the Princess twenty-five years ago.)

Scattered on the bed, along with the brokers' confirmations, Becky saw—as usual—books in six languages: Russian, French, English, Spanish, German, and Italian. No, not Chinese. Princess Lyubov only *looked* Oriental. There was not a drop of blood in her that was not Jewish.

When the Princess spoke, the opulent room disappeared and Becky was back in the Bronx with her mother. *Natalia Lyubov had the same Russian-Jewish accent that Frieda Gelb had had.* So that when the Princess, holding up a magazine and pointing to the smallest advertisement she could find in it, would complain, "Why can't you get me nice little ads like this, instead of those big expensive pages you always buy?" it was Frieda Gelb that Becky heard. Saying why can't you walk ten blocks to the other bakery, where the challah is two cents cheaper?

The Princess spoke six languages, she played world-class bridge, she called film stars and divas by their first names, she was dressed by celebrated couturiers—yet Becky Gagarin, unlike most people who dealt with Princess Lyubov, was never afraid of the old lady. When Natalia Lyubov opened her mouth, it was Frieda Gelb speaking.

"Good morning, ma'am. Did you sleep well?" (At the beginning, Becky had not been sure how one was supposed to address a princess. So she had settled on ma'am, which was what Disraeli had called Victoria in an old J. Arthur Rank film.)

"Sleep? I never sleep." Becky's mother had also insisted that she never slept.

When Becky had first taken over the Lyubov account, Angus Seton had told her that one of her responsibilities would be to appear every morning at the Princess's bedside. At seven in the morning. Because like most extremely old people, the Princess woke very early. Which explained the confirmation slips scattered over the bed and the books from around the world. Princess Lyubov had been reading and planning, figuring and plotting, thinking and scheming since dawn, and by seven o'clock she was starved for someone to talk to.

"Do you play bridge?" she had asked Becky hungrily, on their first morning together.

"Oh, ma'am, I'm sorry, I'm afraid I don't." She would not have admitted it even if she could play. Who would want to joust with those fierce old eyes, that still wily mind?

So Becky Gelb and the Princess did not play cards;

they talked. They had been talking for years now. Mostly, about the Princess's empire.

Princess Lyubov owned a triplex on Fifth Avenue, a forty-five-room cottage in Newport, an apartment in Neuilly, a château in the south of France, an important collection of Picassos, Chagalls, Braques, Soutines, and Matisses, and one of the world's most profitable cosmetics empires.

She had been the first cosmetics manufacturer to decide that a woman's face wasn't just a face. That it was a cluster of competing territories. That the throat and the eyes, the cheeks and the lips, had needs as different and conflicting as Russia and the United States and Japan. And so Natalia Lyubov had proceeded to make a special cream or lotion for each of these territories and package them in cunning little jars, for which she charged ruthless prices.

But today, the Princess just glared at Becky and demanded, "Why don't you come to visit me any more? Why do you send me a cowboy and a bunch of children?"

It took a while before Becky understood that the cowboy was Victor Cameron, and the children were the members of his ambitious young group.

Since Becky had become creative head she no longer called on the Princess every morning. One of the creative groups was always assigned to the Princess instead; it was now Victor Cameron's turn.

"I do not like him," the Princess proclaimed. "He is always making love to his hair. He strokes it and he pats it and he fondles it. I feel as if I am watching the man play with himself in public. It embarrasses me."

From pink satin sheets, she glared at Becky. "Don't bother to invent excuses. I know why you no longer come yourself. It is because you make more money working for other clients now."

She paused. With diamonds flashing from her fingers, and a Picasso peering down on the scene from the wall behind her bed, she announced to Becky, "Money isn't *everything*, you know."

All the paintings in the bedroom were of the Princess, even the Picasso. There were portraits of the Princess seated, the Princess reclining, the Princess full-face, the Princess in profile. One very large painting showed the Princess regal in floor-length sable, ready to go out for the evening, while behind her a little boy stretched a timid hand toward her coat and an even smaller girl cowered behind her brother.

Becky knew they were the Princess's children. Grown now, of course. It had been hard to reconcile the sixtyish man and woman Becky encountered at advertising meetings with the terrified children in the painting.

The religion of the Lyubov empire was nepotism. The little boy in the painting, Michel Lyubov, was now the Princess's manager of research and development. The little girl, Ariane Lyubov, was now in charge of product education. She spent most of her time now visiting stores, upsetting the salesladies behind Lyubov counters.

"Michel and Ariane have mentioned it too," the Princess was saying. "They too think it is a scandal the way you snub us now. The way you never come. They also do not like that cowboy; what does he know about beauty? He only wastes our time babbling about television. I hate those ugly black boxes. I do not even know how to turn one on."

"I'm afraid I agree with the, ah, cowboy about television, ma'am."

The Princess scowled. She began breathing heavily and her eyes flashed. "I cannot believe what I hear! Such nonsense from *you*? Lyubov *never* advertises in television. Lyubov advertises in *magazines*. The best magazines, with nice shiny pages! Even if the ads you buy are too big."

"I am just suggesting we could *add* some television, ma'am. Television is like a magic machine for creating new customers. I can prove it to you, I can show you figures . . ."

The Princess placed a hand over her heart and started to pant. My God, Becky thought as the old lady hyperventilated, what if I kill her?

But when the Princess spoke again, her voice was strong and full of rage. "I too can make figures prove whatever I like. I too can make numbers kick up their heels and dance a kazatsky."

Becky took a deep breath. "It's true that magazines have done a marvelous job for you, ma'am. *So far*. Women of a certain age all know who you are. But what if you are losing fortunes by not telling your story to their daughters? There's a new generation that doesn't like to read, it likes to sit on a couch and eat potato chips and *watch*. Ariane could appear in the commercials, Ariane could speak for you . . ."

Ariane had inherited her mother's photogenic quasi-oriental beauty, if not her mother's brains.

"Speak for me? No one has ever spoken for me. If we must use the power, the authority of Natalia Lyubov for this extravagant television advertising, Lyubov *herself* will appear."

Becky sighed. "Ma'am, how can that be? For years, women all over the world have had fantasies of you. Such romantic, beautiful fantasies. You, suddenly turning up in the advertising, as you are today—charming and wise as you are now, but perhaps a bit older than they expect, wouldn't that upset them? Reality always pales compared to fantasy. And if Ariane appeared in the commercials she could say such marvelous things about you, things so wonderful they would sound like bragging if you said them yourself . . ."

The Princess had stopped listening. She had not sent for Becky to hear such treason. She reached out to pluck a tiny jar from the table beside her bed.

"Have they shown you my newest Lyubov cream? It will be my greatest triumph. There is absolutely nothing in it to disturb the most sensitive skin. It is two hundred percent pure, minimum. So pure you could eat it."

She picked up a teaspoon from the breakfast tray on the bedside table, uncapped the little jar, and gobbled a spoonful.

"Don't forget!" she said, waving the spoon at Becky. "When you advertise my cream, you must say that it is the purest even Lyubov has ever made. As innocent as a virgin."

After that, Becky and the Princess had a good, hard-working session. But when her maid finally appeared to run the Princess's bath, and Becky's hand was already on the doorknob, the Princess beckoned her back.

"Oh, all right. I can see you will keep nagging me and nagging me until you have my permission to experiment with the television. So go ahead and try it. Maybe with Joujou, my new perfume. But if you do stick my poor Joujou into those ugly black boxes, make sure you say, 'Wear it on your furs.' Write that down. *Wear it on your furs.*"

"Furs, ma'am? Television is for the masses . . ."

"Nonsense. *Everyone* has furs."

When Becky's hand was on the doorknob a second time, a very little voice came from behind her. "I still don't understand why you want to use Ariane."

Becky turned once more. "Oh, ma'am, it will be such terribly hard work. Would you want to spend hours upon hours in a grimy recording studio, going over and over the same sentences, to make sure they came out exactly on time?"

"Yes," said the Princess. "Maybe if I lost a few pounds? Couldn't I appear in Lyubov commercials then, instead of Ariane?"

But the Princess did not wait for Becky to answer. She had asked, but she knew what the answer would be. She had known all the answers, all her long life.

She lay back against pink satin pillows. "Anyhow, come back soon. Time crawls for me in the mornings. You are young now, but when you are my age, you will learn that the hours go by very slowly." She closed her eyes. "It's the decades that go fast."

Outside on Fifth Avenue, Becky realized that she had missed a golden opportunity to do some judicious damage to Victor Cameron. It would be gratifying to see Victor fail on the agency's oldest account, and anyway, hadn't Princess Lyubov practically asked to have him removed?

Only, Becky had never done things like that before. And she wasn't about to start now.

The day, which had begun at Princess Lyubov's triplex, came full circle now. It finished with Miranda Gagarin's first dinner party. At 110th Street and Broadway.

Frank—the driver assigned to Mrs. Gagarin by the agency—looked startled when he drove Becky there from the office. In fact, the whole neighborhood looked startled, when they assembled to witness Becky's arrival in the chauffeured car.

Becky knew Annabelle and Wendy would be there. They were Miranda's college chums, and the three girls were sharing the apartment now. She had not expected Seymour, although she was not completely surprised to see him, because she remembered the boarders of her childhood—single men recruited to help a family pay the rent. That was Seymour's function in the apartment now. He was not the lover of any of the girls; he had simply been enlisted to take Karem's place, when Karem had decided he wanted to go home to India, after one week in the apartment. Although the girls were already beginning to consider Seymour a poor replacement. At least Karem had been able to deal with electrical and plumbing emergencies, while Seymour had needed their help the very first day to plug in his hair dryer.

There seemed to be no living room, so the dinner party sat around the kitchen table and drank white wine (except for Alex, who stuck to club soda) while they waited for the casserole that Miranda had in the oven. Miranda said it was an eggplant and rutabaga casserole; she had brought the recipe home from The Zen Master, where she now worked.

Then the rat walked out from behind the stove.

Becky saw it first and climbed onto a chair, and from the chair to the kitchen table. Annabelle threw herself into Wendy's arms. Seymour just stood there, shivering. Alex laughed.

The rat looked at them without blinking, then walked back behind the stove.

"Ciao," Alex said to the disappearing tail.

Annabelle extricated herself from Wendy's arms and said, well, she'd already suspected they had mice. Rats had not occurred to her. She planned to spend as little time at home now as possible. Annabelle was a graduate student at Columbia and usually in classes, or in the college library. She announced that from now on the library would see even more of her.

"I think I'll be putting in a lot of overtime now too," Wendy said. Wendy was doing an "internship" in a lithography shop. New York was not panting for art history majors, and the lithography shop would flesh out a résumé that now had glaringly little listed under *Experience*. Because Wendy was an intern the lithography shop didn't pay her anything. So she didn't expect trouble if she asked to work longer hours.

Miranda was the only one with a *real* job. Miranda waited on table evenings at The Zen Master, a restaurant on East 8th Street that served only vegetarian food. The place had no liquor license. The customers were young, Miranda said, and didn't mind bringing their own wine. She admitted the salary was bad.

"But then, you have to consider the tips," she told her mother.

"How are the tips?" Becky asked.

"Bad," said Miranda.

Before the rat had made his (or her) appearance, while they'd all been making conversation over the wine, Annabelle had told them that her father was a doctor. Wendy had said her father was a lawyer. Seymour's father was in contracting (which made his inability to install a light switch or put up a shelf, let alone handle a plumbing snake, all the more perplexing).

Miranda said her father taught at the Alliance and her mother worked in advertising.

"What do you do, Mrs. Gagarin—write the copy? Design the layouts?" Wendy asked hopefully. An advertising agency might conceivably need an art history major.

"She goes to meetings. And she has *lunch*," Miranda told Wendy. She turned to her mother—"Well, everytime I used to ask you, 'What did you do today?' sometimes you told me about the meetings but you *always* told me about lunch. Who you ate with. What restaurant you went to."

Alex said, "Your apartment is certainly in an interesting neighborhood, Miranda."

Becky stared down at her wineglass. What Alex had said reminded her of an old Chinese curse. *May you live in interesting times.*

Half the buildings on Miranda's block had been

abandoned long ago, the doors and windows either bricked up or covered with steel plates. Although one building, directly across the street, was not completely abandoned. Miranda said she'd noticed people coming and going all day on mysterious errands, through a narrow entrance someone had created by removing bricks from the bricked up door. Miranda's neighbors in her own building had advised her not to be too curious about what the men were doing in the vacant house. "That way, if the police ask, you can always say you dunno."

Miranda's landlord had vanished a month ago. Days afterward, the janitor disappeared too. The orphaned building was now on a rent strike.

Miranda told her parents they'd had a tenant meeting and promised each other to be very prudent and organized about the strike. The rent would be placed in the bank every month, in a special fund labeled *Escrow*, from which they would only make bank-certified withdrawals to buy oil for the boiler and pay the light bills. Except that the boiler had exploded last night. Miranda wondered, might the janitor have sabotaged it in some way before departing? She said that Jesus Garcia, who lived next door, and who had been elected building manager, had spent all day on the phone talking to various city departments about the possibility of the city adding to their funds so that a new boiler (secondhand, of course) could be installed. Before the winter began in earnest. Or even sooner, because without a boiler there was no hot water.

Miranda hugged Becky. "Don't look so upset, Ma. Once we get a few little problems solved, and fix it up a little, you won't recognize this place, it will look so great. I'll knock on Jesus's door right now and ask him what we should do about the rat."

Jesus Garcia accompanied Miranda when she came back. He was a small weary-looking man, who said that

rat poison was not the answer. Other rats would just
come. The problem was the hole in the cellar wall that
had been created by the exploding boiler. When the
boiler was replaced, the wall would be bricked up, and
rats would be discouraged from entering.

He suggested, meanwhile, a cat.

After Jesus left Seymour said he couldn't live in
the same apartment with a cat. Cats made his eyes water
and they made him sneeze. On the other hand, he didn't
think he was allergic to rats. They had just had a rat
visiting, and he hadn't sneezed once.

Miranda said, "Maybe the rat got into the building
through a hole in the cellar, but there also had to be a
way he got into our apartment."

"You mean, somebody has to get down on the floor
and stick his nose under the stove to find a rat hole?"
Seymour looked gloomy.

"Nobody said anything about *his* nose. I thought
of it, I'll do it."

Just as she had suspected, Miranda found a hole
behind the stove.

It took them all an hour to move the stove away
from the wall, locate a piece of plywood, nail the plywood to the wall, and get the stove back into place.

"There are four of us versus only one of him, Ma,"
Miranda told Becky, encouragingly. "It's nothing to
look so *unhappy* about."

Alex looked at Becky. He suggested that maybe
Miranda could save the casserole in the oven for tomorrow, maybe tonight they should all go out for dinner? Everyone liked that idea. Nobody wanted to have
dinner in a kitchen with a thin piece of plywood separating them from a rat. They said that maybe they'd
get used to the idea of the rat tomorrow and it wouldn't
bother them so much, but not tonight.

"Only, it still has to be my treat," Miranda told

her parents firmly. "This is *my* dinner party. I invited you."

At Rivera's Pizzeria on Broadway, Miranda ordered two Super Pies. She specified that the first pie should be half mushrooms (for herself and Seymour, both vegetarians), and half sausage, for Annabelle and Wendy (carnivores). The entire second pie would go to her parents, the evening's honored guests—and for that pie, Miranda grandly ordered the works. Including extra cheese.

Rivera's Pizzeria offered a choice of beverages: orange drink or grape drink. Miranda had had the orange drink before and advised Becky and Alex that it tasted like orange-colored water. So they ordered the grape drink (which tasted like grape-colored water).

Rivera's had no tables or chairs. But there was a long shelf under the window facing upper Broadway where you could put down your pizza and your drink, and the group lined up there.

Miranda stood between her parents. "Be careful not to burn your tongues on the pizza," she cautioned them, as if they were *her* children.

In a dreamy-sounding voice, Becky said, "Pizza always reminds me of the south of France . . ."

"Pizza reminds you of the south of *France*?" Alex repeated.

"Don't you remember? I was doing that campaign for French wines, and the agency was sending me on a trip through the wine country, and we decided that we would add a vacation onto it for the whole family, all of us? You were excited about it because there was a Picasso show in the Palace of the Popes in Avignon that you wanted to see . . ."

Alex remembered *that*.

"Oh yeah, of course! They had all the paintings that Picasso had done in a whole year of his life stretched along the walls in the order he painted them, so you could follow his thinking, see how he developed his ideas."

"Remember, the last night we were in Avignon we promised you kids a special treat," Becky said to Miranda. "There was a little café near the hotel we were staying in, the Hotel de l'Europe, and you and Peter noticed that the café had a sign saying *Pizza*. But when the pizza came it was in little round individual pies, a separate little pie for each of us, with wonderful herbs on top. It was the most delicious pizza I'd ever had in my life, but you kids expected tomato sauce and cheese. You called the herbs 'funny green things,' and you wouldn't taste it . . . Do you remember, we went back to Paris that night by train, in first-class sleeping compartments? Remember how thrilled you were going to bed on a train, Miranda? You must remember, you were eleven years old."

Miranda looked bored and swallowed the pizza in her mouth. She had heard this story before. "Sure I remember, Ma." Then she turned to Alex and said, "Hey Dad, I dropped by your place today to pick up my mail . . ."

Becky thought it was strange how quickly the apartment Miranda had grown up in had become *your* place.

Miranda grinned at Alex. ". . . and I saw that girl who was sitting for you. You sure know how to pick 'em. She's really a dish."

Over Miranda's head, Alex told Becky, "Zoe dropped over for a while this afternoon. A little while. I'm just putting the finishing touches on her portrait."

Alex and Becky lay side by side, and although Alex was breathing evenly, Becky was sure he wasn't asleep.

"It must be a masterpiece by now, you've been slaving over it for so long."

He wasn't asleep. He knew exactly what Becky meant. And *who* she meant. "Zoe isn't the easiest person in the world to paint. She's terribly fidgety, has trouble holding a pose."

"Poor little thing. So young to be so nervous. By the way, how old is she? Older or younger than Miranda?"

"Maybe a little younger, I'm not sure." Alex said. "Incidentally, I know you think Miranda's apartment is the pits, but you could at least *pretend* you like it. *She* adores it."

"I always thought that when Miranda moved away from home, it would be to live in a cute little place." A cute little place that Miranda would decorate charmingly. Broadway and 110th Street could not by any stretch of the imagination be considered cute. Nothing could make it charming.

In the darkness Alex's voice went on. "Given the housing situation, she's lucky to have found it. They have three separate bedrooms, even if they are kind of small."

"Separate bedrooms? They're closets," Becky said. "But they could all have their own separate rats soon. That job she has, I hope it's only temporary. I hope she'll start looking for something with possibilities for advancement soon. There must be an entry-level job in a publishing house or a brokerage or a television network she could get. I offered to help her get interviews but no, she has to do it all by herself . . ."

"You mean, Miranda's apartment disappoints you, and so does her job? Could it be possible that she doesn't have your crazy drive for success, Becky?"

"If I were a man, that crazy drive would be called *ambition*."

Alex sighed. "Since we've got an empty nest, let's make the most of it. I think I'll sleep in Peter's room tonight." He got up and shambled out, trailing his pillow behind him, like Linus in the comic strips.

Becky lay there alone and remembered a little girl

she had once known. A little girl with crazy drive. A little girl who had been as old as Miranda was, when Miranda's parents had taken her touring through France, first-class all the way.

She remembered an eleven-year-old girl in the Bronx, which even then was a ghetto.

Sometimes, when her father wanted to say something to Becky, he would look straight at her and say, "Helen . . . er, Florence . . . er, Becky!"

He always got the last name out after what seemed like a struggle in his mind. When that happened, Becky wanted to say, "Look at me! Look straight at me. I'm not Helen, I'm not Florence, *I'm Becky*." She even wanted to add, "The last one. The special one."

But that night, he had looked straight at her and said, "You can't."

"But I have to go to college." Becky stood there frozen. "If I don't go to college, I'll be *nothing* all my life. I don't want to take a commercial course and be a . . . a . . . secretary."

"A secretary isn't nothing," her father answered. "It's a good job for a girl. Erase that check mark you made where it says Academic Course, and put the check where it says Commercial Course. Then I'll sign it."

Her father was her friend. He was her favorite teacher, her closest advisor. He was her lord of the colors and her master of the words. She loved the way he would sometimes reject a word he himself had just said because it wasn't precisely what he meant, and mutter other words to himself until he found exactly the one he wanted: "Special? No. Exceptional? Maybe. Remarkable, outstanding, extraordinary . . . that's it, *extraordinary*!" She could ask him anything and he always knew the answer. Or he would know where to look it up. "You don't have to *know* everything," he always told Becky, "you just have to know where to find out." Together they had gone to all the museums the city had to offer. He said, "New York is full of miracles. They are called *museums*." He said it was a miracle that there were so many museums and that they were all free. And they had been free, then. They played word games together and took long walks together discovering new neighborhoods, her hand secure in his as she tried to match her steps to his longer ones. How could he be saying this inconceivable thing to her?

Her mother said, "Girls make good money being secretaries."

Becky looked at her mother, then ran into the bathroom and threw up. Of course her mother heard. You could hear everything that went on in any of the rooms of the cramped flat and most of what went on next door, too.

Her mother said that Becky didn't have to eat supper, she was probably coming down with the grippe if not something worse.

That was how Becky's long fast began.

She decided she hadn't made it clear to her father that there was no choice to make. As sure as the sun had to rise and set, Becky Gelb had to go to college.

Every night that week she would place herself opposite her father at the kitchen table, so he could watch her growing thinner. Her mother became frantic and kept offering to make Becky's favorite dishes. Fried matzo, noodle pudding, roast chicken, anything she wanted. Her father kept his eyes downcast throughout, with the *Times* open next to his plate. There was always something to read next to his plate, as if he could not get enough nourishment from just the food. But Becky could see that his eyes weren't moving, and she was sure he wasn't reading. After a while he folded the newspaper. "I am *not* going to sign it."

That night she overheard her father talking to her

mother. "We can't afford to send a girl to college. I get less and less work every day. The movie chains are starting to *print* the Coming Attraction signs, so they don't have to pay local sign painters anymore."

"She just wants to go to Hunter. It's free. It won't cost anything."

"And who will pay her carfare to this *free* college? Who will buy her lunches and her clothes? For *four years?*"

The songs of Becky's childhood said, "I found a million dollar baby in a five-and-ten-cent store." And "Every time it rains it rains pennies from heaven." And "Potatoes are cheaper, tomatoes are cheaper, now's the time to fall in love." And "I can't give you anything but love, baby." Money was always sung about with desperate, insistent sunniness. But there was nothing sunny about the tug-of-war that was going on between Becky and her father. Even though Becky was only eleven, even though she had to go through high school first before she could go to college, there was a five-day war over Becky's future.

Her teacher asked, "Where is your consent form, Rebecca? All the other children have handed theirs in already."

"I forgot it," Becky answered. "I left it at home."

"That's very unlike you," her teacher said. "The Rebecca Gelb *I* know doesn't *forget*."

Becky thought for a second of asking her teacher to help her. But the idea of revealing that her father wanted to sentence her to a Commercial Course was too shameful. It would be like confessing that all these years her father had never really loved her. That it didn't matter that she was the one he chose to go to museums with him, because she hadn't been his special child at all. That the way he kept forgetting her name when he was looking straight at her and called her Helen or Florence meant that he thought they were all just the same. Three girls, basically interchangeable. You could switch them around, as if they'd been stamped out of a machine.

She listened to her parents talking again that night.

Her mother said, "Do you want to read a headline in the *News*, Bronx family starves little Jewish girl to death?"

There was a long silence until her father answered.

"Nobody came into the shop today and asked for *anything*. They're beginning to make their own signs themselves. What do they care how rotten it looks? And my last movie house called and said they're going to start with the printed signs too." There was a funny sound like a groan. "Even a free college is an impossible luxury for us."

The next day her teacher said, "You would tell me if there were a problem at home, wouldn't you, Rebecca?"

"There isn't any problem. I don't know why I keep forgetting. I'll bring it in tomorrow."

She could always kill herself, if she didn't have it tomorrow. If she couldn't go to college, if she had to spend her life answering somebody's phone and typing somebody else's letters, she would just as soon be dead.

Becky told her mother, "He wouldn't be acting this way if I was a boy. If I was his son, there wouldn't be any question about my going to college. And becoming a doctor or a lawyer or even what I want to be, a journalist." Barney Greenthal and Irving Weiss had turned in enlistment papers for Academic Courses, signed proudly by their fathers, the day the forms were due.

Becky's mother made Becky come downstairs to the drugstore and stand on the scale. When you put your penny in, there were always two things on the little card that came out of it: your fortune and your weight.

Becky's fortune read: *Your stubbornness will be rewarded.*

Becky's mother gave a frightened little scream when she saw the weight.

The next day Becky's mother would not let her go to school.

"You look like a ghost," she said, and brought her tea with dried raspberries in it, just as she always did when Becky had a cold, and slices of toast cut into triangles and covered with honey. Becky wouldn't touch the toast, but she had already decided that even in a hunger strike, tea didn't count, so she drank that.

It was dark out, and Florence was home from work. Becky's mother said, "You've been in this bed all day, let me change the sheets, you'll feel better."

But instead of changing the sheets her mother just stood there, staring down.

The three women looked at the blood together. Frieda, gray and nearing fifty. Florence, dark-haired, nubile, seventeen. And Becky, who was eleven.

Becky was horrified. When she'd begun fasting, she'd never dreamed it could lead to this. Why was nobody trying to help her? Did they want her to bleed to death while they stood there staring at the blood on her bed?

It took an hour for Frieda and Florence to make Becky believe that what had just happened to her happens sooner or later to every female. Finally she was able to say, "Well, all things considered, I guess I'm glad to get it over with early."

Then Frieda and Florence had to begin again and make her understand that *it* . . . this blood, this flow, this *leaking* . . . was not going to happen to her just this once. It would happen every month of her life until she was old. Incredibly old.

Her mother warned her never to touch plants when

she was this way, or the plants would die. Never to wash her hair, or her hair would fall out. And never ever to talk to men about what had just happened to her—Becky gathered that men didn't know anything about it. That if she told a man she would be betraying a secret that had been held sacred by generations of women, probably since Eve.

(It wasn't until years later that Becky recalled her mother's warnings and wondered: Could they all have been just disguises for something else? Something more tempting, something more enticing that women must never ever do when they were *that way?*)

Then her mother leaned over Becky and slapped her. It was a light, formal, almost tender slap, but a slap nonetheless.

"It's all right," Florence said, as if their mother were not in the room. "Mama slapped me too when I got the curse the first time. It's to remind you that it's no fun being a woman."

When Frieda Gelb finished remaking the bed, she turned to Becky and said, "Listen to me. Tonight, you will eat."

Her face had become stern, and she folded her arms grimly. "You will eat, and when you are old enough you will go to college. I promise."

Two surprising things happened at the Gelb kitchen table that night. Becky Gelb began eating again. And Frieda Gelb stopped. Frieda would not eat, and she would not talk. She did not say hello to her husband when he came home from work, she did not inquire how his day had been the way she *always* did, and although she passed the salt when he asked for it, she did not smile at him. She sat there in her faded house-dress, arms folded grimly on her chest, and the soft gentle woman they all thought they knew had turned into a fierce implacable stranger.

When Louis Gelb finally signed the mimeographed

form—after his daughter had not eaten for five days, after his wife had stopped speaking to him for only one—it was with his most elegant sign painter's calligraphy. The large check he put next to the words *Academic Course* looked bold and assured. There was not a hint in its flourish of nearly a week of struggle.

When Becky Gelb stopped eating, it had been an inspired action. She had seized instinctively on the sharpest weapon she could have found. Her parents had come from the hungry ghetto towns of Russia where nobody would dream of rejecting food merely to win an argument—presuming the food was available. If she had thought about it for weeks, Becky could not have found a more bravura gesture to prove her point. But it was her mother, her soft sweet timid mother, who had really won her fight for her—that one time, and only that once, she exposed the steel that lay underneath the softness.

And so Becky took college preparatory classes in high school, and after that she went to Hunter College. Hunter was free, and only a nickel subway ride from home. And her father closed his little sign shop, which joined blocks of other closed shops in the Depression-scarred Bronx, and went to work for a commercial art studio that turned out signs for the mammoth downtown movie palaces.

And Becky and her father still visited museums together. And sometimes they still took long walks together, although Becky no longer held his hand as they walked.

When he died, they found a newspaper clipping in his wallet; it had been folded and refolded so often that the print had been worn away along the folds. On the top there was a photograph of Becky. The caption under the picture said that she had just been appointed a vice-president of the advertising agency she worked for.

When they gave the clipping to Becky, she held it

in her hand for a long time and stared at it. She thought that her father must have felt pleased when he saw her picture in the paper, or else why would he have kept it?

He might even have said, "That's Becky. The last one. The special one. The unusual one. No no, the *extraordinary* one."

6

Victor Cameron decided that the time had come to give his first real party. A Power Party, not for his young Praetorians, but for *clients*.

He timed the festivity for Thanksgiving Eve. He did not want clients based in Minneapolis and Detroit to keep thinking of him as an Australian; he chose the most American of holidays to trumpet his arrival in New York.

Becky wanted to kick herself for feeling flattered that he had invited her.

Alex refused to attend Victor's party.

"From the things you've let drop about this Cameron guy . . . even if I were still drinking, I wouldn't want to drink with *him*."

The Gagarins didn't run around the park together any more in the mornings. In fact, they hardly ever saw each other now in the mornings, because Becky was getting to the agency earlier and earlier. She acted as if there were a monster waiting for her there that had to be fed at dawn, that would break out of its cage and wreak havoc if she weren't there to appease it.

And Alex was staying late at the Alliance a lot. He said he couldn't weld in the apartment, he had to use the Alliance studios for welding, after classes were

over. So they didn't see much of each other in the
evenings, either.

Becky put on her go-everywhere little black jersey
dress and black high-heeled shoes, tied a red scarf
around her shoulders, and arrived at Victor Cameron's
party alone.

No cheese-and-beer bash this. She accepted a glass of
champagne from one tuxedoed waiter and a caviar hors
d'oeuvre from another.

Besides clients, Victor had invited: creative "stars"
from other agencies (some of whom mentioned to Mrs.
Gagarin, sure that she must know about it, that Victor
was talking to them about the possibility of their coming
to work for him at Seton & Cecil soon); a waif-thin girl
with titian hair, whom Becky recognized as one of the
American Ballet's new baby ballerinas; and the advertising columnist from the *New York Times*. Who was
making notes every now and then in a pocket notebook,
for the piece on Victor's party that duly appeared in
the *Times* the next day.

The Trowbridge brothers spotted Becky where she
stood, alone against a wall, and joined her. The Trowbridge brothers were portly twins, Dickensian partners
in a Boston bank. They had stopped dressing *exactly*
alike when they were eight years old, but even today
their cold blue eyes peered from similar rimless glasses,
and their suits—while in differing wools—had been cut
from the same pattern.

Twenty years ago the Trowbridge brothers had
bought a small New England bakery that was going
broke specializing in baked beans. The bakery had large
ovens and the Trowbridge twins had vision. As soon as
they bought the bakery they expanded from beans to
New England fruit pies and soda cakes and hearty farm
breads (wheat and oatmeal and corn-molasses) and
chose the then-tiny Seton & Cecil as their agency.

Becky had named the bakery Trowbridge Farm in honor of the brothers and invented Aunt Prudence to appear in the advertising.

Aunt Prudence didn't live on Trowbridge Farm. She had her own farm down the road apiece. But she kept a suspicious eye on the extravagant goings-on at the Trowbridge property. With Yankee thrift she complained darkly about the foolish Trowbridge habit of putting only the best, the most expensive, ingredients in bread destined for city folks. Why, city folks wouldn't even know the difference!

In most food commercials, attractive actors beamed at you from the screen. Vinegary Aunt Prudence scowled at you. The beginning of success in advertising is to invent something different; Trowbridge Farm products were soon selling like hotcakes (which the Trowbridge Brothers included in the line as soon as Becky suggested it). Next to her work on Eve, and maybe the spot where the camera stared at a percolating coffeepot for a full minute, and maybe the spot where a touch of perfume brought a marble statue to life, the Trowbridge campaign was the campaign Becky had always been fondest of.

"The profits last quarter were at an all-time high, I regret to say," Homer Trowbridge told Becky.

"You regret? When have you ever been sorry to see Trowbridge Farm make a lot of money?"

"When we've just sold the company, of course."

Casper Trowbridge stared at Becky over glittering glasses. "Didn't you know we sold out to Consolidated Foods after the second quarter?" He sounded puzzled.

"You must have known." Homer looked at her oddly too. "A lot of you agency people fell over each other buying Trowbridge shares just before ConFood took over."

"I wasn't one of them."

"Scruples about insider knowledge? That didn't

stop your pals. Some of them made a pretty penny on the deal."

Homer consulted the watch that hung next to the Phi Beta Kappa key on the gold chain spanning his belly.

"Casper, I think we must start heading for the airport, if we're to make the last shuttle. Otherwise we'll be stranded in New York overnight."

"Overnight in the sinful city, brother? What a splendid idea, let's stay!"

But they left, first assuring Becky how delightful it had been to see her. Alone against the wall again, she plucked another glass of champagne from a passing tray. She hadn't known that Trowbridge was going to be sold to the mammoth food conglomerate. Even though Trowbridge Farm's success had started in her typewriter, nobody had told her.

What was it that Gandhi had said . . . ?

She wasn't in the club.

Victor Cameron ushered an attractive man over to Becky. Women standing alone against walls do not make a party look like *fun*.

"Want you to meet somebody you've probably heard a lot about, Becky. Hardest director to get in the whole country, the famous Loren Odell. Loren, this is Becky Gagarin."

No Levi's and checked bandanna tonight. In a pin-striped charcoal bespoke suit and Armani shirt and tie, in the beautiful bloom of a virile thirty-five, Loren was easily the best-looking man in the room. Except for a polite social smile, his face was bland as he and Becky were introduced.

"Victor tells me you're with Seton & Cecil too, Mrs. Gregory."

"Gagarin. Yes, I work with Victor. In the Creative Department."

"How interesting! And what do you *do* in the Creative Department, Mrs. Gregor . . . er, Gagarin?"

This was Victor's cue to say, Becky *heads* the department. Or, perhaps, Becky is *my boss*. Or even, in a burst of astonishment, how can you be in this business and not have heard of Rebecca Gagarin? Why, she's Angus Seton's secret weapon.

But Victor could not bring himself to say any of these distasteful things. Instead, he clapped Loren on the shoulder, promised to collect him later "Because I intend to have a long, serious talk with the hard-to-get Odell," and plunged back into his party.

"Bastard," Loren remarked quietly to the disappearing back. "But maybe I shouldn't say that about him to you, Becky. After all, you work for him."

"Is that what he told you? That *I* work for *him*?"

"No, come to think of it, his actual words were that he wanted me to meet someone he worked *with*. Only, you could hear the charity dripping from his tone when he said *with*. The way the Pope might mention a parish priest he happened to work *with*."

Loren Odell and Becky Gagarin remained on the edge of the party, near the door, as Loren gossiped into her ear. Loren said he was sorry he hadn't had a chance to warn Becky he was coming to New York, he was here for a meeting with a few people he wasn't yet free to name, about the hush-hush merger of Odell & Comrades with a much much bigger firm, a deal that would soon be publicly announced. There was a slight hitch right now in the negotiations—they seemed to be troubled that Loren's present setup might lack depth of management—but once that was ironed out . . . ! Becky must come to California in time for the announcement of the merger, which would most likely be in the spring. Becky would be flabbergasted when she learned the identity of the people who were eager to take over Odell & Comrades and make Loren a very rich man.

As he talked, his eyes drifted slowly around the room, moved past the titian-haired ballerina, then returned and fastened on her.

"Look, Loren, if you like the little redhead, go for her. I'm leaving soon anyway."

"Don't be silly. The reason I came to New York was to see you."

"Liar. The reason you're in New York is to do nice things for your net worth."

A plump woman in floor-length ruffled yellow satin hulked past them, carrying a cello. She was followed by two thin men with violins and a bald man with a viola.

Becky groaned. "Now I *know* I want to leave. Victor's gone and hired a string quartet to play through dinner."

"A string quartet? While we *eat*?"

"It's the latest thing. You know what will happen? Everyone will listen respectfully for five minutes. And then the voices will get louder, and then there will be rattling of china, and then it will be Brahms versus a hundred screaming people. And Brahms will lose. While the wretched musicians have to keep plugging away. It's a buffet, nobody will miss me if I duck out . . . go charm your little ballerina."

"I don't believe in cradle snatching," Loren said. "Let's *both* leave. And have dinner someplace pleasant."

"The Carlyle?"

"How'd you guess?"

"You always used to love it . . ." Her voice dropped. "Loren, that girl may be too young for you, but I am too old. Remember what Marchbanks was supposed to say to himself every time he had a hankering for Candida?"

He closed his eyes and frowned a second before he produced it. "Candida told Marchbanks he had to keep repeating, 'When I am thirty, she will be forty-five. When I am sixty, she will be seventy-five.' "

"It's still sound advice."

Loren's eyes opened then and he smiled at her sweetly. "You forgot Shaw's next line. Marchbanks says, 'And in a hundred years we will both be exactly the same age.' "

There had been thick roast-beef sandwiches from room service. Now cheese and fruit and cups of espresso sat on the coffee table in front of them.

"Stop looking apprehensive, Becky. I understand our little fling is History. Even if we are in a wicked hotel, alone, together, I promise not to try to rekindle it."

"You won't? Pity. I was looking forward to fighting you off. At least you'd be a tangible enemy."

They were in Loren's suite in the Carlyle. "I always stay here when I come to New York. It's one of the perks of owning your own business—you learn to pay serious attention to your own comfort. Now tell me about the *in*tangible enemies. I mean, is it all still in the realm of gossip, or has anything actually *happened*?"

Loren's words came in a rush; he seemed very excited tonight. She could understand it. He had been surrounded by seducers all day. His firm was being wooed by a bigger firm; that would thrill any ambitious young man.

He selected a peach from the bowl of fruit. It was a perfect plump hothouse peach, so ripe that when he bit into it the juice spurted out.

"I guess nothing has actually *happened*. Only I feel as if I'm walking on the edge of a cliff all the time. People stop talking when I come into rooms. I suppose word has gotten out that Hamlin is furious with me about something that happened at the board meeting in England."

Loren was listening and at the same time slowly, voluptuously demolishing the peach. And Becky stopped talking. Because a sharp memory had swept over her, an alarmingly precise recollection, a scene from an ancient affair, an affair that they had promised each other must never be resumed . . .

〰〰〰

Becky is thirty-six. Loren is twenty-one, the newest member of Rebecca Gagarin's group, working in his first real job.

Loren's eyes never leave her in meetings. Even in the dark of a screening room she feels him watching her.

Today they will lunch together for the first time. It is supposed to be a working lunch. Loren has offered his apartment for it. He says his place is within walking distance of the agency, they can have sandwiches and really spread out and work there—they couldn't flap layouts around in a restaurant.

Becky does not say, as she probably should, we can flap layouts around in my office too. She prides herself on never listening to silly gossip about office seductions. Besides, it is absurd to think of Loren Odell that way. He is the youngest member of her group. A child, really.

The part of town Loren lives in is too expensive for a junior writer, Becky worries when they get there. Then she scolds herself. Loren is not the Depression child she was. He has grown up in affluent times. He has never been taught to feel guilty when he spends money on himself.

They start out sitting on a couch, layouts spread before them on a coffee table. Loren has brought sandwiches, a paper sack of peaches, and a good bottle of Riesling with them to the apartment.

Becky refuses the wine. "Maybe a glass later," she says, "but first we have work to do."

And for half an hour, they work.

Until Loren says, "I had a teacher in my advertising copy class who kept talking about Seton & Cecil. He said it's the best damn agency in the world; that it may still be small but it's going to teach the whole world what advertising is all about. And he mentioned you, specifically. He said if you want to find out how to write copy, study the way Rebecca Gagarin does it . . ."

"Advertising classes are a waste of money."

". . . he said Gagarin always writes as if she were talking to someone. In the kind of words people use in ordinary speech. Except that when *Gagarin* puts the words together she weaves a spell . . ."

"That's what they pay me for."

". . . he said Gagarin's copy may *sound* spontaneous, but if you study it, you'll find out how disciplined it is. He said he could always tell when Rebecca Gagarin had written a campaign. He said when it comes to copywriters, Gagarin is about the best there is. She may be weaving a spell, but she's also selling, from first sentence to last."

Becky does not look impressed. "Big deal. Writing copy *is* selling, just like standing behind a counter in a store. The only difference is they pay you more, and you get to sit down when you write. And sitting down beats standing any day."

"I was trying to tell you something nice, Becky. About yourself. Why do you always do that, push praise away, as if it might contaminate you?"

"I learned it in childhood. Praise is dangerous. It attracts the evil eye. Besides, sometimes the praise is nothing more than flattery."

Loren picks the layouts up and stacks them into a

neat pile, as if they have finished working. He pours them each a glass of wine. "And you think I was trying to flatter you?"

"What would you get out of it? You'd be wasting your time if you did. Raises have to be approved by the Management Committee, and anyway you haven't been with the agency long enough."

"A raise wasn't what I had in mind."

Becky does not push him away as quickly as she should, although all that happens then is a kiss. Except that somehow, in backing away from Loren, Becky finds herself in a corner of the couch. And Loren is stretched out with his head on her lap.

"Odell," she says.

"Here. Present. Yo."

"That's an Irish name, isn't it? But the Irish are supposed to have fair hair. Not black like yours. And their eyes are blue or green, they have skin that freckles and burns and peels. Not olive skin, like yours."

He grins up at her. "Have you never heard of the Black Irish? Legend says we're descended from Spaniards cast up on the shores of Ireland when the last ships of the Armada were struggling home. But that's only legend. My father always told me that the *real* Black Irish weren't Spaniards, they were Celts. Short, dark, muscular men, laborers who worked the mines and forged the copper weapons. The blonde Irish came later, little souvenirs left behind by visiting Norsemen and Danes. I'm taller than most Black Irish though. There *might* be some Norse blood mixed in with the Celt."

Becky listens, and smiles, and decides that she likes the Armada legend better than the duller truth. Who knows, she might allow herself fantasies about Loren as a Spanish sailor, a man from the sea cast adrift on the shores of Becky's body . . .

Maybe Loren can read her thoughts, because he

sits up, swings his legs over the side of the couch, and takes her in his arms.

And the woman who is so crisp in meetings, who can decide in seconds if a commercial is on track or not, who can pick exactly the right take from a day's worth of dailies on first viewing, does not want to make any decisions now. Alex has been drinking so much lately, studying his paintings bleakly, a bottle at his feet, then passing out night after night on a chair in his studio . . .

As it turns out, she does not have to make any decisions. The twenty-one-year-old stripling, the fledgling member of her group, the callow youth beside her on the couch, proceeds to make them all for her.

Loren selects a peach from the bag he had brought with him. He takes a bite and parts her legs gently and rubs the fruit against her. The peach feels moist and chilly there, and now Becky is moist too. Loren lifts the peach to his lips and eats it and then he says, "Now I want to taste *you*."

～～～

"Becky? Hey, where did you go? You left me all of a sudden and disappeared into your thoughts."

Becky shook her head to dislodge ancient memories.

"Welcome back," Loren said. "Listen, you've been looking so glum this evening, won't you let me make you smile? I used to know how to make you smile . . ."

"Sorry," he said, when she remained frozen where she was. "I thought you would be curious about all the new tricks I might have learned since I was twenty-one."

Outside the Carlyle a tentative early snow drifted down. As the doorman whistled for a taxi, Becky told herself that it was time to close the Loren chapter in her life. She'd always managed to leave that door a little ajar; now it was definitely time to close it.

The night had been a turning point. She could have gone to bed with Loren again. It is almost always the woman's decision after all. But she had chosen not to let it happen. Loren would go back to Los Angeles, where he would eat, breathe, and sleep film. Exactly the life he wanted. And where he would become very rich, something else he wanted. While she returned to her desk at Seton & Cecil. And the increasingly obnoxious presence of Victor Cameron. Who wasn't sure if he worked for her, or if she worked for him.

The doorman had succeeded in finding a cab. And although Becky had planned to tell Loren that they oughtn't to see each other at all any more, not even for lunch, when she looked up to kiss him good-bye she wasn't sure if the kiss should be on his forehead—a chaste, no-nonsense way of closing a chapter in your life—or on the lips, in memory of what they had once shared, such a long time ago.

Because she was wavering between his forehead and his lips, her kiss landed sloppily on his nose. They both laughed. And maybe that was the best way, after all, to end an old affair. In laughter.

7

Wilbur Rank was on the telephone.

"Becky, Ham feels there's something you and I should talk about. Can you spare me some time?"

"Sure. How about right now. Your office?" Since both Gagarin and Rank were executive vice-presidents, there was no clear protocol about who had to do the traveling and who could sit still and wait.

Rank said hurriedly, "Oh, no. No, no. Don't trouble yourself. I'll come to you."

That was a relief because Rank's office always depressed Becky. The crown jewel of the room was a huge antique English partner's desk, its polished surface free of the uncertainties that clutter the lives of ordinary men and woman. Generally, there was not a thing on that desk, except perhaps one carefully centered piece of paper about something Very Important. No IN box. No OUT box. You were meant to think that the man who worked in so orderly an environment must be a whiz at proceeding directly to the heart of problems. Whenever she was in Rank's office, Becky always felt as if her nails needed a manicure and her shoes needed polishing. Which they probably did.

She said, "Well, as long as you're coming upstairs,

I wonder if you'd mind swinging past a coffee machine and getting me some coffee? Light. No sugar."

There was a tiny silence at the other end, and then Rank said, "Of course. No trouble."

Why had she asked Rank to do that? It would conflict seriously with his image of himself. He wouldn't like the idea of Wilbur Rank carrying a cardboard container of coffee, a container that would probably leak and stain his shirt. Besides, the coffee that came out of the machines always tasted bitter and chemical, and Eileen would have been glad to make some for her, fresh.

Rae Ashley's voice came back to Becky, cautioning her: "You talk to them as if they were still the little boys you used to send out for coffee."

"I hear that you went to see the Princess the other day? And talked her into television?"

"I thought we've been trying to get Lyubov on TV for twenty years?"

"Of course. They'll spend more that way."

"Besides which, it's what they *should* do. Was that all you wanted to talk about?" And Becky stood.

"Er, no. I mean, yes, any Lyubov media switch is important, and I did want to confirm it . . . but there's something else we have to discuss."

Tenting his hands and gazing at the ceiling, he moved to the something else.

"You are very talented, Becky. We all know that. From time to time you are even brilliant. But Becky, we are old friends—we have worked together for many years, there's no point in not being frank. I want you to know that I'm not speaking just for *myself* in this conversation. Horatio Hamlin and Howard and I have *all* agreed that we must examine the situation in the creative department dispassionately, and Ham has delegated me to discuss the trouble with you."

"What situation? What trouble? Didn't he like the list of creative stars I sent him?"

"Well, he did mention a list." He stopped tenting his hands, and placed them flat on his knees. "He said what you sent him resembled a *laundry list*. He said that it was just a bunch of names. Too many different kinds of people, doing different jobs, in too many different ways."

"That's what a creative department *is*. Different kinds of people doing different jobs, and the more different the ways, the better."

"Becky!" Wilbur held up a hand. This was his meeting, he had called it, and he was not going to let the difficult woman across the desk kidnap it from him. "Let's try to stay on track, shall we? As I said, Ham has delegated me to discuss the mess . . . the *problems* in the creative department with you."

"Problems? What problems?"

"Well, Ham and I sat together on the plane coming back from London, and we forced ourselves to make an honest, no-holds-barred inventory of the problems in the creative department. As it is structured now. When we got to number twenty we stopped. It was clear the time had come for a major reorganization."

He crossed his knees, first adjusting the fabric carefully so that the crease in his trousers would not be spoiled. Then he unbuttoned his jacket and took a small notebook from an inside pocket. He pulled one page from the notebook. It was covered with Rank's cramped handwriting—it wasn't code, his handwriting was so minuscule it just resembled code. Even so, Becky couldn't imagine how he could have gotten *twenty* ways she had fouled up on such a tiny piece of paper.

Now she knew why he had insisted on coming up here. It was the old rule. Always give bad news in the office of the person who is getting it. That way, you can get up and leave if the scene becomes unpleasant. If you give bad news in your own office, you are trapped.

She concentrated on keeping her voice steady. "What were the twenty ways I failed? I mean, that you and Hamlin decided I failed? Since you were counting the ways, where did it all get so awful that you couldn't bring yourself to go on?"

She knew as soon as she said it that *awful* was the wrong word. An emotional, feminine word.

"Look Becky, we all appreciate the job you've been doing. In many ways, heroic. You've been trying to handle so much, all by yourself. We just want to make things *easier* for you. We're not talking about diminishing your job, just restructuring it so it becomes what one human being can reasonably be expected to do."

He leaned forward and arranged his mouth in a smile. "And we are asking for *your* input on the re-organization. After all, who knows the creative department and its people better than you? Who has struggled more valiantly with its troubles? Won't you give us the benefit of your guidance now and help us to put it together more sensibly?"

Becky stared at a painting on the opposite wall. Sometimes job applicants would notice the signature, *Gagarin*, scrawled in a corner of the canvas, and ask Becky if she had painted it. Unlike the serene gouache that hung over her couch, this other painting was an anguished abstraction of a woman's head. Not so much a head as a mask. With lines of tension etched from the nose to the mouth, from the mouth to the jaw.

"Number twenty," she repeated. "Wouldn't it help me to help you if I knew what number twenty was? Or anything a little *specific* about the horrible way you and Hamlin feel I've messed up?"

Wilbur Rank sighed. "Basically, I suppose we *all* feel that it is time to give some of the younger people a chance. You've sort of, ah, concentrated all decision-making power in your own hands. Maybe younger people need to have a chance to make their own mistakes?"

He was talking to her like a social worker making the rounds in an old-age home. But Rank was only two years younger than Becky. Why was he trying to make her feel senile? Rae Ashley's voice came back to her, patiently explaining. Men get distinguished, Rae's voice repeated. *Women* get old.

"What is it, exactly, that you want me to do?"

"As I said, it isn't what *I* want you to do. It's what many of us, including Ham, have spent the past few weeks discussing at length. Great length, I assure you, and it's what we *all* want. We *all* think there should be some intermediate echelon between you and the people in the creative department . . ."

"I don't understand. Why should there be another echelon between me and my people? It will only delay everything."

". . . a level of real executive importance. A managerial, decision-making level. They could, ah, do the hiring for the department, and assign projects, and represent the agency at new business meetings, and decide what work gets shown to clients. And, of course, handle the creative budget. Raises, terminations, and so forth." He sighed, took a fastidiously folded handkerchief from his breast pocket, and wiped his hands. The tough part was over.

"But you're describing my job. You're describing everything I do. I mean, what would there be left for me to do if all this happens?"

"Why Becky," Rank protested. "Of course everyone would continue to want your *opinion*. It would be a sinful waste not to seek your advice."

"But would they *have* to ask for it?"

"Well, no, not have to. But I am sure they would *want* to. And also," he added, more cheerfully now, "it all depends on the reorganization plan. Which we are asking *you* to work with us on, you know. For example, you might decide that under the reorganization you want to spend more of your time visiting the branch offices. You could be a source of valuable input to the branches. Give them the feedback they need. I'm sure your visits would impact favorably on their product."

"Wouldn't the people in the branch offices hate it? Wouldn't I be just another layer of approval, another grand panjandrum from headquarters getting in their way?"

He shifted in his seat, picked up a letter from Becky's desk, started to read it, realized what he was doing, and dropped it like a hot potato. "Well, no, we don't think it would need to involve another layer of *approval*. You would be visiting in more of an advisory, consultant role."

"You mean, I'd come in and they'd fuss over me and take me to lunch and I would look at their campaigns and make comments but it wouldn't matter because I'd just be *advising* and after I left they could forget everything I said?"

"Why would they want to forget what you say? I'm sure they would *treasure* it, and be grateful for your advice."

"Why should they treasure what I say in Cincinnati and Los Angeles and Dallas if you've all decided they don't have to treasure it in New York?"

Wilbur Rank didn't answer that. Instead he stood up and said in the voice of a man brave enough to face up to the most distasteful missions and accomplish them speedily and without undue fuss, "Nobody can reorganize your department better than you, Becky. Do you think you could give us a reorganization plan in, say, a week? Maybe a few alternative plans? How do you want your door, open or closed?"

"Closed. Please."

When he had left, she shut her eyes and put her head down on her desk. When she made that speech in California in the spring, would they have to introduce her as the creative head emeritus of Seton and Cecil? The amazing new walking talking speech-making figurehead?

She was not going to cry, she was going to *think*. The creative department had been reorganized how many times since she had been in the agency? Every two or three years, at least. She'd set some kind of record, keeping it tranquil for the five years she had run it. Before that, they had played on it like an accordion. Now contracting it, with "decision-making" power in just a few hands, now expanding it to distribute power. So now it would be expanded again. She should have known that something like this was coming after the meeting in England. After the look on Hamlin's face. But she had ridden it all out before and landed on her feet. She would ride it out again.

Besides, Rank hadn't said that Angus Seton knew anything about any of this, much less that he *approved*.

And the little girl inside her whispered, Angus will come home and make it all well again. Angus, her mentor, her counselor, her guide, her beacon, her friend.

~~~~

Dear Becky—
Remember when Hamlet tells Ophelia, get thee to a nunnery? What he should have said was get thee to a faculty. *I feel just as out of the real world here. Anyway, and I almost can't believe it, I'll be in New York Friday! Some sort of academic confer-*

*ence, which I leaped at the chance to attend. Not
because of my thirst for scholarship but because I
want to see* you. *Let's have lunch, you pick the
best place you know for talking. It wouldn't hurt
if they also served food.*

Sheila

The best place Becky knew for talking was La Cour.

La Cour was probably interchangeable with a
hundred other French restaurants in the city, but unlike
most of the others, the tables were far apart. It was
done up to look like the outside, rather than the inside,
of a French inn. There was even a small horse trough
in the corner. Not for small horses, but because a larger
one would have taken away more profitable table space.
The ceiling was painted the kind of sky blue that comes
on crayons, with fat white clouds scudding about among
the chandeliers. The waiters wore long white aprons
with strings doubled around their middles and made
change from oversize leather wallets, just like in France.
The fact that none of them had ever been near France
was beside the point. Jules, the headwaiter, was Gallic
enough to make up for all of them. Becky was convinced
that Jules had been sent over from Central Casting.
Central Casting in *Paris*.

But where was Sheila? Becky studied the room for
the curly cap of carrot-colored hair and the inquisitive
blue eyes but couldn't see her anywhere.

"Mrs. Gagarin, your guest is already here. I have
already seated her." And Jules led her to a table for
two.

"Becky, Becky, you can't imagine how I've missed
you!"

Would the *real* Sheila please stand up? Who was
this impostor? Sheila's hair was red—there might be a
little gray in it by now, but basically it was red, the old
familiar friendly carrot-red. Why, Sheila and Becky

were the same age, give or take a few months. This white-haired woman, this *elderly* woman, was not, could not be Sheila.

"I've missed you too. Terribly." And then to Jules: "Would you pick out a really good bottle for us, please, Jules? I feel like splurging. Mrs. McCall is a very old friend, and we haven't seen each other for years."

Once, Sheila had been a terribly exotic creature to Becky. The only girl in the class who had not been born in New York but in a foreign place called Chicago. The girl who was *Catholic* and not embarrassed to belt out Christ's name loud and clear when the class sang carols in the auditorium every Christmas. Of course, Sheila did not have that magical possession called a father. Her mother did not stay home and scrub floors and then spread newspapers on the floors to keep them clean for at least a week, the way all proper mothers did. Sheila's mother had a job. The floors she scrubbed were in office buildings, where she worked nights.

Becky and Sheila had been best friends in P.S. 42, then in high school, then at tuition-free Hunter. It had been a very close relationship. But Sheila had married immediately after graduation, much earlier than Becky. A handsome young lieutenant who had survived Korea and come home to be killed in a banal accident on the Mass Turnpike. Sheila had never remarried but had gone to California to study psychology and then gone on to earn a doctorate and teach there.

Sheila studied the menu with fascination. She was wearing different glasses now, blatant bifocals, not even the kind where the horizontal line is hidden. "God, what prices. And this is only *lunch*."

"My treat. You're from out of town, I'm the host. Hostess. Have whatever your greedy little heart desires."

"You mean my greedy stomach. And fat hips. And

disgusting thighs." But she succumbed to snails and rack of lamb.

Becky knew Sheila would have a lot of questions, and she did.

Sheila: "So tell me, how is Alex?"

Becky: "Oh, fine. Terrific. Painting up a storm . . ."

That was what Becky said. What Becky thought was more like: Alex? You mean my husband, Alex? Well, I have this funny feeling he might be having an affair with a girl younger than his daughter. He certainly "works" late often enough. But who am I to talk, the other night I felt female for the first time in God knows how long, chatting with an ex-lover. Someone I never did tell you about . . . someone I probably never will tell you about.

Sheila: "And Miranda? She must have her degree by now!"

Becky: "Yes, and an apartment, and a job . . ."

She waits on tables in a fire hazard on the Lower East Side. The apartment has a resident rat, but that doesn't seem to disturb her. She tells me the boiler finally got fixed, sometimes they even have hot water now.

Sheila (compassionate, grave): "And Charlotte? How is she doing?"

Becky: "The doctors say as well as can be expected." *Her sister says she looks like a walking skeleton. It's spread from the lungs to outlying districts. She is in constant tormenting pain. Miranda cries whenever her name is mentioned . . .*

She was relieved that Sheila didn't ask about the office.

She could report stoically about Alex and Miranda and even Charlotte—she wasn't sure how stoic she could be if Sheila started probing about Seton & Cecil.

"Come on, confess," Sheila said abruptly, startling Becky. "The white hair shocked you, didn't it? I could see it on your face. I got tired of running to beauty parlors. It wasn't just the time, the expense of staying a sexy redhead was depressing. So I decided to give up and enjoy being fifty."

"I haven't heard anyone say 'beauty parlor' since I was a kid. I wish I could be as courageous about age as you are."

Sheila guffawed. "No you don't. You've always hated even the idea of age. You were the only person I ever knew who had a midlife crisis at twenty-three. You were weepy about being stuck behind a typewriter in a retail store, and you hadn't written the great American novel yet nor had a play on Broadway, and all the years were slipping by. At twenty-three! I know you don't agree with me, Becky, but being older ain't so awful. It's cheating a little, but I get into the movies for half-price now!"

Sheila could always read Becky's mind. She looked at her friend carefully and stopped sounding jolly. "Becky, Becky. One would think you'd be used by now to the fact that birthdays happen every year. That the thing to do is not to pay too much attention to them, but just blow out the candles, make a wish, and march bravely on to the next year." She reached across the table and clasped Becky's hand.

With her left hand, because Sheila was still in charge of her right, Becky picked up her wineglass and took a gulp to cover the taste of panic in her mouth.

Sheila paused, considered what she had just said, and then edited it. "Except for you, the wishes all came true, didn't they? I read about you in the papers sometimes, and I feel so proud. My Becky is one of The Twenty Women Who!"

"Give me back my hand, I have to knock wood. Don't you know anything about the Machiavellian world of advertising? Maybe by the time I get back from lunch, my desk will have been moved out of my office into the corridor."

Sheila laughed comfortably. "That sort of stuff is only in the movies, isn't it?"

"Right. Yes. Only in the movies." Becky could hear her voice taking on the brisk tone it always had when she was trying to steer meetings headed into dangerous territory onto safer ground. "I see from your letters you've moved to a new address. Does it come complete with hot tub and swimming pool, like all California pads?"

"Hardly. It's just the top two floors in an old frame house. I'm sharing the rent with another woman. But I have a good size room I use for private patients. I'm not only teaching now, I'm building up a practice of my own. After all these years." She dipped bread into the snail sauce, and chewed reflectively.

"Sheila! How wonderful! It's what you've always wanted! My friend, the psychoanalyst!"

"Hey, slow down. Don't throw fancy titles around, I'm nowhere near an analyst, I just do therapy. I try to keep people from jumping out of the boat when they think they can't stand it any more. I try to persuade them to keep on rowing. I even give advice, which analysts aren't supposed to do. If you listen carefully, you can hear psychoanalysts biting their tongues all over America, because they're dying to give advice and they're not allowed. Mmm, Julia Childs would endorse this lamb, it's crisp on the outside, pink and juicy inside, just the way she says to do it on TV. *Alors*, my turn to eat, your turn to talk."

"Sheila, you know what I found out when Charlotte first got sick and I took her to our doctor? Since the main topic of this lunch seems to be age, how old would you guess Charlotte is?"

Sheila frowned. "Well, of course I only saw her a few times. I always thought she was beautiful, there must be a lot of Indian in Charlotte, those wonderful cheekbones. Age? More or less our age, I guess. Pushing fifty by now."

"Well, haha, Charlotte isn't fifty. She's almost *seventy*."

Sheila made a great sacrifice. She put down knife and fork to stare at her old friend. "As Sam Goldwyn once remarked, I have only two words to say about that. Im-possible."

"When I hired her—just before Miranda was born, remember?—she was fifty *then*. And she must have been afraid I'd think she wouldn't be sprightly enough to run around after a toddler. So she lied. And I believed her. And all she did was cook for us and clean for us and market for us and bring up my children and take care of them whenever I was off to Lisbon or London or Timbuktu or wherever Seton & Cecil has offices. She taught them to brush their teeth and mind their manners and fed them so well they never did get used to my rotten cooking. Did I ever tell you she used to iron their pajamas? *Drip-dry* pajamas? And all that when she was in her sixties and then pushing seventy. And I'll tell you something else, if she hadn't lied, I *wouldn't* have hired her. I would have thought exactly what she was afraid I'd think. That she was too *old*."

Sheila said, "It's the unforgivable sin now, isn't it? Age, I mean."

"You're not afraid of it. You flaunt it."

"Maybe I shouldn't." Sheila bit her lip. "Guess who just got passed over again for tenure?"

"Oh, Sheila, no." Becky reached over to touch Sheila's hair. The color might be different, but it felt the same. The same springy, energetic texture. The coat of a small and very alive animal.

"Oh, Becky, yes. Now they keep me on with one-year contracts. There was a prof in the math department they treated like that year after year. Her students adored her. The day she retired the head of the department took her out to lunch and gave her *honorary* tenure."

It was weird. Becky didn't even know the woman Sheila was talking about, yet tears were springing, suddenly, inexplicably, into her eyes. Honorary tenure! How dared they pull anything that shabby, after she'd given her life to that university?

"Excuse me a minute . . . I'll be right back."

In one of the cubicles of Le Cour's elegant rest room, Becky sat drawing slow and careful breaths. She had deflected the tears; in a minute or so she would be able to head back to Sheila.

Just as she was about to lift the cubicle latch, she heard her name spoken.

"Restructure creative? Over Gagarin's dead body!"

"If necessary, yes. He told me there'd be a lot of changes in the place. Time for the new guard to take over. He says Hamlin put Gagarin into that job in the first place, now he thinks it's time to take her out of it."

Becky sat frozen.

"But isn't our creative department supposed to be the best there is? If they asked me I'd have said you ain't supposed to fix things if they ain't broke . . ." The voice giggled. "But they didn't ask me."

There was a little pause. Then one of the female voices asked—and Becky noticed for the first time how very young both voices were—"That guy you're seeing, that Hank, how do you like him?"

"Henry. He gets uptight when people call him Hank."

"Henry, Hank, whatever, is he any *good*?"

Then one of the voices told the other, in startling detail, exactly how good Henry was.

The table had been cleared when Becky slid into her seat again.

"I thought you were never coming back," Sheila moaned. "Protect me, that Jules has been staring menacingly at me for the past ten minutes, I just know he's planning to push that cart full of French pastries right over here . . . How was the ladies' room? As many stars as the restaurant?"

"Worth a detour. Try the *mousse au chocolate*, it's spectacular. You can say I forced you."

Obediently, Sheila ordered the mousse. But as she spooned the rich dark chocolate her eyes stayed fixed on Becky.

"I probably shouldn't say this. It's the penalty of taking a therapist to lunch—we always think we have to pay for it in trade. You rushed away to the john to cry, didn't you? What are you feeling so awful about, Becky? Has something gone wrong at the office?"

"There's *always* something wrong at the office. Don't worry, it will sort itself out. Come have dinner with us tonight? We still live in the same place, although there's this pesky real-estate lady who phones every other day and tries to coax us into selling . . ."

Sheila sighed. "Whatever it is, I can see you're not going to tell me. You've got all the old Becky defenses up. Thanks, but I can't come to dinner. The 'banquet' is tonight, and it's the high point of the conference. Interminable speeches, full of gentle academic jokes."

The two women stood and embraced, and Becky saw herself and Sheila through the eyes of the other diners. The advertising woman, blond and smart but no longer in her first youth. The white-haired lady professor who claimed age was irrelevant. Sheila and Becky. They'd grown up ten blocks from each other, they'd gone to school together, Sheila was the best friend she had ever had or ever would have—so why hadn't Becky been able to talk to Sheila? Why hadn't she been able to cry on the shoulder of her closest friend? Whose *profession*, after all, was getting her shoulders wet?

The next morning Joseph closed the elevator door, slid the metal grate shut, and turned to her sadly. "Well, I never would have expected it of them," he said. "And after so many years, too."

The Building Workers Union had decided to seek a wage hike for its members, and East Side, West Side, all around the town, none of the co-op buildings, and certainly not the rentals, welcomed the idea.

Joe shook his head resignedly. "If it was just between you and myself, Mrs. Gagarin, we'd have this thing settled fast. But this way, you know there's going to be a strike, don't you?"

Becky remembered the last strike and shuddered. Housewives trying to run the elevator. With heart-sickening lurches between floors. Lawyers and stockbrokers rotating as doormen (except when it rained, of course). *Nobody* volunteering to cope with the garbage.

"It's okay, Mrs. Gagarin. I know that against the other votes in the building you can't do nothing. So how's Miranda doing in her new apartment? You seen it yet?"

"Yes, she had us to dinner a few weeks ago."

Joe produced a wry little chuckle at the thought of little Miranda, just yesterday such a cute little baby, giving dinner parties.

Before Becky left she told him, "I hope there won't have to be a strike, Joe."

"From your mouth to God's ear."

～～～～

"Lilah James just called," Eileen said. "She's all upset. There's a rough cut she wants to show you. She's got a problem with it. She asked if you could go down to Screening Room 3 and look at it with her—she's waiting for you there. And Mr. Rank's secretary called, he wants to have lunch with you today. It's about the reorganization."

Eileen didn't ask if Mrs. Gagarin *wanted* to have lunch with Wilbur Rank and talk about the reorganization. She knew that Mrs. Gagarin would. Eileen had been at her desk until ten o'clock every night this week, typing different reorganization plans. And retyping them, as the changes poured back from Horatio Hamlin, by way of Wilbur Rank. Becky knew they were Hamlin's changes: They were fiercely scribbled in orange ink.

"Mr. Rank's secretary asked what was your favorite restaurant? I said La Cour. Is that okay? She's making reservations there."

In the symbiotic relationship that always exists between a discerning secretary and a halfway civilized boss, Eileen knew that Becky was in trouble. And although she said nothing, her face reflected the strain of this knowledge. She was probably also worried about her own status. Because, of course, a secretary's status rises and falls with that of her boss.

"La Cour is just fine."

Far from being just fine, having lunch with Rank there would ruin the place for Becky forever.

But first she had to meet Lilah James in Screening Room 3.

She had expected to find Lilah alone in the screening room, but a whole group was gathered there. Lilah, and the TV producer she worked with, and the art director, and surprisingly, an account man. Not just any old account man but Howard Pullett. An executive vice-president, like Becky. A rajah, in charge of a whole bunch of accounts. Like Wilbur Rank, a protégé of Horatio Hamlin.

Everyone in the agency knew that Mrs. Gagarin didn't like account men present when she looked at a commercial for the first time. If there was something wrong with the spot, she didn't want to have to say so to the group that had worked on it—in front of an audience.

Pullett smiled. "I invited myself here today, Becky. We're on a tight schedule with this campaign, and I wanted to be sure everything is moving along on it."

Becky knew they were on a tight schedule. Her whole life had consisted of tight schedules, ever since her first day in advertising. How would Pullett's being present at the first screening speed anything up? But he was sitting there, sweating slightly, waiting for disaster.

Apprehension always shone behind Pullett's glasses, worry was always in his damp handshake, his memos were always composed in fretful sentences of deep alarm. Between the lines you could read the message: Only Howard Pullett had sense enough to understand the urgency of the problem, only Pullett was perceptive enough to know Seton & Cecil teetered inches from calamity.

Becky had worked with Pullett for years; for years she had her own name for the man. He wasn't a pullet, he was a chicken. He was the famous Chicken Little. He didn't actually run around the agency screaming "The sky is falling, the sky is falling." Mostly he spoke in measured tones, carefully devoid of panic, but you could tell what he was thinking. "We are going to lose this account. We are going to loo-ooo-ose it."

Becky nodded to the agency producer to go ahead with the screening. He did, after first making a little speech about this being a rough cut so the sound track wasn't mixed and the densities weren't matched and the optical effects were not yet in place.

Becky knew he wasn't reciting all that for her benefit. Was he showing off his technical expertise for Pullett?

She held her breath, willing it to be perfect. This was a commercial that had tested exceptionally well in a rough, inexpensive form. What they were going to look at now was supposed to be an even better, air-quality version, with more money, care, and time lavished on it.

It wasn't better. It wasn't even as good. All the spontaneity and charm that had made the original "rough" version test so well were gone. Everybody had tightened up knowing this version was for real; everybody had tried to improve it too much.

The mother in the spot, who was supposed to be your normal average housewife in a normal average tract house, was now wearing a little number whipped up by Trigère. Her hair, which had been in a casual ponytail the first time around, had now been coiffed and teased and sprayed until it looked like the shellacked wig of a store-window mannequin. She was the same actress who had handled the product naturally and easily in the first version, but now she was holding it up, next to her cheek, label artfully turned toward the camera. The way no sane woman had ever held anything in her life. And the children too had undergone their own metamorphosis: Someone had told them to act cute, and they now simpered their way through the thirty seconds.

Becky knew it had only been half a minute, but she felt as if she had been watching for at least an hour when the lights finally came up.

They were all staring at her. Sometimes, when Mrs. Gagarin thought that a spot was exceptionally well done she would applaud. Occasionally she would hug the people who had created it. Now she just said "No."

"No?" Lilah James echoed sadly. "That's what Gandhi said you'd say, when I showed it to her."

"What's *wrong* with it, Becky? It looks fine to me." From Howard Pullett.

"What's wrong with it is that nobody will believe it. This isn't the way people talk or eat or dress. We'll have to review the outtakes and see if we can find more natural readings—there isn't anything we can do about her clothes or hair. And if there isn't anything better in the outtakes we'll just have to run the original test spot on air."

Pullett wasn't wringing his hands. They were folded in his lap. But his knuckles were white.

"We *can't* run the test spot. The client *knows* how much we spent on the remake. It will seem as if we really goofed if we don't use it. I suppose it proves how uncreative I am, but I cannot believe that the way an actress holds up a package or the way a few brats read their lines will make any difference in the final effectiveness of a commercial. Besides," he remembered and grinned in triumph, "we can't run it anyway! It was a *test* spot, we produced it nonunion!"

Becky studied her hands. "We'll call the union and ask what kind of penalty they would want to make an exception. It won't be the first time that's happened. Look, Howard, maybe the client will be a little upset when they hear we want to use the test spot on air. That we *couldn't* improve on it. But shouldn't they be glad to have one good enough to go with, one we feel very happy about, one that tested spectacularly?"

"Ah," Pullett smiled. "You're being logical. Clients aren't logical, they're emotional. You should know that by now."

That was one of Pullett's favorite stratagems. He would use it again and again whenever anyone disagreed with him—accuse them of being too logical. He thought it was an unbeatable ploy, because everyone was supposed to smile and dimple and feel secretly flattered when accused of being *Logical!* They were supposed to cave in at the compliment and do whatever Pullett wanted them to do. He particularly liked to use the tactic in arguments with writers, producers, and art directors. Most of them became putty in his hands when he had explained to them that their problem was that they were *too* sound, *too* rational, *too* methodical in their thinking.

"Look, Howard, I admit it, my department goofed on this one. We wasted a lot of money trying to put icing on a cake that didn't need icing. So let's stop beating our breasts and use the original."

"Sorry, Becky. We can *not* tell this client we haven't achieved what they are expecting. An improvement. And I, for one, think it *is* an improvement. We are all going to line up behind this vastly improved spot, this beautiful spot, just the way we have seen it today."

"Not with *my* recommendation behind it."

"No? Okay. Then with *mine.*"

Becky could feel her face reddening. This had never happened to her before. She had been slapped in the face publicly, by somebody who had joined the agency as a trainee in the account corps when she was already turning out campaigns that sold millions of dollars worth of products for the agency's most important clients. For *this* client, too.

There was silence in the room. The group didn't know who was in charge any more. They had the withdrawn faces children get when mommy and daddy are quarreling.

Howard Pullett was sitting across the room from her, but several rows behind her, so that all through their conversation she had had to twist in her chair to see him. She started counting in her mind. "One Mis-

sissippi. Two Mississippi. Three Mississippi." It was a
trick she had learned in editing rooms: When you haven't got a stopwatch, counting Mississippis will give you
a rough idea of the passage of time. Was Pullett one of
the men Rank had consulted about "all the problems
in the creative department?" Because suddenly Pullett
was behaving like a man who had been dealt powerful
new cards to play.

She counted ten Mississippis, ten seconds, before
she forced herself to turn. "Okay. It's only one commercial in the campaign, and the others are all first-rate."

She left the screening room fast.

Pullett was still there talking earnestly to the copywriters and art directors—*Becky's* copywriters, *Becky's*
art directors, only now somehow they had suddenly
become Pullett's—explaining how important it was for
them all to stick together on this revised commercial.
Because it was a distinct improvement over the rough
original, yes it was, truly it was, nobody must forget
how much better it was, especially when they presented
it to the client.

At La Cour, Jules seemed disturbed as he steered Mrs.
Gagarin to the table in Siberia where he had deposited
Wilbur Rank. Jules whispered in her ear as he led her
to that ghetto: "If the gentleman had only mentioned
that you would be his guest today, I would have placed
him at your usual table, but he didn't *say!*"

Mercifully, they had arrived at the table where
Rank was waiting, so Jules could stop apologizing.

Rank was punctilious about the etiquette of business lunches. He wouldn't approach the real reason they
were there until coffee was on the table.

"About the reorganization plans you sent us," he
said, at the proper time. "Ham and I could see that
you put a great deal of effort into them. But Ham feels,

and I tend to agree, that the direction *I* outlined to you the other day might be preferable."

"You mean, replacing me with *four* people? A quadrumvirate? Team governments have never worked in history, Wilbur. Think of ancient Rome. Think of the French Revolution."

"That was then. This is *now*. Ham and I believe that a quadrumvirate will send a clearer message to the troops of what the basic purpose of this whole reorganization is . . ."

Becky finished his sentence in her mind. To get rid of Becky Gagarin.

". . . to distribute power more broadly in the creative department. And you know, the fact that there are changes in the wind is beginning to leak. Would you believe that somebody in the *mail room* asked me if it was true? Your secretary hasn't been babbling, has she?"

"My secretary never 'babbles.' But the people in the mail room know how to *read*."

"Ham feels the faster we publish the details of the new organization, the better."

"And you tend to agree."

"Right!" he said immediately. And then glanced suspiciously at the woman across the table. "We *both* feel that it's time to round people up for a little meeting and announce the new plan. And Ham was wondering, since you will be moving up to a more advisory role, instead of having to worry about the day-to-day management of a department, if you will still want to bother with Friday meetings . . ."

Friday meetings were when all major problems of the agency were resolved. Rebecca Gagarin had attended those meetings every Friday morning for the last twenty years.

"I would like to continue coming to management meetings. I wouldn't know it was Friday without one."

"Ah, Becky, Becky, why do you want to keep coming to those stodgy old meetings? Why, I'd like to get out of them if I could. They're so *dull*, mostly just crunching numbers . . ."

"But the numbers are so nice and big now. I can remember when they were very small. Part of the fun of being in management . . . in a successful company, anyway . . . is watching the little numbers get big. I would like to keep on doing that."

Rank swallowed his remaining inch of coffee and put out the thin cigar he had been smoking.

"Ham thinks, and I tend to . . ." Stopping in mid-sentence, Rank gave Becky a suspicious look and started over. "Ham thinks that no one should be at management meetings who isn't part of functioning management."

"And you're saying I won't be. Any more."

Rank's voice hardened a little. "Well, you don't act like management, do you? You don't talk like management. You don't even think like management."

Then Wilbur seemed to suspect that he might have gone too far and quickly added in a warmer tone, "Becky! You're *creative*. And as Angus reminds us every chance he gets, that's what this whole business is about. And now you'll be able to devote all your energy to advising us on *creative* problems."

As he signed the check, Rank commented, "I don't believe I'll eat here again. I didn't like the table they gave us one bit. Next to the kitchen, with waiters tripping over you all the time. Oh, Becky, we'd like to have that meeting on the reorganization tomorrow. The new organization charts are all printed up and ready to distribute . . ."

"*Tomorrow?* But I won't have a chance to write out what I want to say by tomorrow. A massive creative reorganization needs tactful handling, or else you panic people, they get scared about their jobs. I'll have to explain it all carefully . . ."

"Don't you worry about that, Becky. Ham thought, and I tend . . . We thought, Ham and I, that it might be best if *I* chaired this meeting. You won't have to talk at all. As a matter of fact, you won't need to come if you don't want to, I'm sure you've got other things to do."

"Won't that seem odd? The creative head sitting in the audience, or not even there, while somebody else explains a new setup in *her* department?"

The check had been paid. He was ready to go. Lunch was speeding to a close while Becky ran behind it yelling, Hey, wait for me.

"I must have forgotten to mention it. You remarked before on our encouraging recent growth. I think you said the numbers were getting bigger? And so they are. And Ham feels that with the agency so large, and what with his having to fly to Japan so often, he has too many people reporting to him now. And he thought it would be better if we included the creative department in the list of things that *I* take care of."

It was eerily silent in the restaurant. All the sound had been sucked away by some invisible vacuum. Nobody moved; a giant freeze frame had fallen over the whole room.

"That means . . . I report to *you* now?"

Rank stood. "I don't think you'll be doing that much. I'll just tell the four new executive creative directors they can bring their problems directly to my doorstep. Think of all the beautiful *time* you will have now, Becky! Time to think. Time to put it all into perspective. Time to *create*."

True to Wilbur Rank's word, the new Table of Organization was distributed the next day.

It had Rebecca Gagarin in a little box all by herself,

with the words *Creative Head* underneath her name.

A dotted line connected her box to Rank's, which was on the same level as hers, except that Rank's box was attached by a thick black line to Horatio Hamlin's. Rebecca Gagarin's box was not. She was a tailbone now, with no connection to the head bone. No, she wasn't even a tailbone, she was an appendix. A vestigial remnant, which in the natural evolution of things would soon flop off and disappear entirely.

The four new executive creative directors (all of them men, and one of them Victor Cameron) had boxes lower than Mrs. Gagarin's, geographically speaking, on the page. But their boxes were linked by thick black lines to Rank's. No line, dotted or otherwise, linked them to Rebecca Gagarin.

She floated alone on the page, alone in her box, with only a dotted umbilical cord securing her to Wilbur Rank.

And now privacy, the privacy she'd dreamed of all those years when she shared a bedroom with two sisters, the privacy she'd yearned for at Omni's Discount Department Store when she'd shared an office with three other copywriters, descended on her with a thud.

Her beautiful office, with the door she could close on the world whenever she wanted to, or open wide to summon them all in when she felt gregarious, had become a cell. The door was closed all the time now. Privacy had become isolation.

The world suddenly felt flat, and Becky was sliding off the edge of it.

The IN box was now empty. Nobody was sending her memos, conference reports, printouts.

The OUT box was empty. There were no longer any decisions for her to make, nobody was awaiting her memos of praise or censure, her opinion was no longer courted. With IN empty, and OUT empty, she almost ceased to exist in her own eyes.

Each day, as soon as she arrived, she found herself looking forward desperately to lunch.

But lunch dates had dwindled too. She no longer had any power to barter over the coffee cups.

And yet, all that had happened was that, in due course and in the manner known to all corporations, not just advertising agencies, Rebecca Gagarin had been kicked upstairs. Shoved out of the way, for younger people. Or, if not younger, at least those who understood the art of shoving.

She remembered a story she had read long ago in the *Times* about the chairman of the board of a major company, a Fortune 500 company. Things had not been going well for him. His company had been headed inexorably for the rocks. So far, only he knew the magnitude of the trouble, but soon the whole world would understand the extent of his failure.

So he had his chauffeur drive him to his office on a Saturday. He went up the elevator, down the darkened hall of executive offices, through his secretary's room, and into his own. He locked the door behind him. The first thing on his agenda that day was TIME TO JUMP. It wasn't written in the appointment schedule on his desk. It was written in capital letters on his brain.

Unfortunately, it was one of those high-rise buildings where the windows don't open, where climate comes to you courtesy of the building engineers. Before he could jump he had to figure out a way of getting a window open.

His attaché case must have been bigger than Becky Gagarin's, heavier than hers, a man's case built on a framework of steel, because he was able to use it to smash open one of the windows.

She could see him now, his glasses off but his suit

jacket still on, as he swung the case again and again, at first with precise rhythmic arcs, but later more erratically. She could see him beginning to sweat from the effort. And finally, triumphantly, the window shattered, and hacking at the shards of glass that surrounded the frame, he had been able to create an opening for himself. He didn't have to perch ignominiously on the ledge. The windows ran from floor to ceiling, so all he had to do was step out, and down.

Thirty stories down.

But what did he do with the attaché case? Did he throw it out the window, and then follow after? Or did he jump with the case still in his hand, the picture of corporate composure, the way he used to look as he strode through airport terminals on his way to his private jet?

Becky thought how lucky she was to work in an old-fashioned building, where you could open a window anytime you wanted. Except that she would probably only break a leg and become a case for one of the clerks in the Benefits Department.

But by the time her leg had healed, even the clerks would be saying Becky? Becky who?

8

Becky was screaming at Alex.

Alex was screaming back.

It was the highest-decibel quarrel they had had in twenty-five years of marriage. The nest was empty now; they could give way to these primal screams. But the Sinclairs, the family that lived in the other apartment on the fourth floor—he from Princeton, she from Smith, he at Merrill Lynch, she at Parke-Bernet—mightn't *they* overhear?

Becky's mother whispered, "Becky, be quiet. What a *shonda* for the neighbors!" All through Becky's childhood her mother had worried that their family's most timid quarrel would scandalize the neighbors.

But—"You were drunk," Becky yelled. "You were lying in your own vomit right on the living room floor when I got back from Milan."

"My God," howled Alex. "Don't you ever close your books? Don't you ever let go of a single grudge? Becky, I want to *help* you."

"I don't need help. I can handle it myself. Haven't I always? Who was up all night that time Peter had croup, and you were in some bar getting plastered?"

Alex slumped in his chair and supported his head in his hands. "Becky, Peter is nineteen. He is in college on the other side of the country. He has a driver's license now, he has a social security card and a bank account. He hasn't had croup since he was four years old. And I haven't had a drink in fifteen. Fifteen years! And what has croup got to do with whatever is going on now?"

He reached out a hand to her. "Tell me. Talk to me. You should see yourself when you come home lately. I hardly recognize you. You look tormented. You look haggard. I'm your husband. I deserve to know what is going on."

"Thanks. That's what I really needed. To be told I'm looking ancient." Since they were assuming neutral corners, she slumped into a chair facing his. She felt their knees touching, and she pulled hers to one side. Away from him.

"So they made you reorganize your department? Is that so terrible? You told me when they made you creative head that nobody lasted long in that job. And you still have the job, only you have to run things a little differently now."

"*Run* things? I don't run *anything* any more. Not . . . one . . . fucking . . . thing. You want to know what my days are like now? I'll tell you. I come in, there's nothing on my desk except junk mail, the kind of mail Eileen used to throw away without even showing me. I guess she puts it on my desk now so the desk won't look so . . . forlorn. I still have the title creative head but I'm a figurehead. A fucking figurehead."

Becky had always thought herself too articulate to need to use words like *fucking*. Now she heard herself repeating it and looked at Alex helplessly.

"You know what humiliates me most about all of this? Eileen. My *secretary*. I'm ashamed of her seeing how little I have to do. So I keep my door closed and every now and then I pop out like a jack-in-the-box and give her something to type. A comment on a campaign. A comment that will go straight into the waste-basket of whoever gets it. It's only been a few weeks since the reorganization, but everybody understands it now. Rebecca Gagarin has no *power* any more."

Alex shifted his chair closer to Becky's, so that their knees could touch again, and reached over to lace his fingers through hers. "So, leave! Why are you still hanging around there? You can probably snap your fingers and get a job in any agency you want."

How could she make him understand the paralysis she felt? It had become hard for her to open the door of her office and walk twenty feet down the corridor to the ladies' room, much less go out into the world and start job-hunting. How could she make him see that Seton & Cecil was more than a job? It was her sanctuary, her refuge, her shelter, her home. It was *Becky*.

"You need courage to come in at a high level in a strange place, and I've been at Seton & Cecil so long."

"You mean, you've *hidden* at Seton & Cecil for so long."

"Maybe so. And if I were a man, I'd be considered at the height of my powers now. A top executive, with all that experience, wow, what a catch. But a woman of my age, suddenly looking, everyone would know it was because I was over the hill. It's like I've gone directly from child prodigy to has-been. With nothing in between."

Alex asked slowly, "And Angus? Does he know how they're treating you? He owes you something, you know. You helped build that place."

She took her hand away from his. She noticed that like Alex's little protégée, just like that Zoe, she had begun to chew on her nails.

"Sometimes I think he must know. New York is the bellwether office, they wouldn't have dared change things so dramatically in New York without telling him. And other times I think no, he doesn't know, this is

Hamlin's doing, Hamlin runs the New York office, Hamlin has the right to move things—and people!—around internally without telling Angus. He'd *enjoy* staging a massive reorganization like this without telling Angus. I've told you how they loathe each other."

Alex grinned. "So, fly over there and talk to Seton yourself. You're important enough to do that, you're a director of the company!"

In a shocked little-girl voice she said, "I can't just pop in on Angus without being asked! Besides, he's coming to New York soon."

"When?" Bluntly.

"I don't know exactly when. Although you can't get in an elevator without hearing that he's due soon. When he comes. I'll talk to him when he comes."

"And meanwhile, you'll go on feeling like shit, and looking like death."

Since they were finally talking about it, she confessed, "Finding things for Eileen to do isn't the worst. I'll tell you what the worst is. There are still some meetings I do go to. Whenever I say anything at those meetings, nobody *hears* me any more. Everyone will be quiet for a second and then go right on as if nobody had spoken. And sometimes somebody will make the same comment or suggestion *I* just finished making, and everyone will nod and say 'What a great idea'—so I *know* they haven't heard me. Or somebody will start talking when I'm in the middle of a sentence as if nobody had the floor. I feel invisible. I feel like Banquo's ghost. As if Becky Gagarin doesn't exist any more—"

"Rebecca." Alex hardly ever called her that. "Let's go out together tonight. I want to take you somewhere. The Russian Cathedral."

She hooted. "Why the Russian Cathedral all of a sudden? Am I supposed to find solace in the church? You're not religious. Neither am I."

"They're celebrating Russian Easter tonight. It's

the holiday of holidays, more important than Christmas
is to the rest of the world. You don't have to be religious
to appreciate how joyous it is. I think it would cheer
you up. You need to be reminded that the world is
bigger than Seton & Cecil."

Alex said the service would start at about eleven and
continue until well past midnight.

A bower covered with white flowers had been built
in the center of the cathedral. "The Tomb of Christ,"
Alex told her. People converged, greeting each other
without modulating their voices, sometimes in English,
more often in Russian. They packed in almost stomach
to buttocks. There were no seats, except a few for the
extremely aged. Everybody stood, and every inch of
floor space was soon taken. But holding Becky's hand,
Alex worked his way toward the front ("Where you'll
be able to see, Becky") and toward the side ("Where
you can breathe").

The priests came in procession from a door behind
the altar. The youngest black-bearded priests were first,
their deep voices clanging sorrow at Christ's death. Behind them older, white- or gray-haired priests filled in
the sound with even more grieving male sonority. At
the end, surrounded by important graybeards who
shielded him like a precious icon, came the most ancient
priest of all. Becky caught the whisper of his voice,
tremulous with belief, quavering with age as he passed.
They all, except for the few who swung censers, carried
tall candles. Like a parade of light they came toward
the congregation and then, to Becky's amazement, continued past them and out of the cathedral.

"Alex! Where are they going?"

"Shh. Listen. Listen!"

The crowd that had been jabbering, chattering,
even shouting to one another such a short time ago was
now silent. Listening.

The voices faded away into the distance, then disappeared entirely.

Silence. Nothing.

But now the music was coming back to where they waited. What did it symbolize, this stillness, then this chanting, this leaving, this return? The death and resurrection of Christ?

The priests had circled the block and were back in the cathedral now. The building shook with the thunder of their arrival. They were skirted in cassocks, yes, but their gray and white and black beards, the tall priapic candles held aloft, the vigor of their chanting—it was like being swept along in the midst of a crusade, they entered like a victorious army. She had never felt so naked of a phallus in all her life. The most ancient priest (archbishop? what?) mumbled something and the congregation shouted back in answer. The priest next to him, somber from head to foot, black hair, black beard, the lowest darkest deepest bass voice Becky had ever heard, clanged forth clearly what the old man had mumbled. Alex translated for her: Christ is risen! And the congregation roared back, Yes he is risen, he is indeed risen! And the third time the priests thundered forth the glorious news, although she wouldn't have thought it possible, the response was even more clamorous, more insistent, a peal of belief from everyone in the church. Including Becky. To her horror.

He was lying on his side facing away from her, so she curved herself to follow the line of his body. "I couldn't even whisper 'Christ' when I was a child. When we sang Christmas carols in school I'd leave 'Christ' out and hum to fill in the gaps. I never thought I'd hear myself *shouting* that He had risen. Lenin was right about religion being the opiate of the masses. I must have been drugged."

"Marx. It was Marx who said it." He sounded sleepy.

She looked at the luminous dial of her watch. "My God, it's three in the morning. I'll be good now, I promise to shut up and let you get some sleep . . ."

"I think I have something better in mind." When he turned over, it was clear that he did.

It had been so long since they had made love that she worried that she might have forgotten how to do sex. At the beginning she felt dry, old, incapable. But it turned out that it was like riding a bicycle, swimming, touch typing, any other physical act that once learned is never really lost. As his hands felt her skin, her own response began. She was liquefying for her husband. She was turning herself inside out for him. She remembered everything that was important to remember.

Their conversation afterwards had been sleepy, amiable, and all she'd done was ask him about Zoe. In a light teasing voice, so he would know she was joking.

"Is there anything going on between you two?" she'd asked.

"I already told you I'm her sponsor."

"I mean, something more serious than that."

"There is *nothing* more serious than that. Helping a person to adjust to life without alcohol. Being there when the person has doubts, questions, problems . . ."

She laughed.

"It may be funny to you. It is *not* funny to me."

Suddenly he was sitting up. "I had to get on my knees today to find out what's been eating you for months now. You never let me into your life, why should I invite you into mine? Anything 'going on' between Zoe and me is private. Plus, it's none of your business." Then he was on his feet, collecting a blanket and his pillow.

"Where are you going?"

"I slept very well in Peter's room that time, I think I'll just move in there. I'll get all my stuff out of the closet in here tomorrow. At least those bloody pigeons won't be screwing on the windowsill at the crack of dawn."

The times after sex had always been cozy and peaceful with Alex.

This was the first time they'd ever gone directly from making love to fighting with each other.

~~~~~~

Even the first time with Alexander Gagarin she'd found herself smiling afterwards.

All of her had been smiling. She remembered feeling the nipples on her breasts curving up, like the clown smiles small children draw . . .

"You wouldn't happen to be Jewish, would you?" she'd asked him, that first time. "Where does the name Gagarin come from?"

She bent over him, her hair swinging into blond panels on either side of his face. She put her hands on his cheeks and let her fingers reach into his hair, felt them becoming part of its urgency, its blackness, its force. It was something she had been wanting to do since she first laid eyes on him two days ago.

"Gagarin? It's Russian. You've heard of Gagarin, the cosmonaut? I'm descended from cossacks. Why? Does it really matter? I'd say I was Jewish if that would please you, only you'd be bound to find out."

Her mother had told Becky about cossacks. Ruthless, feral, sadistic, they rode around on savage horses and raped pregnant women and bashed out babies' heads. She tried to picture the Alex who had just been so tender to her riding and raping and murdering babies, and giggled.

He said, "If we move that mirror to the wall over

there, we could watch each other make love the next time."

"What are you, some kind of voyeur?"

"In a way. I'm a painter, I like to look at things that please me. *You* please me. If we moved the mirror, I'd be able to look at you twice. Closeup, when I hold you in my arms. Then I could glance away and see you at a distance. Get the whole picture, so to speak."

She remembered her father stepping back from paintings in museums, step by cautious step, and the wonderful look of pleasure that would come over his face when he finally "got the whole picture."

"What are you staring at now, Alex?"

"That photograph, on the chest of drawers. It *is* you, isn't it?"

"Yes, it's me. Becky *before*."

"Before what? Oh, I see, you did something to your nose."

"Yes. As the joke goes, I cut off my nose to spite my race. Do you like it, my new nose? It's only three years old."

"Listen, I'm not very good at portraits, likenesses I mean, but I'd enjoy painting you. You probably won't recognize yourself, but I would like to try."

Alexander Gagarin had a cold-water flat. So it was never a choice of "your place or mine" when it came to where they made love. It was always Becky's apartment, with dependable heat and a tiled bathroom. But it was his place that he painted her in. He said his paints were all there. He posed her standing, nude, hands clasped shyly in front of her. There was jazz on the radio and a kerosene heater pointed at her body. Heater or not it was freezing there and she wondered, would he paint the goosebumps on her skin?

Finally he let her see the painting. Alex was wrong, he *could* paint likenesses, her body was recognizable all right. It was the still-narrow body of a girl who would one day become a sturdy woman. The shoulders were slight, the waist still lithe, the rib cage small. But there was surprising width in the pelvis, and the architecture of the thighs and hips warned of heft to come.

Becky's eyes rested briefly on the figure, then returned to the face.

"Why did you do that?"

"I didn't realize I was doing it until it was done," he said.

"You really liked that beak? I can't believe it."

"Well, the nose you have now is very pretty." He traced it with a fingertip. "It's very, ah, cute. But the nose in the photograph, forgive me Becky, didn't anyone tell you? You were *beautiful* then."

9

"I
t's going to be a hell of a good campaign, Gandhi."

Becky took her glasses off and gave Gandhi back the script she'd been reading. They were facing each other in a booth in Lilah's place—the saloon on Second Avenue. When they'd been here before, it had been a sleepy Saturday, but now, at lunchtime on a weekday, it was jammed.

Gandhi stubbed out one cigarette and lit another. "We're showing it to the client tomorrow. It's the first time I've presented anything at a client meeting. I'm petrified."

"Don't be silly, you'll do fine." Becky stared at the inch of coffee left in her cup. It hadn't been very good coffee but it had been hot, so she waved at the waitress for another cup. But the overworked waitress didn't, or wouldn't, see her.

"Why did you want to show it to me a second time?" Becky asked. "You already know I love it—it's the best work I've ever seen for Eve." She laughed. "Aside from my own, of course."

"I wanted to show it to you to be sure I wasn't crazy. Cameron loathes it. He says it's too cerebral, that you can only sell women beauty products when you slather the ads with sex . . . or music. Preferably both.

He's only letting it be presented because he wants to have some different approaches he can shoot down before the recommended campaign is shown. Rae's campaign." Gandhi also waved at the waitress and also was not seen.

"Rae's campaign? That *jingle*?"

"Yeah. Cameron says if you can sing it, you can sell it. Did you know he's asked Rae to do a new Trowbridge campaign, with rock music? And maybe some break dancing."

Becky took a deep breath. She thought of Aunt Prudence's white cotton aprons, of her New England twang lecturing about real milk, none of that dried stuff, real clover honey, the kind bees make, stone-ground flour and . . . Lightly, she said, "I can't imagine Aunt Prudence break dancing."

"Cameron wants to get rid of Aunt Prudence. He says it's ridiculous to use an old hag to communicate with young housewives. Rae's found a cute blonde for the new campaign."

"Well. I'm glad Cameron likes Rae's work," Becky said, staring into her now empty coffee cup.

"Yeah. And he likes Keith's. Sometimes he even likes mine. I guess the only one who's having real trouble in the Cameron group is Lilah. Cameron doesn't like older writers. And she didn't help herself getting caught that way the other day . . ."

"Caught what way? Fill me in, Gandhi. I feel as if I've been living in a cave."

Gandhi puffed on her cigarette with short angry puffs. "Cameron and Hamlin were showing some new client around the creative department. The two of them walked in on Lilah smoking . . ."

"Forgive me, but what's the scandal in that?"

"It wasn't tobacco."

"Oh my God. Why didn't she lock her door at

least?" Then Becky remembered Lilah wasn't important enough to rate a lock on her door.

"Yeah. Cameron had her on the carpet and warned her, no matter how successful her campaigns were, one more stunt like that and she'd be O-U-T, out. I yelled at her too. She has to be careful what she does from here on in, they can use things like that against us when our suit comes to court. Listen, did I tell you, we've really built up momentum now, there are women from Research and women from Casting who've joined in with us . . . it's so sad that *you* can't . . ."

"It isn't that I can't. I won't."

They were both silent for a moment. It sat there between them: Becky would not enlist in Gandhi's feminist crusade. Then Gandhi sighed. "My mother says I've got to change my hairstyle for the client meeting tomorrow. Since I'm going to be onstage. I'll do it but it's a drag. It takes me two hours to take it apart and even longer to get it fixed up again."

Then Gandhi wasn't looking at Becky any more, but at a spot on the table between her elbows. "Mrs. Gagarin. Becky. Why have you always been so nice to me? Or am I the department's token black?"

"Don't be ridiculous. You're not a token. You're an augury. A prophecy of the future." Becky leaned forward and spoke earnestly to the young woman across the table.

"You're too young to remember this, Gandhi, but in the fifties and sixties there was a tidal wave of Jewish copywriters coming into advertising. I was one of them. We were like those slum kids who used to dream of becoming prizefighters in the thirties. It was a way out for us, too.

"And after a while the Jewish copywriters—and their pals, the Italian art directors—changed advertising. Because they started winning all the prizes.

"You see, most of them *longed* for the things they

were advertising, because they'd never had them as kids. They'd spent their childhoods wanting the wall-to-wall carpets and the big road-hugging cars they were making ads for now . . . well, nobody can make a product sound more exciting than somebody who really wants it for himself. And soon the clients began demanding to talk to the Jewish copywriters and Italian art directors directly—not through account men—so they had to let them out of the back rooms. And now a lot of them are running the agencies.

"And I bet you that's what will happen—eventually—to the young blacks and Hispanics who are coming into the business now. They'll make terrific advertising, because that same quality of longing will be in their work. Those kids won't be tokens very long, one day they'll wind up in charge."

Becky sat back and wondered why Gandhi was looking at her with such amusement. "I have to be a good copywriter, because of my poverty-stricken childhood?"

"You're good because you can't help being good. When I edit most of the copy that's submitted to me, I can move the words around any which way I like, and it doesn't hurt. Because the sentences never had any music in the first place. But *your* copy—well, it all hangs together. It's so beautifully crafted I can't edit out a word."

"It's well known, we all got rhythm," said Gandhi, snapping her fingers. But she was smiling. She looked down at her empty cup. "We need more coffee."

She stood up and thundered, "WE NEED MORE COFFEE OVER HERE."

This time, the waitress heard.

When they were walking back to the agency, Gandhi said shyly, "I was just kidding that time I asked you to join us in the suit. You're management, so I know that legally you can't join with ordinary working stiffs in a class-action suit. Listen, I'm on my way to meet with one of the women who *is* in the suit. Would you like to come with me?"

She pointed across the street. "She's waiting in that store."

The tiny needlework shop was clustered with women. Women inspecting fabrics, selecting threads, choosing crocheting hooks and knitting needles, sitting at tables studying pattern books. Becky thought that if they had been planning a revolution this would be the perfect place to do it: Nobody looks twice at a woman knitting.

The woman waiting for Gandhi was Wanda Schiavone.

She looked up from a pattern book but made no effort to shake Becky's hand when Becky was introduced.

"So this is the famous Gagarin! Listen, I worked hard on those scripts I left on your desk. I kept waiting for you to call me about them. Then I heard you hired a kid right out of college for the job. A guy, naturally. Why did I work at the agency for eleven years if I can't get first consideration for a shitty junior writer opening?"

Becky remembered Schiavone's execrable scripts. The woman was standing now, massive and muscular, looming over her, looking at least seven feet tall. Becky would not have liked to meet this Schiavone alone in a dark alley.

"Well, you see, Wanda, everyone thinks he—or she—is a copywriter. I can't go to a meeting without one of the clients, usually one of the younger ones, wanting to rewrite my copy. But not everyone . . ."

"Stop with the bullshit. You didn't like my work because you wanted to bring in another bright-eyed bushy-tailed little boy, from one of your WASPy colleges. We're not talking about *everyone* here, we're talking about Wanda Schiavone. And a chance she deserved."

She sat down again, heavily. "But now that you've clawed your way to the top, why should you help other women get there? It would only make Gagarin less of a success story. Now that you're on top of the ladder you want to pull the ladder up after you. You don't mind letting the good old boys keep the barriers in place, it helps you preserve your own privileged position. Well, I have news for you. Sure, when I sent you my scripts you were somebody, a big muck-a-muck, but everyone knows soon you won't amount to a hill of beans, that it's only a matter of time now before you're out on your ass . . ."

Gandhi apologized for Wanda all the way back to the agency.

Becky insisted she hadn't been bothered by the scene. "But that's why I was never a feminist. I find that kind of anger, that kind of injustice collecting so . . . unattractive. Anyway, what it all comes down to in the end is talent, and the Wandas of this world can't bluster their way around that."

There was a terse note from Rank in her IN box. Becky was to be at Butler Aviation at LaGuardia Airport at three the next afternoon. Stuart Shaw, newly appointed CEO of the corporation that marketed Eve, wanted her in the delegation that would be going to Winosha tomorrow to present the latest creative work on Eve.

Becky sat there, her hands folded on her desk. And remembered Wanda Schiavone's words. "Everyone knows you don't add up to a hill of beans any more . . ."

And although she had mocked Wanda's anger, now she found herself filled with the same emotion. Seething, futile, unattractive anger. At Wanda. For hulking over her and frightening her. At Alex—who had been sleeping in Peter's room since Easter. When they encountered each other now in the kitchen, they would smile dimly, like distant acquaintances. At Rank, for his curt little note. For not inviting her to this meeting until the client had demanded to have her.

She remembered Kathleen Turner in that movie about the mafia. The scene where Turner takes a sweet little pearl-handled revolver from her purse and shoots Jack Nicholson.

~~~~~

Becky put her handbag on her lap and smiled. She was thinking about the gun inside.

If it had been a regular, scheduled flight, they would have had to go through a security check and the gun would have been found. But this was the client's company jet, so a search wasn't necessary. There were no tickets. The pilot and copilot lugged everyone's suitcases on board themselves.

An assistant planner from media, an assistant research director, and three very young account types were buckled into a joking little group in the rear.

Up front, Horatio Hamlin, Wilbur Rank, and Rebecca Gagarin sat together.

She wondered, which one should she murder first, Rank, or Hamlin? She thought how terrified their faces would be when she took the gun from her bag. How their eyes would widen. How they would beg for their lives.

But Rank had decided to throw a few words at her. In his best general-addressing-an-aide voice he said, "Shaw's made a real fuss about your showing up today. Becky, I didn't know you two were pals."

Becky said, "Neither did I. I haven't seen him for years. But we worked together when he was a young brand manager at UniDerm, and I was a junior writer at S&C. . . . We were both pretty young. I guess you could say he was a child, and I was a child, in a kingdom by the sea. There weren't a lot of account men to get between us then."

Rank chuckled. "I'll bet you loved that. Not a lot of account men." Becky Gagarin had been toppled from her place; it was possible for him to joke openly now about her eccentricities. "Well, it was a real surprise when Shaw was brought in as CEO—everyone expected Ed Douglas to get that job. The inside scoop is that they thought Douglas could use a little more seasoning, so they managed to get Shaw. But I hear Shaw's supposed to move up to chairman next year, and then Douglas will be CEO. Douglas is the one we'll be dealing with next year. And of course eventually Shaw will retire and be out of the picture completely . . . but still, it's nice that he remembered you after so long."

He made it sound as if in bringing Becky along, the agency was merely catering to the whims of a sentimental old man. Blood. Blood on that clean white shirt.

Now the engines were starting. Becky raised her voice. "What do you want me to do at this meeting? Give the creative recommendation?"

Rank said quickly, "Oh, you won't need to bother with that. I think we should let Cameron make the recommendation, it's his group. We might only bollix things up if we start adding a lot of extra voices to his show."

It was the first time that Rebecca Gagarin had ever been referred to as a "lot of extra voices" at a Seton & Cecil creative presentation. In the stomach. She would aim at Rank's stomach. And Hamlin, right between the eyes, right into that frosty mechanical brain.

Rank continued, "No, all you have to do tomorrow is just sit next to Shaw and make nice. Smile at him a lot. Don't you agree, Ham? Oh, I'm sorry, I didn't realize you were napping."

Horatio Hamlin always said that one of the things that kept him going was his ability to snatch catnaps on planes and trains and ski trips and mountaintops. Even in caves, when he went spelunking. But he could not have been completely asleep, because his eyes snapped open. "All Shaw wants is to see you in the room." And the eyes snapped shut again.

Rank said, "Well, isn't that cushy? *If* he asks you directly, just tell him how proud you are of the work we're showing. Don't say anything if he doesn't ask! And listen, don't mention you know he's set for chairman next year, I probably shouldn't have told you, it's supposed to be a top-level secret."

Would the pilot radio for help when she shot them? Would they be met by police cars drawn up on the tarmac? Would it make the front page of the *Daily News:* CRAZED ADLADY RUNS AMOK IN EXEC JET. They wouldn't have any problem knowing who to handcuff; she was the only woman on the plane.

She placed her hand protectively over her bag, the bag that was so pleasantly plump with the bulk of the gun, and studied Horatio Hamlin. His mouth was open slightly, now that he was really napping. It wouldn't be fun to shoot him until he was awake and *understood* there might be more risk to tangling with Becky Gagarin than to climbing the Himalayas or shooting white water in a canoe.

Just as her father could never eat without something to read on the table, Becky Gagarin usually would not fly without a book in her hand. But on this trip she was happy without a book. She was content with planning the execution of Wilbur Rank and Horatio Hamlin.

In the end she decided to delay the double murder until the next day. There was too much danger to innocent bystanders on a plane. She would do it *tomorrow*. Right in the middle of the meeting, she would take aim across the conference table and ask everyone else in the room to stand safely aside—while she mowed the bastards down.

The murders in her mind kept her pleasantly occupied all the way to Winosha.

It was dark when they landed. Winters come early and stay late in Winosha; it was already April but snow was still banked on both sides of the landing strip. Inside the terminal Rank headed straight for the public phones, his small notebook in hand and open. He was ready to phone Edward Douglas, heir apparent to Stuart Shaw, with the glad news that his agency had arrived.

"Oh, Becky, you stick with the gang for dinner," Rank said briefly to Becky as he dialed. "Ham and I will be grabbing a bite with Douglas. We'll be laying out the strategy for tomorrow's meeting, we won't need you."

He had given Mrs. Gagarin her marching orders. And publicly strutted the fact that she was reporting to him now.

But after a quick phone conversation, he changed this command.

"Ed wants to bring his wife," he announced gloomily. "Becky, you'd better come along after all. Keep her company."

Edward Douglas was a dark balding man in his late thirties, at least a foot taller than either Hamlin or Rank. This pleased Becky. She liked watching their faces turn up toward Douglas whenever he said anything, like little birds waiting to be fed by a mother bird.

Like many very tall men, Douglas had chosen a petite mate. Ruth-Anne. Except that right now, she wasn't terribly petite. In that endless ninth month of pregnancy, when you cannot find a restful place to sleep in a bed you've found comfortable for years, when the you that used to be lissome is waddling along with bags under the eyes and a pasty complexion, she was a not-so-radiant Ruthie.

"That's an elegant dress," Becky told her. "I remember the times I was pregnant, all the maternity dresses used to have those infantile *bows* at the neckline. But your dress is terrific, you can even wear it after the baby is born. Where did you buy it?"

Rank looked approving. This was the kind of thing she had been brought along to say.

Ruth-Anne blushed. It made her complexion look pretty for the first time that evening. "Do you really like it? I made it myself." She said she still missed New York, where Edward had been posted last. For five years they had had the thrill of living in Scarsdale.

"But it's a wonderful opportunity, for Edward to be posted in corporate *headquarters*."

"Is this your first child?"

Ruth-Anne said no, she had two others, six and seven years old. She looked down at the bulge that used to be her waistline. "They're both in school now. I was planning to do something crazy soon . . . well, I won't be able to do it with the new baby and all. Why don't you put your handbag under your chair, Becky, you look uncomfortable with it on your lap."

"I always keep my bag on my lap, you get used to that in New York restaurants, otherwise it gets stolen . . . What's the crazy thing you were planning?"

Ruth-Anne blushed again, as if confessing a particularly adolescent fantasy.

"My friend Sooky and I were going to start a dress shop. There isn't anyplace in Winosha you can buy anything decent to wear, you have to go all the way to Chicago. We even had the name picked out, Sooky & Ruthie. Although now I guess Sooky will have to find someone else."

She looked down at her swelling middle. "But I'll have the new baby, and that will be much more exciting. Really it will."

"Why can't you have both?"

"Both?"

"The baby and the business. It's not unheard of."

Edward Douglas said quickly, "Of course, we know that *you* did it, Mrs. Gagarin. But doesn't it take a very special kind of woman to be able to balance such conflicting demands? A job and children?"

"What makes you think your wife isn't a special kind of woman?"

She thought she'd said it lightly, but Horatio Hamlin's face went blank, and Wilbur Rank darted fierce unspoken messages at her. *Stop*, Rank's eyes said. *Wrong*, they signaled.

Ruth-Anne lumbered to her feet. "You remember what these last few months are like, Becky. You have to keep running to the little girls' room. Would you like to keep me company?"

Ruth-Anne stared into the mirror, widening and tightening her lips as she repainted her mouth. "Sure, I could handle the shop and the baby too. No sweat. But Ed sulks every time I even mention it."

Becky stood next to her, combing her hair. "I'm sorry if I opened up a can of worms."

"Oh, he's forgotten about it by now. By now they all have their little calculators out, and they're very happy playing with them . . ." She studied her reflection. "I don't know what they mean about pregnancy giving you a special glow. I walk around with special heartburn all the time. I'd sell my soul for some Gelusil. You don't happen to have any, do you?"

"Tums. I have Tums. Cheaper, and just as good."

Becky opened her handbag and rooted around in it. "Don't seem to feel any . . ." She took the handbag, upended it, and dumped the contents onto the shelf below the mirror. Out of her bag tumbled the usual female clutter: address book, wallet, change purse, compact, mascara, lipstick, and a small tube of antacid tablets, which she handed to a grateful Ruth-Anne.

So where was the gun?

There was no gun in Rebecca Gagarin's handbag. Never had been. There had only been the wished-for fantasy gun on the plane. The chimera of a gun that was going to solve all of Becky's problems. That would make *today* disappear and make yesterday happen all over again. The fabled yesterday that she hadn't appreciated while it was happening.

"Don't go in there yet, Becky. There's something you should know before you go in there . . ."

Becky stared at the discreetly dressed woman barring her way to the conference room. Proper business suit, low-heeled Republican shoes, hair brushed trimly back, nails polished a modest Executive Pink. Could this sober, contained, *dull*-looking woman be Lilah James? Lilah, of the taped-together eyeglasses, the inexplicable (or at least never explained) black eyes, the woman who always knew which corner of Bryant Park was the most convenient for the purchase of hard-to-get supplies? Could this be Lilah, curried, combed, and conservative?

The woman continued to bar the way. "Some things you don't expect are going to happen in there . . ." She stopped in the middle of the sentence. Victor Cameron and Wilbur Rank were walking towards them, only a few feet down the corridor. Lilah James smiled at them docilely and trotted into the conference room. It seemed that whatever it was that was so important for Becky to know could not be told while Cameron and Rank were listening.

■   ■   ■

"Becky Gelb! No, I mean Becky Gagarin!"

Stuart Shaw had pouches under his eyes now. Jowls obscured the line of his jaw. The red hair that used to flap into his eyes had turned gray, what was left of it, and instead of darting around the room while he made his points he sat relaxed at the head of the table now, in the seat of power.

"Twenty-five years, and you haven't changed a bit," he lied, and Becky lied right back, "Neither have you! I recognized you right away!"

Twenty-five years ago, Stuart Shaw had been at her first client meeting. It had been at another company, and they were dealing with a different product. The meeting had been in the Glass Palace, the skyscraper that hung like a green icicle on Park Avenue, so pure, so startling in design, that it had spawned other glass buildings to the south of it, and north of it, and in many other cities—none of the others as breathtaking as the first.

Representing Seton & Cecil that day, there had only been Angus Seton and Becky Gelb. On the client's side of the table there had been a lot of people besides Stuart Shaw. Later, Becky had learned that all clients love going to advertising meetings. Not everybody is capable of helping with distribution and production, and meetings on those subjects were rarely over-crowded, but *everyone* was sure he could help with the advertising.

Stuart Shaw had been young and full of beans; she remembered how often he got up to pace the room, and the sharp questions he had asked.

And even though Shaw was the youngest man on the client's side of the table, Angus Seton had talked only to him. The rest of us, we're window dressing, Becky had realized. These two men are making all the decisions between them. (Over the years she discovered that all *good* meetings were like that. No matter how many bodies there were in the room, at good advertising meetings there would really be only two people, one from the client, one from the agency, making all the decisions.)

That day, when Becky had finished reading her copy, Stuart Shaw had smiled and asked her to read it again. And then he had turned and said to Angus, "Where have you been hiding Miss Gelb all this time?"

Now Shaw said, "Sit here next to me so we can catch up on what we've both been doing in the last— my God, quarter of a century? Although I know what *you've* been doing, I know how you zoomed to top creative gal at Seton & Cecil. No, we're not supposed to say *gal* any more, are we? *Woman*, I mean. Anyway, you're doing the same job Angus Seton used to do, aren't you? Creative Head, New York?"

Since as far as the outside world was concerned she still bore the title, it wasn't a lie when Becky nodded. "And *you*. I've followed you for twenty-five years too! It's wonderful to find ourselves working together again."

It's a common belief that advertising men and women switch jobs a lot. The trouble with that is that like most common beliefs it isn't totally true. Advertising people are often timidly intent on clinging to the security of the same desk, the same signature on their checks, and as often as they can will stay with one agency through an entire career. While all around them, with Tarzan-like daring, executives of major corporations swing from corporate ladder to corporate ladder. So that while Rebecca Gagarin had remained loyal and unbudging at Seton & Cecil, never even peering over the fence to see if the grass might be greener on the other side, Stuart Shaw—whom she had known at UniDerm—had worked for Consolidated and Amalgamated and Agglutinated. And now he was chief executive officer—soon to be chairman—of the corporation that manufactured Eve.

The creative group was setting up storyboards across the room. They had arrived the day before and rehearsed until two in the morning, but they had their adrenaline going now and they didn't look tired.

Along the side of the table that faced the cork-board wall, Edward Douglas and Victor Cameron and Horatio Hamlin found seats. Well, not really "found." The seating plan for any important advertising presentation is as painstakingly plotted as the seating plan for a White House dinner. Victor Cameron had been carefully placed next to Edward Douglas, just as Becky had been deposited next to Shaw. The idea was for Douglas and Cameron to make friends during the meeting, while Shaw and Gagarin reminisced. Douglas and Cameron were the wave of the future. Shaw and Gagarin would soon be remembrances of things past.

When they were introduced, Shaw lumbered to his feet and reached across the table to shake Victor's hand. "Nice to have you joining Becky's team, Vic," he said. "The more brains the better."

Victor didn't flinch when he heard Shaw tell him he had "joined Becky's team." Or when Shaw continued, "I hear there's good news today—we're going to see the final print of a new commercial, one that Becky Gagarin wrote for us herself. Bet it isn't every client gets his commercials written by the creative head!"

It wasn't just news for Shaw, it was also news for Becky.

Now she understood what Lilah had been trying to warn her about. The commercial she had shot at the Cloisters with Loren Odell was going to be shown here today, now, in less than a minute. But Becky had never seen it before. Nobody had asked her to approve the rushes, or the rough cut, or the answer print. She clenched slippery hands in her lap. It was going to be a disaster! A commercial needs as much love in the editing room as it does during filming, and who, in Victor Cameron's group, would have bothered to give Gagarin's baby the attention it needed?

But *somebody* must have been watching over each of those thirty seconds. Editing, music, the critical match dissolve—all were perfect. Just as they had marched out of her typewriter months ago, today, on the screen, an army of teenagers paraded boldly down the hill and dissolved into mature confident *women*. In the background there was stirring music while a woman's voice began to speak. The woman spoke quietly, she wasn't selling you anything, she was *telling* you something. She said that while aging was inevitable, it didn't have to be ugly. She talked about the four things that are necessary to keep any woman's skin looking good: enough exercise, healthy food, plenty of good love, and Eve. She said, as the picture on the screen faded to a final shot of the Eve package, that if you had to arrange all those factors in order of importance— she herself believed that Eve would rank second. Right after good love.

A client/agency meeting is like a minuet. Everyone knows when it is his turn to step forward and dance a few measures, when it is his turn to stand silent and watch the other dancers. And traditionally, the top man on the client side of the table does not speak first but defers to his second-in-command. So when the lights came up, Stuart Shaw turned to Edward Douglas.

"Well, Ed, you happy with Becky's new spot?"

Ed was not happy. "Voice-over!" he accused. "Angus Seton's book says that's *wrong*. Angus Seton's book says you should always have someone speaking on camera, directly to the viewer."

Becky thought of all the commandments in Seton's Bible that she had broken over years of writing successful commercials. Of all the commandments that Seton himself had broken. A few months ago she would have cited these precedents. Now she studied her hands and was silent.

But Stuart Shaw said that the commercial looked real exciting to him, and he liked the voice-over and the background music too. "That's a real perky march. Who'd you get to write it, Becky?"

Becky laughed. "Beethoven. It's the *Ode to Joy*."

Shaw grinned at his own discernment. "Well, I guess if it was good enough for Beethoven, it's good enough for Stu Shaw. Okay, that one's approved for testing, now what do we have to test against it?"

So Victor Cameron called on Lilah James to present her slice-of-life.

Keith Andrews came next, with his wordless Eurostyle spots.

And Gandhi Hendricks was third.

The dozens of little braids had been combed into a pageboy, and she wore a demure Laura Ashley dress printed overall with Victorian posies, and a lace Peter Pan collar. But there was nothing else that was shy or retiring about her today. Gandhi focused on Shaw; her eyes never left him. For a while all that was heard was the click click click of slides falling into place on Gandhi's projector as she led Stuart Shaw through the pictures she had taken one day, walking down a New York City street.

Then Gandhi said, "*That's* your market. Eve is the perfect product for women like that, mature women who are as intelligent about skin care as they are about voting, raising children, running households, running businesses. We have to place Eve front and center in the minds of these women, as the product that gives skin the most help when skin really needs help."

Shaw put down his pencil. He had quit sketching little sailboats and was paying grave attention to every word the black girl in the flower-sprigged dress was saying. Becky knew the satisfaction of a client who was seeing something better than he expected to see, and she felt Shaw's body, in the chair next to her, exuding that satisfaction. She would have loved to leap to her feet and prevent anything more from being shown to spoil this moment. She scribbled a note to Rank and passed it to him: *Shaw's in the boat. He thinks Gandhi's work is great. And it is.*

Rank read the note, folded it over once, folded it over again, and then again, until it was no bigger than a postage stamp. He placed it in the ashtray next to him and stared without interest at Becky, his eyes repeating his instructions of the day before: Your job is to sit next to Shaw and smile at him a lot.

Rae Ashley was last. Of course she was last; it is traditional that the work shown *last* at any advertising presentation will be the work that is recommended. (Clients know that too and wait patiently through the also-rans until they are allowed to see what the agency really likes.)

Rae had never believed in underwhelming a client with her costume. Today, she was all in white, her signature color. White leather boots, white leather jacket, white pants.

Smiling, she unbuttoned her jacket to reveal a red T-shirt. On the shirt was printed, in screaming uppercase, 40% SHARE OF MARKET NEXT YEAR!

She gave her audience time to study the guarantee emblazoned across her bosom.

Then Rae said that Eve didn't have to settle for just the older-woman market. Eve should put its logo on exciting advertising! Upbeat advertising! Advertising that would talk to, that would sing to, the *young* women of America.

She pressed a button on her tape recorder and the room flooded with sound. Becky hardly recognized the music she had heard last October. A new track had been recorded that sounded like a thirty-piece orchestra, and the words were sung by one of the year's top female singers.

To illustrate how easy this song would be to remember, when the tape had spun to a stop Rae sang it a second time, a cappella.

"Buhbuhbuhbaby your skin's gonna start livin' with Eve . . . Oh sweet buhbuhbuhbaby your skin never had it so go-ood . . ."

Rae laughed at the end and stretched her arms lazily into the air. "I know I'm not much of a singer. But even I could remember that tune. And in a few months all America will be singing that song, your song, the Eve song!"

Because her hands were outstretched and her jacket was open, they all had another chance to admire the promise stretched across her breasts: 40% SHARE OF MARKET NEXT YEAR!

Which was Victor Cameron's cue to stand and deliver the agency recommendation.

Victor said Seton & Cecil might have done some good work for Eve in the last decades, but it would be as nothing compared to the far better job he could promise for the future. Because he himself, Victor Cameron, had decided to spend most of his time on the Eve account, giving it his own personal attention.

He said that Lilah James's work was "a direction we wanted to explore, but the slice-of-life is the way one sells toilet bowl cleaners, don't you think, not beauty products."

Lilah studied the pink polish on her fingernails.

Victor labeled Keith's campaign "Brilliant. But perhaps a little ahead of its time?"

Keith pocketed the "brilliant" and shrugged off the rest of the verdict.

Victor smiled kindly at Gandhi. He said how heartening it was to see that kind of work coming from a junior. As for the campaign that young Gandhi had shown, well, everyone knew you could not sell beauty products by showing them on the kind of consumers who actually *used* them. Women wanted to look into a *dream* when they looked at an advertisement for a beauty product, not into a mirror.

The days when Victor Cameron only wanted to work on masculine products were over. He had realized that most of the products advertised by the New York office of Seton & Cecil were bought by women, and his interest in such products had soared. He sounded absolutely sure of himself as he stood there in cowboy boots and announced that Rae Ashley's campaign was the agency's recommendation. It was upbeat. It had the excitement of music. The allure of lovely young faces.

With great confidence, he announced, "Hope, not logic. That's what women want."

Freud may not have known what women wanted, but Victor Cameron did.

Stuart Shaw (to his second-in-command): "So, Ed, you happy now?"

Edward Douglas: "I'm not just happy, I'm *thrilled*."

Shaw: "Which particular campaign is thrilling you?"

Douglas: "The one with the music, of course. The one the agency recommended. I can't exactly remember what it says, but it's fun. It's upbeat. It's, ah, hopeful. I like it." He looked nervously at his boss.

Shaw turned to Rebecca Gagarin. "Becky, is that what you think we should do? Put all our money into a jingle?"

"Excuse me, sir. It is not a jingle. It is a *song*." Victor Cameron spoke firmly, with the air of a man who was not afraid to set anyone straight. Not even a client.

"Song, jingle, whatever. Becky, you like that . . . that noise?"

Both Horatio Hamlin and Wilbur Rank swiveled their chairs and stared at her hard.

She thought how miserable these last months at Seton & Cecil had been; she had an opportunity now to make things even worse for herself. Or she could improve her lot dramatically, with a simple endorsement of the party line.

"Like the music? Sure I like the music. It sounds like what my kids sing in the shower . . ."

Hamlin and Rank relaxed. She was saying that the music was *contemporary*.

". . . but it doesn't belong in Eve advertising. Yes, the music is fun. And that kind of music works well for products that are fun. Fast foods. Soft drinks. Amusement parks. But it isn't *fun* to have skin that's drying up and showing lines. It isn't *fun* to get older."

The smiles slid from Hamlin's face and Rank's. But it was Cameron who spoke.

"Of course, Becky, you know more than us men do about products like Eve. Only, I have to tell you that we've already taken Rae's campaign out and done a little research on it, and it performed brilliantly. We didn't come here today with just judgment behind our recommendation. We used *research*."

Agency people are not supposed to quarrel with each other in front of a client. At the very least, it suggests lack of communication within the agency, lack of proper preparation for the meeting. Nevertheless, Becky asked, "What kind of research? Audience research? You played the commercial for an *audience* of women and asked them if they liked it?"

Victor was too smart to fall into that kind of trap. "We asked a lot more than that. We asked if it would make them switch to Eve. And we got a switch that was higher than *any* commercial we've ever tested for Eve before."

It was time to give in. It was still early enough not to count as a major, embarrassing confrontation.

But Becky said, "Sure, as part of an *audience*, sitting there surrounded by other women, they'll *say* they like the nice music. But if you show that campaign to women one at a time—and that's the way they usually watch television, alone in the house, one at a time—I doubt that it will do terribly well.

"And if you let them see the creative work Gandhi Hendricks showed us today, I guarantee it will do better. Because that happens to be a very emotional campaign. It gives women *reasons* to believe that at last there is a serious product which can delay your having to look old. And if that isn't an emotional promise, I don't know what is."

Shaw said, "You haven't changed from that feisty girl I knew twenty-five years ago, Becky. You still stick up for what you believe."

The room was silent. Then Wilbur Rank spoke up. Rank's voice was laden with the importance of a man who knew himself to be the true head of the creative department now.

"Yes. But what Becky believes is, after all, just her judgment. And our *research* has proven that Rae Ashley's campaign is the better of the two under discussion. That's why the agency is recommending Rae's campaign. The jingle, as you call it, sir."

Shaw had been nodding with every word that Rank said. But his answer came sharp and unexpected.

"The *better* of the two? You tested *both* spots?"

"Well, no, we didn't exactly test any other campaign. Because in our judgment Rae's idea had so much going for it . . ."

Shaw laughed the hearty laugh of the young redheaded man that Becky remembered from so long ago.

"So, when it's *your* judgment, judgment is okay? But when it's Becky's judgment, then it's just a hunch? Sorry, I can't go along with that. If we're picking whose judgment to bet the rent on, Becky Gagarin's track record is too good to ignore.

"Okay, young Rank, here are your marching orders: I want *three* campaigns tested against each other. The spot that Becky Gagarin did, the one we saw on film this morning. And the other two we've been talking about, Miss Rae's jingle thing and Miss Gandhi's real women. And while we're waiting for the test results, I want Becky's campaign put into a market too, so we can see how it sells."

Wilbur Rank looked horrified. "It will take us months to field that kind of research. We won't have a new national campaign on the air until the third quarter. Maybe the fourth."

Shaw rose. "But it will be the *right* campaign. Well, I would have liked to break bread with all you good people, but I'm off to Washington now. Little session with Food and Drug."

He apologized for having to preempt the company jet to fly to Washington. "My girl will make arrangements to get you all back to New York. Sorry, Becky, I don't mean girl, I mean *secretary*. And please don't let another twenty-five years slip by before we see each other again."

He kissed Becky on both cheeks and whispered something into her ear. Then he sauntered out, hands in pockets. Because he'd been top man at the meeting he hadn't had to bring any papers into the room with him, and now he didn't carry any papers away. There had been enough people there to take notes assiduously, to write down every word he said, and now all they had to do was exactly what he'd told them.

Only Becky knew what he'd whispered to her. "Us old fogies can teach those smart-ass kids a thing or two about the business, right Becky?" And he'd sent Edward Douglas, his ambitious young second-in-command, a glance that was not loving.

Shaw's secretary had been unable to get them seats in first class. Returning to New York, they wound up in the steerage section of a crowded and dirty plane—it had already made two stops before Winosha, and nobody had attempted to clean it.

The three senior men sat together: Rank next to a window, Hamlin on the aisle, Victor Cameron squeezed between them. Becky was glad not to be Victor, who would have to listen to Hamlin being furious, and Rank tending to agree with him, all the way back to New York.

A few rows behind the account men Gandhi and Keith sat together: the tall black woman and the bearded white man creating a flurry of interest in their immediate neighborhood.

Becky Gagarin, Rae Ashley, and Lilah James wound up in the last row, just in front of the toilets. The Concorde had happened to another woman, in another incarnation.

The stewardess, who might have started the journey looking fresh and pretty, now looked tired and cross. As soon as she had wheeled her cart to the last row, before she could even ask if the ladies wanted anything to drink, Lilah demanded, "Three scotches. Straight. No water. No fizzy stuff. Just plain unadulterated *scotch*."

Rae said, "I don't drink." How could she, and keep slim enough for those leather pants?

Lilah said, "That's all right. I'll have yours." Her new boss, Victor Cameron, was rows ahead of her, and hidden back here she felt safe.

All Becky wanted right now was a book and perhaps a cup of tea. But as soon as she told the stewardess to cancel her scotch, Lilah said, "*Don't do that!* I'll have hers too."

The stewardess looked pleased for the first time. She didn't like these people, and especially not Lilah.

"I'm sorry, miss. The limit is two drinks per passenger. No one is allowed to buy any more than that. That's the *law*."

Lilah looked at her carefully, making obvious note of the wilted handkerchief and the hair that had escaped from the once-perfect coiffure. "I have no intention of *buying* more than one. My friend here," she patted Rae's shoulder, "is buying the second, and my friend on the aisle is buying the third."

The stewardess briefly considered whether the problem was worth taking up with the captain. But she grudgingly passed three little bottles of scotch to Lilah and wheeled her cart away, her back clearly expressing the fact that she never intended to wheel it this far back again.

Lilah lined the little bottles up on her tray. "Airline stewardesses are just *waitresses* with wings. So don't either of you go worrying about what that bitch thinks."

Rae said to Becky, "I wonder what you thought you were accomplishing today?"

"I thought I was persuading our client not to toss out a first-rate campaign."

Rae shook her head. "That's not what I was talking about. Yeah, Shaw seems to love you, and that was nice what he said, about wanting to see you again before the twenty-first century. But you should know by now that it isn't only what your clients think of you that counts. It's also what the powers that be in your agency think."

Lilah sighed softly. She had been up all night rehearsing, and she had just had her first drink in two days. She had dropped out of whatever debate Becky Gagarin and Rae Ashley might be having.

"Seems to me a few months back you told me exactly what they *do* think of me. And you know something, Rae? Every last thing you predicted is coming true. Maybe I should call you Cassandra."

Cassandra/Rae tried to tilt her seat back. And looked grumpy when she discovered that because they were in the last row, it would not tilt.

"Okay. So you spoke up against my campaign. Because you thought it wasn't good enough. And you know something, I actually liked that, it reminded me of the old Becky. I used to love it when you liked something I'd done, Becky, but I respected you even when you didn't. But you know something? I'll respect you again the day you either get up and fight what's being done to you, or get up and get out. Leave. Resign. What the hell are you hanging around Seton & Cecil for? Things can only get worse for you."

Becky took one of those awful little airline magazines out of the seat pocket in front of her and began reading an article about exciting new ways to serve kiwi.

"*Listen* to me, Becky. You not only made Hamlin and Rank furious with your performance at the meeting today, but Edward Douglas, our client's future head honcho, isn't very fond of you either. I don't know *what* you said to his wife, but I have it from a reliable source that he is blaming you, personally, for her renewed interest in becoming a retailing tycoon. He thinks your timing was lousy, considering she's about eleven months pregnant."

Becky didn't inquire who the reliable source was. Without looking up from her magazine she asked only, "How do you like being in Cameron's group?"

"Victor is terrific," was the immediate answer. "He handles the account guys perfectly. He lets Hamlin and Wilbur and Howard Pullett and all the rest of them believe they're *contributing* to the creative product.

Okay, he's not as good a writer as you are, but he can run rings around you politically."

Then—although Lilah seemed safely asleep by now—Rae lowered her voice. "Since I seem to be the only person who's talking to you these days, I'll give you the latest scuttlebutt. Did you know the quadrumvirate is falling?"

Becky kept her eyes on the photographs of kiwi with oatmeal, kiwi with liver, kiwi with bran muffins, careful to hide the hope that this might be good news indeed.

"Already? It only lasted a few months. That's pretty fast for any creative-department reorganization. Even at Seton & Cecil."

Rae shook her head. "It was *meant* to fall. It was always just a caretaker government. An interim step. You should know by now that Horatio Hamlin always has hidden motives, and underneath those, even deeper ones. You could have an interesting archaeological dig, exploring the different layers of Hamlin's motives. Anyway, the new theory is that Hamlin arranged the quadrumvirate to give the Chosen One time to see how the place works. Decide what changes he wants to make, when he takes over."

Becky replaced the magazine in the seat pocket, next to the barf bag. "So the Four are out, and the One is in. Who's the One? No, don't tell me, let me guess. He's bigger than a bread box, and he's sitting a few rows in front of us right now, eating one of those plastic dinners this airline calls food."

Becky's hand clutched the armrest between them, and Rae put her own hand over it.

"Becky, please don't look so sick. After all, it's only a job."

Only a job? Only her life. "Listen, do you think you could get me that third drink from Lilah's tray, without waking her up?"

But Rae had risen in her seat and was trying to see what was going on a few rows in front of them.

"Miss, I already told you, you can*not* do that here. It is against the law."

The stewardess's voice was righteous. She stood in the aisle, arms folded over her chest, chin tilted into the air.

"But smoking has always been allowed in the rear of planes."

It was Gandhi's voice. Stubborn. Unyielding. Loud.

"Not any more. Not for more than a year now. You will be violating federal regulations if you insist on keeping that cigarette." The stewardess's voice took on a distasteful tone as she added, "I can give you some special chewing gum that will help you control your urges . . ."

"I don't have any urges. I just want to have a nice quiet smoke. You want to know what a disgusting habit is? Chewing gum is a disgusting habit."

"Put that out *immediately*, or I will have to inform the pilot."

"And what will he do? Throw me overboard?"

"He can radio ahead for the authorities to meet us when we land. You could be arrested, for creating an interstate disturbance . . ."

"*Me? I'm* not the one who is creating the disturbance . . ."

Becky slid her seat belt open. She walked forward to where Gandhi sat, eyes blazing at the stewardess. On one side of Gandhi, a plump woman in a magenta jump suit was relishing the little scene; later she would tell her family that it was the most interesting airplane trip she had ever taken. On Gandhi's other side, Keith Andrews tried to look as if he had never met this tall black woman before, didn't have the faintest idea how she'd wound up in the seat next to him.

Becky steadied herself with a hand on Keith's shoulder and bent past him to whisper into Gandhi's ear.

Gandhi listened. And looked thoughtful for a minute. Then she smiled and put her cigarette out.

"What did you say to her?" Rae asked curiously, as Becky fastened her seat belt again.

"I said that the stewardess was right, that she couldn't smoke on a plane any more. And that lung cancer is not a fun way to go. And that anyway, she ought to take better care of herself, because if she was still around in five or six years she could be the youngest creative head Seton & Cecil ever had."

Becky knew a lot about lung cancer. Lung cancer was what Charlotte was dying of, painfully and slowly, in Baltimore.

Although Gandhi hadn't put her cigarette out until Becky said the magic words. *Creative head.*

10

"Unfair! Unfair!"

Joseph marched at the head of the picket line. A signboard over his head explained how wretchedly the help were treated in this unhappy building, and he was yelling through a bullhorn.

"Joe, you never said the strike would start so *soon*."

"I *tried* to tell you, Mrs. Gagarin. I guess you wasn't listening."

The chatelaines of apartments 7W and 2E stood inside the building door and watched the demonstration disapprovingly. They looked at Becky talking to Joseph and put her down as a collaborator.

"I've never crossed a picket line before, Joe. But I'll have to cross this one. Either that, or sleep in the street."

He smirked. "Take a good look at the building, Mrs. Gagarin. Notice anything peculiar?"

Becky turned and stared and then it hit her. It was evening, the street lights were already on, but the stately old building on Central Park was completely dark.

Joe explained that something had gone wrong with the electrical system (surprise!) as soon as the strike began that morning. "The Con Ed guys are deciding whether or not it's okay for them to cross the line of a sister union to fix it. Well, you know no electricity don't just mean no light. It also means no water. No toilets. No elevators. You're going to have to lug that up the stairs with you, Mrs. Gagarin. In the dark." They both stood together for a moment, Joseph and Becky, looking sadly down at Becky's suitcase.

Then Joe turned to the others on the picket line and exhorted, "Come on, you guys! If you just tiptoe around out here nobody's gonna know we mean *business*. Let's hear it . . ."

He raised the bullhorn to his lips and shouted, "WHAT DO WE NEED? MONEY! WHEN DO WE NEED IT? NOW!"

Clinging to the banister with one hand, holding the suitcase that had begun as an underseat bag and was now beginning to feel like a trunk, Becky inched her way up the dark service stairs.

Coming down the stairs toward her she heard voices. A man and a woman. A flashlight glimmered toward her. She stepped to one side for the couple coming down.

Then she recognized the man's voice.

His flashlight had been beamed at the steps, but now he sensed someone standing, silent, below him. He raised the light to aim it at her face.

"Becky?" Alex said doubtfully.

Blinking in the sudden shaft of light, Becky saw nothing at first. Then her husband shifted the beam to the woman with him. "Uh, you've met Zoe."

Of course. Alexander Gagarin, and Zoe Anonymous. Zoe of the Catholic Church basement. What a charming couple.

Becky had fast eyes. Eyes trained to look just once at a thirty-second commercial and note every possible flaw. There were no flaws in Zoe today. The flashlight revealed a girl who was a lot happier, and even better dressed, than she had been six months ago. Becky took quick but accurate note. A new Kenzo knit. Low-heeled Ferragamo shoes. Over the fragile shoulders a heather-toned mink, none of your bargain Blackglama.

"Becky," Alex repeated. "You're home early."

"We didn't stay for lunch," Becky said. "Sorry about that."

He must have put the girl into a cab, a subway, a bus, a surrey with a fringe on top, a wheelbarrow, who the hell cared where he had put her, he had disposed of her somehow and they were alone together in his studio now. Alone, with the portrait of the munchkin.

"I didn't know you had a thing about dwarfs. Where did you two first meet, at the circus?"

"You know where we met. She's a student at the Alliance. And she's helping me with the Make-a-Mess Workshop. And she's been sitting for me. That painting. Over there."

Fortunately, Con Ed had decided it would be ethical to restore electricity to the building, so Becky was able to look politely at the painting that Alex seemed to think explained everything. Excused everything. Only, how long did it take to paint one lousy portrait? What was it supposed to be, the Mona Lisa?

Staring raptly at the painting, Becky observed, "She's got a rather low forehead, don't you think? Some sort of Neanderthal throwback, maybe? Short, with a low forehead. So what sort of prehistoric games have you two been playing? Today, *and* that day Miranda walked in on you? And maybe for months now?"

"We were talking. I told you I'm her sponsor. I'm helping her."

"*Helping* her? Goody, a new word for it. The world was getting tired of the old one."

Alex said, "You heard her story, she's been drinking since she was a baby. She was scared stiff of what was happening to her when I got her into The Program. She's been doing very well, but today she got depressed, she was scared she might be heading for a slip. She phoned and asked if she could come around so we could talk for a while. It's dangerous for her to drink. She gets *suicidal* when she drinks. Once she slashed her wrists. And another time she swallowed a whole bunch of pills and they had to pump her stomach. Naturally I said come right over."

"Naturally." Becky looked at the adolescent face and the immense dark eyes in the painting. "So you've just been painting a portrait of the pygmy and leading her down the path of sobriety, that's all you've been doing?"

"That's *all*," Alex said coldly.

She tried to believe him. She wanted very much to believe him. The trouble was, she didn't believe him.

After the successful meeting in Winosha, nothing happened.

Literally, *nothing*.

The strike in the building on Central Park was soon settled, and Joe was back on the elevator. The whole staff had gotten raises, although not, Joe explained, nearly as much as they deserved.

And Becky kept telling herself that Alex was just Zoe's sponsor. He was encouraging Zoe, as once Alex had had a sponsor who had encouraged him. It was like the Big Brother program, Becky told herself. Alex was being a Big Brother to Zoe.

She tried not to think about the incestuous games some Big Brothers play with some Little Sisters.

At Seton & Cecil, the quadrumvirate still ran the creative department. Victor was still only one of four. The dramatic further reorganization that Rae had predicted on the plane had not materialized.

Becky continued to overhear dribs and drabs of

rumors, in the office elevator, in the dining room, predicting that Angus Seton would visit New York soon.

But Seton did not appear.

The three new Eve campaigns were out being researched, and the spot Loren Odell had produced for Becky at the Cloisters was running on all channels in a midwestern city.

She supposed that the creative department must be working hard meeting other deadlines, but since she was no longer invited to meetings, as far as she knew the entire department might have come to a dead halt.

Even her body had arrived at a standstill. Since that last time at Cecil Hall, she had had no more menstrual periods. Exactly as the Indian doctor had prophesied: "One month will be your last, and then there will be no more."

No more blood. No more children. No more work. *Nada. Niente. Rien de rien.*

The months were going by with nothing to mark their passage. Becky was sure nymphet Zoe had periods every month, like clockwork. But the built-in calendar that exists in every woman's body had ceased functioning in Becky's. She had never known how much she had depended on it to measure the passage of time. To predict that just as she had had a past, she would have a future. She had never thought she would *miss* menstruating. But she did.

Although Alexander Gagarin was no longer in her bed, she spent a lot of time there, alone, thinking about him. Remembering the good times they had had together, and the times that were not so good. Even the worst time of all. The Night of the Croup.

~~~~~

Alexander Gagarin had become badly blocked in his work and had begun drinking heavily. Many nights he was not home until three, when the bars closed. On

Saturday nights, he would come home even later. The bars didn't close until four on Saturdays.

The Night of the Croup was on a Saturday. After waiting and worrying until four, Becky had fallen asleep and was awakened shortly afterwards by the sound of barking. Short, hoarse-sounding barks, coming from Peter's room.

Becky swung her legs out of bed and raced for the kitchen. First the ipecac, just a drop, which had to be put into applesauce, to disguise the taste. Peter had had croup every year since he was a year old, but it had never ceased to terrify him. Of course he feels scared, Becky told herself. The poor kid can't breathe. But this was the first time she'd had to cope with croup alone. There had always been Charlotte to help before. Or, more accurately, Becky had been there to help Charlotte.

Only this was the weekend, and Charlotte was off.

"Sit up, Peter, this will make you feel better." But the awful strangled feeling that had awakened Peter in the middle of the night had also stripped him of the dignity of being four years old. It was a very tiny baby boy who sat there in the bed dodging the teaspoon of applesauce.

The next time he opened his mouth to bark, Becky managed to get the teaspoon in. Then she swung him up into her arms, blanket and all, and made for the bathroom.

Shut the door. Turn the shower on. Hot water. Full force. Don't pull out the shower curtain, the whole point is to fill the room with steam as fast as possible.

Putting the lid of the toilet down, she sat on it with the panicked child on her lap. Waves of steam filled the bathroom and condensed on her glasses. Her hair was sopping wet, as wet as if she had stepped into the shower herself. The steam dampened the child's pajamas and turned his curly blonde hair into flat tendrils pasted to his scalp. And then, even as he was still thrashing about on her lap, trying to climb off it—he realized that he could breathe again.

Exhausted, Peter slumped against her.

Becky continued to sit there, crooning to her little boy, crooning to herself.

She crooned that Alex would be home soon, that the fear that he had been run over or mugged was silly, that God looked after drunks and with that God-given assistance her husband would make it home.

Then Peter had to be put into dry clothes, and the vaporizer filled with water, and a tent made of bed sheets had to be erected over his bed to keep the moist air close to him. At first he flailed at the sheets, trying to pull them down, but finally he fell asleep within the tent's embrace. Her watch said it was a little past five. She slumped to the floor next to her son's bed and fell asleep holding his hand.

When she woke the first rays of the sun were slanting into the room. Gingerly she released Peter's fingers and felt his forehead. It was blessedly cool. Legs aching from the weird position they'd been in, Becky staggered to her feet.

Miranda was not in her bedroom. Becky found her in the living room, eyes pasted to the television set, watching the only thing on at that hour: the early-morning farm report. She was sucking her thumb and staring at a man who chatted cozily about early prospects for pork bellies. Miranda was wearing thin pajamas covered with the whole cast of "Sesame Street," but no bathrobe, and she was shivering.

"I had a bad dream and I looked for you. But you weren't in your bed. Daddy wasn't there either." Then, sternly, "I saw you in *Peter's* room."

"It's too early for you to be up. Let me take you back to bed."

Miranda fixed her terms: "You have to stay with *me* now, just as long as you stayed with Peter."

Contorted next to Miranda on the child-size bed, Becky told the little girl, "Charlotte is coming today."

"Charlotte never comes on *Sundays*." Miranda's voice was accusing. Becky was trying to disrupt the natural order of the universe.

"She is today. She's doing us a special favor. Daddy and I have to go somewhere, so Charlotte will stay with you and Peter today."

We have to go to the place where Mommy's father is buried. We will see Mommy's sisters who have comfortably married nice nondrinking Jewish men, and there will be lots of Mommy's other relatives there too, and we will unveil the headstone that Mommy has chosen for her father's grave. We will go, that is, if your father, Alex Gagarin, staggers home in time to drive us to Long Island, where the cemeteries are.

Charlotte was careful not to notice that Mr. Gagarin was not home. Charlotte mopped up the water in the children's bathroom, which last night had become an improvised steam room. She rearranged Peter in bed with his favorite toys. She dressed Miranda and made her pancakes and fixed coffee for Becky.

In a minute she will dress me too, if I don't get organized, Becky thought. She found the black pumps she hadn't worn since her father's funeral a year ago, put on a black dress and then changed it for a black suit, superstitiously deciding that Alex would be home by the time she had finished dressing—and therefore prolonging the dressing as long as she could.

But when she came out of the bedroom, Alex was still not home, so she telephoned a limousine service. A Cadillac complete with chauffeur was at the door of the building in fifteen minutes. The limousine and Alex arrived together. Alex was unshaven, red-eyed, ex-

pecting congratulations on having made it home in time
to drive Becky to the cemetery.

"You are *not* in time." She wouldn't wait for him
to change, but left, alone, in the back of the chauffeured
car.

They drove uptown through Spanish Harlem and
then out of town, past a thousand used-car lots and
stores specializing in discount dinette sets and carpet
remnants. Long before they reached the miles of cemeteries that sprawl along the city's periphery, she
knew that she was going to be terribly late.

The ceremony was halfway over by the time she
arrived. Her aunts and uncles were there, and her cousins, and her sisters. Helen and Florence looked at
Becky and pulled her into the circle of sisters. Three
women in black, standing together near a grave.

The rabbi was talking about the wisdom of Juda-
ism, in that it sets aside the week immediately following
death and devotes it to nothing but mourning, a week
of total immersion in grief. And then, not when that
first week is over but after a whole *year* has passed,
when you have observed four seasons come and go,
when you can bear to laugh at jokes again and smile at
children, when you can accept the strange notion that
life *must* go on, only then are you allowed to mark the
fact that you were no longer helpless with grief by placing a stone on the beloved dead's grave.

It was at that point—while the rabbi was explaining
how wonderful it was that they were now all reconciled
to her father's death—that Becky heard the sobbing.
Then she realized where the wailing and moaning, the
whimpering and hiccuping, the embarrassing rending
racking sounds were coming from. They were coming
from *her*. The aunts and uncles and cousins were all
staring at her. Her body was shaking, her nose was
running, the rabbi was explaining that now the time of

mourning was *over*, but she couldn't stop, the horrible noises continued to spill from her.

She was still weeping when the ceremony ended. The rabbi—a man her sister Florence had recruited for the occasion—looked at her rebukingly even as he patted her shoulder. There was a time to mourn and a time not to mourn, and this woman didn't seem able to grasp the difference.

Suddenly, Alex was there. He had shaved, and he stood at Becky's side in his best suit. "Shall we go home?" he asked her humbly. Her sister Helen still had an arm tight around Becky's shoulders. Her sister Florence was wiping at Becky's face where the mascara had streaked. She wanted to stay with them, still be the baby sister, the youngest of the three, still be taken care of.

She said to Alex, "All right. Let's go home."

In their bedroom Alex put his arms around Becky. "I can't begin to tell you how guilty I feel."

Becky had had to smile for the children and Charlotte. To her husband, she said, "I hope you don't think I was crying because of anything *you* did. I'm past that, Alex. To me you're a *boarder* here. Someone who often occupies a bed, unfortunately it's *my* bed, and who sometimes doesn't turn up all night."

"I wasn't with another woman. I met some friends, and we were talking . . ."

"Not another woman? Listen, there's nothing that would delight me more. Why should I be the lucky one who pays the rent, and the school fees, and Charlotte's salary, and even the liquor store? The owner waves at me now when he sees me passing. We're his best customers. Why should I be the lucky one who *supports* you?"

His arms dropped from around her. "You don't support me. I don't spend my days having lunch, playing games like you do. Maybe I don't make as much money as you, but I don't go to meetings all the time, I *work* for every cent I earn. And if you don't want me around any more, all you have to do is say the word."

Becky hadn't slept the night before. All she'd had today was a cup of coffee. She said the word. "I *don't* want you around. I will raise my children myself."

"Balls. You mean Charlotte will raise your children."

He said that since he was going, he might as well go right away, and began to throw clothes into a suitcase.

I bought that suitcase for him, Becky thought. I bought that cashmere sweater. And those Hathaway shirts. I haven't only been feeding him these last seven years, I've been *dressing* him too.

The sound of the door slamming reverberated through the apartment. It had probably been heard in the kitchen too, where Charlotte was giving the children dinner.

Becky steered herself into the kitchen, a smile pinned on her face. She explained to Charlotte that Mr. Gagarin had had to leave for an unexpected business trip. Charlotte was used to Mrs. Gagarin going off on business trips, but it was the first such journey Mr. Gagarin had taken since Charlotte had come to work for them. But Charlotte didn't blink an eye. Charlotte did not just have Indian cheekbones, she could turn her whole self Indian whenever she wanted to. All of her would become blank. Impassive. Stoic. If Mr. Gagarin seemed to be drinking a lot lately, it was none of her business. If Mr. and Mrs. Gagarin argued a lot, that was none of her business either.

As long as nobody fooled with her children.

The marriage might have ended there, but it didn't.

Alex was home in an hour.

He said it was all his fault. One hundred percent his fault. He said that he needed Becky and Peter and Miranda, and if his drinking was going to take them from him, he would never drink again.

Becky agreed that yes, it was certainly all his fault. And although she took him back, she did not believe for one moment that he would stop drinking.

She was right. It was another year before Alexander Gagarin stopped drinking. It was a whole year *after* The Night of the Croup that Alex Gagarin looked coldly and soberly at his most recent canvases, and for the first time in all the years she'd known him, Becky saw her husband cry. It was *then* that he joined The Program, and went in for Zen, and took up sailing and skiing, and began his daily jogs around the park.

And they all continued to live their separate lives in the big apartment on Central Park West. The children went to expensive schools and grew into tall golden separate people. Alex painted. Charlotte cooked, cleaned, and anchored the household.

And Becky left every morning for her own life, her real life. Which was lived at Seton & Cecil. Where Angus Seton was becoming well known, and then famous, and finally almost mythic. Where Rebecca Gagarin became a group head, and an executive vice-president, and ultimately creative head of the entire agency.

Until one day her hands felt for the next rung and discovered only air.

~~~~~

This week there was, actually, something on her calendar. Even something pleasant—Eileen's anniversary.

It had been eight years since Eileen had begun working for Rebecca Gagarin. Each year Becky would present her with a box of Italian chocolates on this day, or an offering of roses. Today Becky arrived with a charming antique watch to be pinned to Eileen's lapel. An overly expensive gift to make up for her guilt about the paucity of work Becky was now giving her, for how little there was these days for Eileen to *do* to establish her worth in the eyes of the other secretaries.

Before Becky could give Eileen her present, Eileen said, "That Mrs. Schwartz has been calling and calling."

It had been six months since Daphne Schwartz had last phoned Becky. She could not *still* be lusting after the Gagarin apartment. Curious, Becky returned the call.

Far from the confident voice that had tried to seduce her into selling, Daphne was now begging.

"Mrs. Gagarin, please, can't you just let my client *see* your place? Frankly the market is very slow now, and she says she won't look at anything else until she can see yours. She says from what she's heard, it would be perfect for her. Please let me show it, just so she'll look at other places. It would be an enormous favor to me."

Becky could not help responding to the apprehension she heard in the voice. Lately, Becky had been learning a little about fear herself.

"Okay, you can show it. Come around, ah, next Wednesday?"

Daphne was overjoyed. Becky cautioned her, "Don't forget, it's just *show*, not sell."

It was part of the anniversary ritual. Becky would always invite Eileen into her office so they could have their morning coffee together.

Eileen always loved this day. It was the day she was always lavished with praise, told she was the best secretary that Becky had ever had. Usually, she would bubble all day and wear an especially pretty dress for the occasion.

It wasn't until Becky was pinning the watch on

Eileen's collar that she realized what a surprisingly drab outfit Eileen had chosen this time. Dun-colored, long-sleeved, almost matronly.

Eileen thanked Becky for the watch in a dull voice and drank her coffee in silence.

Since Eileen was mute today, Becky found herself chattering. She asked after Eileen's mother. A widow. Younger than Becky. When you are older than your secretary's *mother*, then you are old indeed.

"Mom's fine. But you know, I don't live with her any more. I have my own place now."

"Oh, Eileen, that's wonderful! You must feel so much freer, so much happier on your own."

"Yes. I do." She looked up so that her eyes met Becky's, and her words came out now in a sudden rush. "Mrs. Gagarin, there's something we have to talk about."

Becky thought, *money*. Of course, she needs more money now. She probably was just thinking about the rent when she moved out of her mother's place, now she's discovered that there's also the phone bill and the gas bill and groceries, and all the other things she never had to worry about when she was living with Mom.

"Well, Eileen, you know there is a salary scale for secretaries, and you're already at the top . . . but wait, maybe I could get you listed as my secretary slash assistant? There's only one creative head, and you'd be the only secretary/assistant to the creative head. That ought to give us some leeway for getting you more money."

Becky beamed at Eileen, who sat with her hands folded in her lap, like a good little girl talking to a nun at the parochial school she had attended.

"Thank you very much, Mrs. Gagarin. Of course more money would come in handy, but that isn't what I wanted to talk about . . ."

Her tone was so apprehensive that Becky laughed.

"Uh-oh, I knew this would happen one day. Let me guess: You don't want to be a secretary any more. What other job do you have your eye on? Casting? Production? Writing?"

"No, I *like* being a secretary. It's only, I was wondering, please don't be angry—wouldn't it make sense if I went to work for Mr. Cameron? Like, Mr. Cameron really *needs* me. I mean, he's got a girl now, but she doesn't know what she's doing half the time. But I know everybody in the agency. I know all the clients' names and their secretaries' names too. I know all the production steps any advertisement or commercial has to go through, and Mr. Cameron is new to the New York office, he needs that kind of help . . ."

Victor Cameron. Becky looked at Eileen, who was now staring at Alex's abstraction of a woman's face. Eileen had seen that painting every day for the last eight years, but she was studying it now as if it had just made a surprise appearance in her boss's office. Becky thought, the bastard is trying to steal Eileen from me.

". . . Mr. Cameron told me that I had to speak to you and get your permission. Otherwise you might think he was trying to steal me."

"Why should I think anything like that?" Becky asked, in what she hoped was a tone of amusement. "Listen, Eileen, have you stopped to think that working for Victor Cameron would not exactly be a step up? I mean, you'd be working for a group head, and now you're working for the creative head."

"Well, at first, I suppose. But that would be only for a little while. And later when he, when . . ."

She stopped in midsentence and looked horrified.

Becky put her arm around the girl's shoulders. "He told you that you weren't supposed to mention anything about his maybe taking over as head of the department, didn't he?"

Eileen looked miserable.

"Well, Eileen, I can't blame you for wanting to think about your future. You've got responsibilities now, your own apartment, and you don't know where I stand in Seton & Cecil any more. And if it turns out that Mr. Cameron has been brought to New York to replace me, I can understand why you would want to make your own position more secure. And work for him. Get in on the ground floor, so to speak."

Eileen's shoulders felt unexpectedly frail. Because she probably felt she had made a mess of the words she'd been rehearsing for days, she seemed to be concentrating on remaining silent now.

After all, Becky thought, secretaries get to see the most private papers in any business. One or another of them types the most secret memos. Doesn't matter what you stamp on it. *Confidential. Eyes only.* It was quite possible that very specific plans had been made for Victor Cameron, exalted plans that had already been whispered from secretarial ear to secretarial ear in the ladies' room. Becky cringed as she thought that possibly, even probably, Mrs. Gagarin was the only person in the whole damn place who did not know that, despite the good meeting in Winosha, Victor Cameron had been given a definite date on which he would replace her.

She wanted a gong to sound for an office fire drill. But there was no deus ex machina, nothing would fly through the floor-to-ceiling glass windows, nothing would seep mercifully through the air-conditioning vents to end the awful silence that was happening between Rebecca Gagarin and her secretary of eight years. She had to do it herself.

She took her arm from around Eileen's shoulders and stood. "Of course you have my okay to work for Mr. Cameron, if that is what you want to do. And thank you, Eileen. Thank you for everything. You've taken wonderful care of me for a very long time."

Eileen gave a little sob and rushed out of the room.

Personnel sent a replacement for Eileen. Her name was Kimberly. All girls her age were named Kimberly. Kimberly could not take shorthand. She showed originality in her spelling, however, and she was very punctual— she was out of the office every afternoon at five o'clock sharp. But there was one marvelous thing about Kimberly. She was so unfamiliar with real work, she didn't seem to realize how little of it Becky was doing, herself.

~~~~~

Angus was back.

Becky discovered that by seeing him one day when she went to the Executive Dining Room for lunch.

The Executive Dining Room was the agency's most accurate barometer of the relative standing of those privileged to eat there. It was a civilized room. Low-key. The walls were hung with modern art, carefully selected to go up in value yet not be *so* modern as to disturb a conservative client who might be brought there for lunch. There was an open bar and a comfortable area of leather couches and chairs for drinks before lunch. It was all supposed to be terribly casual and relaxed and democratic. You helped yourself to drinks, you found an empty place for yourself at one of the tables when you were ready to eat.

Everyone mingled. In this room, there was no such thing as rank.

Except that when one of the rajahs poured himself a drink and found a seat on a couch, he soon became the hub of a wheel. Men junior to him, eager to converse with him on the national political or economic scenes, eager to swap tennis stories or golf yarns with him, eager to laugh quietly at his jokes, soon surrounded him.

It was considered bad form to talk shop here.

When the rajah finished his drink and rose to choose his seat at a table, the men he sat between would never pause in their conversation or smile too obviously at the honor.

Of course, there was also a table full of losers. Not any specific table; it formed itself anew every day. The agency bores found seats here, and those who were out of favor.

For years, Rebecca Gagarin could sit anywhere and know that the chairs around her would soon be claimed, and never with losers. Rebecca Gagarin was creative head of the New York office, the only woman on the board of directors, and everyone knew how significant that made her.

But in the last months all that had changed. She discovered that her choosing a table could make it the losers' table of the day. Because being ostracized in a festive room is everybody's worst nightmare, Becky now lunched as rapidly as possible. She would take some salad and a glass of wine, and furrowing her brow with the mythical pressure of nonexistent deadlines, she would gulp her food quickly, demonstrating eagerness to get back to her desk. Back to the empty IN and OUT boxes.

This day the laughter hit her as soon as she came out of the elevator, before she even entered the Dining Room, and she knew that Angus was there. She had been hearing that kind of laughter explode around him since she first traveled uptown from 34th Street all those years ago. Angus had no use for long faces and dreary complaints. His ferocious enjoyment of each day was contagious, warming, gorgeous to be near. His table was, of course, full. Even the tables near him were full. Becky carried her food to a table across the room and waited for him to notice her. In Paris, in London, in Frankfurt, in Milan, anywhere their paths had crossed in the Seton & Cecil empire, he had always insisted that she lunch with him alone, pumped her for the latest office gossip, been nostalgic about remembered quirks of their earliest clients . . .

And now Becky *needed* to talk to him.

She sent thought waves in his direction and *willed* him to see her, just across the room. The manager of the human resources department, one of the certified agency bores, claimed a seat next to her and began droning in her ear about a sitcom series he was following on TV. He had not missed a single episode and was prepared to bring her up to date on all of them:

". . . it's a black family, he's a lawyer and his wife is a doctor, no, wait a minute, it's the other way around, *he's* the doctor and she's the lawyer, anyway they're upper-middle-class and you can see how well the kids are being brought up, all of them with nice manners and respectful . . ."

Becky nodded at intervals. She lifted her fork now and then and inserted food into her mouth.

Across the room, she could see that Angus Seton had almost finished his meal. Soon he would leave the Dining Room. How much longer would he be in New York? Two months? Two weeks? Maybe just two more *days*? He would be on his way to Toronto, or to Buenos Aires, or headed back to England, back across the Atlantic. She muttered, "I'll be sure to watch it next Tuesday" to the manager of human resources and crossed the room toward Angus Seton.

She stood at his shoulder and said, "Hello, Angus."

There was so much laughter at his table that she wasn't sure if he had heard her. He had. He jumped to his feet and grasped her hand, and she thought, he doesn't know. Nobody has told him. He believed that she was still a person of worth in the empire he had created and that had been her life, too, for so long.

"Angus, can we have lunch? Or, if you're booked up, can I come talk to you about a few things?"

Even before she finished speaking, he had taken a small appointment book from his breast pocket. "It seems that I'm no longer very popular—I have lunch free both tomorrow and Thursday. Which would you prefer?"

He did not know. He could not know. This was a man who disliked misfortune, who hated complainers, who feared weeping women. If he knew what she wanted to talk to him about, there would have been no day free for lunch.

Becky said, "Tomorrow."

The manager of human resources followed her out of the room. "It isn't on Tuesdays. It's on *Thursdays*. You'll love it."

~~~~~

Although it was already May, Angus was wearing what Becky always thought of as his Hurok coat. His impresario coat. Long, belted, with a pleat in the back and a mammoth fur collar. The fur seemed to be molting a little—but the fact that it had seen better days didn't keep Angus from wearing it.

He knew the importance of making a statement about yourself with clothes. That was why he wore the same garments again and again, long enough for the least visual-minded of his clients to recognize them and maintain a clear picture in their minds of Angus Seton. The way Roosevelt had used the cigarette holder to establish his identity, the way Churchill had employed the cigar and the bowler hat. All the Seton & Cecil clients had been trained to recognize Seton trademarks. The greatcoat that Angus Seton wore in winter, the two battered English briefcases he carried home every

night, one stuffed under each arm, the green suspenders
he wore with everything except evening dress (and then
his bow tie would be green velvet). She wondered if
Victor Cameron had gotten the idea for his cowboy
boots and silk work shirts from Angus.

She remembered the first time she had lunched
with Angus Seton, and how careful she had been to
order dishes that would present no surprise. She had
wanted to be sure she would know what she was eating,
how to pronounce it, how to tackle it correctly.

But that first time, her pâté, when it came, had
had an ominous black spot in the middle. She hadn't
wanted to cause a scene and call anyone over to complain, so she had tried to eat her way around it. But
Angus had been watching her, and he said, "Oh! You
don't like truffles?" and leaning over had stabbed the
black spot with his fork and gobbled it up. She got used
to that later. Seton was as likely to eat his neighbor's
lunch as his own if it appealed to him more. Like an
imperious child, he regarded everyone else's plate as
belonging to him, too.

Today, she had hoped for the Four Seasons, or the
Côte Basque. Where the tables were far apart and it
would be possible to talk. Instead, they went to a new
place. "I've never been here before, but Wilbur Rank
tells me the food is excellent, so I thought we'd try it."

The food might have been good, but the noise level
was horrendous. The place had become very fashionable very fast. It was jammed with people who were
here to be noticed so they made no effort to lower their
voices. Their conversations reverberated, clattering
back and forth against the hard edges of the room.

Today, Angus was spending a great deal of time
on the menu. And even more on the wine list. But
Angus always brought greedy anticipation to menus,
like a theater lover's excitement before the curtain rises.

Then he discovered that their table was intolerably

cluttered and commanded the busboy—in French—to remove the bud vase that sat between their plates. The busboy looked bewildered; it was obvious to Becky that English was not his language of choice, much less French. The headwaiter hurried over to discover the cause of the flurry that was developing in their corner and then told Juan (or Isidor, or Angel, or whatever his name might be) to banish the offending flower.

Becky sighed in relief. The embarrassing moment was over. There *had* to be one embarrassing moment at every lunch with Angus Seton. People loved to swap stories about them; it was suspected that he planned these excruciating moments in advance.

When would be the right time for her to call upon her mentor, her hero of so many years, for advice?

Obviously, you couldn't ask someone to offer guidance while he was busy spooning soup. He had also ordered trout, which had not been filleted and had to be eaten with attention. It wasn't until coffee that Becky said, "I don't know if you've heard about the changes in the New York creative department."

"Changes? What changes?" Was it possible that the man who had built an advertising empire on the simple premise of brilliant creative work, would not know that the creative head of his largest office had been put on an ice floe and shoved out to sea?

Either he was lying, or he truly did not know. And she had worshipped this man for too many years to believe that he would lie to her.

She told him about the four new executive creative directors. About endless days that went by with nothing for her to do, while around her she could hear the electric hum of an agency working at top speed.

When she had finished talking, their table was an oasis of silence in the trendy clatter of the room.

Finally he spoke. "You know, Becky, you have had a brilliant career."

"A brilliant career for a woman?"

"For anyone. Wilbur Rank told me about the meeting in Winosha. He said that Stuart Shaw still thinks you walk on water."

"All I did was sit there. I wasn't even part of the presentation."

"Whatever you did, Wilbur told me that Shaw's eyes lit up the minute you walked into the room. Listen, Becky, you have had a brilliant career—this reorganization you've been telling me about may be a cruel blow to your pride, but it has *happened*. Why don't you just relax and make your peace with Hamlin and Rank? Accept their leadership. There are no perfect jobs."

"Mine was. I was always surprised when the fifteenth and the thirtieth rolled around and I got *paid* for it too."

"So there. You have been happy in your job. It doesn't happen to many people. Once you decide to stop smoldering and accept that things change, you will be happy again."

Things change. She looked at the strands of gold still gleaming in his hair. A color that had stayed exactly the same through all the years she had worked for him. But then, *her* hair was still the blonde of a young girl. Only Becky and her hairdresser knew the roots were gray now.

Angus Seton's life had wound up just the way he wanted it. He was an international eminence. He was the patron saint of advertising. He had written the Bible that explained advertising to the world. Of course he enjoyed knowing what was going on in the many offices of his agency, but that didn't mean he wanted to become bogged down in unpleasant details . . .

Seton put his napkin down next to his empty coffee cup and stood.

"My advice to you is, pledge allegiance to Hamlin, and Wilbur, and all the other young Turks who are leading our troops today. And soldier on cheerfully until you're ready to retire."

Becky thought of troops whistling as they crossed the River Kwai. Of men slogging across desert sands behind old Monty. Just a few months ago Angus Seton had reminded her that a man's reach should exceed his grasp, or what's a heaven for . . . and now she was being exhorted not to make waves, to soldier on until she was ready to retire.

"Thank you for lunch," she said, at the door to his office. They had been very big on thanking people for feeding them in the Bronx.

"Oh, I'll be sending you a piece of film soon . . . The *Ad Hoc* people have been nagging me to speak at their California boondoggle next month, so I said I'd send some film of me spouting wisdom. Would you take a look at it when it comes and see if it needs any editing?"

He nodded briskly, went through his secretary's office, and disappeared into his own. The man who had elected himself Becky Gagarin's mentor.

Or . . . had he? Or was it just part of the myth she had constructed for herself: that Angus Seton—then a young man, in the thrilling first stages of building his empire—had reached out, and without seeing her, without knowing if she were young or old, male or female, beautiful or ugly, had claimed her as his own? And (this part was so maudlin she never admitted it to herself) just as the prince heads toward the unknown princess, heads toward her over the corpses of dragons and witches, over craggy mountains and through rings of fire, heads for her knowing he must have her—so Angus had seen one piece of Becky's copy and headed straight for her.

Or—had the real truth been that it had been *she* who had claimed him, clung to him, sheltered herself

in the protection of his shadow through the long years
she worked for him?

She must have been a charming find for Seton at
first. So young as to make most of what she said sound
prodigious. So fearless (or naive) as to say whatever
she believed, no matter to whom she said it. But foods
stale, flowers fade, prodigies grow up. Even grow *old*.
And while Angus might have enjoyed feeling that he
had invented Becky Gagarin when she was a bright
junior writer in an office with only one window, why
should he feel as fond, or protective, of the middle-
aged woman she had somehow managed to become?

Joseph was astonished to see her. It was only a little
past four o'clock, and Mrs. Gagarin never came home
until the night man was on duty.

The door to Alex's studio was closed. She knew
he was inside because she could hear Mahalia Jackson
singing "Didn't It Rain?" and Alex always played that
extra loud.

She prayed that she had not come home early to
stumble upon another tryst. She would not be able to
bear discovering dark-eyed Zoe in there with him . . .
but thank God, Alex was alone. He was crouched on
the floor in front of a canvas, so intent on what was
taking shape there that he didn't even realize that she
was early.

He looked up and smiled. "Isn't Mahalia fantastic?
Do you remember the time we heard her sing that in
person?"

As usual, his studio was layers deep in mess. Over
the years she had made jokes to him about the work
habits of the Collier Brothers. Once, she had even
bought a copy of *The Artist in His Studio* and pointed
out the tidiness of the ateliers of Kandinsky and Leger.
Alex had merely flipped a few pages and showed her
the chaos in which Giacometti and Dubuffet worked.

And Picasso. And said he liked their work a lot better than Kandinsky's.

Now he repeated, "Remember? It was a Sunday night at the Newport Jazz Festival. And Mahalia would never sing on Sunday, except in a church, so she wouldn't come on stage until it was past midnight. And remember, as soon as she stepped up to the mike, as if on cue, it started to *pour*? A real cloudburst. A few cowards left, but all the rest of us just sat there, with the rain sheeting down on us, and Mahalia laughed and gave us fifteen choruses of 'Didn't It Rain?' Remember, Becky?"

"It was such a long time ago. Before the kids were born. The whole audience was singing with her at the end."

"You must have been miserable sitting there with me in the rain. We didn't have an umbrella, and your nice hairdo was being wrecked, and you don't even like jazz all that much, but you knew I wanted to stay. And you stuck with me."

She started to shiver. "I had lunch with Angus today. I told him about the reorganization. You know what his advice was? To soldier on until retirement. Cheerfully."

Alex put his brush down and put his arms around her.

There was an old couch shoved into a corner of the room. Alex cleared it of ancient copies of *Art News* and record albums and half-used tubes of paint. He discovered an old four-square that he had been missing for weeks and was overjoyed to see again. He sat Becky down on the couch and sat beside her.

"You're such a *nice* man, Alex. I know I've been awful to be with for the last few months, but I can't help it. I can't seem to let down my guard and be awful to anyone else, and you're stuck with having to put up with me . . ."

The record ended then. "Wait a minute. Don't move. I have to turn it over." When he came back, he folded her hands into one of his and said, "You stuck by *me*, too. And I don't mean through a rainy concert. All those years I was drinking, you were there. And now it's your time of trouble."

"It isn't as if I were fired."

"Weren't you?"

Astonished, she pulled her hands away. But he was right, of course. The only difference between Becky Gagarin's situation right now, and a clerk at Woolworth who had just gotten canned, was that nobody had been honest enough to send her a pink slip. She let her head slide down into his lap. She didn't care about Zoe. Zoe didn't matter. She closed her eyes. She wanted her own consolation, and she wanted it *now*.

In the afternoon stillness of his studio, Alex stroked her hair. She lay unmoving, waiting, quivering with need in his lap.

"Your hair feels so soft, like a little girl's. What do you want to be, little girl, when you grow up?"

"Fifteen years younger than I am now, that's what I want to be when I grow up."

"Younger? What a waste. I like you the way you are." His fingers outlined her shoulders, her arms, her breasts. "I'm painting you, Rebecca. With my fingers."

The denim of his jeans felt rough against her cheek. They had never made love in this room. Maybe because it was so close to the kitchen, which had always been Charlotte's domain. But now Charlotte was not here, the children were not here, there was no one to hear. Was it because the studio was Alex's that they had never used it for love? Had she never been willing to make love in the room he valued most in the whole apartment, just because it was *his*? Because the crazy clutter all over the room was so much a part of Alex, and no part of Becky?

Alex laughed when they were stretched out together on the sagging couch. "This is not the workbench of a craftsman." The couch was uncomfortable, and when they took their clothes off it felt cold in the room. But the bedroom was now an impossibly long distance away.

Becky nestled her head on Alex's shoulder. The tips of her fingers trailed along his stomach, and she asked him if he remembered when they had first known each other, and he had painted her nude? "Do you still have that painting?"

"Of course I have it. As a matter of fact, I was doing some work on it the other day."

Becky leaned on an elbow to stare down into his face. "Alexander Gagarin. That was *my* painting. You *gave* it to me. No matter how good the changes are, I'll still want the original. Why did you have to change it?"

"Relax, Becky. I didn't do very much, just updated it a little. A contemporary version." Barefoot, he walked gingerly across the room and turned a canvas that was propped against the wall, so she could see the new picture he had painted over the old one.

"The old painting was Becky Then. I wanted it to be Becky Now."

It wasn't a terribly good likeness, no one would pick that out in a gallery and say, "Hey, isn't that Rebecca Gagarin?" But she recognized herself. She recognized the insults of age. The sag of her breasts, the thickening of her waist, the extra flesh under her arms, the way her left shoulder slumped from years of hanging the straps of shoulder bags over that shoulder and not the other. She recognized the horizontal lines that time had chiseled on her forehead, the tiny vertical lines that cut at right angles into her lips. Hell, those weren't lines. She was a writer, she should use the precise word. They were *wrinkles*.

And he had painted in a watch. A grotesquely large

wristwatch that looked incongruous on her ten-pounds-
overweight naked body.

If he wanted to paint Becky Now why hadn't he
made *two* paintings? How much would a second piece
of canvas cost, after all? But he wasn't thinking about
how Becky might feel, seeing herself displayed as an
ancient hag—he was thinking of what he wanted to see
on canvas. Right away. She grimaced at the selfishness
he had revealed.

Becky Now stood propped against the wall. Next
to it was the portrait her husband had been working on
for months. A Portrait of Zoe, by Alexander Gagarin.
He must have considered it finally finished, because he
had had it framed, a fanciful wooden frame lushly
carved with rococo leaves and flowers.

As if they had not been just about to make love,
as if she'd stripped herself naked for some reason she
could no longer recall, some whimsical forgotten purpose, Becky began retrieving her clothes from the floor.

She buttoned her blouse and asked, "Why the
wristwatch? On a nude?"

"But you wear your watch all the time. Even while
you're sleeping. As if you're scared you might be late
for an appointment in your dreams."

She had her shoes on before disgust burst from
her. "How could you bear it? How could you even think
of doing what we were just getting ready to do? How
could you contemplate fucking that hag?"

"I wasn't going to *fuck* anyone. I was going to make
love to Becky. My Becky."

And he smiled at the undressed peasant staring at
them from the canvas.

"I'm not. I'm not her. She. That woman. If you
wanted to paint me the way I am now why didn't you
just make two paintings? Tough shit for Becky if she
loved the old picture, if she loved the way she used to
look . . . why did you destroy the beautiful painting

you made of me when I was young and change it to look so revolting?"

Alex stopped smiling. "Revolting? You really can't see yourself, can you? I painted a strong woman, a woman who has done what they call a man's job for years, and done it with a woman's kindness and concern for others.

"So, you're older now, Becky? I have news for you. So am I. When it rains these days, my fingers hurt. But meanwhile I keep on painting. And you know something else, after this whole mess with Hamlin and Wilbur and Victor is over, yeah and the sainted Angus, Angus Dei, after this whole mess is over I believe that you will be strong enough to take a few steps back and see that where Seton & Cecil leaves off, a whole other world begins."

Across the hall, in the kitchen, the phone rang.

The building had become very grand since apartments were starting to sell for many hundreds of thousands. Each apartment had to be phoned now and warned when strangers were at the gate. Joseph said that a Mrs. Schwartz and another lady were here; Mrs. Schwartz said she had an appointment, was it okay to let her come up?

Daphne Schwartz. This was the day that Becky had said she might come. And Becky had forgotten all about it.

"You'd better put your clothes back on," she said to Alex. "We've got visitors."

Becky had known exactly what Daphne's client would look like. Like all the other women buying apartments in the building, she would be young, chic, a graduate of one of the good colleges, a WASP, but rebellious enough to have deserted the proper East Side of her forebears for the trendy West Side.

But the woman with Daphne Schwartz was none

of these things. *She was Ida Ellenbogen*. Thirty years older than when she and Becky had gone to Hunter together, quite a bit heavier now, stuffed into a silk dress and velvet jacket that strained at the armpits, but indubitably Ida.

With her was an army of young children. Four, at least.

"Becky?" Ida said doubtfully. "Becky *Gelb*? I don't believe it."

There had been seven hundred girls in Becky's class at Hunter. And although Becky had not seen Ida since they parted on commencement day (vowing never, never to lose touch with each other), she knew her right away. Ida had been the *star* of the class. Valedictorian. Summa Cum Laude. A Classics major, with a perfect 4.0 academic index.

The thing that had always impressed Becky about that perfect index was not that Ida had had to get A's in all her Latin and Greek courses to achieve it, and in her math and German and philosophy courses too, but to get that perfect 4.0 she had had to get *A's in physical education*. A's in gym!

The gym classes had been Becky's downfall. Okay, there had been two B's in French, because every time she spoke in class she sounded more like the Grand Concourse than the Champs Elysees. But it had been those gym classes, year after year of them, all required, that had dragged her index down to a 3.8. Becky had not been able to jump over the horse. Or climb the Swedish ladder. And she'd never managed to swim the damn pool. (Her mother had always been there, swimming alongside her, pointing out that any minute now Becky was certain to drown.)

But Ida! Not only did Ida get all A's in gym, but while she was working toward a Bachelor of Arts at Hunter she was also working toward a degree at the

Jewish Theological Seminary. *And finished at the head of her class there too*.

Becky put her arms around Ida to hug her. There was a lot more of her to hug now; the girl who had jumped so nimbly over the horse and raced up the Swedish ladder was now a stylish stout. Her bosom had grown so comfortable that Becky thought of the French word for such an endowment. *Le balcon*, the balcony.

There were questions about do you ever see What's Her Name? And do you know what happened to That One, and The Other? The children had to be introduced: they were Leah and Esther and Benjamin and Seth. At four, Benjamin wore a blue velvet skullcap. Seth was just a bit over a year, the bulkiness in his pants indicating that he was still in diapers.

"I always knew you were extraordinary," Becky said to Ida, "but surely these are not *your* children?"

"Grandchildren," Ida assured her. Alex, who was not afraid of children even when they arrived in battalions, distributed Trowbridge Farm cookies and cups of ginger ale. They sat like elves on chairs in the living room, careful not to spill. Well-brought-up kids, these. Charlotte would have approved.

Ida, it turned out, was no longer Ida Ellenbogen, she was Dr. Greenbaum. In fact, she was Dr. Greenbaum twice over. Once in her own right and once in her husband's. After Hunter, Ida had gone to law school, and then on for a doctorate in law, and after that she had acquired Dr. Meir Greenbaum. Becky remembered reading about the marriage in the *Times* and thinking that Ida had caught the dream of every Jewish mother. Meir Greenbaum was not only the rabbi of one of New York City's foremost congregations, he was the author of books that were best-seller combinations of Talmudic lore, psychoanalytic jargon, and old-fashioned horse sense.

"The apartment isn't for us, it's for our daughter, Barbara."

From a large and unfashionable handbag that was as big as a briefcase, Ida produced a picture of a placid young matron of twenty-eight or thereabouts, who looked remarkably like the Ida Ellenbogen that Becky remembered.

"My daughter the rabbi," Ida said proudly. "When I studied at the Seminary they wouldn't let me be ordained. The times weren't ready for me, so I had to switch to law. Mind you, I'm not complaining, the law has been good to me. And studying Talmud was the perfect preparation for it. But a different world is welcoming my daughter! Barbara is not just the wife of a rabbi, she is a rabbi herself.

"And Meir and I have decided to buy them an apartment near us, on the West Side. If they lived out on the island or in White Plains how often would we see our grandchildren? Anyway, your apartment is lovely, really lovely, Becky, but the best thing about it is that it's only on the fourth floor! So they can use the stairs on Saturdays. I'm sure you know that riding in an elevator on Saturday is as forbidden as driving a car. Can we talk price now?"

Becky looked at Daphne. It was Daphne's cue to say that although Becky had agreed to allow her to show the apartment, she had no permission to *sell* it.

But Daphne crossed long legs, smiled sweetly, and gazed out the window at the park.

"Mrs. Schwartz told you, I'm sure, how much we are offering," Ida said, pulling a yellow legal-size pad out of her handbag. It *was* a briefcase after all; Becky glimpsed a whole little office in there, even a staple gun.

"Ida, I'm afraid there's been a misunderstanding . . ."

"We *could* go higher if we had to. Not much higher, what we're investing here is the fee from my last case, plus all the royalties from Meir's last book. But we do want to buy. So what do you say?"

"I wish it were just money . . ."

That was amusing, one ex-Hunter girl saying *just money* to another.

". . . but you see, this is where my husband *works*. He has his studio here . . ."

Alex said, "Actually, I've been thinking lately that I'd really like a separate studio. Maybe a loft. Where I could work with more privacy."

Becky frowned at her traitor-husband, and rushed on. "Also, I can't possibly sell just now because I'm unusually busy at my job . . ."

"Oh, that's right, Becky, Mrs. Schwartz told me you were in advertising. That must be fun! What do you do in advertising, do you draw the pictures or do you invent the slogans?"

Becky looked at her old school chum and thought, thanks, Ida, I needed that. "Well, neither, actually. I sort of supervise the people who, ah, draw the pictures, and the people who, er, invent the slogans. But, as I said, we have been extremely busy lately, and I'm also in the middle of preparing a speech, so if you're in a hurry to buy maybe you should look elsewhere. I'm sure Mrs. Schwartz has lots of lovely apartments she could show you."

"You don't seem ready to make a decision right now," said Ida, who hadn't finished first at Hunter and first at the Yeshiva by accident. "Why don't we meet again in a few weeks? Maybe you'll feel less pressured then, and we can get the price firmed up and set a date for the closing."

Closing. What a dreadful word. A terminus of a word, loaded with finality. Becky could see herself being chased from her apartment with a team of sheriffs at her heels . . .

Ida laughed and said, "Becky, don't look so grim!

It's a beautiful place, but your children are grown, do you really need all those rooms now? Your husband mentioned lofts—have you looked at any? Some of them are very nice, I understand. I'll come back in a few weeks and maybe we'll talk more then."

Ida rose and began to count grandchildren. One little girl—Leah?—was retrieved from Miranda's bedroom, where she had been discovered playing with Miranda's battered Barbie dolls.

While they were waiting for the elevator, Ida said, "Oh, you were friends with Sheila McCall, weren't you? I heard she lost a husband in Korea, that now she's teaching psychology out West somewhere . . ."

"He survived Korea. He was killed in an ordinary automobile accident. And she's not only teaching. She does therapy too, she has her own practice now."

"Really! That's impressive. And you, have you ever wanted to start your own advertising business?"

"Maybe I should have, but I've never even thought about it. I've been working in the same place for a long time, it's rather a large agency, Seton & Cecil."

Ida's face changed. The only way to describe it was that it sharpened. Her eyes narrowed, and her mouth zipped into a severe line. The affable matron who had called on Becky, grandchildren in tow, vanished and was replaced by a different woman entirely, no longer friendly, and in a tremendous hurry.

Swiftly, Ida Ellenbogen Greenbaum buttoned her grandchildren's jackets, muttered a terse "goodbye," and went down in the elevator, the Bronx and Hunter disappearing with her.

Although they had come very close to making love that afternoon, that night Alex slept in Peter's room as usual. By himself, as usual.

Alone in the big bed, Becky found it difficult to fall asleep. She promised herself that she was not going to think about her husband, in celibate seclusion at the other end of the apartment.

Instead, she lay awake and reviewed her lunch with Angus Seton.

She retrieved and examined every word Seton had said.

She told herself that reorganizations happen in every business. Some step down, others move up. And after a while, there is usually *another* reorganization.

Victor Cameron hadn't been formally ordained yet. Maybe Angus was counseling patience, obliquely telling Becky that it wasn't going to happen, that her wisest course would be to pretend to accept the new order . . . and wait? Wait for things to go back to the way they always had been?

That separate studio that Alex said he wanted, so he could have more *privacy*. Was it just to do some innocent welding . . . or was it to entertain the pygmy?

She forced her mind away from that idea.

She thought that tomorrow she probably should drop Loren Odell a little note, just a casual note, letting him know that she would be in California in June.

11

"I t's a short speech, but important. And it's next week, I'm afraid."

In horror, Sam Samson repeated, "*Next week!*" She ran her hands through her short gray hair and plopped into one of the seats arranged, theater-style, in front of a mock-podium.

"You know damn well I always like at least two rehearsals. And I don't have any more openings on my calendar for this whole month."

Just as Seton & Cecil arranged for the physical well-being of its top executives by regular inspections at Corporate Body, it also arranged to have them prepped for public appearances by "Sam" Samson (whose real name was Irma—although she never admitted that on business cards, or letterheads, or in conversation). Most of Sam's clients were corporations; it was the rare individual who could afford her prices. She made no bones about being outrageously expensive, but worth it.

"Okay. Get up on that podium and let's get started. Somebody is introducing you. Today we're honored to have with us Rebecca Gagarin, creative head of Seton & Cecil, the only woman who blah blah blah and the first woman who blah blah blah. Now they're applauding. Clap clap clap. And what are you doing while you're being introduced?"

"Telling myself how happy I am to be speaking to these intelligent people, how wonderful and attractive they all are, that there isn't any place in the world I'd rather be than right here right now."

"Right. And what do you do when the applause dies down?"

"Uh—begin?"

"Wrong! I've told you before, you take all the time you need and compose yourself. They're not going anywhere. The rules say whether they like it or not they have to sit still and wait for *you*. And remember, I want a lot of eye contact up front. Before you say a single word I want you to scan the whole room. Where are your glasses?"

"In my hand."

"Right. You don't want their first impression of you to be a face full of glasses. And remember, head up, *don't* lean on the podium. It's there to hold your speech, not you. Okay, they're dying to hear you, now—go!"

At the end: "Clap clap clap," muttered Sam Samson. "Listen, what the hell is wrong with you today?"

"Wrong with me? I thought I sounded pretty good."

"I have news for you, it was *not* good. You were talking in the most *adorable* little-girl voice, as if you were just begging for somebody to come up and pat you on the head. Let's look at the tape, you'll see what I mean."

Sam Samson always had a video camera recording rehearsals.

"Did you hear how you sounded? Good God, Becky, they asked you to speak to them because they think you have important things to say. You're an important woman, so try to sound like one. And let your voice go down, let your voice go deep, when you're making a point."

"You want me to try to sound like a man?"

"I want you to sound as if you're in charge. Come on, let's do it again and *stronger*. You're preeminent in your field, everyone says you are. Try to remember it when you speak."

An hour later, she let Becky leave. "I'll give you a B-plus now, which you might bring up to an A-minus by the time you get your adrenaline going with a real audience in front of you. Instead of Sam Samson yelling clap clap clap."

"But you still don't like it."

Sam stood there, a stocky little trousered figure, who finally nodded and gave Becky a grudging punch on the arm.

"No, I don't. Mentors. That's the new 'in' topic, isn't it? I must have seen five different articles about mentors in magazines just this month. But teaching, mentoring, that generally involves *two* people. I wanted to hear a little bit about Becky Gagarin in your speech. You're selling Angus Seton in every sentence. How brilliant Seton is, all the wonderful campaigns Seton created to build the agency, without help from a single other human being. You tell some funny Seton anecdotes, and they do make him come alive—but you're the one who's talking and *you* don't come alive. When you read *Pygmalion* it's not just Dr. Higgins you're interested in, it's Eliza Doolittle too."

Becky retrieved the pages on the podium and stuffed them into her attaché case. "I don't have time to rewrite."

Sam Samson shrugged. "Have it your way. You've got a devout eulogy for the Great Seton there. I'm sure he'd be delighted, if he could hear it."

Angus's reel arrived. Becky screened it once, screened it again, then telephoned an S.O.S. to Keith Andrews.

Keith was happy in Victor Cameron's group: They

shared the same ideas about working hours. The day was for drifting in late, gossip, long lunches. Twilight was when you started working. Keith sounded grumpy when Becky asked him to come down to the screening room. It was seven in the evening, and he had just begun on his day's assignments.

Nevertheless, Keith came. He ran Angus's film on the moviola and groaned. "My God, this is too long. Poorly paced. Where was it produced, the London office? Thought so, the English are more patient than we are. An American audience will be bored out of their skulls . . ."

Then he paused and added, "But it *could* be wonderful. With a lot of editing it could show Angus in top form. Only, somebody will really have to wrestle with it. Somebody *else*. Don't look at me like that, Becky. Cameron has me working on three different crises simultaneously."

Becky told Keith that there wasn't another producer at Seton & Cecil with his taste, his instinctive knowledge of what worked on film . . .

Becky said she knew it was Keith who had done the fastidious postproduction work on her own Eve commercial and had done it so brilliantly that the client had approved it on the very first viewing . . .

Becky said that after all, they were talking about a piece of film sent by the *chairman of the board*, who really ought to get to know Keith better . . .

And Keith agreed to do it.

He managed to complete his regular assignments during the daytime, so that during the evening, and into the night, he could labor with Becky over the film that Angus Seton had sent.

She felt like an assassin, editing out so much of Angus. Frame after frame of that magnetic face landed on the floor. When they ran through the reel to decide where to make their cuts, the words would slow down to a groan, each syllable sounding yards long. She thought of all the years that every word from Seton's lips had been so sacred to her that cutting even one would have seemed desecration.

Finally, at half past eleven, on the evening of the third day of editing, they were through.

"We have made, luv, a silk purse out of the proverbial pig's ear."

It startled Becky to hear how fast Keith had picked up Victor's "luv." In New York you called people "Bud" if they were masculine, "dear" if they were feminine, and "Hey, you" if you couldn't decide. Never "luv."

"How do you like working in Victor's group?"

Keith inspected the corned beef sandwich in his hand. That was another sacrifice he had made this week: a corned beef sandwich gobbled at almost midnight, instead of a decent French dinner at a civilized hour.

Keith brought himself to take a bite of the sandwich. So that he doesn't have to answer right away, Becky thought.

"You really want to know?"

"Why do you think I asked?"

"Okay. Victor is exciting. He's resourceful. He isn't half the writer you are, but he's a much better leader."

Which was what Rae had told her on the airplane.

Becky painted her sandwich with an extra layer of mustard. "Do you think he could run the whole department?"

"No comment. I make it my business to stay away from office politics. Listen, the waves close over people's heads very fast in this business. Six months ago nobody in the creative department went to the bathroom without checking first for Becky Gagarin's opinion. Now, I hardly hear your name mentioned. Oh sure, they know you're still with the agency, but they don't know how much power you have left. If any. Right now, we have a quadrumvirate running the department, and I do what I'm told. If somebody else arrives tomorrow from London or Hong Kong or Timbuktu and I'm told that I must follow his flag, I'll do it. I stay away from office politics because I like working at Seton & Cecil."

"So do I," Becky said softly.

"So *did* I," a little voice within her corrected. The pedantic little voice that caught her mistakes when she wrote.

Becky pressed the DOWN button.

When the elevator came Gandhi Hendricks was in it, her eyes half-shut as she leaned against the wall.

Gandhi smiled thinly at Becky. "Know what I miss? Those bourgeois nine-to-five hours we used to work when *you* ran the department."

"I'll take you home," Becky said. She still had the use of an agency car and driver. No one had turned off this convenient perk, and she was not going to remind them about it.

"Have you forgotten I live at the end of the earth? Way up in the Bronx?"

"I haven't forgotten. And I don't want you using the subway at this hour. Or getting into a fistfight with some cabby who refuses to drive you."

Frank was not happy about the journey to the Bronx. He made sure all the doors and windows of the car were locked before they set out.

Becky wondered, what would the Bronx of her childhood be like now? Storefront tabernacles instead of synagogues? Bodegas instead of grocery stores? Check-cashing cubbyholes instead of banks? Restaurants offering soul food instead of knishes?

When they reached the blocks and blocks of

burned-out and blackened buildings, Frank said to Gandhi, "You'll have to direct me from here."

"It's a lot further uptown, just keep going."

Gandhi had to say "further uptown" twice more.

Eventually the raucous life of the ghetto gave way to trees and grass and slumbering colonial houses.

After a while there were larger villas, with two-car garages, set back expensively from the street.

Frank worried. "We're in Riverdale now. Did I pass it?"

"No," said Gandhi softly. "It's right over there, across the street."

She pointed to a house that was more modern than its neighbors. Larger than the neighboring houses too, this house was geometric, flat-roofed, elegantly cool and restrained, but with enormous windows that must have drenched the rooms inside with sun. A path of white stones, shining in the moonlight, led from a side door to a pool.

"You said you lived in *the Bronx*," Becky said. It came out sounding like an accusation.

"Riverdale *is* part of the Bronx. But my parents never admit it. *They* call it Riverdale. I call it the Bronx. To irritate them, I suppose. My father is a theatrical agent, you've probably heard of some of the people he handles, my mother doesn't really live *here*, she lives in Bloomingdale's. When my mother tried to make me 'come out' at one of those fancy balls prosperous blacks give to launch their daughters, that's when I rebelled. I told her I'd done everything she wanted up to then, taken the ballet lessons, learned to ski, gone to the college she wanted—Vassar, did you know? I even learned contract bridge for her. So I could make a fourth at her parties—I was the youngest Life Master in the state of New York. But I drew the line at climbing into a white chiffon dress for a stupid coming-out party.

I started basket-weaving my hair instead and telling everyone who'd listen that I lived in the Bronx."

Gandhi got out of the car and stood there a moment. "Why do I stay here if it offends me so? Because my folks don't ask for rent money. When Seton & Cecil gives me a great big raise, I'll be able to move to a tenement and pay my own way. Sorry to disappoint you, Becky. I know you wanted me to be an ambitious little girl from the Bronx, just the way you were, who would put all the exquisite *longing* she felt into her copy."

Feeling vaguely cheated, Becky asked Frank to drive her home.

12

The voice on the phone had the rote calm of someone who has delivered the same sad message so often that it has turned into words, just words, ordinary words that can finally be recited without tears. It was Osceola, Charlotte's sister.

"She passed, Mrs. Gagarin. Last night. There was no pain at the end, she left this world sweet as a baby."

Becky saw Charlotte's outstretched hands, reaching out for Peter the day she had brought him home from the hospital. She saw Charlotte carrying Miranda around the apartment one long-ago rainy day, pointing out the pictures on the walls, explaining what was in them—"Babies need to see something new every day, that's how they grow."

She saw Charlotte terrorizing the produce men at the market. Only unblemished fruits went into Charlotte Gates's basket. Fish had to be firm of skin and still bright of eye. This was a woman who used all her senses to shop: fruit, meat, chickens—all were smelled and touched and peered at suspiciously. Once Becky had seen her hold a melon close to her ear and *listen* to it.

Becky remembered the scoldings Charlotte could dish out on Monday mornings if she suspected that something her babies needed had been neglected during the weekend. Charlotte always thought they looked a little scruffy after their weekends under Mommy's care, and her suspicion marched in with her on Mondays.

But now Osceola was talking about the funeral. Thursday morning. Baltimore.

"*Thursday?* Oh Osceola, I'm so sorry, I'll be in California on Thursday. As a matter of fact, I'm leaving in just a few minutes . . ."

Osceola didn't pause a beat, and Becky understood that the invitation to Mr. and Mrs. Gagarin had been mostly good manners. It was Peter and Miranda, Charlotte's babies, who were really wanted, in the first row of mourners. And then, because there were still so many people to call, all Charlotte's friends, all the labyrinth of family, she thanked Becky for having been so kind to Charlotte and hung up.

Me? thought Becky. *I* have been kind to *Charlotte?* How could I have stepped out of the door, how could I have gone to *work* without her?

Becky expected Miranda to cry when she phoned, but there was only a minute of silence. Then in a surprisingly steady voice Miranda said, "I'm coming home."

Alex came into the room; Becky gestured at him to stay but kept on talking. "The funeral is Thursday. The trouble is I have to go to California, there's a speech I have to make, the car's waiting for me, I should have been on my way to the airport long ago . . ."

The suddenly mature voice that was Miranda interrupted. "I'm coming home anyway. I just want to sit in Charlotte's room for a while and think about her. Have you phoned Peter yet?"

Peter's reaction surprised her. It was rage. "Damn it. Oh holy hell, damn it to hell." Death had personally insulted him, taking Charlotte.

"Peter, sweetheart. Remember, she was in such horrible pain. And now she isn't anymore. I can't cancel

California, there will be eight hundred people there expecting to hear me . . . I'll be staying overnight with my friend Sheila, but first we can have dinner together, just you and me. Let's treat ourselves to a really elegant meal, the two of us."

When she got off the phone, Alex was staring out the window at Central Park as if he were counting the trees. Without turning, he asked, "What do you mean, you *have* to make a speech?"

She looked at him, puzzled.

"What would happen if someone stood in for you? That Gandhi person you're always talking about? She could explain that there'd been a death in the family so you couldn't be there."

"Alex! I loved Charlotte, of course I did, but *I* have to make this speech. *I* have to do it."

"You mean, whoever else might be there from Seton & Cecil will fall on his knees in the aisle and say, forgive us Becky, we've made a terrible mistake, let us turn the clock back to the way things used to be." He thumped his chest. "Forgive us all that has happened in the past months, ours is the fault, ours is the fault."

She would *not* let him upset her. Alex had never worked in a corporate setting. "I can't welsh out on an obligation for personal reasons."

Yet even as she said it, a nudging little voice inside her asked, would she be worried about canceling if she'd been a man? Men ducked out of meetings to go to Little League games, if a son were playing . . . Except, men were judged only on the things they did that were important to a corporation. A woman was judged all the time, on everything she did, every detail, no matter how tiny. How could she not be there when she had promised she would?

Alex rested his forehead against the windowpane.

"Okay. Go stand on your little platform. Maybe Seton will hear how wonderful you were and change his mind about letting them feed you to the sharks. Be honest, do you think you'd still be on the payroll if they didn't have that lawsuit hanging over their heads? Maybe it would be embarrassing to lose their best-known female employee in the middle of all that."

"You should be glad I'm going. It leaves the coast clear for you and the lady from Lilliput." She picked up her suitcase.

"Her name is Zoe. Thanks for asking how she's doing these days. You'll be glad to know she's doing fine, she hasn't had a single drink since I got her into The Program."

"As her sponsor, you must be proud." She underlined *sponsor* with a snort.

Alex turned back to the window and his census of the trees. Over his shoulder he said, "Thanks for asking about Zoe, and thanks for asking about *me*. No, I haven't done any painting lately. I'm sharing a flat with this dame who reminds me of that character in Li'l Abner, the little guy who walks around with a rain cloud over his head all the time. Hard to live with. Come to think of it, I don't see why I should live with it any more. As soon as I can find a place, I'm getting out."

He did not mean it. It was nothing more than a threat. Like the Night of the Croup, when he had actually packed a suitcase, it was only a threat.

~~~~~

Peter's face swam toward her from the bottom of the escalator. It was a good thing that Becky had one hand firmly clutching the handrail or she might have tripped. He looked so much like Alex, and seeing him there was so unexpected.

"You have the same shape head as your father," she told him. "It was nice of you to come all the way out to the airport to meet me. Have you thought of someplace you want to eat? Someplace grand, where you've always wanted to go?"

"Thanks, that's flattering, Dad's a very good-looking man. A lot better looking than me."

But he made no move to take his mother's suitcase and lead her out of the terminal. "I'm sorry, I won't be able to have dinner with you. I'm taking the red-eye home tonight. I'm going to the funeral with Daddy and Miranda. I phoned and told them. They're expecting me. Uh, I don't have enough money for the ticket, can you lend me some?"

He hadn't met her plane because he wanted to see her. He had met her plane because he needed money. She looked at the thin cotton shirt, the ancient jeans and shabby jacket.

"Peter! You can't show up at a funeral looking like that. Do you at least have a decent suit to change into in New York?"

She heard the horrible, picky, boring words she had lapsed into and seized his hand. It had not been Becky speaking. It had been her mother. What would the neighbors think?

"Oh, Peter, I'm sorry. It doesn't matter what you wear. Charlotte will be . . . Charlotte would have been . . . her family will be so happy to see you there."

They wound up in one of the airport cafeterias. Peter said all he wanted was a Coke. He was staring at the clock and tearing a paper napkin into little squares.

She pointed out, "We can still go out for dinner. Someplace decent. The red-eye doesn't leave until ten."

He began arranging the squares of napkin into precise stacks. "After you phoned this morning, I grabbed my bike and started cycling around campus. I must have ridden around for hours. I wasn't thinking about Charlotte, I was just riding in circles. And finally there I was back in front of my dorm again, and I knew I had to go home."

That was what Miranda had said. "I'm coming home." To a child, home is where the mother is. Both her children were heading toward what they called home, but was really Charlotte's body. Charlotte's dead body. She thought of a grotesque experiment she had once read about, when baby monkeys were separated from their mothers and given *cloth* figures to hug instead. Which the baby monkeys duly hugged. Because their real mamas had disappeared. And the cloth mamas were there. Becky had been gone so often. And Charlotte was always there.

She told herself that she had come to terms with all that years ago. Her children's love for Charlotte in no way diminished their love for Becky. She was glad that they could grieve so for Charlotte. She would have been horrified if they did not feel her loss deeply.

She went with Peter and bought him a ticket on the last plane to New York, the red-eye. Although it was hours until his flight, he refused to leave the terminal. He seemed afraid that the plane would depart without him if he did. Becky tucked his boarding card carefully into the pocket of his shirt and buttoned the shirt pocket over it.

"Mom, you don't have to hang around. You look beat. Dad says things haven't been going well for you lately at the agency."

"The usual political in-fighting. Nothing for you to worry about."

Outside the terminal, a chauffeur held a cardboard lollipop with GAGARIN lettered on it in black crayon. She looked back through the floor-to-ceiling windows and saw Peter sitting where she had left him. A skinny, hunched-over kid, holding a cigarette gingerly between two fingers. He reminded Becky of the emaciated boys who hand out leaflets for massage parlors on New York streets. He wasn't reading any of the magazines she had bought him, he was sitting there quietly, looking frail and alone, a sadder, thinner, younger version of Alex. Why hadn't she asked him about his classes, his teachers, his friends? Had he decided on his major yet? Did he have a girl friend yet? She thought of going back into the terminal and saying, hey Peter, let's just stay together until your plane is called, let's keep each other company, let's *be* together for a while. She could hear herself saying Peter, you're right, things aren't very good for me at the agency now, as a matter of fact things are rotten for me there, but they're not all that good at home either. Did I mention your father is talking about leaving me?

The chauffeur said, "Mrs. Gagarin?"

She let him open the door for her and help her into the car, and gave him Sheila's address.

It was an hour or so outside of Los Angeles, a haphazard neighborhood of rundown houses. Sheila's house, when the driver finally found it, was a wooden structure that might have been held together with staples and Scotch tape. But beside the door there was a proud brass shingle: *Sheila McCall, Ph.D., counseling and therapy, by appointment.* Next to that was another, smaller, far less elegant postscript of a sign: *Ring and walk in. Door is open.*

She rang, and when she turned the knob was amazed to discover that the door *was* open. She contemplated the sublime courage of such a sign: leaving your door open and begging any passing rapist to ring— and waltz in.

In a small waiting room there were the usual chairs, little tables stacked with ancient magazines, and the mysterious door to the inner sanctum of the therapist. And behind that door there was Sheila, whom she was suddenly longing to see. She wanted to bang on the door and shout, Hey, Sheila old friend, here I am, I am here, but instead she observed the decorum of the therapeutic waiting room. Right now, whoever was inside owned Sheila's time. A man's jacket hung on the coat rack. Until the door opened, Sheila belonged to him.

Dr. McCall's patient was a man of perhaps seventy, preceded by a paunch and followed by an elderly spotted dog.

Dr. McCall escorted them to the door and said in a reassuring voice, "I'll see you next week then, Mr. Tessler."

Mr. Tessler chirped, "Yep. Next Monday. Same time, same station. Heh."

Dr. McCall rewarded the joke with a huge smile.

Dr. McCall closed the door and turned into Sheila. She whooped, "Becky, you made it!" They weren't in a restaurant now, they could scream and holler and cry and really let each other know how glad they were to be together.

Later, over a drink in the inner sanctum, Becky asked: were Mr. Tessler and his dog coming at two-fer rates?

"The dog isn't an extra patient. The dog is part of the *cure*. Mr. Tessler is a widower, there were no children, all he has in the world now is that dog. The landlord says no animals are allowed in the building. Mr. Tessler says that his wife was with him when he moved in, that the dog takes up less room and is a lot more fastidious. Without that dog, I think he'd die. I'm masterminding his fight to keep it . . . Hey, do you know I have a pet now too?"

She went out and came back holding a sleepy white cat, barely graduated from kitten age. She held the cat up next to her cheek and purred along with it.

Becky looked at the little love scene and said that once she'd had a pet. A canary. "But it died. My father saw it dead in its cage one morning and wrapped it in

a paper bag. He wanted to get rid of it before I woke
up and saw it. But he left with his mind on something
else, and I found the bag on the edge of the bathroom
sink. Do you think my strange behavior now might have
something to do with that early feathered trauma?"

Sheila consulted her watch. "We'll talk about that
next week, Mrs. Gagarin. That will be eighty dollars,
please."

Becky laughed and stretched out a hand to stroke
Sheila's cat. But the animal, which had been nestling
contentedly on Sheila's shoulder, its white fur blending
into Sheila's white hair, pulled back and lifted a paw
to swipe at Becky.

"Relax. You're scared, and he can sense that. He
won't hurt you, he's only a *baby*. His name is Moishe."

"Moishe? A nice Irish girl like you gives her cat a
Yiddish name?"

"Well, all you people are naming your kids Sean
and Deirdre and Kevin, so I felt I had a perfect right
to retaliate with Moishe. Come upstairs and say hello
to Terry."

"*Terry?*"

Terry had been Sheila's husband. A cat with a
Yiddish name was one thing. Talking about a husband
who has been dead for decades was another.

"She's the girl I share this place with. You didn't
think I could afford elegance like this all by myself, did
you?"

Terry was sitting lotus-style on a slipcovered couch,
watching an "I Love Lucy" rerun. Her hands foraged
in a cardboard bucket of popcorn clutched between her
thighs, and beside her on the couch, facedown, was a
paperback novel. On the cover of the book a blonde
girl ran before a gathering storm, her red velvet cape
streaming horizontally behind her.

Terry took her eyes off the screen only as long as
was necessary to shake Becky's hand. Then she re-

turned her attention to Lucy, who was having a fight with Ricky. Lucy wanted to get a job and go to work. Ricky did not want her to. This was a highly topical situation in the 1960s when "I Love Lucy" was still in prime time.

"We're pretty comfortable here, living over the shop," said Sheila. "This is our guest room . . ." She pointed to the couch Terry sat on. "And that's our kitchen . . ." It had once been a closet; now it was fitted out with miniature appliances that had probably been meant for a ship's galley or a trailer. "And here's our bedroom . . ."

She opened the door to a small room almost filled with a king-size bed.

Becky had assumed it would be the traditional roommates' arrangement, one shelf of the refrigerator is for me, one shelf is for you, we share expenses for utilities, we split the rent. And *twin* beds.

Becky told herself, don't jump to conclusions. People can share a bedroom, even a bed, without it being more than a place to sleep.

"C'mon outside," Sheila said. "Let's sit on the deck. It's cool out there and we can talk without disturbing Terry." Becky noted that Sheila did not seem to care that Terry's loud TV rerun might be disturbing *them*.

Outside, Becky offered nervously, "She's very pretty. I guess I thought, when you said you were sharing, that it would be one of your colleagues. Another teacher."

"Some women on the faculty do live together. I didn't want to get into that. It's rough enough putting up with academic politics, without mixing it up with a personal relationship."

Becky looked out over the railing of the deck. Porch. Whatever. Finally, "Terry is your lover?"

Sheila laughed. "And Moishe is my cat. My, you *are* quick today."

"But—she can't be more than twenty."

"Actually, she's twenty-seven. She looks young because she's so skinny. You'd be surprised how a diet of popcorn and Tab can keep the pounds off. Hardly any calories in popcorn, if you leave off the butter. But she's a terrific Italian cook, too. Her real name is Theresa. I'm glad you made it in time to have dinner with us, she may have been shy when she met you, but watch, she'll make up for it with your dinner."

"Where did you meet her? What does she do?"

"I met her in the bank. She's secretary to one of the officers there. I needed his approval on a car loan, and he was dubious about me. An assistant prof without any tenure? Terry was always talking to me while her boss kept me waiting. When I finally got the car, she helped me learn to drive it. It's my first stick shift, and she's a California kid, they learn to drive shortly after they're weaned. By the time I could pilot that car we were good friends. More than friends. She's very bright, don't let the TV show and romance novel fool you. She always puts on that catatonic act when I bring home somebody from the college."

Becky wanted to ask if there had been other Terrys before Terry, but she couldn't get the words out. She thought of Sheila's skin against Terry's. Sheila's skin would be as dry as Becky's now. Terry's olive-toned arms would be supple and eager and gleaming . . .

"Sure, there were other women in my life before I met Terry. One or two," said Sheila, reading Becky's mind. You couldn't grow up with someone, sit next to her from P.S. 42 through college, without both of you learning how the other thinks. "But Terry is special. She's extremely important to me. As I hope I am, to her."

The Terry who cooked dinner was not the Terry

of the cheap paperback, the bucket of popcorn, the blaring TV set. This was a sensitive, skillful Terry: The warmth she could not put into words, she put into her cooking. (A lecherous little voice inside Becky suggested, *and her lovemaking, too?*)

"Sheila didn't say we'd have a visitor, so I didn't do anything special . . ."

Was Terry *apologizing* for the meal? The salad with its leaves of fresh arugula, the linguine cooked to al dente perfection and combined delicately, not drowned, with a saffron sauce, the tender and succulent osso buco—Becky thought that she too could fall in love with Terry just for the way she cooked. But Terry shrugged off thanks and disappeared into the bedroom with her novel.

"She was married when I met her," Sheila said, as they sat out on the deck again. "He smacked her around a lot. Now he won't give her a divorce because he says good Catholics don't divorce."

Becky searched in her mind for something else to talk about. There must be other subjects besides the girl in Sheila's bedroom. "You'll never guess who I met. From Hunter! Ida Ellenbogen!"

It had always been a joke between them that while Becky never met any ex-Hunter girls, Sheila could not go anywhere without running into them. Once she had met one walking down the street of a village in Tibet. Sheila insisted that the world was teeming with Hunter girls, that the only reason Becky never saw them was that she moved through life with her gaze fixed so sternly on her job.

"Ida Ellenbogen! Where did you run into *her*?"

So Sheila had to hear the story about the apartment that Ida Ellenbogen was convinced she could persuade Becky to sell. So that Ida's daughter, the rabbi, could move into it with her brood.

"It's only on the fourth floor, you know, so it's

very desirable to them. Ida's daughter won't travel on the Sabbath. Not even in elevators."

"I would have loved to have grandchildren already, like Ida," Sheila said wistfully. The cat had stayed close to her all evening, and now Sheila swooped it up and rubbed her cheek along its fur. "Ahh, don't feel bad, Moishe, I know I have *you*."

Becky whispered, "I feel as if I really don't know anything about you. And all those years, I thought I knew everything."

"You never knew because you didn't want to know." Sheila put the cat down and walked to the unsteady railing to perch on it.

"Don't sit there, it's dangerous!" cried Becky. Or perhaps it was Becky's mother.

In either case, Sheila paid no attention, simply repeated, "You didn't want to know. It's a gift you've had ever since we were little girls. Not seeing what you didn't want to see."

Sheila paused, then nodded as if she had decided something. "All those years we were in P.S. 42 together, you knew my father was dead, right?"

"I used to feel so sorry for you . . ."

"I was lying. I can tell you now, the statute of limitations has run out. My mother was so ashamed she didn't want me to tell any of the neighbors, my teachers, or my friends—he wasn't dead. He was in Empire State. The asylum. It took us hours by subway and bus to get there, and hours by bus and subway coming back, but we visited him every Sunday. *Every* Sunday. While you were listening to your father explain the pictures in the Metropolitan, I was bouncing toward the loony bin where my father was stashed. Half the time he didn't know who we were."

Becky shifted uncomfortably. She could not believe that when they had been little girls, the scabby-kneed Sheila had been keeping such secrets. "Is he . . . better now?"

"Oh, he's fine now. He's dead. They wouldn't let him wear a belt or eat with a knife and fork all those years, because he might hurt himself. So he died from a nice respectable heart attack. But I guess they were right about the precautions. Before he went into the hospital he *was* violent. Not physically violent, but he used to say the most savage things to my mother, in this terribly quiet voice.

"When she was eating he'd say, 'Choke on it.'

"When we were all three of us crossing the street together, just the picture of a nice little blue-collar family, the kind the nation is built on, he'd say, 'Don't bother looking at the traffic. Get run over.'

"At night, when my mother was going to bed, with her hair all braided, in one of those long flannel nightgowns she used to wear, he'd tell her, 'Don't wake up tomorrow, die in your sleep.' And he'd say it in exactly the same cheerful tone someone else might use for 'sleep tight.'

"And the funny thing was, she kept on loving him. Even while he cursed her she was loving him. On Sundays—before we took the subway and bus to visit him?—she used to go to early mass to pray for him. I could hear her making bargains with God, you know my mother was a woman who would try to bargain at Macy's. The bargain was that if God would make *him* well, He could make *her* crazy instead."

It was so dark out now that Sheila's face had become a shadow. Becky said, "I was terribly jealous of you when you married so young. Because you'd already found someone who loved you, really loved *you*, and it was years before I met Alex."

"And now I've got my *new* Terry," Sheila said bravely. "At first I thought her being named Terry too was just a coincidence. Then—don't laugh—I decided that it was a sign, a sign that my mother's God was watching and giving me someone to replace the young lover I lost. Do you remember when we got the news about my Terry, my first Terry, and you came to get me, to bring me back to New York? And I told you he was my earth, my country, my home, my land? Well, I feel the same way about the Terry who's in there now. I cling to her when I get scared . . ."

Sheila paused, and smiled at Becky. "The way you once said you cling to your job, when *you* get scared."

"I don't remember saying that."

"No? Well, it's my *job* to remember the things people say, even the things they want to forget. Especially those. So Seton & Cecil is no longer the cornerstone of your existence, the way it used to be? Alex is maybe one-tenth as important now?"

And then it all came out. Becky whimpered that Alex was going to leave her for a new love, but for once she did not try to destroy Zoe with *words*. She didn't lie and paint Zoe as squat and dwarfish and swarthy. She ground the truth out between gritted teeth:

"She has jet-black hair. Delicate, almost transparent skin. And a perfect Waspy nose. The girl is a knockout, damn her eyes. Oh, how could I forget, she also has the most ravishing eyes. Big limpid pools of blackness."

Sheila asked, "What was her name again? Zoe? Well, if Zoe hadn't come into Alex's life, have you ever thought he might have had to go out looking for her? Because you pushed him so far out of it. Alex loves you, Becky. Nobody loves you where you work. That's not what a job is about. Money, titles, power, prestige, that's what you get from a job. Not love."

Sheila had left the railing long ago and was sitting behind Becky now on a peeling wicker rocker. Becky lay on an old chaise on the shabby deck. It was a parody of the traditional analytic tableau. Becky talked, but could not see Sheila. Sheila listened, but did not touch Becky. In this travesty of an analytic session, if Becky had been able to see Sheila, Sheila would have been just her old friend from P.S. 42. Not the detached voice that was helping her to see herself in the darkness.

Becky had never told anyone about Loren Odell. Now, as the evening wore on, she told Sheila. "We were as far apart in age as you and Terry are. Of course, it happened years ago, and it's been over for years now."

Then, with more pain than she had felt talking about Alex's new love, or her own ancient and brief affair with Loren, she poured out the misery of the last months at Seton & Cecil. How it felt to get up in the morning and dress for a job that no longer existed. How it felt to speak at meetings and not be heard. It wasn't until she reached the fantasy she had had on the small airplane to Winosha, the delicious fantasy of smuggling a gun onto the plane and murdering Hamlin and Rank, that Sheila spoke:

"It sounds as if you're finally faced with a decision you can't avoid. Whether to stay in that job or gather your courage and quit."

"What do you mean, a decision I can't avoid? I'm a whiz when it comes to decisions. I'm celebrated for the dazzling speed with which I make them."

"Really? I don't think you've made one important decision since you went to work for Seton & Cecil. Not one."

How could Sheila be saying something so absurd, so patently untrue?

"Once you took that job, it was as if there were no more decisions to make. Those big corporations are set up to take everything you can give, Becky, so that's what you gave. Unthinkingly. Automatically. Without question. Everything. Alex, the children, they all slid into second place. Some people get hooked on booze or drugs; you were hooked on that job. In a way I feel jealous. It must have made things so simple for you."

Becky whispered, "Once I was being interviewed for an article in a trade paper. They asked me how I was able to manage the myriad responsibilities in my life . . . I thought I was being funny when I heard myself say it was easy, I just neglected the children. But it was true. It was so simple to just throw myself into my job, simple to keep on climbing, at least I knew how to do that. And the other parts of my life were so tricky."

~~~~~~

They had been talking for hours. Becky sat on the floor now, her head against Sheila's knee. "And then Angus Seton threw me away, as soon as I became inconvenient."

It hurt so much to admit that, she could not believe it when Sheila laughed.

"Aah, I've got it now. You know what you are? The little girl who never grew up. All those years you were acting the part of the successful V.I.P., with the chauffeur-driven cars and the trips to Europe and the corner office, all those years there was this good little girl hiding in the closet, just wanting to please her big strong daddy. And then, when you get into trouble and Seton comes to New York, and you expect him to put everything right for you . . . he refuses to get involved!"

Sheila was silent for a minute, then said gently, "It must have hurt like hell, Becky. He didn't know he was God. He just didn't want his own life disturbed."

~~~~~~

That night Becky tossed sleeplessly on the couch that
Sheila had called her "guest room." And remembered
the time Sheila had spoken of earlier, when her first
Terry had died and Becky had come to fetch her back
to New York. Could it really have been twenty-five
years ago . . . ?

Sheila has the window seat, which is lucky, because she
doesn't seem able to hold her head up any more. Her
head slumps against the window as she speaks.

"What a stupid way to die. What a stupid, boy-
scout way. Everyone was passing the car with the flat.
The woman in it had two little girls with her, and all
the other cars were just whizzing by. But would Terry
pass? Not my boy scout. He had to get out of his own
car and kneel down in the road and change the tire for
her so some drunken idiot could plow right into him
. . . I want it all now. All the things I used to despise.
I want to hear my mother howling, I want to howl
myself. I want to mourn his death with the noisiest,
most drunken wake there ever was for a darling Irish
boy."

The woman in the seat in front of them turns and
looks at Sheila inquiringly. Becky shoots her a good
strong New York City drop-dead glare, and in confusion
the woman plunges back into her Book of the Month.

"Becky, why did I want to come back to the Bronx
as soon as I found out, why after all these years?"

"I don't know," Becky says. "I guess you can be
happy someone else's way, but you can only mourn the
way you really are, and in the place that you belong."

Sheila becomes terrified. "I *don't* belong there. It's
a horrible place, nothing is green, nothing grows . . . I
live in the country now. I'm Sheila McCall now, I'm
Terry McCall's wife.

"I'll plant a tree for him," Sheila croons. "I'll plant

a tree in his name, and that will be a growing thing. A green thing. And whenever I'm scared I'll go visit my tree, and I'll still be Sheila McCall, still be safe . . ."

"Sheila, won't you try to nap a little?"

". . . still have roots, a country to belong to, a terra firma, *ma terre*, my Terry. See, Becky, there's nothing to worry about if I can still make jokes, did you hear the funny pun I made? *Ma terre*, my Terry?"

"Lean your head against my shoulder and rest now."

"Can we do it tomorrow, Becky?" The blue eyes blaze at Becky. "Can we plant his tree together, will you help me, will you come with me?"

Becky slips her jacket off and tucks it around Sheila's shoulders. "Yes, sure, we'll plant the tree tomorrow."

"Promise?"

"Promise."

Tired, appeased, Sheila allows her eyes to close. In a flat voice she says, "The government pays you for dead soldiers, even dead ex-soldiers. When I get the insurance money I'll try to find a little apartment. And a job that fills my life. Your job gives you a lot, doesn't it? It fills your life, doesn't it?"

"It makes me feel important. It gives me a reason to get up in the morning. It gives me something to hold on to when I wake up frightened in the middle of the night."

"You know something?" Sheila smiles then, and opens her eyes. "All the things you just said you get from your job? They're the things I used to get from Terry."

~~~~~~

"Happy birthday to you, happy birthday to you, happy birthday dear Rebecca, happy birthday to you . . . You didn't think I'd forget, did you? It's your birthday, idiot!"

A barefoot Sheila was standing next to Becky's couch, holding out a mug of coffee and grinning.

Becky sat up and put her elbows on her knees. "Sheila, I didn't tell you—Charlotte died. The funeral's Thursday, in Baltimore. But I'm not going to Baltimore; I'm going to Palm Springs to make a stupid speech."

It had been there on top of Becky's mind all night as she slept. And like something you jam into a cupboard just before you close the cupboard door, and that tumbles out as soon as the door is opened again, Charlotte's death tumbled out of Becky.

Sheila looked down at the steaming mug in her hand. "I couldn't remember if you took cream or not— you don't? Smart girl. Past the lips, straight to the hips. Listen, Becky, you were very good to Charlotte. She was happy with you."

Becky winced. "You mean, I paid her well?"

"You want to feel guilty about not going to the funeral? Okay, feel guilty. But you were good to Charlotte while she was *alive*. You appreciated every single thing she did for you, you thought she was wonderful, you made her feel indispensable."

"She was."

"Of course she was! But how many people go through life without the pleasure of ever feeling it? Feeling indispensable? Maybe that's what's bugging you about Seton & Cecil. You've discovered you're not indispensable there. That the place can just go chugging along without you, making pots of money without you. So, tell me about that speech. What will you be talking about?"

Sheila's brisk tone reminded Becky of Sam Samson. No nonsense, get yourself up on that podium.

"Mostly about Angus Seton. How important it is

for a woman to find a good mentor if she wants to be successful."

As Becky dressed, she recited part of the speech for Sheila. The part where she talked about the origin of the word *mentor* and the important role the original Mentor had played in the life of Odysseus.

"Mentor was always there, you know. Whenever Odysseus was in trouble he was there. To guide, to counsel, to rescue."

Sheila knitted her brow. "Are you sure of that, Becky? Sure that it was *always* Mentor? I haven't read *The Odyssey* in years, but I seem to remember that it was the goddess Athene who waded in and helped when Odysseus was in really big trouble. When the shit hit the fan, it was Athene."

Sheila hunted out a paperback copy of *The Odyssey* and gave it to Becky. "Here, it's a birthday present . . . maybe you should read it again before tomorrow. You want to be right about this Mentor guy—don't give him any credit that really belongs to a friendly local goddess."

Later, the cat named Moishe kept trying to climb into Becky's suitcase every time she wanted to close it. She remembered actually petting him about midnight last night, and when he'd purred and rubbed up against her she hadn't felt the least bit afraid. To her mother, dogs had been menacing biting machines, cats couldn't wait to scratch you, but last night Becky Gagarin, née Gelb, had made friends with a cat.

When Becky waved goodbye to Sheila from the car that would take her back to the airport for her flight to Palm Springs, Sheila was holding the white cat in her arms.

And behind Sheila stood Terry.

Sheila, Becky's friend of so many years, who had had the courage to rebuild her life. To write herself a different script, with different players. Becky's friend who had not been thrown into blithering helpless terror when her world collapsed and she had to accept the idea that things can change.

Becky thought, Sheila, Sheila, how come all these years I never knew you were the stronger one?

"We're holding this folder for you, Mrs. Gagarin . . . and this telex . . . and these letters."

The desk clerk in Palm Springs was deferential: Placidia Brubaker Pennysworth-Klein had reserved a *suite* for Mrs. Gagarin.

In the folder Becky found a saucer-sized button with a foot-long ribbon labeled SPEAKER. And a badge that said REBECCA GAGARIN, CREATIVE HEAD, SETON & CECIL. And a glossy special edition of *Ad Hoc*, with her own face smiling from the cover. The caption under the picture read, *Rebecca Gagarin will speak on mentors: how to get one, keep one, use one to succeed. Ms. Gagarin will also present a film made by Angus Seton.*

The telex was from Keith Andrews. ANGUS DE-TESTS CUTS WE MADE IN HIS FILM. ALAS.

There was also a letter from Angus. Not really a letter, a curt note. "I suggested my film might be improved with a little *editing*. You haven't edited it, you have eviscerated it." Underneath, in green crayon, the initials A. S.

She stood waiting for the rush of despair, the conviction of her own utter worthlessness that always arrived after a message like that from Angus.

Unfathomably, it did not come.

The other letter, also a note, was from Kimberly, Becky's new secretary. "You have to give a deposition for that class-action suit. Next week." Nothing about which day next week, where, what she would have to do to prepare. Becky missed Eileen.

The suite was saturated with flowers. Vases and vases of flowers, all from Loren Odell. She found a note in the largest vase, an overdose of orchids:

> *Candida, I would have liked to come and welcome you to California personally, but I have a meeting scheduled for today that I just can't cancel. Much love, Marchbanks.*

She asked herself, what did she expect? Just because an old flame was in the neighborhood, was the man supposed to drop everything and roll out the red carpet?

To stifle the disappointment she felt, she decided to go out to her private patio and rehearse her speech one last time.

The patio was not so private after all. The hedge running along one side of it merely divided it from someone else's. She was only two sentences into her speech when a surprised voice said, "Becky? Becky Gagarin?"

Around the hedge came her neighbor, flushed with sun, carrying a drink, wearing tennis whites. But the badge pinned to his shirt proclaimed that this short sunburned man, lips shining with Chapstick, feet shoved into old beach thongs, was a person of *stature*. The badge announced that you were looking at HORATIO HAMLIN, PRESIDENT, SETON & CECIL.

"Just get in?" Hamlin asked, zeroing in on the patio's most comfortable chair. "I've been here since yesterday. Had some news that made an early arrival seem worthwhile. D'you know Passport is loose? Passport, the credit card? Both their chairman and their CEO are here now, to take in the convention and maybe some sun. So I decided that's what Horatio Hamlin needed too, a little convention and a little sun . . .

Played tennis with them this morning. The chairman *and* the CEO."

"Did you make sure to lose?"

"You're smarter than that, Becky. I *won*. Both times. But I made them sweat first, so they respected my winning. Got a little extra surprise cooked up for them tomorrow. Big surprise, really."

"What is it?"

"Ah, if I told you, it wouldn't be a surprise any more, now would it?" He pulled another chair over for his feet, sipped his drink (his lips leaving a Chapstick rim around the glass), and said comfortably, "So, how are you getting on these days? Having fun?"

"Not exactly."

A silence fell between them as they sat opposite one another with their drinks, on an expensive patio in the expensive California sun. Horatio Hamlin, a man of fifty. Rebecca Gagarin, as of today, a woman of fifty.

The man lolled in his chair, eyes half-shut. Hamlin never hesitated to say how much he *liked* being fifty. At fifty, a man was in his glorious prime.

But a woman of fifty? Becky thought of all the things everyone knows about women of fifty. At fifty, women begin to smell of age. Their voices begin to thin, like their hair. They begin to walk in brief timid steps, they begin to shrink, physically shrink. They can only be expected to perform in smaller ways, diminished capacities. Those were the things everyone *knew* happened to women at two score years and ten.

Except that Rebecca Gagarin was no longer buying any of that.

What was it that Sheila had said, that Becky hadn't made any really important decisions since she went to work at Seton & Cecil? Well, she had not expected to resign wearing shorts and with a drink in her hand. She had not expected to resign at all, but now she knew that it was the only decision, the right decision. "What date did you have in mind, Ham?"

"Date? What are you talking about? I don't understand you."

Executives at the level Rebecca Gagarin had reached have intricate discussions with lawyers and money managers before they leave a job. They spend months arranging for fat severance pay, fancy consultancies. But Rebecca Gagarin had never thought of Seton & Cecil as a job. It had always been her fatherland, her motherland, her anchorage, her safe harbor. She could not wait for lawyers; the only way to leave was without looking back, and without delay.

In the distance, she could hear the Beatles singing mournfully about Eleanor Rigby: "She is le-e-eaving home . . ." But she could also hear brave trumpets blowing, and angry drums sounding.

"I was asking what date you've got planned for Gagarin to go . . . and someone else to take over. Because I'm going to make things easy for you, Ham. I'm resigning."

According to business etiquette, this was Horatio Hamlin's cue, even if he had considered Ms. Gagarin's contributions trivial, to tell her how sorely she would be missed, the enormous hole her departure would leave in the ranks of management . . .

Hamlin didn't pick up his cue. He scrutinized his drink, and when he finally looked up all he said was, "Well, Becky, you had a nice run for your money, didn't you? Twenty-seven years. That's one for the record books. And it must feel good, being a gal and finishing at the top of the ladder. But the fact is that the needs of the agency have changed. Perhaps if you had asked my advice now and then . . . but you've always insisted on going it alone. Doing everything your own way."

Becky laughed. "And as good creative heads go, she went."

But she had already ceased to exist for Hamlin. She was a problem he had once had but had managed to dispose of. "So, what will you be doing next? Get another job? Open your own agency?"

"I haven't thought about the future yet."

"Yeah, after all, a gal of fifty . . . maybe it's time you got out of the rat race, just took it easy." And he launched into a nostalgic recollection of his own arrival at Seton & Cecil, where Rebecca Gagarin was already a legendary figure, the only woman allowed into the important meetings . . . But Gagarin disappeared from the monologue fast, and soon it was all Hamlin. The accounts Hamlin had captured for the agency. The clients who would not make a move without consulting him. The magnificent job he was doing of leading Seton & Cecil into the Age of Information. He said that while the old days might have been fun, and while he was having difficulties making Angus see the necessity of change, a thrilling New Age was at hand. The Hamlin Era.

Palm Springs is desert country. The sun doesn't descend over the horizon, it plummets. And then almost immediately it becomes cold. Even Hamlin—healthy, tireless, sailing, skiing, spelunking Hamlin—shivered and announced it was time for him to go inside and dress for dinner.

He was at the hedge between their patios when he paused. "Look, when you give your little speech to-morrow, please don't mention your retirement. I wouldn't want it to get out before we've decided how we're going to replace you."

Her voice was steady. "Oh, I'll bet you've already decided. A long time ago."

He looked surprised, then nodded. "Right as usual, Becky. I guess we'll just forget all about that quadrumvirate stuff when you leave. Too complicated, and half the clients can't pronounce it anyway. Better to consolidate power and have one man run the creative show."

"Victor Cameron?"

It was really dark now. She could not see the grin on Hamlin's face, but she heard it in his voice. "Great guy, Vic. We all think he'll do a bang-up job."

Rebecca Gagarin startled Horatio Hamlin again. She said, "I *know* he will."

Inside her fancy suite, she took out the folder she'd been handed when she had arrived and reviewed her cards of identity. The glossy magazine with her photograph on the cover. The badge with her name, and underneath, like a reason for being, SETON & CECIL. She spread it all out on the desk. Her heraldry. Who would she be without all this? Would she be anyone? Would she even exist any more?

Knock Knock.

Who's there?

Becky.

Becky who???

Then she realized it had been a real knock.

13

Cradling a magnum of Moët in his arms, Loren Odell leaned against the doorjamb and grinned down at her.

"The flowers were in your honor, but the champagne is in mine! They're only this far from signing!" He put the magnum down and placed his thumb and index finger an eighth of an inch apart. "Becky, I am inviting you to get plastered with Loren Odell . . . of Odell/Communicorp!"

He did not have to explain what Communicorp was. Who in advertising did not know? The London-headquartered, global communications cartel, Communicorp owned advertising agencies, publishing companies, sales promotion outfits, a television network, direct mail firms, research firms. Communicorp had translators, speech writers, songwriters, screenwriters, joke writers on its payroll. Already the largest advertising enterprise in the world, Communicorp had vowed to make its presence felt in every conceivable branch of human communication. What Horatio Hamlin dreamed in his most ambitious dreams of making Seton & Cecil become, the intergalactic agency of the future, Communicorp already *was*.

And now, Loren exulted to Becky, Communicorp

was heading into film production. Which of course had
led them directly to Loren Odell!

He splashed Moët into two glasses. "I nearly had
the whole thing buttoned up today. They had their pens
out and uncapped . . . only there was this one old geezer
who kept worrying about my 'depth of management.'
Kept on cross-examining me about what would happen
if I got hit by a taxi. Me, who was trained by the sainted
Margaret Odell herself never to step off a curb until
the light turned green! The old fart wants me to show
him a list of people I can bring in 'to insure management
continuity' before they'll actually sign."

Loren puffed out his cheeks to look obese. He
sucked on a phantom cigar. He *became* the dull-witted
fool who had dared to get in the way of Loren Odell's
dreams.

"You don't know what this will mean to me, Becky.
Ever since Odell & Comrades started, I've had to worry
about money. Oh, I painted over the problem pretty
well, with suites at the Carlysle and bluster like that,
but even while we were becoming the production house
everyone in America wanted, it was always a hassle.
No matter how many awards I won, no matter how
much I charged—and I charged plenty—there was
never quite enough money. But with Communicorp behind me I'll be able to do all the things I ever wanted
to do. They've got de-e-ep pockets. Maybe I won't stay
in just production. Maybe I'll get them to back me in
a full-service agency, show the big enchiladas how it
should be done . . ."

"Loren, I've got some news too." She tried to
sound casual. "I quit my job today."

"You what? I don't believe it!"

Loren put his hands on Becky's shoulders and
squinted down at her. "Rebecca Gagarin, you *love* that
job."

"Oh, it was okay for a while, twenty-seven years or so, give or take a decade . . ."

"Seton & Cecil won't *let* you leave. They couldn't. Do you know why I left there myself? I was dying of jealousy. Of you! I knew I'd never be half as good a copywriter as you were. They'd be insane to let you get away, everybody keeps saying how hard advertising is, but you made it all seem so easy . . ."

"They have to say it's hard, how else are they going to justify those salaries? Listen, Loren, in three weeks if somebody calls and asks for me, the telephone operators won't even remember that a Rebecca Gagarin once worked there . . . Seton & Cecil has been hell for me lately. It's past time I got out."

The words were hardly out of her mouth when Loren pulled her into a hug. His hands cupped her face, and the hug became a kiss. It was not a nostalgic kiss. It had nothing to do with old friends.

Twelve Mississippis slid by before he said, "Do you remember our first time? That working lunch, my apartment?"

Her face was pleasantly squashed against his chest. She let her eyes close. "Sure, I remember. I was so nervous about being there alone with you that when you opened a bottle of wine I got drunk on one glass. I guess I thought if I was drunk, whatever happened wouldn't be my decision, it would be a case of your having taken advantage of me."

"Damn right, I took advantage of you. I was daring myself to do it the day you interviewed me. Sitting there so in control behind your desk, asking stuffy questions about college achievements and future goals. I wondered then what it would be like to throw you down on that desk and fuck you right there . . . hey, what am I remembering about *peaches*, ripe peaches, peaches dripping with juice . . . ?"

She blushed, remembering. Loren laughed and

pushed her hair back from her forehead. "Do you
know, Candida, I am starving for peaches, famished
for peaches right now. I'd like to get Room Service on
the phone and tell them to send us at least a bushel
. . . No, we don't want them walking in on us in the
middle of what is about to happen, do we?"

About to happen? It couldn't happen. The affair
of Gagarin and Odell, Candida and Marchbanks, Sep-
tember and May, was over. Finished. History.

Except that he was holding her so closely, right
now.

He was making her feel so unexpectedly sensual.
Now. Loren was here with her, now. Alex was not here.
Alex was busy with a ravishing young Zoe-girl, Alex
was probably with the girl right this minute. Alex had
said he was going to leave her; so she ordered them to
get out of her thoughts, *now*. Alex and Zoe both.

When Loren Odell began to steer Rebecca Gagarin
toward one of the bedrooms, she didn't just let herself
be steered. On her own two feet, she walked with him
there.

She remembered that with Loren Odell lovemaking had
always been lechery, rutting, a wonderful indoor sport,
good dirty fun.

It still was.

It didn't feel as if fifteen years had gone by. It felt
as if they had been doing these things with each other,
to each other, without interruption, for years. Her body
remembered his timing, anticipated whatever he might
want to do. Until he said, "Now, Rebecca. Candida.
Becky. Now, whoever you are!"

Afterwards, he was all contrition. "That will ruin my
reputation, I know I was too quick for you . . ."

She tried to sound as if she had dozens of lovers

she could compare him to: "Don't be silly. On a scale of one to ten I'd give you an eleven."

But he was bending over her again, staring at her while his hands proceeded to explore her slowly, visiting all the places he claimed to have neglected before. He discovered that it was just a hand's span—*his* hand, which he claimed was the only hand that really belonged on her—from her pubic mound to her belly button. He insisted that her breasts were not at all alike. One looked a good deal more wanton than the other. "Open your eyes. Look at me. I like a woman to look at me, when I'm making love to her."

As if she had said it aloud, as if she had voiced her doubts about being able to climax this night, he told her, "Don't be silly. You will. Of course you will."

And she did. Staring up at him, the first time she had ever finished with her eyes open, she *did*.

~~~~~~

When Becky woke the next morning she was alone. Loren Odell, phantom lover, was gone. Had he even been there, or had she dreamed the whole thing?

But on the coffee table in the living room there was a magnum of Moët, most of it left. Becky's mother said, "A waste of money. Such a big bottle, for two people?"

"And now we are privileged to hear from the first woman who . . . the only woman that . . ." The applause came surging toward her. Clap clap clap.

Rebecca Gagarin concentrated on standing straight and establishing eye contact.

The first eyes she contacted belonged to Horatio Hamlin. There he was, in the middle of the first row, perfectly costumed for listening to speeches in a resort hotel. Dark glasses. Chino pants. Tasseled loafers. Knit shirt. No alligator on the pocket, that was last year.

You would never catch Hamlin unaware of the correct uniform of the day.

Not leaning on the podium, sweeping the audience with her eyes, Becky said, "I always wanted to *be* Angus Seton, when I grew up. The closest I've come to that is standing in for him today. I'm sure everybody here knows the Seton legend . . . the fair-haired young Virginian who appeared magically in New York one day and became so successful that advertising had never been the same again . . ."

It was an intent audience. The woman who was talking had been with Angus Seton from Seton's start, and Seton was a man who had built an agency from scratch. A global agency, with dozens of offices and thousands of clients, that people said was the best advertising agency there had ever been. If they listened carefully, some of the magic Angus Seton had used to accomplish his miracle might rub off on them . . .

"What was it like for a junior copywriter, straight out of a retail store, to find herself working for Angus Seton?

"Well, I remember that all through my first year at the agency, whenever I showed him any of my copy, my nose would start running. A terrible handicap, since at the time I was trying hard to look upscale and sophisticated. More Brearley than Bronx. After a year or two I must have gotten more confident because that problem disappeared. What replaced it was the exhilaration of working alongside someone who reached for the stars in everything he did and insisted that you do the same. Who gave you yardsticks a mile long by which to measure your work . . ."

Becky talked about Seton for almost an hour, and the audience inhaled every word. The Seton legend always made good listening.

She remembered to take her glasses off again three minutes before she would finish, and to pause an extra beat before the last sentence. She closed the loose-leaf binder that had held her speech. All that was left now was giving the cue for Seton's film.

Except that something strange was happening. She was suddenly *outside* the woman on the platform. Above the people in this room. Removed from it all.

"My subject today was mentors, and so I've talked a lot about Angus Seton. But he wasn't the first mentor in my life. My first mentor never had any formal education. He said all education can do is teach you how to find things out for yourself. My first mentor taught me how to use dictionaries, encyclopedias, maps, the card index in the public library. He took me to every museum in the city of New York and taught me how to look at pictures. He taught me to *think* about the words I used, to ask myself always—is there a sharper word? A more accurate word? He was my master of the words, my lord of the colors. I was very lucky; my first mentor also happened to be my father.

"When I started to put together what I wanted to say here today, I remembered my father's lessons and headed for the dictionary to look up *mentor*. The dictionary reminded me that Mentor was, in Greek mythology, the man who had advised and guided Odysseus. Mentor, a wise, loyal advisor, a teacher, a coach. *Men*-tor, accent on the first syllable. I stared at that first syllable, men, and thought okay, that makes sense, mentors have always been men. Even for women, men have always been the models for ambition, for achievement, for living the kind of life that others might want to emulate. They had to be. They had the only good jobs.

"In my own life, it was certainly true. I remember everything about my father, but I have to work to remember much about my mother."

The woman on the platform paused and seemed to retreat into herself. The people in the audience glanced at each other uneasily. Sam Samson would have been appalled. Speakers are not supposed to look within themselves. They are supposed to look at the audience.

"I once found an old snapshot of my father and mother. My father's arm is placed shelteringly around my mother's shoulders, and he is smiling into the camera. He looks interested, alert, a man you would ask for advice. My mother's hands are clasped in front of her, she is smiling into the camera too, as she had been instructed to do, but her eyes are frightened. My mother had inherited generations of fear, the fear of Jews in a land that did not want them, the fear of women in a world that disliked needing them, and she passed a lot of this fear onto her daughters.

"But she also passed on courage. Because once, when it looked as if her youngest daughter would not be permitted the luxury of ambition, this timid woman *fought* for her daughter, fiercely, and changed the entire direction of her daughter's life . . .

"This morning I went back to the book where Mentor first appeared, *The Odyssey*, and discovered another woman there. The goddess Athene. Well, a goddess could be anything or anyone she wanted to be. It's one of the perks that go with the job of goddess.

"Sometimes Athene would disguise herself as a misty haze to hide the advancing legions of Odysseus. And sometimes Athene would turn herself into a bird and fly ahead to show Odysseus where to steer his ship.

"And sometimes Athene would decide she felt like *being* Mentor for a while. In fact, most of the time when Odysseus thought that it was good old Mentor advising him, guiding him, it wasn't Mentor at all, it was Athene. It wasn't the classic fairy tale of the little woman standing *behind* her man, Athene *became* Mentor. It was Athene, right there, up front, directing Odysseus in battle, literally calling the shots.

"It's amusing to think of all the young women out there today searching for men to emulate, men to imitate—when the old story tells us that the original Mentor, in Mentor's most heroic moments, was the goddess Athene."

The woman on the platform drew a deep breath and became Becky again. She didn't care how affected it might look: She bent her head and spread her hands in the ancient posture of supplication.

"Help us, Athene. It's hard to be a man, and even harder to be a woman, and we poor mortals need all the help we can get."

There was a puzzled silence, and then—because everyone there was, after all, getting a free California vacation—there was a decent amount of applause.

Then it was time for the treat they had been promised: Angus Seton's film! Becky announced the film and made her way to a seat in the audience. Curtains were drawn against palm trees and tennis courts and sunshine. Here, inside, there was only a big screen and Seton's face filling the screen, filling the room. Even on film he charmed them totally.

And when the lights came up again—*he was there*. Angus Seton. The Real Thing. Smiling wickedly down at the audience. Angus Seton, in the flesh, on the stage.

Now it was not just applause. The audience was on its feet, laughing and shouting, thrilled and surprised. Horatio Hamlin bounced from his seat to join Seton on the platform. Seton hugged Hamlin with one arm and continued to wave at the audience with the other, triumphant prize-winner style, winning-candidate style. These two men, who loathed each other privately, linked themselves publicly now. Because the CEO and the president of Passport Inc. were watching from the audience, and Passport billed many millions internationally. Angus Seton had been summoned here by Horatio Hamlin to charm the Passport decision makers, to seduce them with the flattering thought that Seton had crossed an ocean just to speak to *them*.

Seton descended from the stage to throngs waiting to pump his hand, to be able to say later, "Sure I know Angus Seton, we spent a lot of time together in Palm Springs."

It was a little past eleven in the morning, coffee-break time, but a cocktail atmosphere filled the room.

The crowds were concentrating on Seton. Horatio Hamlin, who had been joined to Seton close as a Siamese twin just a moment before, was jostled aside. So Hamlin made his way toward Becky.

Loudly, he said, "Interesting speech, Becky. You did the agency proud." Then, lower, "I could have sworn I saw you crying when they ran Angus's film."

"You couldn't have. The lights were out."

"Spelunking does wonders for night vision." Hamlin stared across the room at Seton accepting homage. "Yeah, I'm sure I saw tears sneaking down your face while you watched Angus explain how he created heaven and earth and Seton & Cecil. All by himself. With nobody's help."

"I never cry during office hours." But Hamlin was right. She *had* cried, watching the film. Angus Seton never said good-bye to anyone, but today Becky Gagarin had been saying good-bye to him.

Placidia Brubaker Pennysworth-Klein rushed up to Becky to give her a single rose, the year's chic floral gift, much classier than bouquets. "I knew you'd be a terrific speaker, and you *were*! And tonight, at the banquet, you're up there on the dais, right next to Seton."

"I'm afraid I won't be staying for that. I'm catching an afternoon flight."

Placidia was aghast. "Oh, Becky, you *can't!* You'll be missing all the fun. There's an Olympic-size pool! There's the banquet tonight! And don't you want to *mingle*?"

Horatio Hamlin, who was still with them, smiled thinly. "Don't you know that after a speech you're supposed to work the room? Mingle, as Placidia says. You're not supposed to just speak and run, you know. You have to walk around and accept bravos. Do a little business for your agency while people are still admiring you."

He dropped his voice. "Because Seton & Cecil is still your agency. Nothing we discussed last night is public yet. And I have a little proposition for you, an idea I know you'll like. How about we duck over to the coffee shop and discuss it?"

"I really want to make that plane. A personal matter. Family."

Hamlin smirked. "You won't be in such a hurry when I tell you who else is joining us. Only Angus Seton. Interested now?"

~~~~~~~

The coffee shop had a cowboy theme. Branding irons were crossed on the walls, and Muzak played country music.

Angus Seton read the menu aloud.

"Steak and a stack: a pound of beef plus a raft of pancakes. Chili quiche: the only quiche for real men. Dieting without tears: iceberg lettuce smothered in fruit, topped off with low-fat cottage cheese and a maraschino cherry."

Seton closed the menu and looked reproachfully at Hamlin for having brought him to this place. He announced that all he could see on the menu that he remotely wanted was the rice pudding. He asked the waitress—a buxom woman in a ten-gallon hat and boots—if she could arrange to have the raisins removed. He liked rice pudding, but not when a lot of wrinkled black raisins had made their way into it. *Baked* raisins, the worst kind. The waitress, recognizing class, promised to speak to the chef.

Horatio Hamlin turned to Becky Gagarin. "What would you like with your coffee, Becky? Toast? A muffin? A croissant? Don't say you don't want anything, because I happen to have a piece of cake for you. If you're unhappy with the way things are for you now at the agency, I've got a nice alternative in mind . . ."

Grinning, he produced the alternative. "How would you like to *run an office* for Seton & Cecil? Not just be creative head, run the whole damn place. Have final say on everything: media, research, account handling, the whole ball of wax!"

Becky swiveled to look at Seton. The waitress had been successful with the chef, the raisins were gone, but Seton was not eating, only looking suspiciously down at his pudding. She turned back to Hamlin—"Run an office? Which office?"

"A new one. One you'd start yourself. You'll staff it yourself, hire the people you want . . ."

"A new office? Where?"

"Where? Winosha, of course! Think about it. Shaw dotes on you, the Eve account spends thirty million a year. That one account could be the nucleus of a very profitable little shop. Stop laughing, Becky, I'm serious about this."

"Ham, there are five bowling alleys in Winosha and not a single bookstore. Winosha has one movie house, *one*, which rotates porno flicks with karate flicks. And it snows ten months of the year. The lakes freeze over. People die of hypothermia there. Ham, I can't imagine myself in Winosha."

Angus ate a tiny spoonful of pudding.

Hamlin said, "You only saw it in the winter, Becky. Those lakes that freeze in the winter, they're beautiful in summer. People sunbathe around them. And if you got bored without bookstores, you could always count your money. We could make some interesting financial arrangements for you, Becky. A quarter of your office's profits, how does that sound? Becky, you could be *rich*."

The word reverberated against the tiled walls of the coffee shop. *Rich, rich, rich.*

Hamlin's eyes remained riveted on Becky's face. "Okay, a *third* of the profits."

Then, realizing that it was never safe to assume these creative types understood anything about numbers, he explained patiently, "A third is *bigger* than a quarter, Rebecca. Plus—your name on the door. Seton & Gagarin, Inc. Believe me, Becky, we have your best interests at heart. We want to keep you where you'd still be one of the family. In the club. On the team."

There was something wrong with all this. What could have happened between last night and this morning, to make Horatio Hamlin so concerned about Becky Gagarin's sense of belonging?

Suddenly she knew what had happened.

"Ham, by any chance did the research results on Eve come in today? Did you happen to get a phone call from New York saying what they were?"

"Well, yes, they did. And I think you'll like them. Two campaigns did spectacularly well. They both went through the roof on recall, purchase intent, name registration, everything. Your campaign and that little black girl's . . . what's her name again?"

"*Little?* Gandhi Hendricks is six feet tall."

Horatio Hamlin sighed. "Gandhi, right. What peculiar names those people give their children. Anyway, your campaign and *Gandhi's* came in neck and neck. They were so close that it's really a judgment call. Rae Ashley's jingle wasn't even in the running. And your favorite client, Stu Shaw, says that if it comes down to judgment he's never gone wrong betting on Gagarin . . ."

Becky wondered why she kept stirring her coffee. There was no cream in it, or sugar.

"Here's something else you'll enjoy. Remember that toy you were so down on? You were right about that too. There *were* picket lines around the factory as soon as that doll, I seem to be having trouble with names today . . ."

"Radiant Ruthie. The World's First Pregnant Doll."

"She wasn't even in the stores yet, and the picket lines were out." Horatio grinned and raised his coffee cup in a mock salute. "It must be boring to *always* be right. Anyway, your friend Shaw phoned this morning to say how much he enjoyed seeing you again at the meeting in Winosha, and that he wants to see a lot *more* of you. Listen, Rebecca Gagarin, president, Seton & Gagarin Incorporated! You can't let a major opportunity like this pass you by."

"Would you folks like your cups topped off?" The cowgirl was back at their table. These advertising people were always splendid tippers.

Becky seized the interruption to stand. "I have to get back to my room to pack."

Angus Seton said, "Told you it wouldn't work, Hamlin."

He pushed his pudding dish away. "Couldn't eat that stuff. I could taste where those disgusting raisins *had been*. Horrible raisin *ghosts*. Please sit down, Becky. First, I want to apologize for being so crotchety about the way you edited my film. When I saw it again today I realized that you really had improved it. You tightened it up beautifully. People have been badgering me for prints all morning."

From sheer reflex, she asked obediently, "Do you want me to order copies for them?"

He laughed. "Certainly not. We'll get a lot of mileage out of that film at new business meetings. Why should we let other shops get their paws on it? And second, I can't say I blame you for not wanting to live in Winosha. Beastly place. But I promised Hamlin he could try to see if he could lure you there. Now here's what *I* think you should do, my dear. You were kind enough to call me your mentor in your speech this morning, here's what your mentor advises."

"The last time we spoke, you said I should soldier on until retirement."

Angus laughed. The rich, deep, infectious Seton laugh she had worshipped for years. "Did I really say that? What a dreadful thing to tell a *woman*. What I should have said was you will never be as happy anywhere else as you have been at Seton & Cecil. Forget Winosha. Stay in the New York office. Carve out a group of accounts for yourself, whichever accounts you want to work on, and begin *writing* again."

"And Victor Cameron replaces me as creative head?"

"Becky, when will you learn that *titles don't matter*. Organization charts are just works of fiction! The real power in an advertising agency lies behind a typewriter, not behind a title."

He excluded Hamlin as he leaned forward and confided to Becky, "As a matter of fact, I'm thinking about changing my own title from chairman of the board to copywriter. *That's* how important I think it is."

Becky stood again. "Please forgive me, Angus, I have to pack."

Horatio Hamlin was not surprised that Seton had not been any more successful with Gagarin than he had been. Gagarin was always so difficult. Although this morning the woman was downright impossible. He also stood and looked up into Becky's eyes.

"I'm flying to Tokyo from here. But we'll talk more about the Winosha opportunity next week, when we're

both back in New York, and less hurried. Don't make
any decisions until we talk!"

Loren Odell was outside her door, waiting for her.

Yesterday he had been ebullient, almost manic.
Today he was serene, with the smug composure of a
man who has pulled off a major coup, the details of
which he would reveal in his own good time.

As soon as they were inside, he dropped onto one
of the couches and lay there shoes and all, fingers comfortably laced behind his head. Becky's mother whispered warnings about upholstery. It wasn't Becky's
couch, it belonged to the hotel, shouldn't Becky point
that out to her friend?

Loren said, "You were sleeping so sweetly when
I left that I didn't have the heart to wake you. You can
tell me how your speech went later; I can't hold back
my own news one minute longer. Communicorp said
yes this morning! As soon as I told them I had you,
they said *yes*!"

She had been perched next to him on the couch,
ready to hug him in congratulation. Now she sat up
straight.

"What do you mean, you told them you *had* me?"

He seized her wrist and pulled her down again.

"I told them that Rebecca Gagarin was leaving
Seton & Cecil to come and work for *me*. It answered
their only problem, what would happen if Odell got hit
by a taxi? As soon as I told them I had you I was in
like Flynn." He laughed—"Errol Flynn, another of us
sexy Black Irishmen."

"A truck," she said tonelessly. "It's hypothetical
trucks people get hit by in these high-level staffing discussions, not hypothetical taxis. Loren, we never discussed my coming to work for you."

"You want to discuss it? Okay, let's discuss it. Pay
attention, I am about to explain why it will be a dandy

thing for you to do this. Dandy for me, dandy for you, dandy for the randy two of us . . . I told you one of my plans was to expand out of production into a full-service agency, and guess who's going to be my creative head? Won't you adore being in California with March-banks? Working in the office next to him, being near him all day long, taking lovely long lunch hours with him, who knows, some days I may even allow you time to eat . . ."

She got up from the couch and crossed the room to huddle in a chair against the wall.

"Loren, last night—why did you get sexy as soon as I said I was leaving Seton & Cecil? Was that passion, or was it recruitment?"

He crossed the room too and dropped down next to her chair. He squatted there in the cowboy style she'd seen him adopt that time on location. A shaft of sunlight came through the window and targeted his face. In the clear midday light she saw only firmness in his chin, no flab yet, no jowls. And his hair was still thick and black, only a tentative dash of gray at the temples. His eyes glittered with the exhilaration of everything that was happening to him now: Soon he would not just be Odell of a small production house, soon he would be part of the biggest advertising enterprise in the world, Loren Odell of Odell/Communicorp!

He jiggled on his heels, smiling up at Becky. "Well, you recruited me once, and I enjoyed working for you. Think how much more fun it will be when we're part-ners. You'll adore it. You will revel in it. I'll check you every morning to make sure that you do. Listen, Becky, hasn't it ever occurred to you that all these years I've been more than a little in love with you?"

"It didn't. And you weren't."

"Becky knows it all," he teased. "My girl, you don't know *nothin'*. Seton & Cecil, for instance, is over.

You burned that bridge. Time to move on to the next thing."

"You?"

"Us. We'll make an unbeatable team."

"It isn't necessarily over. Hamlin wants me to stay."

But when she told him about Hamlin's offer of the agency in Winosha, with a third of the profits and her name on the door, he sneered.

"You know what that's about, don't you? To keep you from taking another job in another agency, somewhere the Winosha client might want to follow. And remember, little shops have to grow, or they go under. And being part of Seton & Cecil, how much could you grow? Most of the accounts you wanted would be in conflict with something Seton & Cecil already had. And after a few years parked out in Winosha, who'd remember you exist? Come with me, Becky. Odell & Gagarin, the Irishman and the Jew, we'll have all the ethnic bases covered, with Communicorp behind us we'll have all the money we need . . ."

He kissed her then. When the kiss finished, it was because Loren had decided it was time to talk money.

"That salary you've been getting is an insult. If you'd kept an eye on the market, you would have known you could command twice that. Plus the usual incentive bonuses, of course." On the word "bonuses" he traced her lips with a finger. "And oh yes, in L. A. you'll need a car. I'd recommend a Jaguar, I've been really happy with my own Jag."

He touched quickly on stock options and then began leading her back to the couch. Toward what she supposed was the ultimate in executive perks.

When Becky told Loren Odell that she didn't have time in her schedule this afternoon for another session of lovemaking, he looked confused. He was directing this script; he did not expect her to start editing it.

Nevertheless he kissed her once more, a thoroughly Odell kiss, as if he were trying to imprint himself on her memory with his lips.

"They all say you think like a man, but I can tell you—you do everything else like a woman. I'll have my lawyer call your lawyer. We'll let them work out the details."

She was closing her suitcase when the phone rang.

She kept repeating, "Hello, hello, who *is* this?" but no one answered. She was about to hang up when a girl's voice asked, "Is Alex Ga-ga-gagarin there?"

"No, this is his wife, can I help you?"

"Are you sh-sh-sure he isn't there?"

"Yes, I'm sure."

The girl on the phone began to cry. She didn't say anything, all Becky heard was weeping. And even that grew faint as—Becky supposed—the girl began to put the phone down.

"Wait a minute! Who is this? Come on, who's calling?"

The sobs sounded louder now, whoever it was must have lifted the phone again. "It doesn't ma-ma-matter."

"Of course it matters! You can't call somebody and start crying and then say it doesn't *matter*." And suddenly Becky knew who was on the other end of this phone. "Zoe? This is Zoe, isn't it?"

No answer. More sobbing. Many people stumble over the name Gagarin, but Becky remembered Zoe's controlled stammer that night she had heard her speak in the basement of the Catholic church. Only the stammer was not controlled now. Was she drunk? Was this drunken weeping? Alex had said this was a girl who attempted *suicide* when she drank . . .

Becky tried to keep her voice calm, steady, serene, and in this therapeutic tone she asked, "Zoe, where are you calling from?"

A tiny giggle surfaced. "From your apartment. I'm in your k-k-kitchen. Only nobody's home."

Calmly, steadily, therapeutically, Becky asked, "Nobody's home? Then how did you get in, Zoe?"

Another giggle. "Alex gave me a key. Only, Alex isn't here. Where is Alex?"

I'll be angry later, Becky thought. I'll be furious about Alex distributing keys to our apartment later. I don't have time for that now. "Okay, Zoe, you're in our kitchen, you're using the wall telephone in the kitchen, but listen, Zoe—Alex must be in Baltimore now, or on the way."

The sobbing recommenced.

"Zoe, *listen*. Alex isn't home, but whatever the problem is, maybe you can talk to me about it? You know me, Zoe, I'm a nice lady, really I am, I have a daughter your age. I'll try to understand, please talk to me?"

And the sobbing did stop. Even the stammer was gone now when she said, "I phoned and I phoned, but Alex never answered, and I had to see him, I had to talk to him, so I came over and let myself in and I saw this number on the pad next to the kitchen phone. It says *Tuesday through Thursday* next to the number, and I thought, that must be where Alex is. Can you put him on now? Please?"

It was a habit that dated back to the days when the children were small. Becky always left a number next to the kitchen phone whenever she went out of town, someplace Charlotte could reach her.

Since they seemed to be having something resembling normal conversation now, she said, "Alex had to go to a funeral, Zoe. In Baltimore."

"A funeral? Who died? Somebody young?"

"No! Not young! It was somebody old, extremely old, very sick, very tired, very *old* . . ."

"I don't think death should be just for old people,"

Zoe remarked, sounding reasonable. She went on to explain how tired you can feel when you are young, how sometimes even young people just want to give up and lie down.

Becky thought of all the things Zoe might be looking at as she talked. The knife rack on the kitchen counter next to the phone. (*Alex had said, once she slashed her wrists.*) The stove with all the little handles that could fill even a large room with gas in minutes. The food processor with its whirling circular blades. And under the sink, there were cans of drain opener and bottles of bleach and ammonia.

Becky had never realized before that a kitchen was a room designed for death.

"Zoe, wouldn't you like to go into our bedroom and lie down for a while? Have a little nap and when you wake up, maybe you'll feel better."

"Alex never showed me the bedroom. Just his studio, where he painted me."

"All right," Becky said, shifting gears from calm-steady-therapeutic to kind-concerned-motherly, "Now you just go out of the kitchen and turn left, our bedroom is at the end of the hall."

Zoe giggled again. "And when he gets home, Alex will find me sound asleep on his own bed, curled up like Goldilocks, all ready and waiting for him."

If that was what kind-concerned-motherly produced, Becky did not like it. "Zoe? Hello, Zoe?" But now there was no answer. The idea about the bedroom might not have been so bright, in the bathroom next to the bedroom there was a medicine chest, and inside the medicine chest there were tranquilizers and sleeping pills and extrastrength everything. (*Alex had said, once she gobbled a handful of pills . . .*)

"Zoe? Zoe?" But at last the bedroom extension was picked up. Zoe had made it down the hall. She had

even turned the radio on. Becky could hear Janis Joplin
in the background. Music to die by.

Zoe said, in the obedient tones of a very *good* little
girl, "I'm lying down now, like you said for me to do.
On the big bed. I'll wait for Alex here." And then the
little girl disappeared and there was terror: "Oh God
let Alex come soon oh God I'm so alone I'm so scared
I need him I need Alex . . ."

"Zoe, you have *me*. Talk to *me*, Zoe. Tell me,
please try to tell me what happened today that's upsetting you so."

"I can't remember what happened today."

There was a pause. "Or yesterday."

Another pause. "But I remember Monday! I went
to a meeting on Monday and Alex was there . . . we
had ice cream after and it was nice . . ."

How nice? Just run-of-the-mill nice, or especially
nice? Becky didn't really want to know exactly *how*
nice, but on the other hand she had to keep Zoe in that
bedroom, safe on the bed. She certainly didn't want
her to start wandering around. In the living room there
was a cherrywood table with bottles of Remy Martin
and Stolichnaya and Beefeater lined up for company.
If Zoe had already had a blackout, and it certainly
sounded as if she had, there was enough on that table
to send her into convulsions.

Becky remembered movies about people being
taken hostage. She remembered how patient negoti-
ating teams had to be, as they talked to the hostage-
takers. Sometimes for hours. To keep them quiet. To
keep them from *doing* anything. But these crisis experts
were trained for emergencies, Becky wasn't. Suppose
she said the wrong thing? She could easily send Zoe
over the edge.

On the other hand, at this point in time, as Dick
Nixon used to say, Becky was all that Zoe had.

On the third hand . . . Becky giggled to herself.

Only Jews had third hands. To keep them aware of the baffling number of options available in any decision.

The phone cradled on her shoulder, Becky slid down to the floor and propped her back against the wall. This could be the start of a very long siege.

During the first hour, Zoe told Becky about Martha and Bud. Her parents. Becky's mother listened too and tsk-tsked. First names? Her mama and papa she calls by their *first* names?

Then Zoe talked about Wally, the brother. Wally had made it. Wally had achieved what Zoe had so far only attempted. Wally had killed himself performing a perfect jackknife off the high board of a swimming pool. The official verdict had been "accident." Even though he had been fully clothed, and the pool had been empty.

Zoe announced, "I have to go pee now."

While the phone was quiet, Becky crossed her fingers and prayed that the girl would not notice the medicine chest in the bathroom.

Becky had stopped looking at her watch. Her plane must have left by now. It didn't matter.

Zoe came back and began telling Becky about her old life-style. What she liked to drink and where and when.

It seemed she had always been very liberal about *what*. If there were no vintage wines or premium liquors around, she had sometimes resorted to cologne or cough syrup . . .

Where and *when* had also offered few restrictions. Life seemed to have been one long happy hour for Zoe. Except that it wasn't happy, and she was so young still that it certainly hadn't been very long. Becky's goal now was just to get the girl through *today*.

Zoe talked about Alex.

What would those kids do if "I mean" and "like" were taken from their vocabularies? They would have no narrative skills left at all. Nevertheless, from what Zoe said, Becky encountered an Alexander Gagarin that she felt she didn't really know—even though she was married to him. All those years Becky had been occupied with scrambling up the Seton & Cecil ladder, Alex had been creating himself anew. Alex had been the father figure, the sponsor, the guide who stood at the door of safety and sobriety for Zoe, and beckoned her over the threshold.

Alex was Zoe's mentor.

Was he her lover, too?

Right now it didn't seem to matter.

It was chilly in the room, and it was beginning to get dark outside.

In the last hour, the pauses on Zoe's end had become longer and more frequent. Now, in New York, there was only silence. Zoe was no longer answering.

Bones aching, Becky staggered to her feet. Maybe Zoe had just fallen asleep. Nevertheless, when she awoke, *someone had to be there with her*. It was not safe for the girl to be alone.

Miserably, Becky tried to think of whom she could summon to stay with Zoe. Someone who could get there right away, someone who had a key . . . Of course! Joseph had a key . . . Wonderful, marvelous, pilot of the elevator and soon-to-be-hero, Joseph had a key!

Fumbling through the pages of her address book, Becky found the number of the house phone in New York—the phone the new tenants had had installed next to the elevator, so guests could be announced in style.

She dialed the number and prayed for Joseph to answer. And he did, on the very first ring.

Becky explained that there seemed to be a slight emergency in the Gagarin apartment. There was a young girl there, a friend of theirs, a girl who might need help. She might be drunk. She would certainly be depressed. Joseph would find her in the master bedroom. Could Joe use his master key to go into their apartment and check on the girl? If it was necessary, would Joe call a hospital—or the police?

Joe was thrilled. Nothing this juicy had happened in the building since the strike. He was at the end of his shift anyway, the night man was already here. He declared himself ready and available to cope with any and all emergencies in apartment 4A. Perhaps he should collect Dr. Halperin in 1A and bring him along? Maybe a doctor would come in handy?

"That's a good idea. Do that, Joe. Only please, do it *fast*."

"Gotcha," he said. A marine, speeding to the shores of Tripoli.

"Call me back!" Becky screamed, but too late— he had already hung up.

When Becky tried the apartment again, the line was busy. Zoe had probably not hung up the phone when she had fallen asleep. *If* she was just asleep.

When Becky called again, ten minutes later, the line was no longer busy. But nobody was answering. Whatever emergency had been happening in apartment 4A had adjourned to another site. Becky saw Zoe being carried though the lobby on a stretcher, blood seeping through bandages on her wrists, paramedics trying to revive her and then giving up in despair, saying if they had only been summoned sooner . . .

When she phoned the third time, the voice that answered was ponderous, deliberate, medical. Dr. Halperin, apartment 1A.

He said that Zoe had been discovered, not in the master bedroom, but curled up with her thumb in her mouth in a room that he thought must belong to Mrs. Gagarin's daughter? One of Miranda's old Barbie dolls lay on the pillow next to her, and a bottle of Stolichnaya was on the floor next to the bed. It was a good thing they hadn't gotten there much later; Dr. Halperin didn't know if the bottle had been full when she started on it, but it was certainly empty now. She might be one sick young lady soon . . . But she was breathing well and her blood pressure was all right. And of course she had youth on her side. Nevertheless, a hospital should look at her . . . there was a certain clinic he'd used before for similar, ah, problems . . . did Mrs. Gagarin happen to know if the young lady had Blue Cross?

~~~~~~

The man in the seat next to her cleared his throat. "Excuse me, you're Rebecca Gagarin, aren't you?"

"Yes, I'm sorry, I don't recall . . . ?"

"No reason you should. I was one of a dozen guys in the room when you pitched our company twelve, fifteen years ago. But I remember *you*, of course. You were the only woman in the room. You . . ."

And as they flew through the night together, he told Becky how much he liked dealing with "creatives." Creatives always told him he wasn't like most clients, he understood them. Becky nodded and smiled and concentrated on helping the pilot fly faster.

". . . so why are you headed east? Business, I suppose?"

When Becky told him she was on her way to a funeral, it was as if she had turned a switch. He said, "Oh, I'm sorry," and burrowed in his briefcase, silently, for the rest of the trip.

Charlotte lay in an open coffin before the altar, her hands folded over the talisman of her Bible. Seeing her so shrunken it was hard to remember how majestic she had always seemed in life.

Becky had last seen her in the hospital, wearing her own wrapper, not one of those hospital gowns which she claimed were indecent.

Cancer takes old people slowly. They get nibbled

at, then gnawed at, then chewed away, inexorably becoming less and less themselves while it is happening.
But Charlotte, in her own chenille wrapper, had always
been Charlotte, right up to the end. There had been
two Bibles on her night table. One, clean and hardly
thumbed, Charlotte said "came with the hospital." The
other was her own, worn with years of reference, the
book she was taking with her now.

Becky stood with other latecomers in the back of
the church.

She saw Alex in a pew in the first row, between
Miranda and Peter.

"If religion was a thing that money could buy," the
sopranos sang . . .

The contraltos warned, "God's gonna trouble the
water . . ."

But the sopranos shot right back with, "The rich
would live and the poor would die!"

The contraltos warned again, "God's gonna trouble the water."

Then it was the whole choir, men and women together: "Wade in the water, wade in the water children,
wade in the water, God's gonna trouble the water!"

Miranda felt Becky's gaze and turned. Her eyes
widened and she stood to wave her mother towards her.
Becky made motions to signal no, there wasn't room
for her. But Miranda waved insistently, yes there was.
There was!

Alex didn't look startled when he saw her. Becky
thought he didn't look particularly glad, either. But he
shifted a little to the left, Peter moved a little to the
right, and Becky was able to squeeze between them.
Miranda reached across Peter's lap to grasp her mother's hand.

A trio of pretty young women offered "Jesus is
alive and well," and then Osceola rose and said she
wanted to sing Charlotte's favorite song.

"My big sister used to sing me to sleep with this, when I was a little tiny baby."

And Osceola sang "His eye is on the sparrow, and I know he watches me." Miranda's mouth opened and closed as she whispered every word along with Osceola. Osceola wasn't the only little tiny baby who had been rocked to sleep with that song.

They were standing on the steps of the church when Osceola found Becky. "I thought maybe you'd like to have this back. Remember, you sent it to Charlotte? At the end it seemed like she was always looking at it."

It was the snapshot of the Gagarin family gathered around a birthday cake, on Miranda's fifth birthday.

~~~~~~

"I have a funny feeling the apartment was broken into while we were gone. I know somebody's been at the liquor."

Alex was always acutely aware of precisely how many bottles there were on the cherrywood table in the living room, and exactly which brands they were. Even though he never touched any of them.

That was when Becky told Alex about the marathon phone call from Zoe, and about Joseph and Dr. Halperin speeding to Zoe's rescue.

Alex listened in silence. When he finally spoke he sounded so miserable that Becky found herself feeling wretched for him. "That clinic Halperin took her to, I've heard a lot about them. They're supposed to be very good. But she'll be scared when she finds herself there. I'd better go see her first thing in the morning."

It had been a four-hour drive back to New York from Baltimore, and Miranda rubbed her eyes and announced that it was too late to go back to her own apartment. Peter said he'd try to get a plane back to California the next day, as early as possible, he didn't want to miss too many classes. So that night both the

Gagarin children slept in the rooms of childhood, while Becky and Alex went off together to the bed they had shared for twenty-five years.

But they arranged themselves on separate sides of the king-size bed, with enough space between them to put another body. Zoe's body, Becky thought.

Becky lay chastely on her side of the bed and thought that tomorrow morning, her husband would rise early to comfort his new love, his true love, who might be frightened when she found herself in strange surroundings.

Black black black was the color of his new love's hair.

14

The note on the kitchen table was printed in pencil and held down by a jar of instant coffee and a coffee mug, which was empty except for a cold inch of brown liquid. *Off to airport. Want to be first on stand-by line. Peter.*

Alex announced he too had to leave immediately; he had to see how Zoe was doing. "She'll be petrified, first week in a rehab," he explained, although Becky hadn't said a word.

Becky turned to Miranda. "And where are *you* rushing to?"

"Me? I'm not rushing anywhere. I want to talk to you about something."

"But why? Why *Hunter*?" And why *social work*?"

Miranda knit her brows. "I guess you could say it started with Jesus. I felt so useful, so absolutely blissful helping him, then suddenly one day I realized it's the kind of work I want to do for the rest of my life. Only, I have to learn how to do it right." In the morning sunlight her eyes looked huge, sanctified, otherworldly.

Becky thought Miranda was confessing she'd joined some born-again religious cult.

"Don't be silly, Ma. You remember Jesus Garcia, the head of our rent-strike committee? I've gotten to know everyone in the building through him . . . Maria on the second floor and Lupe on five, they're single mothers, Jaime on the ground floor, poor guy's got AIDS, and in the apartment next door to me there's this beautiful little autistic boy who screams all the time, I mean *all* the time, his parents can't understand why he's so different from their other five kids . . ."

Becky had made real coffee, and Miranda paused and stared at her mother, her eyes devout over the rim of the cup.

"When I realized I didn't have the slightest idea what I could do to help any of them, any practical steps I could take, I went over to Hunter and persuaded them to let me talk to the dean. She said I was missing some courses but I could make them up and get my MSW in two years. That's a Masters. In social work. Please don't look so horrified, Ma. I know you wanted me to go into advertising or broadcasting or something like that, something that wasn't grubby and unglamorous, something that would pay well and give me a nice office and opportunities for advancement . . ."

Becky repeated: "Social work."

"You're thinking, why would I want to go to Hunter after you shelled out all that dough for Bennington? But I've figured it all out—if I can sign up for morning classes, and keep my job at The Zen Master, and live without spending more than I spend now, I'll be able to manage. And if I can make a difference in the world, even a little tiny crumb of a difference, won't it be worth it?"

Becky said it again. "Social work."

Then she reached across the table and took her daughter's hand.

"I'm sorry if I looked . . . horrified, Miranda. I didn't mean to. It's just that while you were talking, I couldn't help remembering that social work was one of the careers they were always holding out to us as proper goals for women at Hunter. Attainable goals. Noble goals. You could be a teacher! You could be a librarian! You could be a social worker!" Quietly, she added, "I would never even consider them. I couldn't afford to even think of them. I had to do something that would make people stare at me and say, wow, look at her go, look what she's done with her life."

She squeezed Miranda's hand and said, "You said that I wanted you to go out for something that would give you a nice office and opportunities for advancement . . . that's not totally true. I want you to do whatever will make you happy. Sometimes I think why didn't I go into law, like my friend Ida Greenbaum, or become a doctor, do something that would help people . . . only, I am who I am, a Depression child. I had to bring in money to feel good about myself. I suppose it helps to have had money as a kid, to be able to turn your back on it later." She laughed. "And the rat? Has he, has she, shown up again? I'm only asking since it seems you'll be in that apartment for a pretty long time . . ."

"I haven't seen it since we got the cat Jesus suggested." She giggled. "The cat was a terrific investment. It got rid of Seymour too."

Nobody at the office asked Becky if she'd made any decisions yet about her future.

Nobody was there to ask. Angus Seton was supposed to stop in New York before returning to England, but he hadn't turned up yet. And Horatio Hamlin was still in Tokyo.

But Loren Odell phoned constantly. She had never heard a worried Loren before; his voice was high and strained. He refused to listen when Becky kept saying that no, she did not want to come to California and work for him. Or be his partner, as he sometimes enticingly put it.

But when Loren called early on Thursday, his voice

was funny and flirty and charming again. He was Loren again.

"Communicorp decided they don't need another advertising agency. They said they'd been tempted when I first started talking about it, but then they counted and realized they already owned eleven *agencies*. They said what they need now is a *production house*, that's what they'd been shopping for when they first came after me . . . what? Sure, they still want Odell! If Communicorp buys a production house, you can bet it's going to be the best . . . Of course I said yes!"

"But Loren, you told me you wanted to run an *agency*. Show the big enchiladas how it should be done."

"You must be thinking of someone else. That doesn't sound like me. It's *film* that turns me on."

There was something of a pause.

"Hey, listen Rebecca, Becky sweetheart, I don't know how to say this . . ."

"So let me say it for you. Since Communicorp doesn't need an advertising agency, you won't need a creative head. It's all right, Loren. Don't worry, I'll be okay."

He was still making relieved little noises when she said good-bye gently and put down the phone. In the background there was the welcome sound of a door being closed. She was grateful that she had been the one who closed it.

Her calendar said that this was the morning she had to give a deposition at the offices of Greenbaum Feinstein & Giordano, lawyers for the plaintiffs in the class-action suit against Seton & Cecil.

Ida Ellenbogen Greenbaum liked her life.

She liked being Meir Greenbaum's wife. Even though she wasn't crazy about the tendency of strange women to coo over Meir at parties and babble about how much they admired his two best sellers: *Mid-Life Mishegas*, and *How to Be the Perfect Balabusta Without Making Your Whole Family Hate You*.

She was proud of her daughter, the rabbi. Although it had been hard not to feel jealous now that Barbara was living the dream that Ida had only been able to long for, when Ida had been Barbara's age.

But most of all, she adored being the person everyone thought of first when looking for a lawyer to litigate a case that had anything to do with feminism. Although Meir would stroke his clean-shaven chin (Meir was a Reform rabbi) and tell Ida that hers was a classic case of compensation: She was trying to capture for other women what she herself had been denied.

She even liked her office. It was on one of the worst streets of Broadway, near squatting places of the homeless, and prostitutes and their handlers, and teenage boy and girl runaways from Minnesota. Ida said that the location of the office helped her to remember that the world didn't live only in law books, the world lived out there, on the streets. She said a fancy Park Avenue office would have made her feel embalmed.

Now she sat in the somewhat shabby conference room of Greenbaum Feinstein & Giordano, smiling at her old friend Becky Gagarin. Becky Gelb it had been, when they had gone to Hunter together. Ida planted two plump elbows on the conference table, leaned toward her visitor, and let her voice drop to the dramatic near-whisper she often used to underline shocking facts for juries.

"Most people do not realize this, but air-conditioning is the country's leading cause of nervous breakdowns."

"Uh, how so?" Becky asked warily.

Ida leaned back and placed folded hands over her stomach. "Think about it! Used to be you'd work like a bandit nine, ten months of the year. Then you were

entitled to relax, step back, take it easy during the
summer. Everybody was *expected* to slow down then.
Nobody was surprised if you weren't your usual brilliant
self when newspaper photographers were running all
over town frying eggs on sidewalks. But now, what with
air-conditioning everywhere, not just in the movie
houses but in all the offices, all the courtrooms, all the
stores and apartments and maybe soon in the zoos, you
have to keep going at the same crazy pace all year
round. You don't dare slow down *ever*. The human
constitution wasn't meant for it."

Her voice deepened into the accusatory pitch she
saved for closing arguments: "And so I put it to you,
Air-conditioning Is the Number-One Cause of Nervous
Breakdowns!"

Today, Ida wore an orange silk foulard blouse and
an orange silk skirt with broomstick pleats all around.
Plus her favorite brown space shoes, the ones that really
understood her feet. Although she was beginning to
have doubts about today's outfit. Silk foulard was really
too heavy for the record-breaking heat spell they were
having. (It was about this time every morning that Ida
always regretted whatever clothes she had selected for
that day.)

She studied her watch. "So, where is everybody?
This proceeding was supposed to start at ten-thirty."

Becky smiled. "I thought *I* was a workaholic. Relax, they're only a few minutes late. Although I hope
we can start as soon as they get here—I have a meeting
later that I want to be on time for."

It was a mysterious emergency meeting of Seton
& Cecil's international board. It had been called suddenly, just the day before, and there had not been any
word of what the subject would be.

Ida shook her watch and scowled at it. "Stopped!
It's supposed to wind itself automatically whenever you

move. Could it be that I don't move enough? Well, let's *use* the time. I owe you a big apology, Becky.

"Remember that day I came to look at your apartment? With the realtor, Mrs. Schwartz? I must have seemed horribly rude, running away like that without a decent good-bye. Only, I was absolutely flabbergasted when I found out where you work! Here I am representing a bunch of women who are suing Seton & Cecil, and it turns out you're part of Seton & Cecil management! Could my offering to buy your apartment be construed as a bribe to a witness? All I could think of doing was to get out of your place fast, before I wound up prejudicing the whole case.

"Anyway, Lou Feinstein and Howie Giordano—my partners?—say I have nothing to worry about. They say the purchase was already in progress before we found ourselves on opposite sides of the table here . . ."

She skidded to a halt and asked Becky searchingly, "The purchase *is* in progress, isn't it? I really want your place for Barbara, Becky. It will be perfect for her."

Becky didn't have to answer. Dropping briefcases, shedding jackets, wiping brows, the lawyers for Seton & Cecil wilted in. They were Barton (Bart) Depeu, Schuyler (Sky) Carruthers, and Patricia (Tish) Hempstead. The new arrivals represented a prestigious firm that ordinarily did not get involved in class-action suits. They looked surprised at finding themselves in a run-down-looking office on a seedy Broadway block, facing a vast matron in orange silk, who improbably enough had a formidable reputation for exactly this kind of litigation.

Bart Depeu settled into the seat next to Becky. "We stopped by for you, but they said you'd already left."

He kept the smile on his face, but his voice dropped to a whisper. "Why'd you come here alone? This is an adversarial proceeding. A lawsuit. Even a deposition is part of the record. Who knows what Greenbaum may have wrung out of you before we got here."

It always amused Ida when even fellow lawyers failed to understand that a whisper is the loudest sound you can make in a crowded room. The whole room always hushes immediately to eavesdrop.

"I didn't wring anything out of her, counselor. And she isn't under oath yet anyway," said Ida, amiably.

"Are you ready for me yet, Ms. Greenbaum?" A woman stood in the doorway, carrying one of those three-legged Rube Goldberg stenographic contraptions.

Ida Ellenbogen Greenbaum nodded. "Now that everyone's managed to get here, it's possible that we can get started. All right, Becky, I mean Ms. Gagarin—it's time for you to be sworn in."

She looked at Becky sympathetically. Old school friend or not, Ida intended to be tough. Becky was a woman, with a top job at Seton & Cecil. She could be the most damaging witness Seton & Cecil could bring against charges of antifemale bias.

The following excerpts were taken from proceedings in the Direct Examination of Rebecca Gagarin by Ida E. Greenbaum, attorney for the plaintiffs in the suit of Schiavone and James et al. versus Seton & Cecil, Inc. Note: These are only excerpts. The actual proceeding was much longer.

Q. Ms. Gagarin, is the name Wanda Schiavone familiar to you?

A. Yes. She was in the media department, then she decided she wanted to be a copywriter. I came in once on a Saturday, and she'd left samples of her work on my desk.

Q. And given your responsibility for staffing

the creative department of Seton & Cecil, naturally you examined these samples with care?

A. I glanced at them.

Q. *Glanced?* That doesn't sound like the action of a creative head searching for brilliant
writers.

A. It didn't take me long to decide she wasn't
someone I wanted. The first few samples I looked
at were . . . tasteless.

Q. Could it have influenced your opinion of
Ms. Schiavone's talent when you read, in a note
attached to her *tasteless* samples, that she had
worked in the media department of Seton & Cecil
for eleven years? So this applicant was not just a
woman, but most likely a middle-aged woman?

A. I'm a middle-aged woman.

Q. Yet when you find a woman who has given
eleven years of service to the agency, and who is
asking just to be considered for a transfer to an
entry-level junior writer's job, you dismiss her
samples with a glance. All right, let's move on
. . . does the name Lilah James ring any bells?

A. Of course. She's a senior writer at Seton
& Cecil. One of our best.

Q. You consider Ms. James talented?

A. Very. Lilah has a tough mind. Plus unusual understanding of the consumer. She does terrific, consistent, hard-hitting work.

Q. Then why does the hard-hitting Ms. James
remain a writer? Why hasn't she advanced to
group head or whatever it is you call your next
higher echelon?

A. A group head has to understand people.

Q. You just said that Ms. James has unusual
understanding of the consumer.

A. She also has to understand the people she

works for. Sometimes Lilah pays no attention to things that might upset clients.

Q. Would you be more specific about that?

MR. DEPEU, ATTORNEY FOR SETON & CECIL: I think we should go off the record here.

(*There was a twenty-minute discussion off the record. The questioning resumed.*)

Q. You wouldn't accept Wanda Schiavone as a junior writer because you were worried about what you perceived as her lack of talent. And you wouldn't promote Lilah James to group head because you were worried about her, er, life-style. All right then, let's move higher in the creative department. Ms. Gagarin, your present title is creative head?

A. Yes.

Q. Would you kindly examine this organization chart of the Creative Department and point out your name to us?

(*Pause*)

Q. I asked, would you please . . .

A. I've never seen this chart before. It's brand-new to me.

Q. Then would you please read us the name in the box at the top? The box labeled Creative Head?

A. Victor Cameron.

Q. Could you speak a little louder, please.

A. VICTOR CAMERON.

Q. Now Ms. Gagarin, you may not know that in legal jargon, the kind of questioning we are doing here is called a "discovery." And I think we are beginning to discover some interesting things about Seton & Cecil personnel policies. We have discovered that a middle-aged woman, even though she has worked for the agency for eleven years and has had excellent evaluations, has little chance of being *hired* in Seton & Cecil's creative department. And that another middle-aged woman, even though her superior says she is one of the best, and calls her work terrific, has little chance of being *promoted*. And now we discover that a third middle-aged woman, a member of the international board and an executive vice-president, after a long and celebrated career in the agency, can wake up one bright day to find herself fired.

A. Fired? What do you mean?

Q. Fired. Surplused. Displaced. Discharged. Phased out. Excised. Dehired. Terminated. Canned. Laid off. Bounced. I don't think I can make it much clearer than that.

A. I wasn't fired. I resigned.

Q. And why did you resign? Or could it be that they found a way to *force* you out?

A. It wasn't like that at all. I no longer had enough work to do. My advice no longer seemed . . . needed.

Q. But aren't those classic corporate techniques for getting rid of an unwanted executive? The executive is assigned less exalted projects, the executive's advice is no longer needed? Why were these time-honored techniques suddenly used on *you*? The fact that you could no longer be considered young, which—in a female executive at least—seems unforgivable, could that have had anything to do with it?

A. It was more complicated than that . . .

Q. Ms. Gagarin, answer the question. You are still under oath, you know.

A. I know I'm under oath. What I'm trying to say is that sometimes the truth isn't neat and simple. I wasn't fired, I resigned. But I was asked to reconsider.

Q. Be that as it may, you've just seen the latest Seton & Cecil organization chart, from which your own name is omitted. (*Pause*.) As I understand it, Rebecca Gagarin is a well-known figure in the advertising world. I am told the word that has been used about your career is "legendary." And suddenly the table of organization no longer lists your name. You are sure this had nothing to do with your being a woman, a no longer young woman, a woman with grown children . . . ?

A. My children never interfered with my work! In fact, the day we landed our very first large package goods account, Angus Seton called me into his office to say that he wanted to take me to lunch with the client the next day . . . and I was six months pregnant at the time! Well, of course, maybe he hadn't noticed because I was always there just as usual. Always coping, just as usual.

Q. Seton hadn't noticed that you were six months pregnant?

A. Angus Seton never lets little things distract him from whatever problem he might be working on. Well, I suppose that day I wasn't a *little* thing any more. Because he did, suddenly, stare. Then he said that he didn't see how he could introduce someone as pregnant as I was to a brand-new client. (*Laughs*.) As it turned out the client rejected the first campaign the agency submitted, that somebody else had done, a man, so I was called into it anyway. At the last minute. And the client didn't faint when he met me, although I was even bigger then. We shot their first spot the day before my son was born.

~~~~~~

When the questioning was over, Barton (Bart) Depeu
marched with Ida Greenbaum into her office and remained closeted with her there for nearly an hour. Then
a furious-looking Depeu stormed out, collected his
crew, and left. Without saying good-bye to Becky.

Becky knocked on Ida's door. She had to know what
could have changed the warm-hearted Ida she thought
she knew into the nasty inquisitor she had just faced.

"I didn't recognize you in there. You turned into
someone else."

Ida smiled. "First things first. Let me make one
phone call, *then* we can talk. There's this terrific little
blintz place around the corner that delivers. Don't say
you're not hungry, you haven't tasted their blintzes.
Cheese blintzes, Becky, the dairy food of the gods. And
these are so light they almost float . . . okay, okay, but
you'll be sorry."

She picked up her phone and placed her luncheon
order tenderly, before turning back to Becky.

"Of course I was someone else! You've just seen
Ida the Advocate in action! Ida Greenbaum, the best
lawyer in the whole U.S. of A. when it comes to feminist
causes. Not Ida Greenbaum, precious wife of Meir,
sweet mother of Barbara, doting grandmother of Seth
and Esther and Leah and Benjamin. That's the trouble
with women, they think they have to be the same adorable person all the time. To everybody! They don't
realize that the kind and gentle ways that work in the
nursery, and in the bedroom, don't necessarily work in
the conference room. The guy who's darling daddy at
home doesn't mind behaving like a shit in the office if
it serves him better. Pardon my English. It's good I
never became a rabbi, not the way I talk. So I was a
shit just now? Well, it worked."

She smiled a tiny smile. "Depeu says he's decided not to call you as a witness for Seton & Cecil."

"*What?*"

Ida had not changed her tone at all, just tacked that last incredible sentence to the rest of what she was saying.

"Listen, Becky, if I were Seton & Cecil's counsel, I wouldn't want you up on that stand either. You should have seen yourself when you were describing the way Seton acted when he happened to notice that you were pregnant. Okay, okay, you couldn't see yourself, so I'll tell you: You had this look of complete *disgust* on your face. You were holding your hands out in a huge circle as if you were describing a pregnant elephant. If you did that in a courtroom, your friend Seton would have come across looking like the worst kind of macho bigot."

She began to make room on her desk for the arrival of lunch, piling books and folders and legal pads into a precarious tower.

"After you did your little act, I was thinking that maybe *I* would subpoena you. Then I decided that no, I can't risk calling someone who's likely to testify that one of my plaintiffs is untalented and practically says her work is garbage . . . And who says that another of my plaintiffs is a lush . . . Okay, okay! So you didn't actually say it until we went off the record. You've changed a lot, Becky. You'd make a rotten witness for anyone now. *Nothing* is neat and simple for you any more. All of a sudden you see too many sides of everything. Anyway, you're well out of it, these feminist suits can be an awful bore, some of them drag on for years. And we don't have the courts on our side any more."

Becky stared at her hands, feeling oddly disappointed. As with any party you haven't been invited to, the class-action suit had suddenly become the glittering event of the year.

"If you think feminist suits are such a bore, how come you specialize in them?"

"How come I specialize in them? How could I do anything else?"

Ida's voice became flat and quiet. "*You* may have made it, my friend. The first woman creative head of a top-ten advertising agency. *I* may have made it. A woman who starts her own little law firm when she can't make partner in a big one. But there are millions of other women out there who need our help.

"Take your typical female college graduate. The rules of the game say she'll have to work twice as hard as the man at the next desk, even to be considered for any decent promotion. And her chances at the really big jobs will be over much, much sooner. Promote a man of fifty to sales manager? Sure, that's a guy who really knows our business! Promote a woman of fifty? Wait a minute, the dame's decrepit! Do you realize what that does to a female's career, if she gets her first promotion years later, and is shoved out of the race years earlier? It's as if every girl baby has ten years lopped off her life before she's even born, we go over the hill that much sooner."

Ida got up and peered down the hall. "They must be delivering by way of Haifa."

She returned to her desk and transferred her gaze back to Becky. "Then there's that last lovely hurdle. The one *you* came up against, my friend. If I seemed a little hard on you, Becky, it's because you're a perfect illustration of the woman who works her head off, does everything that's expected of her and more, things nobody even thought to ask for, does it all brilliantly, and then the way she finds out about the invisible glass ceiling for women is when she bangs her head on it . . ."

Ida's face lit up. "Aah, food, food, be-yoot-iful food!" A delivery boy was at the threshold of her office, one hand dangling a brown paper bag, the other extended for a tip.

Becky watched Ida unfold a paper napkin and tuck it into her neckline, the better to protect the orange silk blouse.

"Ida, you've got it all wrong. My problem wasn't sex, or age. My problem was just that I was unbelievably stupid about office politics."

Ida chortled. "And that has nothing to do with sex? Sorry, Becky, I can't go along with that. One needs teaching in office politics, like any other office skill. Only it's the kind of teaching men don't like to waste on women."

Later, she was to chase Becky down the corridor to the elevator, clutching a small manila envelope. "Shh," she whispered, shoving the envelope into Becky's hand. "Take it quietly. Don't make a fuss. It's a bribe, my friend. A brazen, unashamed bribe. I want you to remember that if you ever, *ever* move, your apartment goes to my Barbara!"

In the manila envelope, carefully wrapped in waxed paper, was a cheese blintz.

"And I only ordered two," Ida said sadly.

You can always find a cab in New York. Except during rush hours. Or when the theaters let out. Or on holidays. Or when it rains or when it snows or when it's too cold or when it's too hot.

Now it was July and there was a record-breaking heat wave, so Becky had to walk twenty blocks through the sweltering city.

When she got to Seton & Cecil's offices, she was panting. She didn't feel like going directly into Conference Room 1. All the directors would be there, or at least those who had arrived in time for this mysterious emergency meeting. First she would catch her breath in the projection booth . . .

When she dropped onto the folding chair in a corner of the darkened cubicle, it was as if she were watching a play. Through the projection-booth window the
conference room was a well-lit stage. There was Angus
Seton, at the head of the table. He had unbuttoned the
top button of his shirt and pulled off his tie. It lay there
on the table next to him, a puddle of rejected green
silk. His elbows were planted on the table and his bowed
head rested on clenched fists. Strangely, he was unshaven. The white stubble on his face looked incongruous against the miraculously still-youthful blonde of
his hair. Becky had never seen him look so discouraged.

Ranged down the table, some of them dizzy with
jet lag, were those directors who had managed to get
to New York in time. More than a few seats were vacant, including the chair at the end of the table opposite
Seton, where Horatio Hamlin should have been.

Seton was talking. "They remind me of nineteenth-
century colonial powers. They think their ability to invade another country gives them the right to invade.
They march in, grab what they want, destroy what they
don't. Substitute 'company' for 'country' and you've got
a picture of the world of business as it is conducted
today. Raids. Forced mergers. Hostile takeovers. Corporate colonialism, that's all it really amounts to."

After a while, Becky pieced together what Seton
was talking about.

At the board meeting in England, Horatio Hamlin
had volunteered to form a committee that would begin
the necessary steps to protect Seton & Cecil against
takeovers. Everyone had breathed more easily when
Hamlin shouldered the responsibility. It had been comforting to know that it would be Hamlin, stern, implacable, ruthless Hamlin at the drawbridge, guarding
their castle against marauders.

The trouble was that Hamlin had not done any of
the things he had promised to do. A few of the directors

claimed that they had just been on the verge of getting in touch with him to ask why nothing seemed to be happening.

Perhaps Horatio Hamlin felt bitter at not being voted CEO at the meeting in England. Or perhaps he was revenging himself for ancient grudges against Angus Seton. In any case, when Hamlin flew to Japan from California, Seton & Cecil *still* did not have its poison pills in place. Nor had it begun buying back its own stock. The agency was an unprotected fortress, naked of defenses against being seized by another company.

There were those on the board who felt that it was not an accident that a Japanese raider had chosen Seton & Cecil as its target. They even suggested that Horatio Hamlin had gone to Japan *to complete arrangements with the raider, arrangements that he had already started*. Because within days of Hamlin's arrival in Tokyo, a trans-Pacific phone call had been placed from the offices of Hiro Motors in Japan to Angus Seton in the United States.

Ichiro Yamaoto, the chairman of Hiro Motors, was not fluent enough in English to deliver the ultimatum himself. So it had been his second-in-command who gave the grim news to Seton. In stilted sentences that were obviously being read, he announced that Hiro Motors had already bought 5 percent of Seton & Cecil's stock and intended to purchase as much of the rest as they could get their hands on until they had control of the company.

And because the American government had done such a clever job of forcing down the value of the dollar, thereby making American real estate and factories and motion-picture companies and retail stores and advertising agencies dirt-cheap for foreign investors, Hiro Motors would be able to offer *double* the current market price of Seton & Cecil's shares to any shareholder willing to sell.

"Mr. Chairman? Angus?"

One of the Canadian directors raised his hand. He was always an optimistic man; more so than usual today.

"Maybe they're just trying to scare us?" he proposed. "Maybe we should offer them a little money, you know, a little greenmail, and then they'll go away quietly? I mean, what could a Japanese automobile company *do* with Seton & Cecil? I could understand them wanting to get their arms around one of those new high-tech outfits, or a chemical plant or an industrial firm, or land, forest land or farmland, but why on earth would they want an *advertising agency*?"

Seton's laugh, usually so warm and charming, a Zeuslike shower of gold, today sounded more like a cackle.

"Tell me please, sir, why do you want to climb Mt. Everest? Because, my child, it is there. Maybe they want to buy us simply because we are *here*. And why should a Japanese automaker buying a U.S. advertising agency be any stranger than half the other lunatic events that have taken place lately? Who would have expected a little accountant who was peddling wire shopping baskets five years ago to scoop up Ogilvy & Mather? Next to Seton & Cecil, the most prestigious agency in the business! Who would think an outfit with a name like Pantry Pride would wind up owning Revlon? Or that some Canadian upstart no one ever heard of, some parvenu who got his start building little ticky-tacky houses, would take over *Bloomingdale's*?"

Seton looked around the table and groaned in frustration. "We can't waste our time worrying about *why* they're doing this. We have to concentrate on what we can do to prevent it. What a time to be short of a quorum."

It was then that Rebecca Gagarin realized she should not be on the outside looking in, hiding in the darkened projection booth. If anyone belonged at the table, inside, fighting for Seton & Cecil, she did. She had done as much—or more!—for the agency as any of the men at the table. Her arrival would deliver a quorum so they could get on with considering steps that might save Seton & Cecil.

~~~~~~

The room filled with smoke. Around seven o'clock, sandwiches and drinks appeared. All the directors stayed on until midnight debating measures of counter-attack, in tones that became increasingly despondent.

~~~~~~

The other directors had left. Except for Rebecca Gagarin, Angus Seton was alone, glumly collecting his papers. He stuffed them into a worn leather briefcase, as his tone switched from bitter to maudlin.

"You know who I remind me of now, Rebecca? Lear. Lear wandering in the storm, threadbare and freezing on a lonely heath, alone, near madness, muttering to himself. 'A poor old man, as full of grief as age; wretched in both!' "

Advertising is theater; the best admen are almost always skilled actors. Even though she knew Seton was playing this scene to the hilt, Becky could not help feeling touched. These last months had taught her how it felt to be evicted from the place you thought was home. She knew that Seton would be a richer man than he already was, if Ichiro Yamaoto bought all his stock and took control of Seton & Cecil. She also knew that the center of Seton's life would be gone.

"I have an idea," she said. It had come to her as the other directors were leaving; it was the reason she had remained behind.

"You do? How wonderful. I can't imagine why I was worried."

She ignored the patronizing words. "What's the

most important asset of any advertising agency? Besides its creative people, I mean? Its *clients*! Who owes us more than our clients? Somebody at this table was talking about white knights a while ago, investors who come in to rescue a company that's in danger of being taken over, without insisting on control of the way the company is run. So why can't we—"

Seton did not allow her to finish the sentence. "You want us to crawl to our *clients*, admit we've gotten ourselves into this mess, and beg them to bail us out? I can see them wanting our opinion on anything after that. Besides, even if they wanted to, they wouldn't be able to. Our most important clients are all *public* companies. They'd have to get approval from their own boards on any major investment. I can't imagine an American board of directors allowing a firm to pay more for us than the Japanese seem enthusiastic to do."

"But they're not! They're not *all* public." Becky heard her own voice, more excited than she had ever heard it. "At least one of our clients never needs board approval for anything, because the person who founded the firm still owns it. And still runs it!"

An hour later, when Angus Seton and Becky Gagarin had finished talking, they had the beginnings of a plan. She remembered the glorious feeling from the old days, when she had been a very young copywriter, working with Seton to build a campaign. They were building something together again. Something thrilling, out of nothing.

The next morning Rebecca Gagarin walked once more through the ebony doors of a triplex apartment on Fifth Avenue.

Angus Seton was with her. And also a young woman Becky had asked to come along with them.

The three went up a curving marble staircase, down a corridor lined with recessed cases of African and oriental art, past many closed doors and one open door—revealing a bedroom that had been turned into a shrine. A man's hairbrushes stood in place on an inlaid ivory and teak chest, a man's slippers were lined up solemnly on the side of the bed, a silken bathrobe was reverently draped on top of a coverlet already turned down for the night.

When the little group arrived at Princess Lyubov's bedroom, they discovered they had missed the morning levée. The Princess was already up, although her immense glass bed, a swirl of pink satin sheets and pink cashmere blankets, had not yet been made. The Princess was not only out of bed, she was already dressed, her long black hair coiled into a bun.

She did not turn to greet her visitors but placed a warning finger to her lips and remained erect on a hard-backed chair, her eyes fixed on the television set that had been installed in a corner of her bedroom.

"Shh! Serena is deciding whether or not she will remain with Cornelius. If she asked me, I would advise her *not* to stay. She will be much better off with Dimitri. When Dimitri returns from that safari, of course. I wish she had worn one of her de la Renta dresses to receive Cornelius, no one does more striking afternoon costumes than dear Oscar . . ."

Becky remembered the time, not terribly long ago, when Princess Lyubov had railed against television and claimed that she did not know how to turn on a set. But she must have gotten the hang of it somehow—could it have happened when Becky had persuaded her to put the Lyubov advertising budget into television, and that media shift had brought Lyubov a staggering 10 percent increase in sales?

But that was not all television had done for the Princess. The black box had opened a new world to her. Elegant men, exquisite women, lavish houses, events so juicy and so intricate that one could ponder them for hours. Now she was particularly concerned about the latest occurrences at Serena's château. The Princess was worried that Serena might not know how deceptive servants in the south of France could be. Serena's year as mistress of the château might have been too heavy a burden for a twenty-year-old girl. Of course, at not much more than twenty, hadn't Natalia Lyubov herself owned a château? And not long after that, the places in New York and Paris and London and Cannes? And what is more, she had bought them with her own money, money she had made herself . . .

It was not until the half hour she spent every day at Château Incroyable was over, and the Princess had had time to digest the latest happenings there, that she turned her attention to her visitors.

"*You*. You, I have not seen for years," she said freezingly to Angus Seton.

And to Rebecca Gagarin, "So, you condescend to call on me again? Or are you here to collect my gratitude? *Eh bien*, I am grateful. Those television commercials you urged on me did work well, after all."

Gratitude isn't all that we're here to collect, Becky thought.

"Ma'am, I don't think you've met a colleague of mine . . . I would like to present Gandhi Hendricks, ma'am."

Afterwards, if you had asked Princess Lyubov to describe the young woman who was introduced to her that day, she would probably have begun with the striking coiffure. Dozens of intricately woven braids sprang in all directions from the girl's scalp. Whenever she moved her head, the little braids would whirl around the fresh young face, while gold and silver beads woven into the braids clicked softly against each other. It reminded Princess Lyubov pleasantly of headdresses she had glimpsed while traveling with the Prince through parts of Africa so many years ago . . .

She probably would not have bothered mentioning that Gandhi Hendricks was black. Natalia Lyubov was a truly color-blind woman, one who never troubled seeing beyond her own interests. She was not interested in this new young woman's skin color, only her sense of fashion, her cleverness, her willingness to work extremely hard for the Princess, if that was what she had been brought here to do . . .

When Becky promised that Gandhi Hendricks—whom Becky described as an unusually talented copywriter—would be coming to assist the Princess every day, early every morning, the way Becky Gagarin used to do, the Princess was pleased. Of course, she was not going to admit that too easily. That was not Natalia Lyubov's style at all.

As if Gandhi were not sitting there next to them, the Princess demanded of Angus Seton: "Is this new one clever? Does she have *ideas*? Can she play a decent game of bridge? It was always a disappointment to me that *this* one . . . ," she poked Becky's shoulder, a surprisingly fierce poke for a woman in her nineties, ". . . pretended that she did not know the game."

"I promise you that Miss, er, Hendricks is clever," Angus Seton swore. "She is a superb copywriter. In fact, she reminds me of Rebecca Gagarin, when Rebecca was young . . ."

(Actually, he had never laid eyes on Gandhi Hendricks before this morning, nor did he understand why Becky Gagarin had insisted on dragging the girl along on this important visit.)

"And she plays *brilliant* bridge," Becky supplied. "She was a Life Master at eighteen! The youngest ever!"

The Princess's eyes glittered. She swiveled and for the first time spoke directly to Gandhi. "You were the youngest? Well, *I* am the oldest. We will see who is better." And pattering back to her bed, plopping into

the nest of pink satin pillows, she scrabbled in the
drawer of a bedside table for a deck of cards.

"Seton here will make a third. I will soon know,
young lady, if you have *any* brains at all."

While Princess Lyubov dealt the cards, Angus Seton brought up the true purpose of their visit.

The Princess had been peering at her cards all through
Seton's speech, and yet she still seemed to be listening
to him. Becky wondered how she could follow a cruel,
intricate game like bridge and at the same time pay
attention to a business proposal.

As soon as Seton finished, she put down her cards
and grumbled, "Of course I will have to review everything you have just told me with my most trusted ad-
visors . . ."

Becky looked at a glass chest of Chinese porcelain
figures across the room. Angus Seton looked at his
cards. They both knew that the only advisor Princess
Lyubov had ever trusted was the Princess, and it was
important that they not catch each other's eyes. Or they
would be unable to keep from laughing.

". . . but who can tell, Seton & Cecil might be as
good an investment as any in these crazy times. I believe
you've never once omitted a dividend? And that building you have your offices in, Seton, it must be under-
valued now, the real estate market has grown so much
since you bought it . . ."

The Princess giggled then and asked whether it
might not be an embarrassing demotion in rank, going
from Princess to knight? (Becky had never heard her
laugh before; the sound was alarming.) Although she
rather liked the idea of being a *white* knight. White had
been the color of the anti-Red forces in Russia, the
Romanov forces. And a century or so before that, white
had been the color of Marie Antoinette's supporters.
Royalist ladies had worn white cockades in their hair,

sometimes mounting the steps of the guillotine with the cockades still in place, so that when their heads bounced into the basket the white ribbons were still waving . . .

The Princess picked up her cards, squinted at them again, and returned to the slightly less gory twentieth century. She said she quite understood that the role of a white knight was behind the scenes, not getting mixed up in the actual direction of a company. Nevertheless, if she agreed to go ahead with Seton's proposal, she did want agreement on one small change in her advertising.

"You know I never interfere in details . . ."

Angus Seton and Rebecca Gagarin were still careful not to look at each other. Nothing took place at Lyubov without the old lady's advice, consent, and constant meddling.

". . . but I *would* like to appear in my own commercials. I think it was a mistake of you to discourage me when first I suggested it."

Becky was about to leap in with Yes! Sure! Of course! It seemed a small enough concession to make to someone who would soon be the agency's major investor—when Gandhi Hendricks spoke for the first time.

"You *should* be in the commercials," Gandhi said. "It's the personal touch the campaign needs. Only I don't think we should put you on *film*. I think we should find the world's best print photographer and have him take the most fabulous still pictures of you. Then we could open every spot with an elegant portrait, to pull the viewers in, and fade into another portrait at the end—leave them with a stunning visual promise. A visual *guarantee* of how much Lyubov products can do for any woman . . ."

The Princess rang a silver bell on her bedside table to order coffee and croissants for herself and her new young friend.

Becky thought—somewhat ruefully, although it was all going even better than she had hoped—she's forgotten all about Seton and me. She's forgotten we're here.

"You'll see, it will work," Gandhi said. "Just slathering her with makeup wouldn't make her look any younger, it would make her look grotesque. And if we depended on soft focus, the viewers would think there was something wrong with their sets and start jumping up and fiddling with dials . . . but with photographs we'll have complete control, we can retouch and retouch until she doesn't look a day over forty. Okay, sixty."

Becky Gagarin and Gandhi Hendricks had had a three-hour celebratory lunch at La Cour, and now they stood together outside Becky's office door. The account men assigned to Lyubov were inside the room, waiting for them. Becky had volunteered her own office because all the conference rooms were booked, and Gandhi felt it was important to have an immediate meeting: "We've got to tell them right away about using the Princess in the advertising—we don't want to give them any chance to start complaining about being left out of decisions."

"You've learned a lot, working for Cameron," Becky said. "Remember what I told you on the plane, about your being Seton & Cecil's youngest creative head someday? You've taken a giant step towards that, this morning."

Gandhi grinned. "I know. And did you notice that I've stopped smoking? Totally. Not just on airplanes. Since my mentor told me it was the only obstacle to my brilliant success . . ."

Becky blushed. She had never thought of herself as Gandhi's mentor.

"C'mon, let's go in . . ." Gandhi was eager, her hand on the doorknob.

"No, you don't need me for this. Oh, listen, don't

forget to have someone check on whether the Princess needs to join the union. I'm not kidding, still pictures or not she'll be on camera, so have it checked."

"You want me to talk to them *alone*?" The girl's brows were raised.

"Yes, alone. You can handle it." But it wasn't until Becky said, "Seton wants to see me, his secretary said it was important" that she went into Becky's office, alone, and sat down. Not behind Becky's desk, but on top of it, swinging her legs.

There was a burst of laughter inside the room. Gandhi had evidently opened the meeting by saying something the young account executives found entertaining.

Becky watched her for a moment. Gandhi was laughing now too. Whatever she did, Gandhi was going to do it with joy. She was not a young Becky Gagarin. She was a new and gutsy kind of woman, one who would allow herself to relish success—because she knew she deserved it. A kind of woman who hadn't been invented yet, when Becky was her age.

It is considered very chic in the classier advertising agencies to have an English voice answer your telephone. Angus Seton, as usual, had gone the other agencies one better. Seton's secretary was English, and *male*.

"Mr. Seton's on the terrace. He must have asked me five times where you were . . ."

Angus Seton wasn't alone on the terrace. Victor Cameron was there too, looking oddly pale and uncertain for Victor. And Wilbur Rank was also there, leaning against the terrace rail, his eyes trailing Seton as Seton paced back and forth.

Seton turned to her. "Becky. You won't believe this. Hamlin's dead!"

At first she thought he was speaking metaphorically. Dead to the agency. Dead as far as our plans go.

Then she saw there was nothing metaphorical about it. Angus meant every word, literally. Horatio Hamlin was *dead*. Deceased, departed, gone.

She understood now why Cameron looked uncertain. Suddenly she found herself feeling uncertain, vulnerable, even a little frightened. Horatio Hamlin's death meant everyone was mortal. If that much energy and ambition, if that kind of ego and raw physical courage could die, then they *all* must die.

"The news came this morning, while you and I were with the Princess. The cable was on my desk when I got back. I would have thought you'd have had to shoot Hamlin with a golden bullet to kill him. Or drive a silver stake through his heart. Which I'm told is pretty much what happened . . . a stake through the heart. He had a full-blown coronary, massive, sudden, the kind type-A villains like our friend Horatio are *supposed* to get. Don't look so shocked, Rebecca. I don't believe in that pious cant about not speaking ill of the dead. Not when they've done so much mischief to us while they were living."

Nevertheless, they all stood in silence for a moment, while Seton stopped pacing and sucked thoughtfully on his pipe.

Fifteen stories below them New Yorkers scurried about. A historic heat wave was suffocating the city, but they were still New Yorkers and they still had things to *do*. To inaudible martial music, a black meter maid strode down the block ticketing overparked autos. An enterprising Korean hawked both sunglasses and umbrellas: Rain was forecast for later in the day, so he had diversified his inventory. A taxi stopped in front of the building and spewed forth a knot of agency people. Becky couldn't make out their faces from up here, but she knew they were agency people. They were carrying the oversize portfolios that are specially made for storyboards, and they were waving their arms and talking about the Very Important Meeting they had just attended. When had she stood with Seton like this before, staring down at little people leading their little lives? In England. On the roof of Cecil House.

Seton sighed. He had given Hamlin his minute of silence; more would have been hypocritical.

Briskly he said, "That was an interesting notion of yours, Rebecca, to talk the Princess into becoming the agency's white knight. I was hoping it would give us extra time to fight for our survival—but it's unbelievable how fast things have been moving. The Japanese insist they are still going to seize control of the agency . . . even with the Princess behind us, even without the help of their pal Hamlin, even if it costs more than they'd originally intended. And all the publicity has already made us a target for other sharks. Communicorp is interested now. And what Communicorp wants, Communicorp generally gets. It looks as if Seton & Cecil may soon be the target of an international bidding war, Communicorp versus the Japanese . . ."

Seton shook his head but oddly enough did not look displeased. Fate had eliminated Hamlin, the man he had mistakenly elevated to second-in-command. He was in complete control of his realm again, and he relished it—even though the barbarians were outside, howling at the gates.

"But first, we have to get the New York office back in order. I don't want to have to worry about it while we're fighting for our very existence. Hamlin's death leaves New York leaderless—I've just talked to Wilbur here about replacing him."

Becky remembered how Angus himself had once described Wilbur Rank. "Such a tedious, wishy-washy little man, always trotting along in Hamlin's shadow." But the tedious, wishy-washy little man was convenient now, and Angus bestowed a radiant Seton smile on him.

"Now, as for the creative department, how about you and Victor running it in tandem?"

Angus Seton beamed at both of them. Although he was not a man who generally liked to touch people, now he slung one arm over Becky's shoulders and draped the other around Cameron's. Cameron stood next to Seton smiling back dutifully—but his eyes were wary. The idea of his not being alone in the box at the top, of working in tandem with anyone, let alone Rebecca Gagarin, must have been a bitter pill to swallow.

Becky said, "Angus, yesterday someone showed me a new table of organization for the agency . . . and I wasn't even on it. Victor was in the box labeled Creative Head. *Only* Victor."

Seton walked to the end of the terrace . . . to think? . . . then wheeled and returned. "I'm sure that was Hamlin's doing. He was so set on exiling you to Winosha, getting the agency structured exactly the way he wanted it before he handed us over to the Japanese . . . But Hamlin is out of the picture now. We can make the boxes on a chart any damn size we want. So we'll just have a whopping big box on top and put you and Victor in it *together*!"

She had once read about a particularly grisly kind of medieval death penalty. You took the condemned, sewed him up into a huge burlap or hemp or somesuch fiber bag along with a live ape, and threw it all—man, ape, and bag—into deep water. It was always immensely entertaining for onlookers. They could enjoy the frantic heaving of the bag as the prisoners inside struggled, ape clawing at the man, man flailing in helpless terror, until the waters rushed in and drowned them both.

The whole scheme was pointed toward disaster. It would be dirty fighting all the way, no holds barred, until one of them, Gagarin or Cameron, would wind up destroying the other. But Seton had to know that.

And right now, *he simply did not care*. He was merely buying time again. He was not worried about what it might do to the two inside the bag.

"Angus, do you remember—last week, in California, I tried to resign? And you asked me to think it over? Well, I just did."

~~~~~~

The four of them had been on the terrace for almost an hour. The air was getting heavier, the clouds hanging low and sullen, refusing to yield a drop of the promised afternoon rain.

Cheerfully, Victor Cameron said, "Where are you going, Becky? Y&R? Burnett? Or have you struck your own little deal with Communicorp?" It was clear that he didn't care where Becky went as long as she *did*. The faster, the better.

Angus Seton said, "Could you be planning to open your own shop, Rebecca? And maybe take that writer you admire so much with you, that girl?"

Wilbur Rank spoke for the first time, actually interrupting Angus Seton. "It isn't a matter of *who* she wants to take with her, it's *what*. She thinks she can take the Lyubov account. And probably Eve too." He glared at Becky. "You may not know there are laws about that sort of thing, Mrs. Gagarin. If you try to steal a dollar's worth of business from S&C, one hundred copper pennies worth, we can and *will* sue."

Seton said, "I am having trouble believing that you would leave us without any plans at all for your future, Rebecca. I've always said you think like a man, you wouldn't do anything as foolish as walk out of here naked. Or are you planning to consult? Half the people who go into consulting don't have the faintest idea what they're doing; you should be a raging success as soon as you hang out your shingle."

There was a crash of lightning, and rain sheeted down on the terrace. Everyone who had been on Seton's terrace dashed inside, into his office. Becky went with them but kept on going. Into Seton's office, then straight out the door.

15

Becky sat on the lumpy couch in Alex's studio and waited for Alex to get home. She'd seen hardly anything of him all week. He'd been in and out constantly, mostly out. The visiting hours in Zoe's clinic must have been spectacularly liberal.

Once Alex had complained to her that she never let him into her life.

Well, today she was going to open the door wide and welcome him in. She would ask him all the questions she should have been asking all along, and had not. Was he selling any more of his work? The babies in the Make-a-Mess Workshop, had he discovered any budding Picassos there? *How long had he been in love with Zoe?* Could Zoe need him as much as Becky did? Did Alex have the slightest idea just how much Becky needed him? That when it came to Alex, Becky might be one of the city's hundred neediest cases?

Outside, summer lightning stabbed the sky. The windows rattled from thrusts of rain. A naked middle-aged woman stood across the studio from Becky, keeping her company. Alex's full-length canvas of Becky Now. Somehow, the picture didn't look as depressing today as it had when Becky first saw it. Nudity was not the best costume for a middle-aged woman, but the woman did have intelligent eyes, and a nice quirky smile. Even her enormous wristwatch looked right somehow. It was the sign of the Workaholic, Becky's sign. It made the portrait look a little comical, and a little rueful; it was Becky Now, seen through the eyes of the person who knew her best.

Then she noticed that the portrait of Zoe, baroque wooden frame and all, was missing.

She stared at the bare rectangle of wall where the painting had hung and tried to think of logical explanations for its disappearance:

The picture had self-destructed. Alex had put so much passion into it that one day it had gone up in a flaming burst of spontaneous combustion . . .

No, the picture had not self-destructed. It was hanging in some gallery now, and the face in the portrait was so luminous that the gallery owner was asking a higher price for it than any of Gagarin's previous work . . .

No. Alex had simply transferred the painting to Zoe's apartment. Because he too would be living there soon. Bingo. Home run. She didn't have to dig further for explanations; she had the answer. She curled up on the ancient couch, shut her eyes, and tried to vanish into sleep. Sleep would fill the gaping space on the wall and the jagged new hole in her heart.

Alex was shaking her shoulder. "You shouldn't sleep in the daytime, you'll screw up your circadian rhythms. Sleep in the daytime, toss all night. I have a surprise for you in the kitchen. I bought you a cake."

She sat up, dazed. It had stopped raining; rays of late afternoon sunlight slanted into the room. "A cake?"

"For your birthday. Mocha between the layers. You've always been a pig about mocha. Plus, chocolate on top."

"My birthday was *last* week."

"I know. But you weren't here *last* week, and I still had a hankering to celebrate it with you."

In the kitchen Alex cut the string of the cake box, the special blue-and-white string you only get from bakeries, then pulled open drawers searching for wherever it was that Charlotte used to keep birthday candles. He found them finally, a box of pink candles and a box of blue, in a bottom drawer that also held a child's battered tinfoil crown.

"Forty-nine, Becky. Where did the years all go?"

Fifty, she nearly corrected him, but thought better of it.

He was putting a pink candle into the center of a chocolate rose when she blurted, "Alex, why did you give Zoe a key to our apartment? You don't go around distributing keys to every passing stranger, do you?"

He arranged plates and forks with scrupulous care. He took a container of milk from the refrigerator and shook it before opening it. Becky always did that too, it was a habit left over from days of glass milk bottles, but he was taking such a long time about it. Frowning, he filled two glasses to a level he seemed to judge exactly right. Finally, he answered.

"Zoe isn't a passing stranger. I used to be her sponsor, you know. I gave her the key to remind her that when she absolutely *had* to have a drink, she could come talk to me instead. And that even if I wasn't home she'd always be able to get in and wait for me."

Becky seized on the important words. "*Used* to be?"

"You have a milk mustache," he told her.

He'd been so calm and funny up to then, speaking in his usual Alex voice, that she was astonished when—right after warning her about the milk mustache and handing her a paper napkin to deal with it—he hunched over and put his head into his hands.

"It was stupid of me, Becky. It was a conceited,

egotistical, arrogant thing for me to do. And dangerous
besides. They *caution* you that it's always best to sponsor someone of your own sex. They *warn* you, men
should sponsor men, women should sponsor women.
But no, oh no, Alex Gagarin didn't have to worry about
nit-picking rules like that, not kind, funny, considerate,
compassionate Alex.

"You asked me once if there was more going on
between Zoe and me than my just being her sponsor.
Well, there wasn't. There wasn't time for anything else.
My idea of being her sponsor was to be her social
worker, her employment advisor, her doctor, her God,
I guess. I filled her up. And her need for me was so
flattering it filled me up, too. And even when I realized
that she was falling in love with me—I knew it was
happening, I wasn't that blind—I didn't have the sense
to end it right away. I thought we'd discuss it reasonably, and I'd talk her out of it, and then we'd go on.
She could go on being my worshipful little Zoe and I'd
go on being . . . her God. A sponsor isn't supposed to
be a God, Becky. A sponsor is a mentor. Someone who
just helps you stay sober, which by itself is a big enough
job. There I was, dealing with a kid with suicidal ten-
dencies, so what did I do? Handed her another problem
she couldn't deal with."

All that jabber about birthday cakes was only a
cover, Becky told herself. The poor guy is miserable,
he's absolutely crushed, and you didn't even realize.
She rushed around the table to kneel at his side, her
hands creeping around his waist as she hung on to him.
"Alex, what are you saying—Zoe didn't kill herself, did
she?"

Almost dazedly (he was deep into his mea culpa
now, not holding a conversation) Alex looked down
and repeated, "Kill herself? No, she didn't kill herself.
But you can't imagine how devastating a slip can be for

an alcoholic. After months of not drinking anything, to make a bottle of vodka disappear in an afternoon!"

He sighed, picked up a fork, and began nibbling on the piece of birthday cake in front of him. Nodding absently—because even when one is wracked with guilt, chocolate and mocha do make a fine combination— he said, "That's a good place Halperin got her into. She's made friends there, friends her own age. She's been talking about moving to New England when she gets out. Once she's located I'll put out feelers in the network and find her another sponsor, a woman this time . . ."

He stopped, put his fork down, and pounded his chest with a closed fist. "There I go again. Alex the Omnipotent is playing God, all over again."

They talked for hours that night.

When Becky told him she was leaving Seton & Cecil, Alex said only, "Praise the Lord."

"Praise the Lord? That's all? Aren't you going to ask me what I'm planning to do? Everyone else has. Angus Seton asked me. Wilbur Rank asked. Victor Cameron asked. I understand they were Horatio Hamlin's dying words: What is Gagarin going to do?"

"So, what are you going to do?"

"I don't know. Give me a second and I'll think of something."

And they both laughed. She realized how long it had been since she had heard that optimistic sound coming from Alex.

"Remember that portrait I did of Zoe? Well, I gave it to her today. As a farewell present. I admitted I wasn't the right sponsor for her, that it was time for her to move on to someone else. She cried a little, then she said the portrait was the best gift she'd ever gotten."

"Of course it was. You're a good painter, Alex."

"What do you mean, good? You're a writer, writ-

ers aren't supposed to settle for anything that pedestrian. Have you thought about brilliant? Powerful?
Penetrating? What about seminal, great word seminal,
have you considered seminal?"

Later, when they were in bed—in the same bed,
in the same room—she said, "Alex, can I tell you what
this last year reminds me of? Remember that summer
we were in France with the children? And the afternoon
we sat outside the maze in the Bois de Boulogne and
watched Peter and Miranda inside?"

The maze had been made of glass, so they had
been able to watch the children trying to find their way
through.

Peter and Miranda had been old enough to solve
the riddle of the labyrinth quickly. But sometimes a
child, especially a really small child, would get lost and
keep retracing the same route, bumping into the same
glass pane over and over. Sometimes you could see one
of the children, lost and frustrated and frightened, burst
into tears. Then a parent or a nursemaid would hurry
in and scoop up the panicked kid and take it outside,
into the sunshine.

"For months now I've felt as if *I* were in that maze,
and I didn't know my way out, and I kept bumping into
the same invisible barrier. And nobody was rushing to
take me out. And then I realized that I was all grown-
up now, that the only person who could get me out of
the muddle I was in was me. Myself. Becky."

Alex didn't answer. When she propped herself on
an elbow to look at him she saw that he was lying on
his side, asleep. She turned on her side too, and arranged herself so that they fit together, her toes turned
up against his heels, her stomach against his buttocks,
her breasts against his back. When she'd fitted all of
Becky onto him, there was still a great deal of Alex left

over. And grown-up as she was, somehow that was comforting.

It is not a good idea to try to go through a revolving door when a cardboard box is thrust out in front of you like some late and peculiar pregnancy, and both your hands are occupied hanging on to the box. And then some Speedy Gonzalez behind Becky pushed the door so fiercely that she was whirled around too fast and spun out into the street and up against the stomach of a man waiting to go in.

It was Loren Odell's stomach.

Of course she dropped the box. Papers, glossy photographs, bizarrely shaped statuettes for assorted prize-winning campaigns, all lay scattered on the sidewalk. She had closed the door on Loren; what was he doing here?

Becky knelt and crammed fugitive papers back into the box. "What are you doing here? If you'd phoned, you'd have found out this is my last day, not the best time to come calling."

"I'm not calling on you, I'm here to see Seton." He squatted opposite her to help. When they'd managed to cram everything back into the box, he teetered on his haunches, slo-o-owly rose (Loren's special patented Gary Cooper rise), and consulted his watch. A Rolex, Becky saw. Not one of your ostentatious twenty-thousand-dollar diamond-and-platinum Rolexes, just a simple everyday gold Rolex, only five or six thousand. Indeed, Loren's whole outfit was casual today. He always wore jeans and a windbreaker on location. It was the first time she'd seen him wear them in New York, only these were custom-tailored. Knotted around his neck, instead of the checkered cotton kerchief of location days, Becky saw a heavy silk scarf.

He caught her staring and flushed. "They *like* me

to dress this way. I'm one of their showpieces now, one of their expensive crazy creatives, and they like me to look the part. I'm half an hour early, can I buy you a drink?" He didn't say it, but she understood that he'd decided he couldn't go upstairs half an hour early. Whatever this meeting was about, he didn't want to look *too* eager.

～～～

Loren led her into a nearby bar and ordered martinis. Martinis had been in fashion when she first went to work at Seton & Cecil and learned that you were *supposed* to have a drink at lunch. Then they'd gone out of fashion. If Loren had just ordered them, they were probably back in.

"I'm generally not invited to this sort of thing," he confided to Becky about his meeting. "It will be mostly Communicorp's financial types, all set to persuade Seton to lie back and let us have our way with him. And if they don't get what they want via persuasion, I suppose they'll move quickly on to threats . . ."

When Becky was growing up financial dealings like this were supposed to take forever. They were supposed to be pondered over interminably by wise and prudent men. Now the whole thing was more like shooting dice on a street corner while keeping a wary eye out for the police—huge financial dealings were done with a kind of frantic, almost furtive, speed. It was only last week that the Japanese automobile manufacturer had decided not to get involved in a bidding war with Communicorp after all. Not because they didn't think they could win. Because they were interested in buying some of downtown Dallas instead. And only a few days ago Princess Lyubov had pulled out too. "Maybe if I were eighty again," the *Wall Street Journal* had reported her as saying, "but all this is happening too fast for me."

And now, Loren told her, Communicorp was moving swiftly in for the kill.

". . . The London office wanted me at the meeting today because they remembered I used to work for Seton. They thought a familiar face in the crowd might relax him, reassure him that what was happening to Seton & Cecil—and therefore to him—wasn't crass or ugly or brutal, it was just another ordinary good-natured business deal among friendly businessmen." He laughed. "I neglected to tell them I was only one step above the mail room when I was at the agency, and Seton wouldn't know me from a hole in the wall."

It was the old easy, effortless, Loren patter. If you just listened to the words you would think that all was right with his world, that Loren Odell couldn't be happier. Becky looked into his eyes instead and bluntly asked, "How do you like working for Communicorp?"

"Not much," he answered, as bluntly. He stared down into his drink, spotted an olive in the glass, plucked it out, and put it on the side of the plate. Even if martinis were back, he made it clear that olives weren't.

"Communicorp is the biggest now and I suppose I should feel delighted being part of their act." He tasted the martini and nodded. He forgave the olive; the drink itself passed muster. "They've got tentacles all over the world, but of course the important decisions are made in London . . . I'm beginning to understand what my father used to say about the English. He said they were the greediest, most money-grubbing race on the face of the planet. He said they worship money, rake it in as fast as they can while keeping their noses in the air and talking about something *nice*. You think Americans are materialists? The English make us look like a bunch of starry-eyed romantics."

Becky had never heard Loren speak with anything resembling a brogue before. Now his voice sounded more and more Irish. Was it outrage at the English he was feeling—or at Loren Odell, for having become one of their belongings?

"You'd gotten so used to running your own show," Becky said slowly. "Could it be that you don't like being a small frog in a big puddle?"

"Could be," he admitted, looking at himself in the mirror over the bar. He made a minor adjustment to the scarf around his neck, then nodded at his reflection approvingly. "Unfortunately the contract I signed with them has a no-compete clause. If I leave, I'm not allowed to work for anyone else for two years . . . that's a laugh. Loren Odell being in competition with Communicorp!"

He checked his Rolex. "I can't show up for another ten minutes. I've heard you really are leaving Seton & Cecil—where are you going?"

As soon as Loren said *where*, Becky said the rest of the sentence with him, so that it sounded as if there were an echo in the room.

"Everyone's been asking me that. To tell you the truth, I hadn't looked for a job for so long that I wasn't sure I remembered how one went about it. Finally I forced myself to call a few agencies, places I respected . . ."

To her surprise, there had been an immediate and lucrative offer. And then two others, from bitterly competitive headhunters.

"I couldn't decide which offer to take. I was just about ready to start tossing coins, when I realized the reason I couldn't decide was that I didn't want any of them. I wanted something different, something harder, even if it was riskier . . . I picked up the phone and called Stuart Shaw."

She removed the olive from her drink too, but she swallowed it. Unfashionable or not, she *liked* olives. "Shaw came on the line right away. He said it was a

wonderful coincidence, he was just about to phone me.
He said that although none of my colleagues at Seton
& Cecil had seemed in a hurry to tell him, he'd found
out via the grapevine that I was leaving the agency."

Shaw's voice had sounded more than a little an-
noyed. *"First they kept saying they were going to set you
up in a little shop out here . . . Then suddenly nobody
was talking about that any more. But I liked that idea,
whatever happened to it?"*

*"What happened was I turned it down . . . I have
another idea now. One that I think is better. I'd like to
try it out on you."*

"I'm listening."

*"How would you feel about my crossing the great
agency/client divide and coming to work for you?"*

On the other end, there had been silence. Not even
what you would call an interested silence. Just a blank,
bleak, discouraging silent silence.

Gamely, she had plowed ahead. *"Clients never hes-
itate to offer us their, uh, guidance on creative matters,
so I wondered what would happen if you had a pretty
good creative mind on your payroll, ready to help at the
very beginning of projects . . . before everything is set
in stone . . ."*

The silence erupted into shouts of laughter. She
hadn't thought the idea was quite that crazy.

*"What do you have in mind for a title? Would you
want to be called? Our Marketing Guru? Our Resident
Genius?"*

This was not going the way she had hoped. Shame-
lessly quoting Angus Seton, she'd said, *"Titles don't
matter. The point of the idea is that we'd be able to cut
through the million layers of people who have to get
involved in every decision, and who slow everything
down. Think of the time we'd save on meetings! But it
would be an unconventional thing to do, I can understand why you wouldn't . . ."*

Shaw wasn't laughing any more. *"Why I wouldn't what? Listen, I love the idea! In a few weeks I'll believe I thought of it myself. I was laughing because I could see all the faces when we announce it. Ed Douglas's face. Not to mention the faces of your own chaps, when they realize suddenly you're a client, and they have to behave around you. But I'd want you involved in more than Eve. I'd want your help on all of our products, new and old, in all the divisions . . . I'll phone you in a day or two and we'll work out details like salary."*

"And did he? Did he phone?"

"The next day. He even sent the company jet for Alex and me so we could tour Winosha together. He said he'd discovered in these times you have to woo the spouse too . . . suddenly, the whole transaction had shifted from a proposal I'd made *him* to his pursuing *me*. And Alex is happier about the whole thing than I'd have ever expected. The state university is less than an hour by car, and with his background in the Artists' Alliance he's already been promised a job there. And he found this empty old factory building with enormous windows that he's rented for a studio, ten thousand square feet! He's talking about starting a new art colony in Winosha, he's going to spread the word in Soho about the midwest light and all these old factory buildings going for next to nothing. He says that's how Provincetown got started, and Springs, out on Long Island. Artists wanting more space and a better break on rent . . . And you know something, I discovered that for once Horatio Hamlin did tell the truth. Winosha *is* lovely in summer. Those lakes I'd only seen frozen before were surrounded by the tallest, greenest trees, and people were *swimming* in them."

"Becky, I can't believe what I'm hearing. You're going to spend the rest of your life in *Winosha*?" Loren sounded horrified.

She looked at him steadily and shoved her drink

away, most of it undrunk. "I always thought Seton &
Cecil would be the rest of my life. Then, when it seemed
that I couldn't climb any further at the agency because
someone had taken away the ladder . . . at first I was
paralyzed with shock. It was my agency, my ladder. I
almost fell apart back there. Hell, I did fall apart. I
even had fantasies of murdering Hamlin and Cameron
. . . Well, now Becky can think again. I already understand the agency side of our business. If I go out to
Winosha, in a few years I'll know the client side too.
I'll have something so special to offer, I'll be able to
write my own ticket. Listen, Loren, I'm a Depression
kid, I'm programmed to keep working. Hard. Who
knows, maybe I'll grab Gandhi Hendricks then and set
myself up in business with her . . . I'm lucky that Shaw
will be retiring in a few years . . ."

Loren eyed her warily. Everything Becky had said
in this conversation had astonished him, this most of
all. "Are you setting your sights on Shaw's job, down
the line?"

"No, I don't want Shaw's job. I'm lucky because
if we won't be working together very long I'll be less
tempted to turn the poor guy into an instant icon the
way I did with Angus. I seem to have a need for these
Big Daddy figures in my life . . .

"Loren, you said before that Communicorp might
be the biggest, but it wasn't the best. Well, Angus Seton
was the best. And I'll always be incredibly grateful to
him. He taught me how to think, how to judge my own
work as ruthlessly as if it were someone else's. I even
lost a lot of my Bronx accent, listening to Angus Seton
talk. I was part of his agency's glory years, when Seton
was teaching the world that advertising didn't have to
scream, that it could be quiet, intelligent, charming,
and still work. Work *better*, in fact."

She stood, and swung her bag over her shoulder.
"Well, the glory years are over. It doesn't matter who

buys Seton & Cecil now—either Communicorp or the Japanese can improve it out of sight and mind in financial soundness. Only, the Ranks and the Camerons will inherit a duller, bleaker, sadder world. Come on, Loren, you don't want to be late for your meeting. I left my box in the checkroom, I mustn't forget to collect it."

Although she wouldn't need a cardboard box of souvenirs to remember Seton & Cecil.

The lusty pigeons that used to carry on outside their bedroom window must have found another ledge. The air-conditioner they had doted on was gone.

The room was stripped bare of rugs and pictures. It looked eerily empty. the way it had—all those years ago—when Becky and Alex first moved in. Except today the Gagarins were moving *out*.

Becky pulled on shorts and a T-shirt and repeated to Alex what she had told him the night before: "This is crazy. Nobody runs around the park on moving day."

Alex grinned. He could *taste* the old factory building where he would soon tackle the mammoth new projects that were still in his head. "The moving men do the moving. Our job is to get out of their way and worry a lot. We can worry better in the park. Besides, they promised they wouldn't be here until eight."

Joseph kept the elevator door closed an extra minute when they reached the ground floor. The Gagarins had to know how much he was going to miss them. Although he did like their friends, Mrs. Greenbaum, and her daughter, and it would be nice to have the apartment full of children again.

Studying the elevator buttons, he asked casually, "Uh, so how much did you get for the place, Mrs. Gagarin?" But he didn't seem offended when Becky only smiled and wouldn't tell him. Enough, anyway, to

buy a house on a lake in Winosha, and to finish putting
Peter through college.

On the path that circled the reservoir, Alex slowed to
match Becky's pace, while Becky tried to move faster
for him. She had gotten better at this running business.
When she stumbled now she did not resign herself to
falling; she would right herself and start running again.

They were halfway around the running path now.
On the other side of the reservoir Becky could see their
own apartment house.

She remembered the hard-working young woman
who had lived there, the woman who had been a pi-
oneer, but too busy to stop and think about it.

She heard women's voices offering counsel. Rae
Ashley warned again that men get distinguished, but
women only get old. Sheila McCall said that age was
the new unforgivable sin, the best way to deal with it
was to make believe it wasn't happening. Natalia Lyubov (sounding startlingly like Frieda Gelb) complained
that the days went by too slowly, it was the decades
that went fast. And why didn't anyone come to see her
any more? Ida Greenbaum talked about glass ceilings.
About reaching the point where nobody expected you
to climb any higher, if you were female, no matter how
good you were . . .

And now there was a man's voice, Alex's voice.
Alex said, So you're older now, Becky? I have news
for you, so am I. When it rains, my fingers hurt. But
meanwhile, I keep painting.

And Becky thought, it had been nine months since
her life at Seton & Cecil had started to unravel. Nine
months since the day Rae Ashley had picked up a pencil
and turned the two *C*s in *Rebecca* into two zeros. The
whole terrifying interlude had felt like an eternity but
had only been nine months. Long enough to give birth

to a baby. Could she, Becky Gagarin, have fooled them all—and given birth to a grown woman instead?

When they came out of the park, two enormous vans were parked in front of their building. Muscular men in white overalls were looking up and down the block, impatient for the Gagarins, eager to start packing their vans with the Gagarin lives. Becky reached for Alex's hand and together they crossed the street.

WHAT HAPPENS WHEN THE PRIME OF A WOMAN'S LIFE TURNS OUT TO BE UNMAPPED TERRITORY?

Becky Gagarin is a woman who seems to have it all. She is creative head of one of the world's largest advertising agencies, calling the shots in mammoth multi-media campaigns. She's a wife, a mother, and she can play hardball in the old boy's network, while being both task mistress and mentor to young people hoping to follow in her footsteps. But Becky's seemingly perfect life is not without its perils: a career-threatening international takeover...vicious office politics...and a lovely younger woman to whom her wildly attractive husband is inching closer and closer....

This savvy, deeply moving novel, with a heroine who is both achingly vulnerable and fiercely determined, is a vivid portrayal of the way women live, love and work...and a wise reflection on what it costs a woman to stay on top.

17165

0 71162 00499 1

ISBN 0-451-17165-9